GRAND OAK BOOKS

Acadia Lost

Published by:
Grand Oak Books Publishing, Ltd

ISBN-10: 1937727181
ISBN-13: 978-1-937727-18-5

Library of Congress Cataloging-in-Publication Data:

Hodge, A.M./Acadia Lost

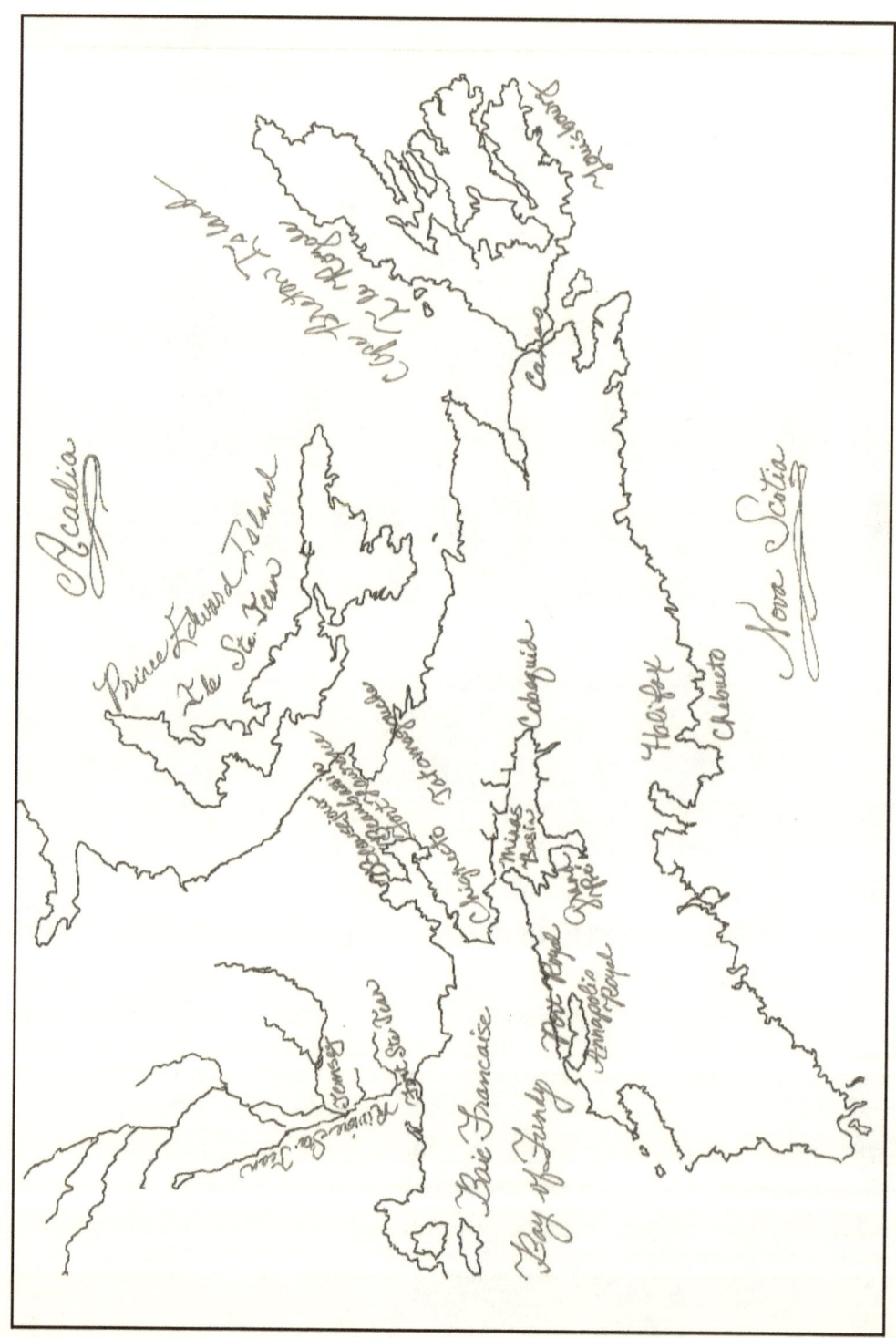

Acadia Lost

by A.M. Hodge

Grand Oak Books
2012

DISCLAIMER

This novel is a work of historical fiction. Some of the characters are historical and where they have been included in the story the author has tried to be faithful to how they are known to have been both as men and as historical figures. Any errors in their portrayal are strictly those of the author. The same is said regarding Native American characters. The author gave them English names for ease of both reader and writer to follow and took some liberties with their ways of thinking about nature and the spiritual world to emphasize their relationship with their natural environment. I'm grateful to those Native Americans who shared the thoughts and ideas with me over the years that influenced those elements of the story.

AUTHOR'S NOTE

In September 1995 I visited Nova Scotia on a week's vacation. Driving from Yarmouth with no particular itinerary or destination we came to Grand Pré late one afternoon when the rays of the late afternoon sun slanted across the fields and our next thought was about where we might stay for the night. Standing in front of the reconstructed church of St. Charles-les-Mines. I felt dread and anxiety as if they rose up through the ground and enfolded me. I stood there feeling what I believed was the pain and suffering others had endured. I didn't understand it and only wanted to get away from it. The next day when I bought my souvenir copy of Longfellow's epic poem EVANGELINE and read the compressed history of the expulsions in the introduction it made my skin crawl. I'm not an Acadian descendant at least not that I know of, but for about half my life I've lived within a short drive of John Winslow's home in Marshfield, Massachusetts. The story of the Acadian expulsions remained with me from 1995 on and finally drew me to research the history of what happened to the habitants of Acadia/Nova Scotia and then write this novel. Many heartfelt thanks to everyone who helped and encouraged me in the writing of this book. I couldn't have done it without all of you.

This book is dedicated to the memory of Nancy Ann Dawe (1931-2012), photo-journalist and friend who always saw the best in anyone and everyone she ever met.

ACADIA LOST

He shall return no more to this house;
neither shall his place know him any more.
- Job 7:10

PROLOGUE

Thus the whirligig of time begins its revenges.
- Shakespeare, *Twelfth Night*, Act 5, Scene 1

The evening fog rolled up from the harbor thickening so fast I feared I might lose my way. As I turned the corner to go down Inglis Street my heels beat the familiar rhythm of my name on the weathered pavers "E-van-ge-line, E-van-ge-line."

Down the block a way I saw the spreading glow of a light snapped on above a doorway. A blurred figure came from the opposite direction, reached the entry and went inside; radiance spilled through the opening and made the droplets of mist outside glisten for a few seconds before the door closed.

I was in Halifax Nova Scotia because my uncle Henri called from his home in North Carolina while I was on a research trip to tell me he'd loaned some history professor our family treasure – the surviving pages of an old journal written by his eighth great-grandfather in the years leading up to the Acadian Deportations. Liam Butler, the scholar who'd borrowed them, was to speak about the publication of his work on the journal this evening in the back room used for such gatherings at Schooner Books.

I expected Professor Butler to be an older man, the kind that sports a goatee and wears one of those Indiana Jones hats that historians and archeologists seem to favor. But I was wrong. He was middle-aged and handsome with a full head of dark curly hair and a ready smile that made his eyes glow. I caught myself wondering was he married.

Butler wasn't always famous; in fact he was a relative unknown until he completed the work he'd come here to speak about. Now he could scarcely go anywhere in the Maritimes without being lionized by his peers.

I was a year or so into my own research so I made it a point to be in Halifax to meet him. When I stepped through the door and slipped off my coat I saw another woman in the crowd, but she looked like she was the athletic rather than the scholarly type and seemed out of place here. She had Butler's ear and was energetically making a case to him. I wasn't trying to eavesdrop but a few words cut clearly through the conversations that thickened the air in the room – her ancestor; some-one named Daiell; the British army; Halifax; the deportations, and something about a duel. Butler's facial muscles tightened when she said that. But then the gathering was called to order. Introductions were made and it was time to start.

He picked up the pages he was to read and said it was a short se-lection so that we could have as much Q&A as we wanted. He cleared his throat. A couple of others coughed and chair legs scraped against the wood floor as we settled back in our seats to listen as he began to read.

As he spoke I watched him in fascination. His expressions changed like cloud shadows chased by sunlight. I saw how he used his body, slim and lithe as a dancer's; his gestures and movements seemed to flow un-consciously with the words. The intonations of his voice and the way he used his eyes to draw each of us into Guillaume's story so deeply we felt we sat there with him and his family listening to their quiet con-versation at the end of the day made me wonder how many women who ever saw him perform – because that's what he was doing –had sexual fantasies about him.

At that moment he looked up at me as if he knew what I was think-ing. When I blushed he turned his eyes back to the page. I detected a small crinkling at the edge of his lips like he was suppressing a smile. The girl with the ancestor was enthralled by him and I wondered if he had groupies. Hardly the sort of thing you'd expect in a crowd of schol-ars waiting to pounce and argue their own theories and finer points of interest.

From time to time over the years I'd listened to Guillaume's jour-nal, sometimes in French and other times English depending on which of my relatives was reading. I'd grown used to the old story and knew it inside out. But Butler changed it for me. He made it live and now I wanted to use his work for the basis of the family history I'd begun to write. I looked across the room at the 'ancestor' girl and saw the gleam of determination in her eyes. She had a note or something she wanted to show him and by the way he was looking back at her I knew I'd best get to him before she did.

When I went up and introduced myself his expression changed as though he'd expected to see me; he excused himself while he dug some papers out of his briefcase including a copy of the translation he'd just read.

"Here," he said, "take this. Once you've had a chance to look it over give me a call." He said he'd be at the Marriott for the next couple of days; we could meet for lunch if I had time. I opened my mouth to answer but his attention was already on the woman who stood behind me and for him I wasn't even in the room any more. I sighed and picked up my stuff and went back to my hotel. Not as nice as the Marriott but at least I had a minibar stocked with a couple of bottles of a good dry Canadian white wine. I poured a glass and sat in the single armchair, pulled the papers from my briefcase and settled back to read the manuscript and plan my lunch with the professor.

Excerpt from the BOOK OF GUILLAUME BANCOUER, entry date 1744

Late in the afternoon while the women cook the evening meal, I sit on the bench in front of my house with the sun warm on my face and my pipe in my hand and enjoy one of the few pleasures left to an old man. I close my eyes to think of other times and places. A puff of air caresses my face as delicate hands once did.

The tall oak in front of me has sheltered our thatched-roof house for as long as we've lived here. As the sun goes lower its light will be dappled by the leaves that chatter when the breeze gusts across the wide meadows. The song of a distant bird and the buzz of insects gathering nectar from the nearby garden comfort me and soothe my thoughts. I lean my back against the whitewashed boards that wall the house to hear the sounds within more clearly and listen to the familiar hum of women chattering and the clatter of pottery as they move about preparing the food. I'm troubled about my first-born son, Paul Dancing Crow. Since the English came last spring to break the French siege on Annapolis Royal I've had no word of him and pray he survived. I remember when he was a boy how he'd grab at my leg for me to lift him up. I feel a pull and as I reach down still living in my memory of him, there's one of the puppies from the barn tugging at me. I pick up the wriggling bundle of fur. Its pure joy at being held and stroked brings back the ache of my emptiness.

"Hungry? Supper's almost ready." Jerusha's voice summons me from my reverie. I put the puppy down and watch it run off to join its fellows. My wife stands in the doorway wiping her hands on her apron and gives me an appraising look. "Ye seemed so far away. What's on your mind?"

I think what answer to make to please her. "I recall your father when I first met him. He convinced me that once the land was diked to curb the tides there'd be many more acres ready for the plow. And he said that if I married you, we could live here for the rest of our lives and never lack for bountiful harvests." I gesture toward the broad expanse of bottomland that stretches before us all the way to the sea.

"Do ye remember when ye first saw me?" She often asks this, as she did in the time just after we were first wed. Her face softens and makes her look as young and tender to me now as she was then. "Aye, I do that." I wink at her. "Such a beautiful young woman I'd never seen in all my life." Her smile still inspires springtime within me.

When the meal is finished we go outside to enjoy the beautiful summer evening – Jerusha, our daughter Virginie and our sons Armand, a recent widower and Guillaume-Honoré come with his son Mathieu to help in the fields.

Honoré was the first of my sons that I watched grow all the way from a babe to a young man; now here's his boy coming along. Jerusha was so pleased her first child was a son she couldn't let him out of her sight. At eighteen years of age he struck out for the high marshes to claim land, build a farm and marry. She's never forgiven him for leaving her.

Just a month ago Father Germain came to Beausejour to hear confessions and say mass for the farmers. The chapel sits on a grassy knoll overlooking the fields. The Black Robe's a gentle man with the Acadians. Whenever I look at his face and recall how kind he was during our family's troubled time I can't believe the fierceness rumored of him when he goes to lead the Indians. He sat in the sunshine on the bench in front of the priest house picking some sticky burrs from the hem of his cassock as I spoke to him of Jerusha wanting to know about my years among the Indians and how reluctant I was to tell her. I didn't expect the priest's response. "Secrets have power," he said looking up at me, his eyes darkening. Confused I answered that I didn't fathom his meaning. I stammered as I asked, "Why do ye speak so?"

The priest fingered the wooden cross that hung on his breast. "You're keeping something secret that Jerusha wishes to know but can't unless ye tell her. That keeps her in thrall to you and to your secret."

"But when I die my secrets will die with me."

His eyes flashed as a cloud crossed the sun and cast a momentary shadow on us. "That's my point," said the priest. "Rather it'll outlive ye, and always have power over Jerusha's memory of ye for as long as she lives. Is that what you want?" His words surprised me. But as I've become older I've learned that many times things aren't as I expect them to be.

Jerusha became my second wife several years after I arrived in Acadia. While I was among the Indians I married and fathered a son, Paul Dancing Crow. Whenever Paul came to visit me, he and I would go off for a day or two into the forest. Once Armand saw us camped in the wilderness and sitting by the smoldering em-

bers of a fire as we talked. He later told me that he felt he witnessed something very special, a bond between his father and the eldest son that made him feel a hot pang of jealousy, something his Acadian brothers didn't arouse in him. He said he knew it was unworthy but he couldn't help it. I love him for confessing that. I told him that I love all my children each in the same way. But in my heart I know that no father ever feels so.

For a time I measured the Abbé's words, turning them over in my mind. Then I agreed to tell Jerusha those things she wanted to know. I've never understood why they made her suffer over and again all through our years together. When I tell her about Song Sparrow I want Jerusha to know that I only tried to shield her from the effects of the terrible pain and anger I suffered because of her loss. When I finish the telling I want us to be together again as man and wife. I want to be at peace with her when the circle of my life finally closes and know that at last she has the contentment she deserves.

- Translation by Liam Butler, A.B., M.Ed., Ph.D.

PART ONE: 1698 to 1747

NORMANDY, 1698

King William's War was finally over and the army disbanded at last. In less than another day the Bancouer brothers' long journey home to the family farm would end. As Guillaume straightened up from breathing a spark of life into a struggling campfire, he spotted a stranger picking his way along the forest path that led toward him. He called to Jacques and Henri gathering wood nearby; they put down their bundles of twigs and sticks and went to the clearing to watch the man approach.

He wore dark clothing that was of finer wool than the usual, a wide-brimmed felt hat and a pair of stout leather boots and his bearded face was creased by an expectant smile. "Halloo! Halloo!" he called out as he neared them. "Peace to ye. I'm a friend. Pitre LeBrun."

They had neither seen nor heard another person for the past day and didn't expect anyone to wander into their camp, but this one didn't look like any of the other tramps that had crossed their path and he called out in their own Norman dialect.

"I'm alone," he said as if reading their thoughts. "What're ye doing here in the forest? There's a village only about a mile away. You could spend the night in a bed at the inn."

"No money for it," Guillaume shrugged. Jacques and Henri nodded. They stood like three moldy peas in a pod, garbed in clothes picked from battlefield corpses and stared at the well-dressed stranger wondering what business he had to do with them.

"Me neither," Pitre admitted. "Mind if I join you?"

Henri broke the brothers' hesitant silence. "You're welcome. We're soldiers from Rouen going home from the war. You a Norman?"

"Yes," Pitre said. The brim of his hat shaded his eyes as he turned his head. "I'm heading home too. Work for the *Compagnie du L' Acadie*. You're probably not interested but I'm searching among soldiers come back from the war for recruits to go to New France to learn to trap and trade furs. But I can see that you men are headed home to your family's farm to live happy and cozy and never feel hunger because of the bread you'll have from the harvests of your fields."

Jacques laughed. "Was that so we'd already be there."

"Well," Pitre said with a wide smile, "Then it may be I've something better to offer you."

He pulled two loaves of bread from his bag and then dug out a large piece of cheese. "We'll talk while we eat." Pitre bent over to brush away some soil before settling on a rock by the fire. He broke some chunks off one of the loaves and handed them to the boys.

"Ever hear anything about New France?" he asked as he chewed on a piece of bread. He lowered his head as he worked his jaws and rolled his eyes upward; he crinkled his nose as he looked at them. "It's a wild place where men can make fortunes. From the sea it's the cod fish; from the land it's the pelts that bring in the gold. That's the *Compagnie's* trade. They need more men in New France to trap furs."

Pitre hawked and spat; he wiped the back of his hand across his mouth before taking a large bite of the cheese and handing it along to Henri who hesitated a moment before taking his knife and cutting off a large chunk. Henri passed the cheese to Jacques and he broke the remaining lump into two pieces and handed one to Guillaume. Pitre's gaze followed its passage and rested on Guillaume as he was about to open his mouth and eat the last bit. He hesitated as the cheese was about to pass between his teeth and slowly extended his hand to Pitre who snatched the morsel and popped it into his own mouth.

As they ate the boys told him they wanted a life of adventure and wealth but not the kind of adventure that comes of always living the military life and not the kind of wealth that comes from pillaging and that ends in spending on drunken orgies.

Pitre broke the second loaf of bread and passed a chunk to each of them. Now that they had some food in their stomachs they were all ears to what he spun to them and his vision of fortunes to be made gripped their imaginations. They took the earnest expression on his face as testament to the truth of his words. After a time Pitre fell silent.

"If he was so inclined," Jacques took an off-handed tone which his brothers recognized as a sign of interest, "how's a man to join this *Compagnie?*"

Before he answered Pitre studied each of them with an expression like that of a bear sniffing out its surroundings.

"D' ye think this is a hoax?" he finally bellowed. "Well it isn't. For all the *Compagnie* offers it expects very little. All it wants of any man who accepts its help to establish himself in New France is to spend his first three years there working for it. Payback to the *Compagnie* is a mere sixty beaver pelts each year after the first year. That's a time for learning the country and the trade. Any pelts taken in that year will go to the *Compagnie*. After that ye may trade as ye wish."

"How'd we know that number of pelts ain't so high it can never be paid?" Henri was suspicious of everything. During his time with the monks he'd overheard more than one confession about ways a man could use to cheat another by manipulation.

Pitre replied as if he had his answer by rote. "I myself have gone to New France and lived and trapped with the Indians. That was the bounty the *Compagnie* expected of me. Each year I'd more furs than that. Even saved some money to bring back to France."

"Why come back?" Henri was quick to ask. "If you've done so well with the fur trade why didn't ye stay there and keep at it?"

"I'm to recruit some new blood for the *Compagnie's* work. They want to control the fur trade and need more men for that."

"And soldiers who can fight can be trained as trappers," Jacques concluded.

"What d' ye think?" Pitre asked them. "Look to you like a better prospect than staying here in France to soldier or join the priesthood or be a tenant farmer?" He looked into the eyes of each one of the brothers as he spoke.

Henri started. "How'd ye know I was with the monks?"

"Hands give ye away. Soft and no calluses. Who else has such hands as they, I ask you?"

Guillaume snorted to suppress his laughter. "And how're we supposed to get there? Ye haven't told us that piece yet. *Compagnie* pay for us to go?"

"Up to you to talk it out when ye meet one of their ship captains."

Next morning Jacques offered to walk along with Pitre, who saw he was prime to sign on and was certain the younger brothers would follow his lead. If Pitre had a taker at that moment he might have bet his last gold sovereign against a livre that he would have all three recruited by the forenoon.

After they signed the papers Pitre told them to travel to La Rochelle and find Captain Ambrose Hébert of the *Fleur de Lis*. He was expecting Pitre to send him some recruits but they'd have to negotiate their passage to Acadia directly with him. Then Pitre wished them good fortune and went off on his own.

When the brothers reached La Rochelle which seemed a town of fair prospect until they came close enough to catch their first whiff of it, they followed narrow winding lanes that led to the crowded waterfront where fishmongers hawked their stinking catch yelling and cursing when anyone passed by them without parting with a few coins. They elbowed their way through crowds gathered by the booths of farm women come in to sell their produce and gawked at the towers and fortifications along the harbor's entrance.

Guillaume followed behind Henri and Jacques as they walked along a narrow lane that linked one busy commercial shipyard to another and saw vessels being provisioned or repaired and men shouldering their way toward gangplanks carrying tools or barrels or chests of goods destined for foreign ports.

Jacques grinned and danced about. "We'll make our fortunes in no time if all this business is for trade with New France!"

Just beyond the last of the shipyards Henri spotted a wooden sign that creaked on a hinge above a weathered entry. "That must be the place." He pointed toward the *Duck and Dragon*.

The brothers pushed through the heavy door and stood in the tavern's low-ceilinged common room. As their eyes adjusted to the dim light they picked out the innkeeper, a tall man who stood above most of the crowd. His wife was short and round and argued with a customer who was trying to shortchange her. Her face blackened with anger and she let out a stream of invective so powerful the man dug into his purse and threw some coins down on the table. He pushed the brothers aside as he made for the door. "Now we see who's the 'Duck' and who's the 'Dragon' of the place," Jacques laughed. "Ain't she something?"

The two barmaids ignored the fuss and kept waiting on the patrons and taking food and drink to the tables. Loud conversations were pierced with shouts of sudden laughter as one or other of the giggling women pushed by a group of men to deliver food to an appreciative customer. Two men sat before a board of draughts never taking their eyes off the table as they sipped from glasses of whiskey. A card game with a large crowd of onlookers was being played; on the side a couple of bystanders made their own wager.

The innkeeper approached the brothers and Guillaume asked for some beer. They found a place near the fire to seat themselves and began to talk about a strange adventure they had experienced the day before. Each of them felt an undercurrent of something else going on in that farmyard besides that farmer being attacked by his sow. Guillaume was sure the wife tried to back out of her offer of a meal in exchange for their help to rescue her husband because she saw the way Jacques looked at her daughter and how she'd looked back at him. Henri teased, "Jacques' lucky he didn't wind up in the muck with that pig alongside that oaf of a husband she called us to come rescue."

"Did she even say it was her husband?"

"Maybe was she that pushed him in when she saw us coming."

"But now there's the daughter."

"As sweet and fresh as she could be. Mother tried to keep her hidden away."

"Didn't know us very well did she?"

"Well..."

Their laughter carried above the din.

Captain Ambrose Hébert sat quietly amidst the hubbub with his napkin tucked up under his chin and ate his dinner while doing his best to eavesdrop. He began with chuckling at their adventure and ended by laughing out loud when they did. Then he heard Jacques say his name and he turned to look them over.

They paused and looked back at him. Their stomachs growled at the sight and smell of the rich stew he had been spooning into his mouth. Satisfied these hungry youngsters were Pitre LeBrun's most recent recruits, Hébert introduced himself and invited them to join him. He waved to the innkeeper and held up three fingers and pointed to his own dish with the other hand. More food was quickly brought and the brothers dove into their first true meal in more than a week, tearing apart bread fresh from the oven and using it to scoop up great mouthfuls of stew. The captain plied his knife and spoon as he began to entertain them with stories of his adventures sailing to ports in the New World.

"Last year I shipped cargo from La Rochelle to Sainte Domingue. French planters were happy to see salt cod and good French cloth," he paused to take a swallow from his tankard. "Then I sailed to Acadia and traded coffee, molasses and rum for pelts. 'Twas a very profitable run." He popped a piece of bread into his mouth and chewed furiously.

"Your business usually like that?" Henri asked between mouthfuls.

"I go wherever I see the chance to pile up the gold. At Minas I saw their supplies came from New Englanders by way of French privateers. Can't compete with goods like that. No point to try. But there're ways to get the pelts – that's where ye make the big money – and I know how to do it." He winked at Henri as he took a swig of beer. "My secret. I'll hang onto it for now."

"This voyage the war's ended. Still we must sail wide of the British. Bound to be a ship hasn't heard about it. Don't want to meet them in the middle of the ocean. You'll have enough excitement when ye get to Port Royal. You'll see action when the British come to call."

That explained the *Compagnie's* interest in recruiting soldiers for their work in New France. They looked at each other as if to say they should have guessed as much. Hébert's stories confirmed what Pitre said about gold to be gained from the fur trade. But they weren't rich yet and had only a few coins left by the time they met the captain.

Henri turned to him. "It's taken most of our money to travel to La Rochelle to meet you." Hébert raised an eyebrow as if inviting him to explain himself.

Jacques and Guillaume nodded. "Any work aboard ship for us to help earn passage?"

Hébert expected that question – recruits for New France were always poor and starving. After all why would any man of means wish to leave behind a comfortable life in France for the unknown dangers of the New World?

He looked each of them straight in the face as if to take their measure before giving his answer. "Two of my crew shipped on to another vessel. Landsmen aren't the most welcome replacements but go and apply for work to James, the ship's mate. And if we do run afoul of any British during our crossing to New France, you'll be a great help."

Jacques grinned. "If only half what we've been told about New France is true we'll be rich before we know it."

Hébert's hearty laugh rang out and some men seated nearby turned their grinning faces for a look. "Pitre's beguiled ye with a rosy picture," he boomed.

"Then in spite of your successful trade you've yet to see it happen," Guillaume observed.

"Not yet but one day it may. Pay attention to your own safety – that's the first thing ye must learn to do. If ye last the first winter you'll certainly survive. However ye prosper will come by the work of your own hands."

As Hébert turned to gesture to the innkeeper, the door opened and the ship's purser entered the tavern. "Captain," he shouted to be heard above the noise as he elbowed his way toward their table. "The ship is fully provisioned. James says we're ready to sail at the turn of tide." He looked at the brothers. "These the new men? I'm Adam. Glad to see some new hands."

Hébert nodded and lowered his voice. "Anyone come from Pitre LeBrun direct to the ship?"

"No, sir. But I thought ye expected someone else."

The innkeeper approached with the bill. As he did so the door swung open again and a gust of wind blew inside. A group of workmen entered, found seats and were soon engrossed in some conversation. One man was dressed in what looked like the remnants of a military uniform. He remained by the door and searched the room. The innkeeper called to him, "Lookin' fer some'un?"

When the brothers heard him answer "Captain Hébert" they exchanged knowing smiles, certain he was yet another of Pitre's recruits.

As he paid the innkeeper the captain asked him to fill a napkin with some food and provide a bottle of beer for the man to take along when they left the tavern. Then he pushed back his seat and faced the newcomer. "I'm the one ye seek. And who might you be?"

He approached the group with his eyes riveted on Hébert's face. "Pierre-Jaspar Montard at your service, Captain." He stood at attention with his heels together and his hat in the crook of his arm. "Pitre Le Brun told me your ship's ready to sail for Acadia."

Hébert's features relaxed and a smile spread across his face. "You arrived just in time, sir. Welcome. Take that food and drink from the innkeeper." Then he leaned toward Montard and lowered his voice. "We can talk in my cabin once we're aboard and away from La Rochelle."

The Fleur de Lis was a small frigate that was formerly a ship of war. She was now in use as a supply transport and her crew was hand-picked by the captain. The holds were loaded with food, cloth, dry goods – mostly gunpowder and shot; the ship also carried trade goods for the Indians

— beads, knives, iron pots and axes. Once everyone was aboard long boats attached lines to the bow of the ship and towed it out into the roads. When the lines were dropped and the first sail hauled up the mast, the vessel gave a shudder like that of a large animal awakening from sleep. The timbers came alive as the ship began to move and when it reached the stone towers it coasted smoothly between them and out of the harbor.

While they still sailed near enough to the coasts of England and France to be sighted by British patrols, the captain pressed everyone aboard not needed to man the ship into duty as lookouts. Between the handling of the ship and the search for enemy sails on the horizon, there was more than enough work to keep all hands busy. That gave Hébert the opportunity he was waiting for to invite Montard to his cabin to explain both himself and the furtive messenger who came to the docks only two days before the ship was to sail to book passage for a "noble gentleman." From remarks Jacques overheard between the captain and the mate, the messenger had hinted at interests of some highly placed people at court who wished passage to New France for one Pierre-Jaspar Montard.

Guillaume was nearby when James reminded Adam that the last such passenger the captain had agreed to take aboard turned out to be a Jesuit. By the time the ship lay off Port Royal, the priest had the crew so inflamed they were ready to mutiny. "Remember what that 'un did?" James laughed. "Threatened the crew with excommunication? Thought they'd feed him to the fishes he got 'em so mad with him. And there's always some big 'un down under the keel where cook dumps the offal just waiting for such a morsel."

Adam chimed in, "Served him right they did that. Cap'n wouldn't like it though. Only gets paid for passengers as finish the journey." Both men laughed at the joke.

Montard's reserved but pleasant mien and lack of references to holy things indicated he was certainly not a priest. The brothers wondered could he be some kind of spy? But what would be his purpose if he was? The war seemed not to have ended in peace but rather in a stalemated continuation of hostilities. According to Hébert, Port Royal was unprotected and suffered raids. The fish-drying and processing businesses in places called Chedabucto and Le Heve had been destroyed by an adventurer from Boston named Phips. In Hébert's memory that was the most costly of all the outrages the French had so far suffered at the hands of the English. Perhaps they would learn of some new and even more contemptible thing from what passed between the captain and this Pierre-Jaspar Montard. Henri found a way to observe some of Hébert's meeting with the man. A light rap on the bulkhead announced the visitor. "Maybe he's just who he claims to be," Henri thought. For the time being he reserved his judgment.

"Please enter," Hébert said in a pleasant tone. Montard opened the cabin door and slipped inside. "I've been waiting to chin with ye." Hébert gave him an appraising look.

"I can imagine. You've a visitor just as you're about to cast off who demands passage for a mysterious guest. Of course you wondered who and what ye were letting yourself in for."

"That's the face of it," Hébert said. "But I'm sure there's more to the story than just a bored young nobleman seeking adventure in New France until he can safely return home."

Wood rasped against wood as Montard pulled up a stool. "Do ye mind?" he asked. Hébert nodded and also took a seat.

"I'm no nobleman nor rich man in case you've been given that impression," he began. "My father's a well-to-do merchant who expected his oldest son — my brother that is — to take over the family business one day. Decided I'd have use for my talents fighting the British. I advanced by battlefield commission to the rank of captain. Toward the end of the war I fell in love with my company commander's daughter. Her father sent me off on what he thought would be a suicide mission. Got some cuts and bruises but still got back to the willing arms of my lover. Old man took it like a stalemate.

"Now her father thought could I be persuaded to go, I'd be very useful in New France. He contacted Pitre Le Brun. That worthy set himself to cross my path and offer me a mission to Quebec attached to the staff of Governor Vaudreuil. Of course I saw through the bribe. What man wouldn't? But no matter. I agreed to take the post and leave Europe. For that I received some gold sovereigns and passage aboard the *Fleur de Lis*."

Hébert gave him a penetrating look. "Well made, sir. It's certain you'll find your new life far more rewarding than whatever sort of adventure ye could've hoped for in France. I'm sure that in time you'll return back to France if that's your wish. How can I serve you?"

"I've several assignments but only one to reveal to you. I'm to make a full report on conditions at Port Royal, and send a copy with you on your return to France. Then if goods are being transported to Quebec, I'm to travel along and report there. Otherwise I'm to get there as best I can." Montard shrugged and smiled as if to beg excuse for a poorly made joke.

"Smacks of adventure don't it?"

"I'd call it promising." Hébert pointed to a place on the chart that lay unrolled on the table. "Do ye ken the New Englanders patrol the waters of Baie Française? Some of them come to trade and some to attack and loot. No one knows for sure till they land on shore whether they mean to do the one or the other. Ye must've already heard Governor Villebon fights with the British all the time. They keep trying to shoot down his fort on the St. Jean."

"I had no local briefing. If you could show me the charts and where these places are I'd value a full discussion of these things." They leaned over a table in the middle of the cabin to look at the charts. They kept talking in a low murmur until the noise of the watch changing on deck broke their concentration.

"Perhaps I'll go now. Another meeting with you to pick this back up?" Montard smiled at Hébert and he nodded his assent. "Wish ye luck, Sir. Wouldn't be in your shoes for all my weight in gold. You'll be challenged to survive your mission. But then that's true of all who venture to New France."

Henri scuttled from his hiding place and joined the other sailors as they ran to their watch stations. Later he told Jacques and Guillaume what he heard, but when they talked about it they found it offered them little insight into whatever Montard's true purpose might be.

One evening after clearing the British coastal patrols and with a steady wind speeding the ship along its course, Hébert invited the *Compagnie's* recruits to dine with him and some of the officers. Newly at sea the ship's provisions were reasonably fresh and the wine more than acceptable. Inside the small stern cabin the unfolded table nearly filled the compartment. Cutlery and crockery rattled as the boards vibrated with the ship's motion. The bowl of biscuits that awaited their pleasure was soon moving from hand to hand and glasses clinked a cheerful musical counterpoint to the conversation as wine bottles went around.

"I can tell ye only what I recall from last summer," Hébert said in answer to a question posed by Guillaume. "Things in Acadia change so quickly I can't be sure any of this still holds true. Good example is news we heard about the treaty just before we sailed."

The cook chose this moment to push his way into the cabin and interrupt the talk by placing a steaming salver of meat surrounded by root vegetables in front of the captain. "Anything more, sir?" he asked as he wiped his greasy hands on his apron. Hébert smiled in anticipation. "Later."

The men eyed the meat and inhaled the aroma of it. Every one of them salivated as Hébert speared a juicy piece for himself. He shoved the dish toward James who sat next to him. "Help yourselves," he said. The platter quickly went round the table.

"And how long do ye think that treaty might last?" A cryptic smile passed over Montard's face as he swallowed a bit of food and sipped from his wine glass.

"The treaty?" Hébert waved his knife and pointed it at Montard. "People like Baptiste on both sides, it won't last any longer'n the meat on this platter."

"Who's Baptiste?" Jacques asked just as the serving dish reached him. He paused to dig around the bottom of the dwindling pile in case some choice morsel had been overlooked.

"Man's a privateer who sails under the French flag. Before the truce he was good at taking British supply vessels. Now the British Navy's out to get him. Nearly did a couple of years back. Come on him in a cove near the St. Jean River. Bottled him in. Baptiste and his crew ran *Le Bonne* onto the rocks. Man loved his ship. Was truly desperate to escape. Which they did by staving in the bottom of the ship and then running fast as they could go through the forest."

"Sounds like a truce mayen't have meaning to such as him," Guillaume said.

"Always use for men like Baptiste. Governor sees to that. Now there's another cut from the same cloth. So far Villebon's fought off the English and kept his fort secured. Had time for little else. While the war was on he could depend on privateers like Baptiste to take British supply ships and divert them to Port Royal and Beaubassin to help feed the settlers. Now he'll have to worry about whether the farmers can raise enough crops to do the job for themselves. And the New Englanders still come raiding up the coast."

"Do ye say the peace treaty could be violated?" Henri asked.

"Well of course. This is the New World. There'll be raids and other such things happening. One side or other will take offense at something they think warrants revenge. It's just how 'tis between the British and the French no matter where they are. Even sometimes between the French themselves."

"French fight each other? Why don't they stick to fighting the British?" Jacques banged the handle of his knife as he put it down on the table.

"Greed and power," Henri said with a sanctimonious look on his face and his lower lip extended as if in a pout.

"And so the *Compagnie* recruits former soldiers to come to Acadia and learn to trap furs?" Jacques asked. "This seems to give them an army of sorts to keep their trade with the Indians under control and defended from the enemy. Is that the story? Is that why we're brought to Acadia? To fight another kind of war?"

"Men must always be ready to defend what's theirs." Hébert spoke as if he was explaining a point of law.

Henri said, "Perhaps it's a matter of gaining enough power to uphold a treaty by collecting an army of men like us inside the country. Then a truce would have to be respected."

Montard smirked. "Might makes Right." That retort convinced Jacques more than ever that he was going to Acadia to become embroiled in some conflict he didn't want to try to imagine. The table fell silent; the brothers exchanged uncomfortable glances. Montard raised an eyebrow as he held up his glass to them. Hébert decided to shift topics by indicting the English. He picked up the conversation with the story of a French fishing fleet taken on the Grand Banks by a warship from Boston.

"But that's insufferable!" Jacques pounded a fist on the table hard enough to make the cutlery and the platters jump. "How can they invade our waters and take our people off as they will? No law in this place?"

James looked at Adam and giggled. Henri gave them a smoldering look.

The captain smiled. "Such happens. Fairly common. Was it such a strictly law-abiding place there wouldn't be the adventure ye seek or so many ways to make your fortune. You've to be clever about what ye do and careful who ye trust."

A large bowl filled with a steaming gelatinous white pudding appeared as the cook made his way into the cabin, bracing himself against the ship's motion. The fragrant mass trembled as he came as if, given the chance of any false movement by the bearer, it would hurl itself out of the bowl and onto the laps of the nearest diners. The cook's performance and the confection itself drew all eyes and paused the discussion.

"Your favorite, sir," the cook said landing the dessert as carefully as he could on the table in front of the captain. The pudding quivered.

"Blanc mange," the cook announced as he left the cabin.

Hébert acted as if he barely noticed the shimmering presence and continued, "Last year when I sailed up the St. Jean I heard the Acadians were in dire need of provisions. The winter was harsh and supplies were running very low." The diners stared at the confection and inhaled its delicate odor of sweet spices. "There were no puddings like this," he gestured as if to give way to the men's desire to get on with the eating of it. "Help yourselves gentlemen."

As of a single mind they reached across and dug into the shaking glutinous mound. Once the pudding was finished, right down to the last bit of it scraped up from the platter and licked from the spoon, there was a satisfied silence. Hébert's benevolent smile shone upon their appreciative faces.

The men prepared to listen to Hébert spin yet another from his endless store of yarns. He poured himself a glass of brandy before passing the decanter around the table. The smokers in the group puffed away on their pipes.

"A few years back war's always simmering up to the boil. Villebon speeds toward Port Royal to take up his new post as Governor of Acadia and captures an English fishing vessel just off the coast. Questions them close about the strength of the English and are there raiding parties abroad at the time and then lets them go." He drew on his pipe.

"Sails into Port Royal and sees the British flag flying from the fort but no ships of war nor troops in sight. His own sergeant La Tourasse meets him as he comes ashore. Says Phips had only to land his forces to take the place and chose him to govern the fort when they sailed away."

"And how was the fort taken? The French can't fight?" Jacques shook his head in disbelief.

"Fort's in bad repair and garrison's too small. English overwhelmed them and French surrendered. Naught else to be done. 'T isn't Europe. Here when a man dies, there's none to take his place. No New World commander would ever risk the needless sacrifice of his men."

"Surely Villebon did something about it," Jacques' eyes darkened with anger. "Surely no Governor runs away when the enemy's about?"

Hébert continued affably. "He's a remarkably good soldier and dedicated warrior but he's no young hothead" – he paused to give the brothers a significant look – "to go chase after a fleet much stronger and better armed than his only ship. People of Port Royal begged him to do nothing to attract the English back. So Villebon took himself and his men across the bay to the St. Jean River and went to Jemseg to set up his headquarters."

"Why'd he go so far away from Port Royal if they could need him to fight the enemy?" Jacques persisted. "None of what ye say makes sense."

"Had his reasons," Hébert reflected. "At Jemseg he's in the middle of the Indians' territories. Give him some control over them. With Father Thury's help he could easily gather braves for war parties against an English threat to Port Royal and send out scalping parties to attack settlements in New England."

"And what do priests have to do with scalping and war parties?" Guillaume wondered.

"Once the priests make converts they control them and the Indians daren't refuse when the Black Robes order them to war on Protestants. Taking enemy scalps is a practice of both sides. There's a handsome bounty for them. Beware of that when you're in the forest. And it doesn't stop with men – women and children get scalped too. So far as British and New Englanders are concerned Acadian scalps are the same as Indian or French."

Instinctively Henri crossed himself. "We understand the British are the enemy. Fought them ourselves. But I don't want to ever see the day when priests would set Indians on us."

"Whatever ye do, mind the priests. They're more in control of war parties than any governor." The brothers exchanged glances. Montard drew on his pipe and watched them; a smile twitched about the corner of his mouth.

"Priests hate Protestants as much as Protestants hate Papists." Adam piped up to break the nervous silence. "Was in Boston for a time. At the peril of my soul I listened to some Protestants sermonize to ken what they was preaching. People pickled in vinegar those are. One of the ministers was the Reverend Cotton Mather. Relentless against Catholics that one. Preached death and destruction to all Papists and especially French Catholics of Acadia. Protestants're dedicated to drive us away. Call us a blight on the land."

Hébert's eyes twinkled as if something humorous had just occurred to him. His sudden laugh broke the somber mood. "Thus was it ever between the English and the French. No different in the New World. Now I think about it, Villebon's also in the right position on the St. Jean to control the fur trade. That may have more'n anything else to do with his decision to fortify Jemseg. I deem you'll meet the governor soon after ye set foot in Acadia."

On the sixty-fourth day out from La Rochelle the fragrance of New World forests stalked the Fleur de Lis to the delight of men starved for the sight and smell of green things that grew rooted in soil. Guillaume searched the unbroken horizon and willed the land to appear.

At the first sight of shorebirds Captain Hébert reminded the men that now they sailed in waters heavily patrolled by British warships. The recent treaty was too new to trust that every vessel had word that the war between England and France was ended and he ordered extra lookouts on each watch. "Can't be too careful," he told his crew. "Better we be safe than sorry."

That night the brothers had the watch and paced the deck shivering with the cold. Against the clear black sky stars glittered with an austere gem-like quality. Guillaume recalled just such a night toward the end of King William's War when the French attacked a line of English pickets. At first the French eked out a tenuous victory; then they had to retreat when a larger force of regulars charged them. Henri voiced his thoughts that the land they were sailing to might prove to be the death of them. Jacques, who had hung on every word Pitre had said about the opportunities for young men like them in Acadia, growled, "France might've also been the death of us don't ye recall? If we're to live we've got to keep moving ahead. Not spend worry and regret over any thing we left behind. It'll be better once we're on shore and see the place for ourselves."

As the rim of the horizon brightened, faint swirls of warmer air came riding the northerly current that pushed them toward Baie Française. James smelled the salt in it and called for the sails to be trimmed. A blast out of the southeast snapped the canvas taut and the ship charged ahead; the rigging moaned as the helmsman brought the vessel to a new heading. As he walked past Jacques the mate clapped him on the shoulder. "Now we're running a prime course straight to the mouth of the Baie. Won't be long 'til the land shows itself."

The change of course brought the captain out of his cabin. Just as Hébert stepped on the deck a lookout spotted a British warship on the horizon. He called for his spyglass, snatched it from the cabin boy's hands and took it over to the rail.

"Shit!" Hébert took away the glass and looked around. He saw the mate holding his hand up to shade his eyes, straining to see the enemy ship. "James come here! It's the fookin' bloody *Wolfhound*." He studied the vessel for a few more moments and yelled, "They've seen us. They're changing course to chase us down. Call out all the men and tell the cook make us a good hot meal. Might as well do our running on full stomachs."

Hébert yelled to the helmsman, "Go more west. Make a course around the shoaling islands." He looked around for the navigator. "Michel! Bring the chart here. Need ye to watch and be sure we give them a wide enough berth."

Michel traced a line across the chart with his finger. "We stay on this course, we're like to kiss the edge of where we seen shoaling last time. We'll take it wider to be sure."

"Any chance we put the shoals between us so as to make the British change course?"

"Could be. They ought to know about how sand shifts around over there; changes every tide. Enough British ships wrecked out there as didn't know any better."

"We'll run west, then we come round and head for the cove at Cap Fourchu. Maybe they'll worry about the shoals so they'll stand off and we clear the point before they get around. They see us enter the cove and it's all over. They'll have us boxed." Hébert looked up to the tops of the masts. "Them sails need to be taut as ye can make them if ye don't want those British over here drinking our rum."

James yelled to the crew. "Hop to it!"

Hébert watched the *Wolfhound* begin to close on them. "We could use the help of a subterfuge in this situation."

"Aye, sir. Run up the British colors?"

"They see that, they might call off their chase. Do it now. Wait too long and they'll smell it's a ruse."

The *Wolfhound* ran off the wind and began to close the distance between them. On this heading and with her greater speed, she would change course once she cleared the shoals and then she would have open water to run them down and take them. The British ensign gave them just the slightest chance she would spot the flag, take them for a New Englander and head back offshore.

They rounded the shoals with a great clatter of canvas and the ship slowed as they changed course.

"Head for Minas. That should look like we're a New England trader."

"Their move now," James said. "Wager?"

"Bad luck," Hébert growled at him. "We'll see soon enough."

The tension mounted as the men went about their business and tried to control the temptation to watch the ship pursuing them.

"Act like you're bloody Englishmen used to seeing British ships in Boston's harbor. No fookin' gawkers at the rail!" Hébert paced the deck and spoke to the men. "Just go about your business. You've nothing to do, then get yourselves below. Don't want them counting more men on deck than a New Englander would have on a normal watch."

A half-hour later they watched the *Wolfhound* change her heading to go seaward.

"We'll stay this course until she's gone away. Then head down for Cap Fourchu."

Hébert spoke to the cabin boy, "Tell the cook and the purser we'll have double rations of rum all around. Ye can start bringing it up now." He called to the brothers, "This is a prime welcome you've been given!"

"Look at them," James said. "They've seen they won't have it easy here. Pure luck we escaped those British this time."

"Now just wait a minute. Seamanship had something to do with it," Hébert insisted.

ACADIA, CAP FORCHU

The Fleur de Lis sent up a red rocket as it stood off the rocky shore of Pubnico and the helmsman steered the vessel toward a small overgrown cove. Hébert called for the sails to be lowered and for the crew to stand by to hoist quickly if the red rocket was answered by a blue. When no counter signal appeared the Fleur de Lis slid through the entrance into a cove and dropped her anchor. After weeks of the relentless din of the journey and the excitement of being chased by the British – feet pounding on deck as sailors ran to and from their posts, men shouting orders and responding to them, the constant creaking of the ship's timbers, the unrelieved slapping and pounding of the sea against the hull, the relentless dirge of the masts as the sails drew the wind – there was an eerie silence.

Trees crowded the rocky outcropping that edged an anchorage large enough to serve several ships even when the tide went low. As the noises of the vessel quieted they heard birdsong wafted toward them by the light breeze. Ducks swam near the shore. Herons stood in the rocks that jutted out at the water's edge and waited for small fish to come near, so still they were all but invisible until they moved to strike. A pair of fish hawks circled in the sky, their cries pulsing as they flew above the ship. About a quarter-mile from the ship lay a small rock-strewn beach where some large boulders parted just enough to allow landing room for one or two long boats. Behind the beach a break in the trees showed where a trail led off into the forest.

"*Compagnie's* messenger's to meet us here. We agreed that instead of sailing blind into Port Royal first we'd learn is the fort still in French hands," Hébert told the crew. "While we wait James'll take a watering party ashore." The captain pointed at Jacques and Guillaume. "You'll go with them."

Two of the ship's long boats were lowered, each with an eight-man crew and all the barrels and assorted containers it could carry. They would put one boat at a time ashore to water.

As the men landed on the beach an Indian armed with a knife and hatchet stepped from the trees onto a rocky ledge just above them; he looked straight down at the mate. From that vantage point he could have easily sent his knife plunging into the man's heart.

James looked up in surprise and his face paled. He was unarmed and stood knee deep in water holding the line he was about to use to tie off the boat. One of the crew near Guillaume muttered, "More of them close by if this one showed himself. Ready to move fast we've to be."

A single word issued from the stranger's lips. "English?"

"French," James replied.

The Indian turned and melted back into the forest. The second long boat backed farther off as James waved them away. He quietly ordered his men to back their boat out from the beach. Another voice whispered, "They was attacking us already done it. Be dead we."

A voice boomed from within the grove of trees, "Who are ye? Why come ye here?"

James shouted his reply, "We're about watering our vessel, the *Fleur de Lis* of La Rochelle. She rides at anchor there." He raised his arm to point to the ship. "Who're you? Will ye show yourself?"

The man emerged from the trees. His large body was clothed in leather skins; his head was covered by a round-brimmed hat trimmed with fur. A long dark beard hid most of his weathered face. He stood with his feet spread apart; a knife was tucked into his belt and he raised his hands to rest them on his hips. "Could've killed ye all had we a mind. More heedful you've to be if you wish to live."

James exhaled with relief. "I know you! Simon Desjardins, the *Compagnie's* agent."

"Ye sport with me? You've come from the *Compagnie*? Who's your cap'n then?"

"Ambrose Hébert."

"Delightful!" Desjardins crowed. "He coming to shore? Chief Rising Hawk wants to chin with him."

"You're to come out to the ship with us." James ordered the men to unload the barrels and make room for their guests.

Spyglasses aboard the *Fleur de Lis* glinted as the captain and the purser monitored the long boat's return. Adam watched the vessel leave the shore; he was the first to identify Desjardins and his Indian companion.

As Guillaume rowed he had the chance to look more closely at the chief. He had skin the color of almond. His face was hairless and the expression on it was one that told nothing of his thoughts. The man was even handsome by European standards. A jacket of creamy moose skin covered much of his upper body and a knife was strapped to his thigh. As he watched the Indian scale the side of the ship Guillaume thought he was accustomed to boarding vessels like this. He imagined him doing so with an axe stuck into his belt and a knife between his teeth. His strangeness made him a fearsome sight even without the further help of his imagination. The chief stepped aboard the ship and looked straight at Hébert. In clear but guttural French he said, "Welcome back Captain."

"Rising Hawk, my friend," Hébert's face pinked with pleasure. "The fookin' British been more aggressive than usual?"

Rising Hawk reached toward Hébert and touched a lock of hair that swept his forehead. "British pay big scalp bounties for all Indians. Biggest pay for braves' scalps. Don't care if scalps be Indian or French. Same bounty."

"French pay more for British hair?"

Rising Hawk nodded. "Joke with your friend, Captain? Best pay for yellow hair and for red hair. But those can bring bad luck."

"Bad luck for any man who loses his hair. Any color."

"Bad luck if British catches Indian with yellow hair or red hair."

"Well," Hébert adjusted his belt. "We send back a long boat for your men? Take them aboard with us?"

"We go away tonight."

"James," the captain called out to the mate, "tell the cook to get up the best meal he can for us." He turned to Desjardins and Rising Hawk. "We're at the end of our journey and there's little left of our stores. But there'll be something for us, nonetheless."

Hébert turned to his passengers and beckoned, "Come along if ye like."

Inside the captain's cabin they wedged themselves about the table as comfortably as they could manage. The purser uncorked the last cask and sent filled glasses all around. Hébert took a sip and admired the wine before he asked his guests what news they had of Port Royal.

Desjardins began, "Hear about the new treaty?"

"Aye. Heard about it leaving La Rochelle. Appears whatever it's to mean in Acadia depends on what the British have got up to. Port Royal still French?"

"Not with Villebon's help. Still hard at it to build his new fort up the St. Jean River."

"Abandon Jemseg altogether now is he?" Hébert was wide-eyed.

"Quebec sent orders to move his fort nearer Port Royal. Settlers complain about it not being safe enough for them if he's not to rebuild fortifications there. Governor moves to new Fort St. Jean." Simon shrugged, "Port Royal will be left to molder. Farmers and tradesmen settled there for protection of a French garrison. Now they're wide open to attack whenever fookin' English come." He milled his arms in wide gestures as he spoke.

"Careful," Hébert said as he ducked to avoid being cuffed.

"Even so the settlers made new roads and dikes to drain more marshlands. Even there's a new windmill. Some farmers have a bit of overage now. *Compagnie* would trade it – that and the green cod – to New Englanders. But Villebon's forbidden so-called 'trafficking with the enemy.' No matter. Boats come up from Boston to load in secret. *Compagnie's* the King's own monopoly and our very business – so we have to only trade with the French. Pretend money's not changing hands behind our backs and we can't take our share," Desjardins sighed.

A brief smile played about Hébert's lips. "Seems nothing's changed here."

The cook entered with a large pot of pea soup. "Last of it, Cap'n", he reported. "Biscuits coming right along." The cabin boy entered behind him with a large bowl of hardtack and set it down between Simon and the captain.

"Any sweet for us after dinner?"

"Everything's used up. Need provisions." The cook shuffled his feet.

"Bring a ladle and some bowls. We supposed to look at this or eat it?" The boy ran off to the galley to get the tools.

The captain took up the conversation. "Ye deem we'll have visitors in this cove tonight? This one can hide and rewater a vessel. Others must use it."

"We'd seen a ship here when ye come in we'd warned ye off."

"How'd ye know if we was friends?"

"Englishman heads right up the bay. We know who's about in these waters. "

"How about the *Wolfhound?* Seen her about in these parts lately?"

"Now ye mention it we did sight her yesterday coming up into the Baie at high tide. Must've been chasing someone. You see her?"

"Was us they wanted." Hébert smirked. "We're flying the English flag."

"No, sir." Simon was surprised. "Was you they was running after?"

"Lucky they left off us when they did. Had to sail farther down the coast to get away. Only then we came back up to the cove. Most adventure I've had in a while. Could do without any more like that. Caught us, they'd probably hanged me. Throw the crew in irons. Sorry start for those coming here to make a new life for themselves." Hébert gestured toward the young men. "They've traveled all the way to New France to work for the *Compagnie* and make their fortunes. What advice can ye give them being as they're new to Acadia?"

"Be this a caution to ye." Simon waxed to his subject. "Fighting between French and English means attacks on our settlements. Before the truce Canadians and Indians raided villages in Massachusetts. Instead of chasing them back to Quebec, New Englanders revenged on an easier target – the innocent farmers of Acadia. Our land's but an easy sail down the wind from Boston. Quebec's a long hard slog over mile on mile of rough country. French run there and hide. Set Acadians up to take their beatings."

Simon fell silent and the men thought he was finished. Then he erupted as if anger propelled his words from somewhere deep inside him. "Ye ask how they treat Acadians? Benjamin Church brings his Bastonnais militia. Fookin' bounty hunters the most are. Like the chief says, there's no difference between scalps. They come and lay waste and hunt our people to get rich on bounties." Simon grimaced and took a swig of wine. "No place here to settle and not expect such from the fookin' English."

PORT ROYAL

Next morning the crew weighed anchor and the Fleur de Lis began the final leg of its journey. During the day the wind shifted and the salt tang of the ocean replaced the green smells of the land. They arrived at Port Royal and found its waterfront rank with the pungent odors of fish and sweat and decay. Compared with all the brothers had heard about it, Port Royal seemed a place of little consequence. Its buildings hugged the ground as if hunkered down for protection from a sky filled with bulky gray clouds that marched like ranks of soldiers in monotonous progression toward some distant battleground. The sailors disappeared below decks once the vessel sat at anchor; occasional laughter came from the crew's quarters.

The brothers rowed ashore with Simon, Pierre-Jaspar and a few of the crew. When the long boat shoaled on the beach Henri jumped from it into the ankle-deep water and ran onto the land. He knelt and kissed the earth and then unbent himself to raise his hands to the sky and thank God he was off the pitching, rolling ship. Then he stood up and looked around him. "What a cabbage patch of a place this is," he pronounced. "Just look at it – small and dirt-poor."

"Aye. It makes our farm in Normandy look fit for a king," Jacques grumbled. "Maybe we didn't rightly know the worth of that."

A pang of homesickness hit Guillaume. Images of his childhood sweetheart came unbidden to his mind at Jacque's mention of their farm. Their neighbor's daughter Bess had played with him in the hayloft, rolling about with first one on top and then the other. It was the first time a girl had aroused his sex. His father's voice had called from below and ended the game. He remembered that clear voice of authority and how it had echoed through the barn. Guillaume had pulled himself together and climbed down the ladder; Bess had stayed still in the hay hoping not to be discovered. Armand had put his arm around his son's shoulders and firmly walked him away while she made her escape. "But there's no escape from this and no father to bear me away from it." Guillaume felt saddened.

"Ye'll learn to love the place," Simon chided as he marched them toward the truck house.

Port Royal bore no resemblance to what they had last seen of France. La Rochelle had watch towers and stone ramparts protecting the harbor entrance. Port Royal had some wooden piles driven into the ground. The place was a collection of huts and hovels gathered about a small chapel and all were enclosed by a flimsy palisade. Jacques' expert military eye scanned it with misgivings. "That's the kind of protection offered against the British, no wonder the place fell without a fight."

Montard said bitterly, "Must frustrate the Governor to have everything he's built up destroyed by the British. Then he has to build again to repulse the next attack. If the King sees no reason to send troops to keep the country safe but rely on men like Villebon and whatever alliances they can make with the Indians to hold on to these settlements then no matter how great the effort, France will lose Acadia to the British."

Guillaume asked, "Ye sailed with us but aren't of the *Compagnie*. What's your purpose here if ye don't mind me asking?"

"I'm here to study the Governor's work. He's very capable. In some quarters he's taken to be an honest man. But rumor and doubt have tarnished his name in France. Most likely that's the result of jealous gossip. I've met him before and disbelieve the stories about him circulating in the court. That's more than I should've told you."

"Who'd we tell it to?" Jacques sounded resentful.

"Will ye leave us once we've reached the governor's fort?" Guillaume asked as if there had been no interruption.

"Yes. My orders will eventually send me off."

"To Quebec?" Henri asked.

"Possibly. Our paths may cross again somewhere in the wilderness. Your hunting will take you along the rivers toward Quebec and maybe even farther west."

"You've been in Acadia before."

"Returned to France last year. I'm back to clear up this situation regarding Governor Villebon. I'll stay with him for the time being."

Later Captain Hébert came ashore and saw them walking about, legs wobbling as they tried to adjust to being back on dry land. "One look and anyone'd tell you're new here. Be fine in a few days. Takes time to get used to being back on land." He laughed. "Bunch of drunks, ye seem."

They followed Simon into the truck house expecting to learn something about the *Compagnie's* business in Acadia. Henri moaned when they walked inside and saw confusion all about them. Iron pots and axes lay willy-nilly behind the counters. Furs lay about in great piles on the floor. Barrels of foodstuffs were opened and their contents exposed. Simon turned from his conversation with another trader and asked Henri, "Ye feel off?"

Henri swallowed before he answered. "This place is a mess such as I've never seen before. How do ye know where any thing is or if any stuff's missing?"

"Just talking about that. Clerk died over winter. No one to replace him." Simon rubbed his chin. "Did you say ye read and write? Do sums too?"

Henri looked at him confidently. "Yes I can. Kept books for the monks. What happened to your clerk? He get sick with something and it killed him?"

Desjardins looked at the other man, "Best we tell him it right out."

"Aye. See can he take to hear it."

"This is a good place but you're new to it." Desjardins chose his words with greater care than usual. "Clerking here's a good job but ye need take care how ye handle it."

Henri nodded. It seemed reasonable so far.

"Recall chief Rising Hawk?"

Henri nodded and began to wonder where the conversation was headed.

"Chief forbids braves to have liquor. By *Compagnie* rule no liquor's allowed in the truck house. Clerk thought otherwise. Brought a jug of rum inside. Sold it by the glass to some braves. Some of them get drunk and go to sleep. Some go on the warpath instead. Get my drift?"

"Aye, I think so. Clerk killed by a drunken man?"

Desjardins exchanged glances with the other trader; he shook his head ever so slightly.

"Ye understand then." Desjardins came toward Henri, reached out and clapped him on the shoulder. "We'd make better use of your pen here than your knife or gun. Didn't fancy you as a woodsman. Truck house work's better for ye. Keep the books. Sell stuff to trappers and exchange goods for furs. Better use for you than traipsing the forests."

"But if I work here how will I make up the number of pelts I need to pay the *Compagnie* for my indenture?"

"Five of every hundred pelts brought in goes to your account."

"Ten."

"Seven," Simon countered.

"Eight and a half."

"Ain't no such thing as half a fookin' pelt. Eight."

"Done! When do I start?"

"How about right now?" Henri rubbed his hands and chuckled. Then he added, "By the way, how'd he die?"

"Who?"

"Clerk I'm replacing."

The other man stepped forward. "It's like this. He's selling rum to the braves. One man has a mean temper – pays for his first glass, then a second. Comes back again but has no coin nor nothing to trade for more. Clerk refuses him. Man gets angry and makes threats. Clerk tries to push him out the door but he pulls a knife and threatens the clerk who reaches for his musket. No time to load. He's already dead." The man snickered as he saw the color drain from Henri's face.

"No, no," Desjardins shouted. "What're ye telling? Trying to scare the new clerk with your stories?" He gruffed at Henri, "Just don't go getting any liquor in here is all. No side trading with anyone and ye'll be just fine. It ain't here then none'll come to look for it.

RIVIERE ST. JEAN

September was full of the lush green ripeness of summer shading toward the dun colors of the harvest - each day brought sights and discoveries that added to their patchwork of knowledge about their new country. Along the shores of Baie Francaise Jacques and Guillaume saw men patrolling long stony beaches lined with ladder-like flakes and keeping watch over their drying fish to protect their catch from human and animal thievery. The sun-warmed air of the day rode the cool undercurrents that heralded the coming season; migrating birds crowded the broad marshes and rose on thrashing wings and filled the air with their cries.

Where the trees came right to the edge of the water there were sometimes paths that led from unknown places inside dense forests down to small beaches. The tides were the greatest they had ever seen. They were even more powerful than those that washed the shores of Normandy. Flats of red clay stretched for miles at low water and made it impossible to land a boat until the tide once more filled the bay.

On an unseasonably warm day they arrived at the mouth of the St. Jean River and found Governor Villebon in the midst of supervising some final buttressing for the fortifications to house and protect the headquarters he and his men would occupy during the coming winter. With his sleeves rolled up above his elbows, he looked unlike anything they expected of a governor.

Villebon was a wiry man with an unruly head of salt and pepper hair. He was no taller than anyone else but stood out from the others by the way he held himself and used the power of his eyes to hold easy sway over his battle-hardened men.

Guillaume asked who it was that built the old fort and Villebon stopped for a moment as if to consider whether to take the time to respond. Then he wiped his chin with the back of his arm and looked around at the others hard at work before he began to tell the story.

"Some years ago there's a war over the fur trade. Court's favorite d'Aulnay pitted himself against de La Tour, King's appointed Governor of Acadia. Two Frenchmen that should've settled their differences and found a way to share. They did that Acadia'd be a rich place now. But they're jealous of each other and headstrong. So they fight. La Tour's beaten and runs off to Boston. Gets help from the Protestants."

Villebon spat on the ground next to his right foot and cleared his throat. "D'Aulnay captures his fort and takes his wife prisoner while he's gone. Executes La Tour's soldiers and makes his wife stand by with a noose about her neck to watch them die. Soon after that she dies, some say 'twas by poison." He paused to look out beyond the fort as if scanning the harbor for enemy ships. The breeze stiffened to a steady blow and the tide rolled landward in waves that came on like a herd of great white horses. As if satisfied that this day no vessels rode their backs Villebon continued his story.

"D'Aulnay gets control over all Acadia and the King's blessing to boot. Hardly has the chance to enjoy his triumph before one day he falls from his canoe and drowns. No sooner he's in his grave than La Tour's back from exile and marries the widow d'Aulnay. They go off to live right here at the old Fort La Tour. King reinstates him as governor of Acadia. Should've been peace then but that wasn't in the cards."

"D'Aulnay's major creditor in La Rochelle, Le Borgne shows up to claim his holdings at Port Royal that were mortgaged to pay for his war against La Tour. Fight with Le Borgne only lasts about a year. Then the British show up and take Port Royal and Fort La Tour. Both." He shook his head. "British come and find the French fighting among themselves and with no defenses. Not about to happen while I'm governor."

Campfire talk mostly concerned the details of finishing the fort but as the evenings lengthened the men spun yarns about the New Englanders and how they treated the Acadians; about Indian attacks on New England settlements led by the Black Robes; about English Rangers making attacks for retribution on Acadian settlements; and about the grisly trade that sprang from the notorious scalp bounties set in reprisal by both sides.

"Powder and shot," Villebon told them. "That's what we give our Indians as presents. Give them food such as dried peas and corn. Some dried fish. Gave them all we had after the winter to get the raiding parties moving. Left us near high and dry of supplies. Off they went with the Black Robes leading them on the war path." His mouth formed a sardonic smile. "Not civilized like how they war in Europe where you boys come from."

Jacques sputtered, "What's so fookin' civilized about killing a man over there? It's a bloody awful business. Screaming and crying when men're shot or cut. Bodies lay on the ground bleeding out in their own shit. Was the worst thing I ever seen."

"Families killed here as well as fighters. Women and children are butchered and scalped. English and French both guilty of that. Take scalps to change for money." Villebon stopped when he saw the expressions on the boys' faces. In a gentler tone he said, "You've a lot to learn as I can tell." Then he changed the subject. "When the *Fleur de Lis* sailed into the bay we thanked God you're here in time for us to get some winter stocks. Lacking your supplies there'd be little food and ammunition for our men staying here to defend the fort."

"Is it regular?" Guillaume's face had almost regained its color. "Give powder and shot to the Indians each year?"

"Price we pay them as allies to fight the English," Villebon replied. "How far do ye think we'd get with only Frenchmen when there ain't that many of us? You're different because ye come from the *Compagnie*. They send you here to trap and trade, not to war with the enemy. But if ye meet any English while you're off in the forest, they'll be quick to go against you."

"So," Jacques repeated, "there's no truce here in spite of the recent treaty."

"Count on nothing that happens in Europe. Only what ye find here."

CHIGNECTO 1699

Guillaume noticed Song Sparrow, Rising Hawk's youngest daughter on the very first day he and Jacques entered the Indian encampment. She was tall for a girl, with glossy black hair pulled back in a single braid that fell between her shoulders. She wore a loose shift of soft deerskin that fell to her knees; a small child tottered by her feet grasping the hem of her dress to try to keep its balance.

"You've caught me little girl," she cooed; the child's body wriggled with anticipation. Song Sparrow put her hands on the baby's waist and picked her up. The child spread her arms in pleasure as Song Sparrow swung her out and rewarded her with a delighted laugh. Then she drew the little girl in and squeezed her. The two grinned at each other. At that moment a young woman ran up and claimed the child. Guillaume was enchanted and surprised at himself for feeling glad the baby wasn't hers; she blushed at his notice and turned her face away. He saw the flash of a smile and felt alive for the first time since he set foot in Acadia.

The men in the camp were not so friendly. They looked the Frenchmen over with scowling faces and muttered comments. "It's like when we went off to the war, ain't it?" Jacques said to his brother as they looked around the camp. "Looking us over like we're so much meat. Ugly bunch here, you ask me."

One man walked up to Guillaume and brushed his shoulder, glaring into his face. As he did, Guillaume locked eyes with him. It was a gesture that any fighting man would recognize. Rising Hawk saw them and called to the man. "Flying Squirrel, these are French – with us. English are enemy."

"Man looks upon your daughter," he pointed at Guillaume. "Not like it." The Indian spat in the dust near Guillaume's feet as he walked away. Guillaume followed him with his eyes and kept his hand on his knife.

Over the first winter the brothers learned to trap and pull loaded sleds over trails packed with snow as the clan traveled to their hunting grounds. There the men went out in parties to spend days roaming the forest, trapping furs and bringing down game which they dressed and packed to take back to the main camp.

One of the early hunts was on a day of flying clouds and blue sky with the wind soughing in the treetops and making its own music of dried rustling leaves and crackling branches. The quiet movements of animal feet in the litter and the anxious calls of small birds as they descried predators – things that speak of hidden danger to the wary – were masked by the creaking and squealing of large tree limbs. That was why Flying Squirrel unexpectedly came upon a bear almost ready to hibernate.

He was caught off guard, reacted by throwing his spear and hit its shoulder. The animal roared in surprise and reared up to its full height. Flying Squirrel and the bear stared at each other. The bear's hackles rose and its forehead wrinkled as it opened its mouth and growled; the man backed a few steps and then turned to run.

"Spears! Throw! Quick!" The men moved as fast as they could to get close enough to help him. The bear's front feet dropped to the ground and their spears pierced the air. The enraged animal charged, thundering through the underbrush with blood spurting from the spear's gash. Even though it was wounded, the bear was faster than the man and it caught Flying Squirrel, scraping his back with long fierce claws. Then the man's foot wedged into a pair of rocks that rose from the ground to form a stirrup and down he went. His leg twisted and he screamed in agony as the leg-bone snapped.

The man howled as he lay trapped and in pain. The animal reared above him and men shouted at the bear to divert its attention. They circled it with drawn knives and tried to close in to slash at it. Gore from the bear's shoulder ran down its foreleg with the animal's every motion. Blood dripped from its raised and extended claws. Its labored breath came from its mouth in bursts of steaming pink froth. Flying Squirrel let out a terrified shriek and turned his face away from the bear's claws as the animal hovered over him, poised to strike.

Guillaume steadied his musket; just as the creature took a final murderous swipe at Flying Squirrel, he fired off a shot that hit the bear square in the face. The huge paw fell slack and the bear toppled with a groan onto the ground beside the injured man, its tongue falling out of its shattered jaw. The heat of its final breath caressed Flying Squirrel's face and he fainted. Guillaume stood holding his weapon with slack hands, staring fixedly at the dead animal and the unconscious man. Others ran forward to tug the carcass away from Flying Squirrel. They freed his foot and twisted his leg to straighten it.

When Flying Squirrel finally regained consciousness, he was surrounded by the braves and the center of their attention; the first face that came into focus was Guillaume's. He clenched his jaw, determined not to give the Frenchman the satisfaction of seeing him in agony. The men trussed his leg with sticks wrapped inside strips of rawhide to hold it still and laid him on his side on the ground. A couple of the braves bent down to speak to Flying Squirrel in low voices, but he soon lost consciousness again.

They worked in silence – each knew what needed to be done. Some of the men cut saplings and made litters to carry the wounded man and the bear. Others skinned and trimmed the kill to ready the meat, fat and hide for the trip back to the camp. Guillaume and Jacques helped carry the meat and walked ahead of the litter that bore the wounded man.

The party was nearing the encampment when one of the men broke away to run and tell Rising Hawk and Flying Squirrel's mother of his injury. A large crowd was gathered by the time the hunters reached the camp; they swarmed around to see the injured man, poke at his wounds and hear his story. Flying Squirrel's mother pushed her way through to her son and burst into tears when she saw him.

"Be still, woman," her son hissed in a weak voice. She reeled as if he slapped her hard across the face. The chief ordered everyone to get away and leave him to the shaman's care.

The women took charge of the animal's remains and readied the kettles. For days afterward the smell of bear fat being tried to separate the fat from the gristle hung over the camp. The hide was scraped clean and stretched, the legs unrolled entire from the bones and given to Guillaume for leggings. During the days that followed, Flying Squirrel's angry eyes tracked the brothers' every movement as he watched them through the open flap of his wigwam.

Dogs fought over the bones, snarling and snapping at each other and dragging them about the camp. When the last of the bear's leg bones lay on the ground in front of Flying Squirrel's wigwam, two dogs claimed it and pulled on the ends. Then one of them let go of it and attacked the other. After a fight that left both dogs bleeding, the larger dog bared its fangs at the smaller dog and threatened it with a deep vicious growl. Howling, the smaller one retreated with bleeding flanks and the skin of an ear hanging in gory shreds. The winner clamped his jaws around his prize and dragged it away into the underbrush.

After Flying Squirrel's leg healed and he began to hunt again, he approached Rising Hawk and asked for Song Sparrow to be his wife.

"My wife and daughter must know what you wish."

"Women? Doesn't matter what they think. Chief decides."

Rising Hawk closed with him, his forehead taut with anger and his eyes hardened. He growled, "Be it as I say."

Flying Squirrel looked back at Rising Hawk and absently handled the hilt of his knife. "You be sorry, she marries Frenchman." Rising Hawk looked at his hand and then at Flying Squirrel's face. The young man took his hand away from his knife and stalked off to disappear into his wigwam to sulk.

"No good when man act like that," the chief thought.

One night they sat in the wigwam talking across the fire pit as hunters do at the end of the day and Rising Hawk made an observation that startled Jacques and Guillaume. "Indians think Black Robes have strange magic."

His words floated in the air as if sent by some presence on the other side of the spirit veil. No one spoke. Rising Hawk studied the brothers through slits of eyes as he took a puff on his pipe; its smoke curled above his head and mingled slowly with the smoke from the fire as it rose and wafted out the opening at the top of the wigwam. Dark shadows formed beneath his eyes as he looked at them across the fire pit, his face as still as carved stone. They waited for him to speak again.

"White man's god. Priests say they eat his body. Iroquois defeat a man of great strength and honor. Eat enemy's heart to take his spirit and make them strong." The fire flamed up and crackled. The brothers sat still and stared at the ground in front of their feet.

"But what god gives his own flesh for men to eat?" Rising Hawk took another puff of his pipe and turned his solemn face toward the brothers. "You have answer?"

"What says Black Robe?" Jacques asked.

"Black Robe calls it great mystery of faith. Says we must believe it so if we wish to join in their religion."

"They teach all the same. Same for French. Same for Indian. Same beliefs go as far back as anyone can tell, even to the time long-ago when our God came to live and die on earth and then rise up to glory," Guillaume said.

"Never seen our gods. Believe they watch us. Call our spirits to them when we die."

"Many Christians believe the same."

"Aiee, Guillaume. But what of the priests? They suffer like other men. Eating their god not save them from dying when they be sick or killed. Some priests even tortured by men who want to see will their god come to save them. But Christian god not save those."

Guillaume lay his hands on his knees with palms open to show he hid nothing from Rising Hawk. "The priests are men like us and give us the example of their belief. Christians are taught to have faith in God's love, no matter what happens to their bodies."

The chief frowned at the answer and decided to consult Smiling Otter before the time came when he must tell Guillaume about the prophecy.

1702

Guillaume and Jacques continued to court Rising Hawk's daughters in spite of the open malice they saw in Flying Squirrel's face and the un-spoken resentment of some of the other men. On a warm and sunny afternoon, Guillaume walked with Song Sparrow in a wildflower meadow where he bent down from time to time to pick a blossom for her. Soon her arms overflowed with a large colorful bouquet. A huge oak tree stood nearby and they went to sit in its shade. Guillaume sighed with contentment, looking at the sky and then at Song Sparrow sitting with her lap filled with flowers. "I feel I've come alive," he whispered. She looked at him with love in her eyes.

"These're beautiful, Guillaume," she smiled running her hands through the many-colored blossoms.

"Not as you are, my dearest girl. I hope they'll speak to ye as I would."

He took some of the flowers and tried to wind the stems into a chain.

"What'd they tell me could they speak your very words?"

He wove more flowers but now he was nervous and his fingers were thick and not used to such a fragile task. After he pulled a few of the heads from the stems, Song Sparrow put her own delicate fingers to work with his. Their fingers intertwined and he raised her hand to his lips and kissed it. "They'd speak of my love and how I wish to make you my wife."

"Oh," her breath caught and she looked at him. They leaned toward each other and their lips met in a sweet and tender kiss.

"Song Sparrow," he wound the chain of flowers around her shoulders. "Will ye marry me?"

"Yes. What else would ye think?" A tear ran down her cheek and he wiped it away with a light caress. Then he put his arms around her and drew her close to give her a lover's kiss.

When they returned to the camp, their glowing faces told the whole story. Song Sparrow told her mother of Guillaume's proposal. White Heron and Rising Hawk talked long into the night about their daughters and what might happen once the clan knew they both wanted Frenchmen for husbands.

Next morning Rising Hawk went to speak to the shaman. The chief stood at the flap of Smiling Otter's wigwam to be recognized and invited inside. The shaman took one look at the chief's face and beckoned. "Join me, my brother." Spears and shields were stacked opposite the shaman's seat. Ceremonial masks hung above them. Smiling Otter's spirit skin lay on the top shield as if to observe visitors from its perch. Its eyes were closed and Rising Hawk was glad the spirit chose to ignore him.

Bunches of grasses and herbs hung above the edges of the fire pit and as smoke rose up from the hearth toward the opening, wisps of it trailed around the masks and played about their empty faces. One had a beaked nose and the smoke curled up into it before drifting back out through the mouth slit. The shaman smiled as he followed his friend's gaze. "When I see this I think it must be an ancestor returned to enjoy what pleased him as a living man."

The shaman packed a pipe bowl with tabagie laced with herbs and handed it to his friend. He lit a straw in the fire and touched it to the leaves. The chief drew on it and when the tabagie took the light he stood and raised the pipe to the mask to offer the spirit the first puff of its fragrance. Then the men shared the pipe in amiable silence for a few minutes to let their minds clear before taking up Rising Hawk's dilemma.

"You're here because of your marriageable daughters," the shaman observed.

Rising Hawk started.

"No surprise, my friend. No magic needed to see what troubles your spirit. Many threads wait to be woven into cloth strong enough to protect the clan from being divided by bloodshed."

"At first I was angry, horrified those French wish to marry my daughters. Then I think of the young men of this tribe. Surely once I'm dead, husbands of my daughters be rivals to take my place. They be enemies and split our people apart and make war against each other."

"But now ye think if your daughters marry those French that can't happen?"

"One of them could never be chief."

"What about the omen? What if she dies?" It was bad luck to mention her name.

"All the more reason for her children to have French for father."

"Ye know there're men who'll be angry enough if ye give one daughter to a Frenchman, but for both to marry those brothers..." Smiling Otter's words trailed off as he shook his head. "Envy makes men dangerous when they crave something. What'll ye do if any threaten to leave our clan because of it?"

"There are other marriageable girls among the clans, even chiefs' daughters. Men of a clan should look to girls of other clans. You've said so yourself. One of my daughters marries a Frenchman and the other marries a member of our clan. Ye see how there'd be a fight when that one sets himself to be the next chief. Maybe everyone wouldn't agree about that man. Flying Squirrel wants to marry Song Sparrow. She spurns him. He hates the Frenchman who loves her and would try to kill him had he a chance. Do you think he'd be a good chief for the people?"

Rising Hawk glanced over to the spirit skin and was startled to see that now it seemed to be wide awake. Its yellow eyes pierced him and made his skin crawl. He looked about hoping to see that its glass bead eyes just reflected some stray beam of light. The shaman furrowed his brow. "I don't argue with ye, my brother. Just think about this before ye answer the Frenchmen. Say no to them and they'll find other wives."

"Say no to them and my daughters say they'll marry no one else. Then what'll I do for grandchildren? And who'll be the next chief after me?" He frowned. "I know my answer. And I know I'll have to defend it before the clan. Will you at least stand by me?"

"My brother, you can depend on me. These French better be worth your trouble."

As the shaman spoke, an old dog with his face and back covered with scars from fights he had won or lost when he was younger, pushed his way past the flap and curled himself at his master's feet. The shaman absently patted his head as the dog looked at Rising Hawk with the same intent yellow stare as the spirit skin. The chief turned to look for the skin but now it was lost in the shadows. The dog yawned and closed his eyes and the shaman fell into a meditative silence. The dog nestled closer and kicked its legs out as if it dreamed of chasing something. Then it stopped and sighed in its sleep.

Rising Hawk wondered if the spirit had taken over the dog or was this just the way of an old animal? He shook off those thoughts and continued. "Another knot in this rope – I've to tell Guillaume about the prophecy. He'll have to protect her now."

"Aiee, brother. Does he respect what our ancestors tell men in sacred council or does he think like the Black Robes and spurn such as superstition?"

"Black Robes have magic in their rites. Frenchmen say they believe in Black Robes' teachings about their god. Lived with us long enough to see we honor our old ways even as we pray to Black Robes' god. Doesn't bother them like it does the priest. Most of all they want to marry my daughters."

"Let it be on ye then," Smiling Otter said as he stroked the sleeping dog.

Rising Hawk called his women together and forbade the brothers to approach the wigwam until he called them to come. Jacques and Guillaume went into the forest to search for game birds while they waited for his call. They hunted in silence using hand gestures as their only communication. For a time they sat concealed in some bushes.

Near their hiding place a squirrel sat on a branch of a tree and looked about through dark mischievous eyes. Its head jerked back when it saw the men. Then a sudden movement in some high branches of a nearby oak drew its attention and the squirrel leaped from limb to limb toward a young hawk that landed there and held a tiny bird's egg in its mouth. The squirrel flew through the branches toward the hawk and the bird retreated, raising its wings to protect the egg. The squirrel sat on a nearby branch and scolded. Then it attacked the hawk and the egg fell to the ground and its shell was smashed. The squirrel ran down and licked up the yolk and the hawk swooped at it, screaming. The squirrel escaped into a thicket of prickly vines. The brothers got up and moved to another blind. "Too much racket," Jacques spat.

Once they had a brace of quail, they began their walk back to the camp.

"What's it seem that Rising Hawk'll do?" Guillaume broke the silence.

"Don't see him letting one girl marry one of us and not the other, so I'll say he either agrees to both or to none. If he says none, we'll have to leave. Braves'd think we wasn't in good stead with the chief and they'd find ways to provoke us to fight. Best not wait for it to happen. Agree on furs we trapped and take them with us. Travel fast to get them to the *Compagnie's* warehouse. Henri counts them in. We be near finished with our indenture."

"All or nothin'. He says one daughter to marry one of us we've both to leave. Got it right?"

"No half-loaves. Don't nivver do."

The wigwam flap was open when they carried the birds into the camp. White Heron came outside and made a fuss over how beautiful and plump the birds looked. She beamed when they gave her the quail and Jacques winked at his brother.

Rising Hawk called them to come inside. A pipe stuffed with tabagie was lighted and passed to each man; the chief took a long pull and slowly exhaled. "Ye pleased my wife with your gift. My daughters will hear no word about ye but to your good. Other men want to marry them but both refuse to listen to any others."

Jacques asked, "Ye say this because you're going to let us marry them?"

Rising Hawk nodded. "We've to be very careful when I tell the clan of this. Much depends on how you act, so ye must speak to no one of what I say."

A few days later Rising Hawk went off on a hunt with one other man, a friend whose son wished to marry Patient Moon. That evening each man came back with a deer. The whole camp tried to read their faces for clues as what had been decided.

The following day the deer meat was spitted and roasted and all in the camp were invited to a feast. When the food was nearly eaten, Rising Hawk stood in front of his wigwam and made his announcement. Most of the men expected to hear he agreed for his daughters to marry the Frenchmen and muttered so. But only one man remained angry, his pride bruised by what he saw as the chief's affront to him. Flying Squirrel took his weapons and his bedroll along with some food and left in the night.

Rising Hawk woke Guillaume just before sunrise and gestured for him to follow. They went off into the forest to a secret place the Chief sometimes used when he needed to think and where they would not be overheard when he told Guillaume about Smiling Otter's prophecy. They collected twigs and branches to make a fire. The chief took some smudge sticks from his pouch and threw them into the blaze. The incense smoked and its fragrance embraced the men. Rising Hawk stared through the flames at Guillaume, his eyes as distant as if they looked out from within the spirit world. After a few minutes the chief's eyes refocused and he told Guillaume the shaman's prophecy for his daughter.

From the time she was a baby Song Sparrow seemed like an old spirit in a child's body and Smiling Otter and Rising Hawk watched her closely. One morning they entered the forest with the day dawning behind them after a night spent chanting prayers for the child whom they would ask the ancestors to name and protect.

They walked among ancient trees to a wide circular clearing. As they went, the far-off sounds of birds calling and the crackle of twigs as animals foraged came to their ears. Near the opening to the sacred place a crow clattered; its voice sounded like dry bones rattling against the inside of a gourd. As they passed its perch the crow fell silent and watched them through slitted yellow eyes.

They paused at the entrance to the clearing while the shaman took the skin of his spirit animal from his pack and asked its blessing. He hooded it on his head; the front legs hung down the sides of his face so that its front claws rested on his shoulders. Rising Hawk followed him as he danced through the opening between the sentinel trees, his arms by his side and his body swaying to mimic the otter's fluid movements. He sang a high whistling song as they approached the place where the ancestors waited for them.

An oak stood among the tall dense firs that hedged the sacred clearing as if this single tree that knew the cycle of birth and death stood among the evergreens to show how the living world was held within the world of spirit. Inside the circle they faced giant trees that seemed to be the roosting places where all the souls that had gone to the Above returned to sit in council with the living. The glass bead eyes of the otter began to take on the spirit of the shaman as they brightened and his dulled. The golden eyes glowed softly as the shaman made a song of the otter's chirping noises. The song turned to grunts and a fierce fire-colored light flashed in the otter's eyes and the beads that decorated its claws glowed red and hung like blood dripping from their tips. The boughs of the trees rustled and their tall heads seemed to bend down as if the ancestors crowded the branches to watch the men. Slowly weaving their way, their feet moved to the rhythm of the shaman's chants as they circled the clearing and approached the sacred rock at the eastern side. When Smiling Otter finished his song only the movement of pure soundless air throbbed against their eardrums.

They burned some smudge sticks of fragrant pine to please the ancestors. Then they seated themselves with their backs to the rock and looked out across the clearing; the animal eyes were still fierce with the light of the spirit that had crossed into the otter's skin. The forest barely breathed and the scent of the burned smudge sticks lingered in the air. The door to the ancestor world opened and its breath rustled a leaf that swung wildly about its twig for a moment and then stopped. The stillness returned.

The shaman waited for something to direct them. A small bird landed on the twig that held the leaf that had spun about and began to sing, at first a small trilling of liquid notes and then a full joyous song that quickly ended in a few chirps. Once more peace descended. The bird sat silently as if considering its song and then lifted from the twig with a harsh squawk. As the bird flew off into the forest the twig and the attached leaf fell to the ground.

Rising Hawk did not dare breathe or move. He saw the omen clearly but waited for the shaman to speak. Smiling Otter opened his eyes as if returning from a dream; the otter skin's eyes were once again yellow beads. The shaman read the fear on his friend's face.

"You're right to be worried about your daughter." He began to speak his prophecy. "The way to the ancestors' place is open but she's not yet invited to go there. The bird carried her spirit here to visit us. She'll not remain in our camp many years. Her life will be short. She'll be happy until death comes to claim her. She's to be called Song Sparrow. As the small bird flies with grace and speed and spreads joy with the music of its voice, so she'll spend the years of her life. As the bird disappears into the forest so this child will leave our clan when the ancestors call her spirit to fly to them."

Rising Hawk was deeply troubled by the shaman's prediction and resolved to protect his daughter. But what could he do to defend her? He was brokenhearted. How could he keep her from the fate the ancestors decreed? He felt they were even now ready to welcome her into their domain. Better to keep the shaman's prediction from her mother. As they walked back through the forest toward the encampment, he bound the shaman to keep the prophecy a secret between them.

When Rising Hawk finished his story, Guillaume felt himself thrust deep into something dark and hopeless that lurked beneath Song Sparrow's life and now his. But soon after returning to the camp Guillaume became so caught up in the joy of their marriage that the dark thing swam away from the edge of his mind. Even as he promised Rising Hawk to keep the secret between them, he willed himself to believe the thing could not withstand the light of their happiness.

Rising Hawk told Guillaume the story of her naming but withheld his premonition that their marriage would likely herald Song Sparrow's death. He didn't want to give her up to the ancestors but he knew that no matter how he tried to stop them from claiming her, he couldn't succeed. And anything he did to obstruct them as they wove the strands of all creatures' lives together into a single great net, might just lead to greater suffering for her. No such fate cast a shadow over the love between Jacques and Patient Moon.

The wedding day dawned fair. Song Sparrow emerged from her father's wigwam wearing a creamy moose skin dress covered with shamanic designs promising happiness and a life filled with children. She was adorned with colored beads that were strung into necklaces with feathers and shells; the shaman's gift of a small red carved bird hung on a leather thong about her neck.

Guillaume couldn't pull his eyes away from her; they followed wherever she walked. Her long dark hair hung loose and cascaded down her back. It swung this way and that as she danced her passion for him and, as if his body knew how to do what his mind did not, his feet took him to her and at last he abandoned himself to dance his love for her.

She took his hand and led him to stand with Jacques and Patient Moon; the couples were joined in the ancient way before the shaman. The feasting went on into the evening until Smiling Otter rose to lead the couples away and sing his blessings on their lives. While he listened to the chanting, Guillaume thought of what Rising Hawk told him of the shaman's prediction and he frowned in worry, but then his wife reached to his face to smoothe his forehead and her caresses soon made him forget his concern.

That night when he saw her body for the first time, he couldn't believe a woman could be so radiant; they held each other with their limbs intertwined and loved each other throughout the night. In the morning he rose early and stoked the hearth fire. Then he went outside to collect some water and herbs to prepare a tisane. Song Sparrow stretched herself with the languor of a contented cat and laughed with pleasure when she saw his smitten look. The pot was long cooled and the herbs steamed to sodden muck before he thought of it again.

It wasn't long before Song Sparrow told Guillaume she carried their child; he was transported with happiness. She gave birth early in the following year to a son he named Paul. When the child became old enough to walk about in the wigwam Smiling Otter gave him his real name, Dancing Crow, for his joyous movement and constant chatter.

For that moment Rising Hawk felt that the prophecy was distant; he prayed that marriage with the Frenchman had somehow wielded a magic of its own powerful enough to erase it altogether.

1704

War once again broke out in Europe between England and France. At the start of the winter Rising Hawk led the clan deep into the forest on a long trek inland toward Quebec. They traveled by canoe up the St. Jean River to the Indian fort at Medoctec and then went on to Nashwaak to visit the French fort before setting off for the St. Francis River where they could reach a short portage to the St. Lawrence that could take them to Quebec if they decided to take their furs to the truck house there.

Early in April snow was falling again. After the last storm the men had gone out on snowshoes to look for game tracks and seen those of a deer. They had trailed the animal, which was thin from lack of forage and taken it; now the meat was nearly gone. They hoped for fresh tracks to follow after this new storm.

The smoke of their campfire drew two travelers trekking on snowshoes through the forest toward Quebec. Pierre-Jaspar Montard and Simon Desjardins were surprised to find themselves welcomed by old friends and to learn Jacques and Guillaume had married Rising Hawk's daughters. Once they thawed themselves out and the women served them a hot meal, a stew that contained the last of the deer meat mixed with some dried peas and corn, they relaxed around the fire. Paul lay deep in contented sleep nestled in a pile of furs next to his mother.

"Lucky ye find us tonight," Rising Hawk said.

"Aye," Simon agreed. "Storm might've been our death. But praise the ancestors and all the holy Saints! We're with friends. Warm and dry with bellies full of good hot food." His face creased with pleasure as he stifled a belch. "'tis the best of life. Just this." He waved his arm about. "Contentment."

Song Sparrow smiled at him. "Good ye say that Simon."

"Not just me." He waved a hand at Pierre-Jaspar and he blushed.

Jacques looked like a cat that had just claimed a mouse. "Best tell us the news."

"I got a letter from my darling girl I left behind in France. She's coming to Quebec and we're to be married."

"She have your child?"

Pierre-Jaspar looked pained. "Of course not. It was that her father was opposed to our union but he died in battle not long after I sailed with you. The eldest son being heir, he moved into the father's house and his sisters of course inherit nothing. She sent me a letter and I wrote back offering marriage. With my letter went one from the Governor's wife offering to take her in and act as her chaperone. All right and proper."

"When's she coming?"

"May be already at Quebec when I get back there." His face glowed.

"Ain't he the very picture of a man in love and on a secret mission and all at once?"

"Don't try to deny it, Pierre, "Guillaume teased. "So ye came to Acadia to escape her father's bad temper."

"That wasn't the only reason," Pierre-Jaspar insisted. "There was another and then this came about, the reason we're traveling now. You may not have heard this news."

"Dudley, the governor of Massachusetts said that Baptiste – you recall all the stories told about him when we were aboard the *Fleur de Lis* – though the English captured him as a prisoner of war, when the war ended they said he became nothing but a common criminal and he'd be hanged as such. English refused to exchange him. Wouldn't budge on it. Past two years there's been lots of talk about whether or not Dudley would actually carry out the execution. Then Governor Vaudreuil found someone so valuable to the English they'd surely preserve Baptiste to get their own man back. He sent us to Montreal to tell that fighting maniac Hertel to recruit some Indians for a raiding party to run to Deerfield in Massachusetts and take prisoners from the settlement. They attacked in the dead of night and set fire to the town and took the prisoners Vaudreuil wanted. Couriers sent ahead to Quebec to tell us the attack was successful."

"Ye don't say," Jacques was astonished.

Pierre-Jaspar nodded, "I did just now say so."

"Governor wanted Reverend John Williams and his family to offer in exchange for Baptiste. Won't be easy to negotiate. Those Bostonnais are angry as a stirred-up nest of hornets about the attack. In the end they'll have to agree to an exchange. They won't leave such an important man in French hands. Nor will they stretch the neck of our man while we hold the Reverend. Went to Port Royal to tell Governor Brouillan and warn him to expect New Englanders to try to revenge it. On our way back to Quebec now."

"I've nothin' to do with it," Simon protested and held up his palms as if to ward off a spell. "Headed to Quebec to meet *Compagnie* men coming in when the snows end. Travel, trade for pelts with any Indians we meet. You have pelts to take to the truck house for the *Compagnie*? That pile ye got looks big enough to clear away the rest of your indentures."

Jacques remained content to live with the clan and move about with them as they changed camps in spring and fall, and wandered the wilderness expanses of Acadia and Canada. They traveled endless forests thick with game, canoed wide rivers dense with fish and visited the occasional truck house where they exchanged some of their skins for tools and other necessities.

Guillaume was increasingly determined to establish himself in an Acadian community. He and Song Sparrow had discussed it often and each time she insisted she wanted to stay with her family.

"We've all we need here with our clan."

"Among Acadians we can work our own land and build a house of our own. Many families among the Acadians are like us, French and Indian together."

"But Acadians live at the mercy of the English. They come in ships and attack their villages. How can ye think that's better than how we live?"

Each time it ended in a draw. Guillaume was insistent. Song Sparrow didn't resist what he had to say but she deflected his arguments and left him feeling stalemated.

One brilliant fall day the early morning clouds were alive with hues that shifted from deep pink to the vital colors of the salmon's flesh. As the sun mounted the sky it turned from twilight to deep blue and the forest blazed with a glory of orange and gold. Song Sparrow held her son in her arms and glowed with motherly devotion. Guillaume's heart swelled with pride and love and he thought himself the luckiest man alive. Paul made soft baby noises as he toyed with the bird totem necklace that Song Sparrow had worn since the day of her wedding. She had not taken it off before, but now she placed it around her son's neck and covered his face with soft kisses.

Jacques had already bid his own wife adieu and called to his brother with some impatience. "We're ready to leave." He and several braves stood waiting. Reluctantly Guillaume turned to Song Sparrow. A tendril of hair wisped down the side of her face. Gently he wound it around his finger and looked deep into her sparkling eyes, whispering his love to her. Then he kissed his wife and son good-bye and left with the hunting party.

The people turned to their day's tasks. With the hunters away there were only a couple of braves, a half dozen elderly men and a handful of women with their children left in the camp.

As the people busied themselves, a prowler with a face blackened by war paint stalked the camp. Where he found brush thick enough to conceal him he rose behind it just enough to peer through the branches. He followed Song Sparrow's movements and watched as she handed her child to her sister. He ducked back as Patient Moon turned her head and looked straight at where he hid. He held his breath and dared not move. She mustn't have seen him – she walked away with the child and didn't raise the alarm. He slipped down to hide his face in the dirt and when he raised his eyes again she was gone and the one he wanted stayed near the fire and watched the children at play.

With the hunting party away he saw only a couple of braves, men he'd played with when they were boys and now left behind to guard this camp. He motioned to a man concealed behind him and they quickly took stock of the situation. They saw no opposition once they had done for the two braves standing guard. The rest of the Rangers waited for their English leader to give the signal to move. The intruders crawled through the underbrush and advanced on their unsuspecting prey. They crept near to the lookouts – one was surprised by an attacker who spoke his name before killing him quickly with a knife to the throat; the other was garroted.

The attackers all stood at once, screaming and running at the unarmed camp. Fear and confusion overtook their victims. Pandemonium erupted as old men and women and children shrieked in fear and tried to run for their lives. The brunt of the attack was swift and brutal and no quarter was given. The English Rangers who hunted the people with their Iroquois braves and the renegade who felt spurned by his clan made short work of their defenseless prey.

Knocked to the ground by a screaming child trying to flee from his attacker, Song Sparrow knelt in the dust and was still dazed from her fall when she heard the growl of a man bending over her, "You're going to suffer, you whore of the French! I would've made an honorable husband, but ye refused me. Now you die. Know I'm your killer." Flying Squirrel rested his foot on the back of her leg to keep her on her knees. "You're not so proud now, ye see Death come to take ye. I want to hear you beg me, let ye live."

Too terrified even to scream Song Sparrow felt his grip relax for a single instant as if his pity began to get the better of his anger. But then his anger hardened again and he pulled her head back and she saw his face. He dropped his axe and hatred born of his lust for her filled his eyes as he drew the knife from his belt and slashed her throat. With each beat of her terrified heart her warm blood spurted from the wound. Her head fell forward and she collapsed into a bleeding heap. His breath caught in a sob as he wound his hand tightly into her black luxuriant hair; his shoulders heaved as he finished his gory vengeful act, pulling her head back and looking into her eyes already gone dim and seeing her face smeared with blood and dirt. "You're mine now," he whispered in an orgiastic fury.

He made a few quick cuts to pull away the forelock of her hair and reveal a patch of bare bone. He screamed as he took her scalp and held it up so that bits of gore fell against his face. Her head fell forward into the pooling blood still warm as the pulse from her body slowed to a trickle. He picked up his knife and wiped it across the back of her dress. Then he thrust it into his leg wrapping and the scalp into his belt and ran off into the brush and never looked back. The long strands of her hair waved as he ran and bounced each time his foot struck the ground. His axe with his totem animal incised in its butt lay forgotten on the ground next to Song Sparrow's body.

Hidden a short distance away under a pile of leaf litter banked up next to a fallen tree, Patient Moon lay terrified. She bit into her fist to keep from wailing and tasted her own blood. Dancing Crow uttered a cry and she covered the boy with her body to quiet him. They lay hidden from the men of the war party who were now intent on taking scalps and scavenging the bodies for prizes. The leader, an English officer, ordered the Iroquois to leave the bodies and move on, but they refused until they had chopped every head and collected every last scalp, even the small ones. The sun stood in the western sky when the killers were finished as if it waited to guide the souls newly released from their bodies toward the land of the ancestors. Silence broken only by the occasional groan of someone still lingering on the threshold of death descended over the forest.

Patient Moon lay numbed. Next to her Dancing Crow lay on his back looking up at flies buzzing in the warm late afternoon sunbeams that slanted through the trees; a bird alighted in the tree above him and hopped from branch to branch as it trilled out its song in clear liquid notes. His waving arms and gurgling laughter at the bird's antics roused

Patient Moon from her stupor. She gathered the boy in her arms and warily looked around before she crawled to another hiding place. The sight of her sister's blood-smeared corpse sent shudders of grief and fear coursing through her body. She lay down with the boy and concealed them before she fell into a deep sleep of shock and exhaustion.

When the men returned to the camp at the end of the day, they saw no sign of smoke from cook fires and smelled no food. Fearing the worst as they drew closer, they caught the metallic smell of blood and then the grisly sight of the massacre greeted them.

Guillaume ran about looking for his wife and found Song Sparrow's crumpled body, her face turned to the ground. His face went white with shock and he fell to his knees beside her; her blood soaked through his clothes and stuck against his skin. His fingers touched her skull that was bared where the scalp had been ripped away and an animal moan rose in his throat and turned to a gurgle as sobs began to wrack him.

Jacques searched for his wife and looked for Paul in the sad wreckage of the small bodies but neither of them was to be found. "They must be together," he tried to convince himself and encourage Guillaume.

Guillaume was mad with grief and heard no voice but his memory of hers crying out for him. Jacques saw the axe lying on the ground. He picked it up and saw Flying Squirrel's mark on it. Enraged, he took the weapon and stalked off still frantic with worry about what might have become of his own wife. He was certain she had not been taken prisoner, especially if she had a child in her arms.

One of the men heard the hoot of an owl and another that answered it from somewhere far upwind in the forest. Alerted to the chance the attackers might not be a very long way off, he approached Jacques.

"That filthy traitor will pay for this," Jacques growled showing the axe. The men soon picked up the trail and went to hunt the enemy.

Guillaume stayed behind cradling Song Sparrow's body and keened his grief.

Patient Moon stirred at the sound and disturbed her camouflage of leaves. Guillaume heard the rustling and looked up. Her eyes focused first on his tortured face with its bloodied cheeks and lips and then on her sister's broken head lying in his lap. Song Sparrow's arm was extended; her hand was opened as if to beckon her sister to join them. Patient Moon lay back down not daring to move; then Paul began to whimper, his breath catching in sobs. As if from some far-off place Guillaume heard his son's cries and turned to look for him.

Patient Moon groaned; tears streamed from her eyes as she raised herself and the boy and crawled forward to touch her sister's lifeless hand. Guillaume pulled Patient Moon and his son into his grieving embrace. He looked beyond them and as if for the first time saw scattered about the campsite bared skulls of all sizes that shone in the dimness of the night like the iridescent nacre of mollusk shells whose living creatures had been ripped from inside them.

Somewhere far off in the forest there were faint shots and the muffled noise of a distant fight, the faint decrescendo of men's voices and cries of ebbing lives.

Some time later Jacques and the braves returned. Under the fading light of the moon now glowing through a light mist as the day began to approach, the returning men looked like the risen ghosts of the dead. Jacques gently claimed his wife. He wrapped his arms around her, his jaw clenching and tears flowing. No words passed between them.

As the day waxed Jacques carefully drew toward Guillaume. He squatted next to him and looked into his brother's face. Guillaume had held Song Sparrow close throughout the night and through the rise and set of the moon. Somehow he believed that as the sun rose it would bring her life back with it. As Jacques put his hand on Guillaume's shoulder a soft dry sob racked his chest and when Jacques put his arms inside Guillaume's to lift his wife and take her from his embrace, he knew his hope was false and let his brother draw her gently from his arms. She was slight and never a burden and his arms felt limp and empty with the loss of her.

They buried the dead and sang their souls to go Above. The words caught in Guillaume's throat as he felt her spirit perched in the trees about the campsite with all the others watching and waiting for the men to perform their final acts of respect. It was cold comfort to know there'd be no such consolation for the Englishman and that the soul of the traitor would wander forever and never to find its way home.

Jacques chose four men to escort Patient Moon and Paul Dancing Crow back to Rising Hawk's camp. They took the traitor's head wrapped tightly in a skin, along with his axe to show Rising Hawk they'd revenged his daughter's death.

Guillaume didn't care to go on because it meant leaving her behind but Jacques refused to let him stay by his wife's grave and got behind his brother and shoved him. Guillaume stumbled a few grudging steps and the others began to trot to encourage him to keep up with them. Soon he felt his feet were moving faster than his grief could bear.

VECHCAQUE

A few days later as they slogged through the forest they heard sounds of gunfire echoing off a layer of clouds that stretched above them like a lid made of pewter. They ran faster and came to a jumble of brush at the edge of a salt marsh. Through a tangle of vines and branches they could see a sloop anchored near the shore. On board it sailors were bringing a single cannon to bear on a small village.

Two braves crept through the underbrush to the water's edge; they slid beneath the surface and swam out to dive under the sloop and cut its anchor lines. The rest of the men crept toward the buildings and used their shelter to advance.

A gang of armed seamen was grouped on the beach near their long boats waiting for the cannon to fire at the village before they attacked the small band of men who stood ready to defend their families with fowling pieces and whatever farm tools they could muster for weapons. The men stood in front of a house where they had put the women and children for safety. A baby of about Dancing Crow's age leaned out a window and shrieked, "Daddy, Daddy." A woman reached out and clutched the child to pull him back inside. Terrified cries rose from the other children and the men on the beach pointed to the house and laughed. Guillaume heard a shout, "There's women there! Ye know what that means!" Anger as he had never felt it before built into a rage that blotted out all else.

It was then the ship swung free of its bow anchor. An inshore current caught the hull and the cannon lost its bearing and pointed toward the trees. The craft began to move and shouts echoed across the water. Jacques gave the signal to attack.

Indians erupted from behind the buildings shooting and yelling and running past the surprised villagers. The attackers broke their lines and ran toward the shore; they screamed at the men aboard the ship to toss over an anchor and ran for the long boats. Some threw down their muskets to run faster; they clawed like trapped animals at anyone in front of them to get on board a boat and escape from the beach.

The villagers rallied to pursue and fire at the intruders as they rowed like mad men to reach the sloop before it drifted farther off into the bay. The wounded were left behind on the beach. Guillaume sprinted and caught up with the last long boat to push off; furiously he grabbed at a man in the stern and caught him by the breeches. He pulled him backward into the water and held his face under until he went slack.

The long boats were sucked away from the shore by the outgoing tide; the escaping men rowed frantically. Blood-curdling war calls flew in pursuit of them. The Indians shouted their anger and shook their fists at the men escaping in the boats. Then they turned their attention to the terrified men left stranded. The metallic light cast by opalescent clouds onto the shimmering quicksilver of the gently undulating water glinted in waves of dark and light reflected in the blades of the scalping knives the men now pulled from their belts.

A man screamed as Guillaume's calloused hands sought the soft flesh of his throat and pleaded for his life. "My wife's to have another child soon. Have three others to care for. Please..." his voice trailed off.

Guillaume looked at the man as if seeing the victim's humanity for the first time and then his face clouded and he saw the man through a red haze. "No one spared my wife," he grunted as he shoved the blade home.

Soon the beach was quiet except for the sounds of men's footsteps sucking in the muck as they moved from body to body. They worked quickly and took the scalps of the dead and dying. They searched the bodies for valuables and one of the braves held up a pocket watch. It glinted in the pale light; the hour hand clicked ahead and it chimed. Men nearby turned to look and their dark laughter chilled the watching villagers. Jacques paused in his work and looked around.

Once they were finished with them, they pushed the bodies into the water and left them to float as the retreating tide willed. The water shone like an undulating sheet of polished silver with the dark hull and masts of the fleeing sloop far out and the long boats chasing it with their rapidly dipping oars etched on its surface like a fleet of waterstriders desperately trying to catch an escaping beetle. The bodies drifted faithfully behind like a macabre flotilla of jellyfish slowly following in the vessel's wake.

Exhausted from the fight and smeared with the blood of their victims, the rescuers now turned toward the villagers who stood motionless with expressions of mixed horror and relief on their faces. Instinctively they shrank together in fear, not knowing what to make of the strange blood-soaked band of Indians and French that appeared out of nowhere and fought off the English with such ferocity.

A baby's cry broke the silence and its mother, whose face was streaked with the tracks of dried tears clutched it close to her breast. She looked at Guillaume with fear in her eyes. He turned away from the woman's terrified stare and continued to scrub the blood from his hands.

An older man walked along the beach toward them as they washed their faces and clothes. "You've saved us," was all he could manage to say. "You've saved us and done to those bloody English what they'd have done to us, plead as we might that we've nivver done any thing against them."

Jacques took the man by the elbow and walked him back to the waiting villagers. "We're glad we're nearby enough to hear the noise of those fookin' English. Few less scalps here and ye could've done it for yourselves." The sight of their shocked faces quieted him for a moment and his face creased with a grimace. "It's all right. French 'n Indians stick together."

He waved his arm toward the beach. "This's the hard sad truth of how English come to visit. Lucky we wasn't so far off when they come to you."

Like a sudden thaw melts the ice and unlocks the water to flow again, the village leaders began to come forward and thank their rescuers. They designated a barn to shelter them and delegated men to see them fed and settled. The women made an impromptu meal of bread and cheese and cold meat pies that were downed with great mouthfuls of hard cider.

Even Guillaume finally slept that night, beneath a sheltering roof and wrapped securely in his cloak. Toward dawn he heard the faint crow of a rooster but instead of awakening to it he turned over and dreamed, feeling enclosed by a great love. Radiant warmth eased his limbs as he felt Song Sparrow's presence. Memories of his wife flooded back and consumed him. Again he saw how beautiful and felt how desirable she was, how loving and passionate their embraces were. He wound his hands in her thick black hair and tasted her lips. Still in the dream and just as he was starting to awaken, she bore him a son and the child cried out for him as his wife faded away. His eyes fluttered with tears. Grief consumed him with knowing that his son was all he had left to remind him in this living world of his great love for her and hers for him.

A hand gently touched his shoulder. He still clung to the edge of his dream and he thought it was her and called out her name. Then he heard Jacques' voice, "Guillaume? You all right? Time we was moving about."

René Theriot and Ismael Breau were nearly breathless when they ran into the village to tell how Benjamin Church's New England militia attacked Grand Pré. As his friend spoke Breau became worked up and tearful. He shouted, "No matter we're at peace. Church orders his forces to loot and burn. Shoot anyone tries to make them stop. We come to warn ye that Church and his militia's sailing this way. Doubled the scalp bounty. No difference – Indians or Acadians or French."

Jacques said, "Those that just come here must've been part of his force. Now they'll be sure to bring Church here to revenge their dead. You've to go now to escape more punishment. Leave soon as ye can. Turn the animals loose. Chase them off."

Within a day ships were sighted in the bay headed toward the village. People took whatever they could carry and set animals free from their pens. Men shouldered young children and women clutched toddlers. Older children carried infants or pulled younger ones along. Jacques and his men followed at the rear of the settlers and obscured their tracks to conceal the route they took as they fled into the forest.

From a distance Church, a large man wearing a white coat and a broad black hat was seen in a long boat headed for shore and followed by more boats so filled with men that their gunwales nearly swamped. They came onto the beach screaming and firing their guns.

The first man onto the land grabbed the scruff of a dog that wandered too close to get away and with rough hands, clutched the animal's furry neck; its whines were cut off by a knife plunged into its chest and the carcass was tossed aside onto the sand that greedily drank the warm blood. Other men ran up the lane and merciless as wolves in a blood-lust frenzy, they fell upon the settlement.

A horse trumpeted in fear and reared up pawing the air; a musket boomed and the animal fell blocking the lane; it trembled and cried in fear as men surrounded it and bashed its head with the butts of their muskets. A cow's insistent mooing turned to moans as it was felled by a bullet and dispatched by hard blows to the head. A sheep tried to run with one leg that was broken and twisted, blood running down its white fleece; a shot exploded and the creature fell.

A man ran outside a looted house holding up a Sevres porcelain teacup that was once a wife's proud possession screaming, "Look what I got!" Before he could thrust it inside his jacket, another man dashed it from his hand and snarled, "What do ye need that Frenchie stuff for, mate?" The cup hit the ground and shattered.

"Get yourself some of that buried Acadian gold!" someone shouted. Men staved in doors and violated homes. They pulled up hearthstones looking for family hoards; their triumphant shouts sounded the death knell of the village.

The New Englanders torched the mass house and the refugees saw flames racing skyward from the steeple. Then more flames rose and fire consumed all that was left of their village – houses, barns, animal carcasses, stores of grain, tender herbs that filled kitchen gardens. A cloud heavy with the noisome smell of carnage hung like a shroud above the destruction.

With their blank eyes fixed to the ground the villagers drifted like insubstantial spirits. Jacques, Guillaume and their small band of braves headed back to their own encampment at Haute Tintamarre, moving like the rearguard of the displaced Acadians who ghosted their away through the great marshes.

BEAUSEJOUR

Benoit Ruisseau was working in his fields when he saw the procession of the refugees. He approached with two of his sons and invited the French to join their settlement. He was a farmer, muscular from his work and with a weathered face; his bushy hair and beard were streaked with white. His sons stood by him, suspicious of the brothers and seeing them as a couple of leather-beaten squaw men.

"Plenty of good land to claim here. Dikes finished and soon farm fields will be where ye see tidewater now." He gestured toward the diked marshes with a wide sweep of his arm. "We help each other build. Ye could settle here with us."

This should have been what Jacques and Guillaume had risked everything to win, what they had come all the way from France to achieve – a place where they could live at peace and be neighbors to others like themselves; where they could be comfortable and happy simply by the work of their own hands. Guillaume had yearned for such a place to settle with Song Sparrow and raise a family. Here was the opportunity for him to have what he wanted but without his precious wife to share it with. He looked at the farmers' faces. The older man's was open and inviting but his sons' were guarded and withdrawn. He wanted to stay but now the well-intentioned invitation seemed nothing but a mockery of the hollowness inside him.

"I've pledged to my wife I'll live with her clan." As Jacques spoke Guillaume felt someone staring at him. He turned and saw a young woman. From beneath her cap wild curls of dark hair escaped to frame her heart-shaped face and emphasize her dark searching eyes.

Following Guillaume's startled look Benoit smiled as he saw one of his daughters standing nearby. "Jerusha," he called to her. The girl took a hesitant step forward as if she were about to dip her toe into a pool of water to test its depth. Then her mother called and she drew back and hurried off to a nearby house. Benoit grinned at Guillaume and said, "My daughter seemed interested in our talk."

BAIE VERTE

Throughout the rest of the season Guillaume wandered the shores of the great bay catching rabbits and grouse, squirrels and fish, and even found an occasional root vegetable missed by earlier foragers. He picked the last dried berries left behind by migrating birds as if to nourish stragglers. On the first day of winter he crossed the isthmus and went to Baie Verte to stay at Simon's truck house with Jacques and his family and warm himself at the edges of another man's household. He watched his own son Paul Dancing Crow follow his cousins Albert and

Theo as they ran about the place and tussled like a litter of playful puppies; his eyes teared whenever he thought of the children that ran about Rising Hawk's camp. Sadness filled his face when he watched Patient Moon scoop the boys up and put them to bed.

Through the late winter nights fireside conversations turned around Simon's attempts to convince Jacques and Guillaume to keep on hunting and trapping.

"Makes no sense no more," Jacques said each time Simon broached the topic. "Fur trade's locked up. King's appointed men own it. Whoever they may be. It's they as make the money and not the trappers. Look at something else, namely surpluses of grain and animals. Trade and sell to them as need what Acadian farmers have. New Englanders come from Boston to buy grain. France sends ships for grain and beef. All need more than the green cod to live on."

"And both English and French are angry when Acadians trade with the other," Simon chuckled at the symmetry of it.

Their talk made sense to Guillaume and over the winter he became drawn into the scheme and took an active part in the planning. His thoughts turned more toward the future and one day it just came blurting out of him. "Maybe it's time for me to start again and marry."

Jacques looked at him in surprise. Then he said, "You've got to live your life. She'd want that for you."

BEAUSEJOUR 1705

When Benoit saw Guillaume crossing over the dikes at the bottom of his fields he went out to welcome him. The spring planting was nearly done; Guillaume joined Benoit and his sons to help them finish and at the end of each day he sat at the long oak table inside the family's common room eating a meal prepared at the large hearth. Whenever he looked at Jerusha she avoided his gaze.

She was small and lovely with hair usually piled up on her head. But she was so energetic that it would come apart in wild masses of tendrils that fell about her face and framed the most beautiful eyes he had ever seen. There were times he couldn't bear to think about marrying again, but he knew he must. Otherwise what would he do with Paul? He was growing up fast, and seemed content to live with his aunt and uncle.

When Guillaume remarried, his son could come to live with him. But would a stepmother give him the care he needed? He was sure that if he was interested in marrying Jerusha others would be looking to wed her.

He worked with the men and ate the noon meal the women carried to them in the fields, yet he wasn't at ease with the community. While they shared their common meals the farmers' talk was all about their families and the crops, things that belonged to a life that lay outside his experience. The quarrels between the English and the French and all else that had happened to him so far seemed to belong to some world other than this fruitful Eden.

Few things escaped Benoit's grasp once he decided to latch on and he was not about to let Guillaume, who he thought was a hard-working eligible young man and good husband material, escape his clutches. Jerusha was showing all the signs of needing a man like that and here was an acceptable candidate. He pressed the other farmers to help build a house so the couple would have a place to live once they married.

But, Guillaume asked Benoit, as he as yet owned no land, how or why would they build him a house? Immediately Benoit offered to help him claim some fifty acres of land next to his own farm on the Beausejour Point that opened when one of the original settlers removed farther up into the marshes. In his mind Benoit saw it all as a done deal and that was how he put it to his prospective son-in-law.

Now Guillaume got cold feet and wanted to slow things down so he asked Benoit, "Ye told Jerusha about this plan?" He wondered how she might react to her father sealing her choice and her future like this.

"She's willful but she'll come around. Just give her a bit of time to think about it." Benoit was certain she would do as her parents wished. "Marie-Josephte was just like her when we married and look at the fine wife she's turned out to be." He puffed out his chest and looked at him with a gesture that said as sure as words that Guillaume didn't understand how much of a favor Benoit was doing for him.

Thus Guillaume became a settler at Beausejour. He could farm and then after the harvest he would be free to go into the woods with his brother and trap. That would get him some pelts to trade for whatever goods he might need. In a year or so he should be ready to marry.

Benoit thought that was a terrible plan. If he went back into the forest Benoit thought it would be too tempting for Guillaume to lapse back into his old ways. So he was of no mind to put off any wedding; Marie-Josephte agreed. She prodded Jerusha to get better acquainted with Guillaume.

Guillaume overheard Marie-Josephte one evening as he sat on his front step carving a piece of wood. She was usually a soft-spoken woman but when she was excited or exasperated her voice became high-pitched and penetrating.

Jerusha was defiant. "He's widowed. His wife was an Indian. They're different. What if he expects I've to be like her? She was killed in a raid because she was out in the forest without his protection. His child is lucky he lived. I'm scared to think of that kind of danger."

"He's not going to put you in any danger," Marie-Josephte paused for breath. "What're ye, jealous because he's married before?"

Jerusha stamped her foot. "Of course I'm not. Mother! How could ye think it?"

Marie-Josephte eyed her daughter. "I know you, girl. Guillaume's not a foolish simple man like some about this place that give ye the mooning look. He's a fighter; he's a strong man and a hard worker such as a girl like you needs to take care of her. What's wrong with you that ye don't see it? By God's grace you've got him for the taking."

Jerusha faced her mother, pouting. "What if I just don't want to marry him?"

"Your father built that house for him expecting you to live there as his wife. Ye won't be going to live in the forest in any wigwam made of sticks 'n hides. Ye don't marry him that makes you a greater fool than I ever thought. One way or other your father's determined he's to be part of our family. Your sisters like him well enough."

"Mother!"

"Your father approves of him. If you're not interested your sisters are. Just go ask them."

Jerusha stormed out of the house and nearly knocked Guillaume to the ground. "Why are you avoiding me?" he called out to her as she fled. "Why won't you even look at me?"

Marie-Josephte followed her daughter to the door. She shrugged her shoulders at Guillaume's puzzled look. "Don't know what to do with her anymore."

BAIE VERTE   1705

During their indenture to the Compagnie Jacques and Guillaume learned that even though they were free to roam the forests, the fur trade itself was so controlled by middle-men they could never become rich as mere trappers. Once that was understood they knew it didn't matter whether or not they were indentured to the Compagnie – they still had to bring their furs to the King's monopoly by selling them to the traders who ran the truck houses.

When the rumor of the King's proclamation that the *Compagnie* was no longer the fur monopoly came true, it was officially disbanded and Simon was no longer as powerful as he was as the *Compagnie's* agent. But he was hired to work under one of the established traders of the newly chartered company and when that man returned to France a short time later Simon found himself once more an agent of the fur monopoly, and that protected his truck house as a profitable business.

Samuel Watkins was a Boston trader who befriended Henri in his early days at the truck house at Port Royal. He tracked him to Chignecto and showed up at Baie Verte. Henri, who came to live with Jacques after the *Compagnie* closed down, rushed to embrace his friend; glasses and whiskey appeared and they spent the afternoon gossiping about the changes to the town.

Simon began his campaign as they ate their supper. "Why not consider a new truck house there? Partners with us?" he ventured to Samuel. "Henri knows Port Royal well."

Samuel's ears perked up. "Worth a look."

They gathered around the table and laid out all the trades they had made in the past year. Henri kept a journal of all they discussed. At Baie Verte the truck house mainly served the trappers and the French; sometimes they traded some European goods that came in through Quebec. Jacques mentioned, "There's some small trade with New Englanders for molasses and liquor. Many truck houses use strong spirits to cheat the Indians out of their pelts but Rising Hawk's stern again' the liquor. Don't allow such kind of trade to be more'n a tittle of our business and no selling liquor by the glass."

Samuel said he had something much larger in mind. "We'd do very well with rum and whiskey and such in Port Royal. Traffic there's different – we see fewer Indians. But pelts're quite valuable."

Simon nodded in agreement. "Well ye ken it." His voice was prideful.

"With the flow of furs through here and the gold they'll bring us, we can build any kind of trade we want at Port Royal," Samuel concluded. "Have a base for trade with Boston while we're at it."

"I see it could work," Simon agreed. Turning to Jacques, "You of the same mind? Furs come in here and we trade them for French gold. From Acadians we buy surplus animals and grain that we send on to Ile St. Jean, Quebec, and maybe even New England. Take molasses and brandy from the English and European stuff from the French."

Jacques took it up. "We offer English goods to Acadians and some of the stuff from Europe. New Englanders always want European goods they've no way to get without having to pay English importation fees – unless from traders like us."

As the men talked everything seemed to fall into place. Jacques and Simon would operate the truck house at Baie Verte; Simon would handle the fur trade with the Indians. By the time they finished talking about their plans the whiskey was finished and their faces were flushed with anticipation.

Samuel had a surprise waiting for Henri when they returned to Port Royal. He had bought a building near the waterfront with an office, a separate room to live in and another to use as a store and gathering place. It connected to a second building that served as a warehouse. A bright new sign hung out in front to announce the new firm: Watkins & Bancouer, Merchants of Trade.

For Henri it meant that now he could earn enough money to buy a warmer coat, rent a house and marry. He'd always known he was never ordained to be a priest. Samuel laughed and his eyes twinkled when he heard Henri admit it and he wondered what his friend Samuel might be scheming.

BEAUSEJOUR 1706

Guillaume was passionate about getting his son back; when Jacques and Patient Moon brought Paul to live with him Benoit was relieved that Jerusha was quick to take a liking to the little boy.

Patient Moon was as attached to her nephew as if he was her own child and couldn't bear to think of leaving him behind at Beausejour. The first night they slept in Guillaume's house she insisted to her husband, "We can't leave the boy here. No good for him. Jerusha's a girl, not had any children yet. How does she know what to do for our boy Dancing Crow? He's to grow straight and true as an Indian, not a Frenchman. She can't raise him like that."

"Guillaume must decide," Jacques told her. "Rising Hawk says it's his choice. Paul's his son – you've not forgotten that?"

"But every time Guillaume looks at his son he sees Song Sparrow. That's not fair to the boy or to Jerusha. Once she understands that, she'll hate Dancing Crow. It's too much for them if he stays. And wouldn't you miss him?" Jacques read the sorrow in her heart. He pulled her close and whispered to her, "Aye. I love the boy just as you do. But however it pains us we must do what his father thinks is right for him."

Guillaume courted Jerusha to the point where she knew she had to make a decision. If she didn't marry him soon he would be free to go to another, most likely one of her sisters and each was very willing to step into Jerusha's place in his affections. She never thought of herself as jealous but Jerusha decided she couldn't let that happen and competition from her sisters firmed her decision.

Guillaume asked Benoit and Marie-Josephte for Jerusha's hand. Benoit held his breath as his wife encouraged her daughter to accept him and was relieved when she agreed.

Guillaume came with his family to share supper with the Ruisseaus the next evening. Jerusha's sisters lingered at the table after the meal, listening to Jacques and Patient Moon converse with their parents and hoping to hear Guillaume propose. Marie-Josephte knew that game and ordered them to stay away when Jerusha led Guillaume into the parlor.

He nervously cleared his throat once they were alone. Jerusha said, "Uneasy are ye, Guillaume?"

"I don't know what to expect from you. Making me nervous," he admitted. She smiled, pleased with herself and teased, "Want me to propose for ye?"

He paced a few steps. "Course not. What're ye saying? Ye think I'm afraid?"

"Then why don't you just go and get it out?"

He barely uttered the words when she gave him her acceptance. Her face flushed and she laughed and that made Guillaume chuckle, "You're blushing, girl."

"What if I am?"

He held her at arm's length and studied her expression; then he pulled her close to embrace and kiss her for the first time. It wasn't a peckish kiss given by a nervous lover but one that made Jerusha wonder what made her put this man off for so long. They walked out the door and stood holding hands. He leaned over to kiss the top of her head and then found her lips again.

Jerusha looked over his shoulder at the star-filled sky. As she stared outward and felt the heat from his hands pleasantly radiate through her body, she saw faint pinpoints of light sparkle across the heavens and a mischievous smile curved her lips; she leaned into him and felt him harden for her.

Quickly the marriage preparations went ahead and it was celebrated in the fullness of the season when the harvest was in and the sugar maples stood decked in gold and the sun's mid-day warmth made the air languid and golden. The sky was mirrored in the water of the distant bay and glowed deep blue. Fair weather clouds floated high overhead, all white and ivory like fluffy piles of swans' down.

Long tables groaned with the good things of the harvest; they bowed with platters of roasted meats – venison, pork, beef, fish, fowl – and squashes, peas, corn and beans. The guests sighed with pleasure at the sight of it as they waited for the bride to appear.

Jerusha wore her mother's white lace bodice brought from France and a light colored wool skirt striped in red and cream, with a band of red felt encircling her waist; her sisters wove a wreath of wildflowers that she wore on her head.

Guillaume dressed in woolen pants and a linen shirt that Marie-Josephte gave him to wear. He was nervous and Paul clung to the leg of his breeches. "Daddy," the boy pleaded. "Pick me up!" He swung his son up into his arms and kissed his apple-colored cheeks.

Then Jerusha stepped into the doorway of her father's house and Guillaume handed Paul to his aunt and went to stand by his bride, proud in his love. Abbé Felix Pain had come to Beausejour to bless the harvest and now he performed the wedding. He stood in front of a table brought from the house to serve as an altar and offered the mass. Before the bread was broken to share in communion he bound them in marriage.

Paul clung to his aunt's skirt all through the ceremony and Patient Moon laid her hand on the boy's shoulders, squeezing him as his father made his vows to his new stepmother. A wild tendril of hair escaped the ribbon of flowers that framed Jerusha's face as she turned to her husband. They looked at each other and she blushed as Guillaume bent to kiss her.

The music, toasts, feasting and dancing lasted long into the night. Around midnight a procession of well-wishers escorted the newly-weds to the door of their home, joking and teasing. They seemed as if they might spend the night camped on the doorstep but Marie-Josephte sent her husband and sons to round them up and make sure they all got bedded down somewhere else.

Guillaume's eyes warmed at the sight of his wife, so lithe and beautiful with her dark eyes sparkling. Her white teeth flashed as she smiled at him; her translucent skin shone like the smoothest creamy alabaster. At about two o'clock in the morning the last flame of a torch in the yard flickered out and the deep silence of the night sky finally reigned.

Before the month was out they had their first fight. Jerusha was uncomfortable with Paul living with them. Every time she put her arms around her husband he seemed to be there and she felt like the boy's mother was standing by him and watching them. When she went to her parents to talk over her feelings about the child, Benoit offered to take up her case with Guillaume.

Being a direct man Benoit knew of no way to handle it except to tell Guillaume what Jerusha had revealed to him. "She looks at the boy and sees his mother. The boy's an innocent of course, but just by him being in your house – and you expect Jerusha to raise him – it poisons your love for her and hers for you."

"How can ye say that? Why should Paul be a trouble to her? Aren't all females natural mothers?" Guillaume was puzzled. He told Benoit about the children who ran about the Indian camp, little ones taken up and kissed and tickled by adults who did it just to see their childish joy.

"That's not the point," Benoit insisted. "Paul's such a good and beautiful child she's worried that all ye see when ye look at him is how much ye lost when his mother was killed and how much ye still grieve it and whether you'll ever get over it. Jerusha's young and sometimes foolish but she means well and always comes around. Still I see this is outsized for her to handle and she feels overwhelmed." Benoit paused to take in Guillaume's distress and thought he had been too brusque. When he spoke again his voice was gentler but his words were to the point. "She needs you to help her. Can't ye understand what she's feeling?"

Guillaume was stricken; it showed from the expression etched on his face to the way his body seemed to have shrunk into itself. He whispered, "O' course I've to help my wife."

Benoit drew a deep breath. "Ye must take the boy back to his aunt and give yourself wholehearted to your wife. Your life's with her now. She's young and she needs you."

"But I love Paul too, you see. I married thinking now there's a home for him where I can have him to live and he'd have a mother who could raise him with the children she'll have with me. He needs a place to be with me that's safe and protected."

"I don't ask this of you lightly. Sometimes it goes this way with a second family. Children can see their parents. It's not like they go so far away they're lost. My brother was in a like situation – sent two children off to live with their aunt and uncle. Grew up with their cousins. No one seems to have lost by it. Maybe you'd be at least willing to give it some thought." Benoit put his hand on Guillaume's shoulder. "Hard decision to make but think it over. Ye may see it's best for the boy and for Jerusha."

When Guillaume told Paul he had to take him back to Jacques and Patient Moon, he could see the boy's obvious delight. Patient Moon's happiness to see Paul come back to her and the joy with which he ran to her arms stabbed at Guillaume's heart and made him feel abandoned. Leaving Paul again was an unbearable heartbreak that felt as terrible to him as if he had lost Song Sparrow all over again and now his son was gone from him too. He wept all the way back to Beausejour.

Guillaume's feelings were rent to shreds but he expected this would mend things at home and so he didn't expect Jerusha to act as she did. As soon as he came back from delivering Paul to Baie Verte, Jerusha began a campaign to try to force him to tell her all about his life among the Indians and especially about Song Sparrow. Each time she broached the topic the pain of reliving Song Sparrow's death and the absence of his son burned unbearably in his chest. It wasn't long before he looked at her with eyes as hard and black as stone. One day he told her he would leave her if she ever asked him again.

Then when he thought he had his grief under control enough to try to explain it, Jerusha refused to credit his feelings. "Ye think I've to be like her," she shouted. "I'm not her. You've to realize it. How can a man marry a second wife and live his life together with her but always long for she that died? Your grieving will nivver let ye live as a husband with me. How can ye when you're always yearning for her?"

Once she started she couldn't seem to stop and picked at him constantly to give her what she wanted. She was used to winning when she spatted with her siblings about small matters and she didn't understand that it was a far different thing to pick an argument with her husband so targeted to the burden of grief and guilt that weighed on his heart. When she shouted at him he felt as if he rode a wave of pain to the edge of a dark abyss. It was more than he could bear and he finally shouted at her in a raw voice, "Enough!" and turned his back on her.

After a few days of truce when each treated the other with awkward courtesy, he found her lying across the bed weeping. She raised her tear-stained face from the pillow. "I'll nivver ask ye again." Guillaume looked at her gravely. "Dearest wife," his voice softened. "There must be peace between us if we're to live together." He bent down and kissed her tenderly.

Before the winter came she carried his child.

BOSTON 1709

Samuel found a pretext to invite Henri to visit Boston and stay at his home. A bachelor, he had inherited the care of his sisters and his family's well-appointed house on Summer Street near his company's dock. The house had large flower and herb gardens hedged by yews that separated them from a wide lawn. Farther out stood a small stone building that served as a smokehouse. Wild bushes of berries grew thick along the edges of his land. Apple and pear trees provided sweet fruits for pies, compotes, and preserves. The house itself was of brick and had large sun-filled rooms furnished with beautiful draperies, chairs and settees, cushions of embroidered wool and silk and fine furniture of cherry, maple and oak, from cabinet makers in New England.

Samuel's single piece of English furniture was a walnut full-bonnet highboy topped with torch finials that was almost a century old when his parents brought it with them to settle in Boston. It stood in the entrance hall. A bullet hole in the wall opposite the highboy still held the ball that had been fired through a window when two rowdy gangs of sailors met in the street and fought, leaving a dead man on their doorstep. The projectile barely missed his mother who had walked in front of the highboy just as the gun was fired. She outlived the incident by a few decades and was grateful for every day. The neighborhood was more gentrified now that other merchants had come to build their own fine houses.

Samuel had three living sisters. The eldest was married to a ship captain with a large home in the town of Salem. The youngest was married to a lawyer who practiced in the court at Boston. Marie was the middle sister and she lived with Samuel. She was without either a suitor or immediate prospects. Henri knew Samuel invited him for a reason; now he understood but didn't find it objectionable. In fact, a day or so into the visit he found himself perfectly charmed.

Marie took an immediate interest in him. She was a lovely woman and much to Henri's taste. She enchanted him with question after question about his life in Acadia and about the truck house business and one afternoon he let down his guard when she extolled his personal bravery, living as he did and doing business with all sorts of dangerous men – Indians, privateers, trappers, soldiers, hunters.

"It must be so romantic," she crooned. "At Boston we only hear tales of the strange characters that you see walk into your truck house every day."

The figure of Rising Hawk on the first day he saw him came to mind, how fierce the Indian had seemed and how bravely Henri had taken his scrutiny – it was too much of an exaggeration to tell it like that but it still pleased him to hear Marie say how exotic she found the mundane things of his daily life.

"It can be exciting at times," he admitted, reining in his imagination, "and I'm perfectly happy to stay as I am – if I'm to stay a bachelor – by a warm hearth in the winter and farming my bit of land in the summer, trading with the locals and the New Englanders who sail to Acadia in search of all manner of things. It's as good a life as any can be and a happy one. But I feel it's incomplete without someone to share it with."

The moment the words escaped his mouth he regretted them. What was he thinking? He was just being honest with her but he hadn't realized all that such sentiment added up to when expressed in quite that way.

"Now I've done it. I've led her on to think I was going to say.... What?" He took one look at her and his face reddened.

She looked like a cat sitting guard at a mouse hole and was as focused on every word he spoke as any cat would be who knew there was a mouse inside that was ready to come out. She certainly expected to hear something more and waited for him to say it.

He froze in fear and his mouth opened as if to speak but then he clamped it shut and said nothing. He stared at the intricate design of the rug on the floor as if it would reveal the answer to his predicament. His heart pounded as if it might knock its way through the wall of his chest; he coughed and used that as an excuse to take leave of her to find some water. He needed to be alone so he could try to pull himself together. What had he done? He couldn't believe this of himself.

Marie sat in a daze and felt deserted by Henri's sudden exit. She tried to calm herself enough to mull over what had just happened. She concluded that Henri said something he hadn't meant to let slip. But if his words were true – and what she knew of him made her think they were – then he was in love with her and he either didn't recognize his feelings or he had just then made the discovery and become unnerved by it.

Samuel saw her and came into the room. "Something the matter?" Marie turned to him and finally reacted to Henri's exhibition with a mix of tears and laughter. "It seems there may be something amiss with our friend."

She told her brother what had happened and Samuel threw back his head and laughed as if it was the most wonderful joke. "Got him now, ye do, and he's not used to being the fish with the hook in his mouth. Good for you. Told me he was never intended to be a priest in spite of him living with the monks for a time when he was a boy and now he's found someone he could marry. Just give him some time to think it out and he'll come around. He'll be here a bit longer." Samuel winked at her.

"In fact, he'll be here as long as it takes. Bide your time and you'll reel him in."

Marie decided to leave Henri alone and be cool to him when their paths should cross, so when Henri next saw her she almost entirely ignored him. He was tense and didn't know what to say to her but after a few days their friendship resumed as it had been and it appeared that she looked for nothing more from him.

Every time Henri said it was high time for him to return to Acadia, Samuel found one reason after another to delay him in Boston. Henri felt he had been away for too long; he should go home and resume his place in the truck house. Anxious as he said he was about the business, he was also reluctant to leave Marie. He believed that if he left without her she would soon have other suitors and he might lose her to another man. There was naught but one thing to do to resolve the matter.

"Marie," he approached her one afternoon. "Could we walk in the garden? I'd like to speak with you if I could." She nodded to him and they went out the door. The afternoon sun warmed the flowers and the fragrance enveloped them. She felt the tension in him and asked, "What is it, Henri? Are you trying to think how to propose to me?"

Startled by her frankness he squirmed like a worm being stuck onto a hook. He stopped and turned to stare into her laughing gray eyes. "Well I am, although I'm making a confusion of it. Since ye can read my mind to know what I'd ask, at least you could tell me will ye have me?"

"Dear Henri. What more could any woman hope for than to marry her best friend? Will ye take me home to Acadia as your wife?"

"Oh, yes," he crushed her in his embrace and planted a kiss on her forehead. Marie cupped his chin with her fingers and drew his lips to hers to put a more passionate seal on the bargain.

Over the days following the proposal Henri painted a picture of himself as a completely happy man who has finally met the woman of his dreams and he crowed about his good fortune to anyone who would listen.

Samuel gave them a wedding that was all anyone could have imagined. There was some discussion about religion – Henri being Catholic and the Watkins being a family of Protestants. Finally they all decided that if Marie and Henri were to live among the English in either Boston or Port Royal they should marry in the Anglican Church. Henri was aware that his ambitions now rode a fast-rising tide and pronounced himself a Huguenot when the question was hinted.

The wedding took place in Boston, relieving Henri's Catholic family from the need to attend. Marie wore a dress of filmy white embroidered muslin over a shimmering silk underdress with a hint of the delicate pink one often sees in the outer fold of a seashell. Her light brown hair was curled in ringlets around her heart-shaped face. Her bow-shaped lips were drawn up in a confident smile as she entered the church on her brother's arm and Samuel gave the bride away, his smiling face ruddy with pleasure.

Their guests were mainly the merchant princes of Boston. With her sisters' families and some naval officers in their dark blue uniforms setting off the brighter hues of the women's dresses, the wedding party was a colorful lot. There were toasts frothing with champagne that left some of the guests at least a little tipsy with the frequency of them.

Gossip was inevitable because Henri was new to their society. Not being so well known meant he was a ready subject of speculation. The women looked him over and whispered their comments, one to another. When the words, "He has Indian relatives," were spoken, eyes turned discretely in his direction.

"What's Marie thinking to marry into a family like that?" an older woman's voice asked in a stage whisper. Heads turned toward her. "Shush or else she'll hear you." Eyes turned to look at the happy bride.

To shut down that line of gossip one of Marie's sisters declared, "Henri's one of our brother's partners and in charge of all Samuel's business in Acadia."

"She's going to live in the wilderness? With all those savages hiding among the trees?" a lady asked her husband.

"Acadia's not a bad place. I'm going there once in a while like the other traders. Good enough place for Alden, Adams and the Faneuils to trade and own property, then it's good enough for me." Samuel had come up behind the couple and overheard them.

The woman said, "Oh. I didn't know that," and tittered nervously.

"You making the kind of money they are?" the husband asked; Samuel winked at him and walked away.

"Look at old man Bluestone over there. Ever think he'd wind up with that young lady on his arm?" one of the officers nodded toward his subject. Heads turned to study a well-dressed man leading a blond woman out a door into the garden. Both held champagne glasses.

"Who's she?" a man asked his wife who was turned to whisper something to her friends.

"She's one of those new rich folk. Her father came over to New England because he went bust in London; now he's started a business here. Folks say he's done pretty well. Look at the airs she puts on."

"What business is he in?" a man asked.

"Ship transports." Another man answered. "Heavy investment to buy a ship or two. But once you get a good captain and start to get the business, you can make good money."

"Where's his business come from?" The two men moved closer to talk more about their interest in the topic.

"Small traders as need to band together to fill a hold; some work for the governor, such as troop transports. Two ships sent to Virginia last year carrying men to help fight off the French and Indians on the frontier and make room for more English to settle." They swigged their champagne.

"At least she's not an Indian," an elderly lady commented.

"Of course she's not," a man said smoothly, "Not with that yellow head of hair." They all laughed.

"Do ye admire her?" a lady asked the man and he sighed, "Bluestone's a lucky old boy if he marries her. Only heir to the family fortune. All goes well for him and he'll be sitting pretty."

The orchestra played without seeming to ever need rest. Many of the couples danced, whirling about like so many colorful and exotic birds. Henri and Marie disappeared some time after sundown and from their hideaway they heard the party take on new life.

A week after their wedding they got word the British had attacked and taken Port Royal. By the time they left Boston the old Acadia was no more. It was to be called Nova Scotia from then on.

BEAUSEJOUR 1711

A messenger whipped at his horse and they went from one farm to the next, barely stopping long enough to catch their breath. They came to Guillaume and he grabbed the horse's bridle and asked the man, "Why're ye here? To tell us it's about lands the French must give over to the British?"

"French and British both saying they own all of Chignecto. Habitants called to meet about it and decide what they're to do."

"Ye mean to tell me the French say my farm's in their territory and the British say it's in theirs?" The man nodded. Guillaume rubbed his chin. "No good news there. Countries always send armies to fight over who owns the borderlands."

Like a flock of birds that seems to rise without any audible or visible signal and spiral skyward to wheel and turn as with a single mind, the farmers at Beausejour gathered as if instinct drove them together. Some of them were former soldiers and called for the Acadians to form an army to defend themselves and fight the British. A few drops of rain fell on them and the sky grew dark but the men just drew closer together to hear what their neighbors had to say and bark angry words of their own.

"Can't allow them to come here and take over our farms and lands," one of the men shouted.

"We've worked too hard to build the dikes and drain the marshes to get these fields producing," another voice growled.

"Aye! Aye!" they roared or muttered at each thing anyone said. Fists were raised as if daring the storm clouds – or the British – to attack. The pattering drops became a light shower that quickly ended; the farmers ignored the rain and persisted to speak their own thoughts and competed with each other to be heard.

"Ask the French. They'll send men to help us. Don't want the British here any more'n we do," one of the former soldiers yelled.

"Won't get here by the time we need them, the French. Have to raise our own defense. Who's in it with me?" Abraham Gaudet shouted. He was powerfully built and aggressive, with coal-black eyes that could fill in an instant with bottomless anger. His hair was black and straight and his beard reached down to his chest. His nose was broken in a fight and left to heal as best it could.

Abraham's wife lay sick most of the time. In spite of the rumors whispered about him by the women of the village, he treated her with tenderness. The men thought he'd once been an officer in the French army. No one knew for sure because no one dared to ask him.

Lightning flashed and the clouds opened in a downpour. "Be ready when I come to call ye out." Abraham pointed at individual men as if to mark them as his confederates.

Guillaume went home soaked to the skin and wondering what would happen when the British came. He didn't doubt they would; the only question was, how soon. Brooding as he dried himself off, he looked out the window across to the rain-soaked territory opposite his fields that the British had gained by the treaty. He rubbed his forehead and wondered how soon they'd try to extend that claim to Beausejour.

The answer to his unspoken question came not a month later. It happened on a morning when fog rode up the bay on the tide and tendrils of mist drifted ashore like white smoke.

A ship lay at anchor near the mouth of the river, concealed by the murk. Oars rattled and voices gave orders that clearly echoed in the fog as long boats were lowered and filled with men. Farmers who went to the fields early that morning heard them and sent a man to warn the village. Gaudet called for his volunteers and when the messenger came to fetch Guillaume, three-year-old Honoré ran into the yard shouting he wanted to go, too.

Jerusha ran after him, "You're just a little boy. Not time for you to go off to fight the soldiers." She grabbed him by the ear and marched him back inside. "For once ye can learn to think of your mother. I need you to stay here and take care of me. What if the English come and your father's not here? What'd I do without you to protect me?" His face became grave at the thought of this new responsibility and it was all Jerusha could do not to laugh.

Guillaume made for the woods to join the rest of the farmers where they waited for the enemy to land.

As the British rowed for the shore the sound of oars became fainter and the men knew that meant they were being swept by a current that would likely put them on the beach about a half-mile from the town, on a point where the forest came almost to the water. Gaudet decided where to set the ambush and they ran as fast as they could to get ahead of their quarry and position themselves before the British landed and got organized to march.

As the redcoats made their way along a stretch of road that led through the wood the fog lifted above the trees. Guillaume watched from a thicket as the line of soldiers marched past. Acadian faces hidden in the brush where they could peer through fringes of wet leaves to look upon their enemy came uncovered as the British passed. A slight movement attracted the eye of one of the soldiers who turned his head and shouted in surprise.

The Acadians ducked down and slipped away as the column came to a confused halt. Gaudet motioned for the farmers to get ready for an attack and waited to see what the English would do now.

The officer in charge ran back along the line to the man who yelled and asked what he had seen.

"Men's faces, sir. One, nose all mangled and bent. Looked out at us from in the bushes."

"Where'd ye see them?"

"Right in there," he pointed. "Gone now."

"Anyone else see them?" the officer demanded as he paced back and forth along the line. He sent a couple of men to thrash through the underbrush and flush out anyone they found hiding but they found no one lurking nearby.

"Back in line," the officer shouted and ordered them forward. Ahead of the soldiers the crook-nosed man jumped from the trees onto the road. He fired his gun and hit the officer in the shoulder. Men in the front of the line loaded their weapons as fast as they could and fired into the trees while the rest of the attackers made their way through the underbrush along the line of soldiers. They fired as they went and killed two soldiers and wounded others before they scattered and disappeared.

A couple of soldiers escaped the ambush and ran back to get help from the ship. After a time another detachment of recoats landed and brought the ship's doctor with them.

The fresh troops marched carefully along the path and searched the woods to each side. They kept on along the trail and came out of the woods at the edge of Beaubassin where they found some farmers working out in the fields.

Guillaume saw them when he reached the boat he left at the river and rowed back across to make his escape. When he reached the house Honoré came running out, "You shoot a redcoat? Get shot or anything?"

"No, I didn't. Let me catch my breath and tell your mother I'm back with no holes punched in me."

However they prised out the information, the English learned the name of Abraham Gaudet and put a price on his head. Then they entered the village and kicked in doors. They turned people out of their houses and ransacked them looking for weapons.

At Gaudet's home two redcoats pounded on the door but his wife was too ill to leave her bed and lay there trembling with fear that her husband had been found out and arrested. One of her young sons opened the door and the soldiers pushed their way in, shoving the children aside. They yelled, "Where's he? That devil as set that ambush on the trail?" One of the soldiers grabbed the boy who let them in and pushed him against the wall, slapped his face and shouted, "Ye'll tell us now. Where's he gone?" The youngster burst into tears and the man threw him down onto the floor.

The soldiers turned over furniture and opened chests. They threw things everywhere. They pulled blankets from a trunk and wiped their muddied boots on clean white wool, all the while shouting at the frightened bedridden woman and her children.

Abraham and his friends took no chances after the attack; by the time the soldiers were breaking in the door of his house, they were already escaping to Quebec.

ANNAPOLIS ROYAL 1725

On the street in front of the truck house, a soldier in full uniform attended by a boy beating on a large drum stood to attention as he read out the Governor's summons: all Acadian men were called to gather at the end of the day in the town green. Then he fastened a copy to the wall of the building. Henri asked the man what it was all about; the soldier just shrugged and answered, "You'll be there to find out. Don't know myself."

Jean Cormier, the first customer who came into the truck house that day asked Henri, "What's the British up to now? Ye hear anything?" That day everyone who crossed the threshold voiced the same question. Henri could only say, "Don't know, but nothing good ever comes when the British put on their dress uniforms to talk to Acadians."

That evening the sun lowered beneath a cloudbank so it was underlighted first in gold and then in darkening ridges of scarlet that looked like bloody welts. When it finally dropped below the horizon it left the sky with a thick rumpled skin of clouds the color of bruises.

With mixed curiosity and dread the nervous Acadians stepped from their houses into the early darkness to go see what the Governor had to lay out upon the anvil.

At this time of day the men usually looked forward to being at home. Inside their cozy houses lighted by the comforting glow of hearth fires and candles and filled with women's chatter as they prepared the evening meal, the men usually sat with their children playing around them, giggling and laughing. This night the Acadians walked in a solemn group; their faces were filled with resignation as they advanced from the lower town. Their numbers steadily grew as men came out of their houses to join the ranks as they passed by. A light rain shower moved quickly overhead and was soon gone. Light from the lanterns some of the men carried was absorbed by the gloom.

Like fine gossamer threads spun by a legion of tiny spiders, soft questioning murmurs strung their way through the crowd as Placide or Michel anxiously asked Ysidore or Josef did he know what this was about? The whispered words were punctuated by the sound of their feet as they walked the inevitable route that took them to the green. No one was willing to voice his own fears. So troubled were they that even the homely and usually comforting smells of cooking that escaped through opened doors and lingered in the air failed to distract them from their dread of the governor's mysterious intention.

Some soldiers stood outside the ranks mustered on the parade ground and held torches to light the place. Once the Acadians were assembled the British closed ranks and hemmed them in. By torchlight they looked completely different from the half-starved raggedy men that went about the garrison during the day. The light flickered across pale faces now set with menacing expressions. Their red coats, black cockaded hats, white breeches, black boots, shining brass, and rifles held across their chests made them look like the very guardians of the gates of Hell.

The swarthy compact-bodied Acadians were dressed in their daily working clothes and stood in a cluster as if they were the captives of some bloodless coup. A few took rosary beads from their pockets and lifted the crucifix to their lips to ward off whatever evil they felt stalked among them.

With a flourish the drummer beat a tattoo ending with a roll to announce the Governor and his aides. Doucette stepped to the front of the ranks and looked around the crowd as if to mark each of their faces. He ordered an officer to step forward and read the summons in English and in French. Then he spoke.

"Ye recall how Indians have attacked this town during the past several years. We must do all in our power to protect our citizens, their lives and property. To that effect all of you know there's an ordinance that no Indian shall be welcomed to any Acadian home after curfew. We know that some of you've broken that law; here among you tonight there's a man to be brought to account for it. Ye ken the punishment. You Acadians must keep to the law. When you flout it you'll pay the piper." Then he commanded the man who'd read the summons, "Bring the witness forward." The captain shouted an order; soldiers parted ranks and the witness was brought forward by an escort on either side of him and with his head hanging down like a ragdoll's. They placed him beside the Governor and turned him to face the Acadians.

To them his was a familiar English face. The Governor gave him a look that as good as said, "You'll not back down from this." Again Doucette scanned the faces of the Acadians who stood nervously before him. He turned to take another look at the witness before he motioned to the captain to proceed.

He asked, "Do you see here that man ye saw open his door to an Indian?" The witness became agitated; the flesh of his face jiggled as it jerked from side to side pretending to look closely at each of the Acadians standing nervously before him. He suddenly reddened and pointed wildly and shouted, "There! That be him!"

The captain screamed out a command. "Take that man!"

Henri stood in shock with his feet rooted to the ground like lead weights. The witness was pointing to him. He felt himself become warm in the crotch as a wedge of soldiers detached from the front rank and shoved their way through the crowded Acadians, yelling at them to make way as they rushed toward him. He was packed so tightly into the dense bodies moving backward and forward as men struggled to get out of the way that he couldn't move. He trembled with the certainty he was the one to be arrested and thrown into chains because Paul Dancing Crow had made his way through the town on the night before and come to his house. He closed his eyes and waited for the soldiers to grab him, bind him and drag him away. But they shoved him roughly aside and gave him a clout on the shoulder for good measure as they cleared a space around the man standing next to him, his neighbor Prudent Robichaud. They seized him. He had a large family, many of them Indian or mixed-blood who often visited him.

Henri almost shouted, "It was I!" to protect his friend from what he thought was his guilt; but then he realized they would have taken them both and not released Robichaud. He felt the weight of the accuser's eyes staring at him. Henri saw his red-faced rage and realized that the man had tried to get back at him for discovering him trying to pilfer some goods at the truck house. That would-be thief and liar knew they seized the wrong man but realized if he tried to correct them now, he risked being taken to suffer the same fate as he had brought upon Robichaud. Henri scowled and locked eyes with him. Neither man dared to speak. The witness tried to shrink from Henri's glare by burrowing into the protective cover of the soldiers but one of the redcoats growled, "Get back out there!" and shoved him toward the Acadians.

After the English took Robichaud away the rest of the Acadians were released. The red coats pushed them along to clear them out of the green. Henri stumbled on weakened legs and moved along in the middle of the crowd. They made their way down the lane until they were out of the sight of the soldiers and then stepped into the middle of the street and pulled together into a tightly knotted group.

"He's using this so-called witness to take revenge," one of the men whispered so low the others could barely hear him. "Acadians chose Robichaud to serve on the council. Doucette rejected him. Rest of the council members come hat in hand, very humble they was, shuffling their feet and complaining. Doucette come all shouting. Angry. Said they're defiant. Stamped his boot on the floorboards hard enough to make them shake. Shouted at them, 'Do as you're told.' "

"What do ye think will come next? Will they try another oath; do they reckon we'd swear without the exception?"

"Aye. They do this to set the example to what'll happen should we refuse it."

"Give us the choice to take their fookin' oath or leave all our worldly goods behind and go to exile at Ile Royale or Ile St. Jean is what I'd wager."

"Nothing should surprise us after what they do to Prudent."

Soon they broke up to get home before curfew, each man to cross his own threshold and be received by a family thankful to see him back safe.

No one in the town slept that night.

At dawn three drummers beat an echoing cacophony loud enough to wake the dead as soldiers chained Robichaud's wrists and suspended him above a platform in the marketplace. All day long soldiers stood guard near the prisoner. Of the few people who came to the market that day none dared approach the platform.

At sunset they let Robichaud down. His wrists were lined by blood from cuts made by the sharp-edged cuffs. The soldiers marched off carrying the chains he'd worn and left him lying on the platform to be claimed by his wife and children.

ANNAPOLIS ROYAL 1726

The sun shone through the tall side windows brightening the dining room. Every time Henri came into the room he remembered the argument he'd had with his wife over the silk damask that covered the walls and gave the room such a warm and welcoming feel. Marie was right to insist on having it. From its glistening light pink of early morning to its deep peach by evening candlelight it softened faces and promoted easeful thoughts. Henri had argued that they didn't have her brother's wealth and couldn't duplicate his house – at least not right away. He finally gave in and warned her, "This is the one extravagance you're allowed in this house. Don't ask for anything else." But in the end he was glad he agreed to let her have the silk and later on he was man enough to tell her so.

Now he felt like she had gotten him to agree to something else and he just couldn't remember what it was. He groaned and rubbed his temples. Samuel and Marie sat at the table with a newspaper spread out in front of them, drinking their coffee and chatting. Henri came over and kissed his wife's forehead and sat down. "Must've been some night," he groaned. "Catching up on the social news?" She raised an eyebrow at him.

"You were in a wonderful mood. Never better – wine or anything else." Marie smiled at him. Henri knew something was up but he was so desperate for a cup of coffee that he would be willing to give her anything she wanted if she would only just pour him some.

"Where can I get some of that?" It almost sounded like he was pleading with her.

He looked at Samuel as if to appeal for his support. "I've a feeling I promised Marie something last night over dinner, but for the life of me I can't recall what I said. Do you?"

"Remember when Samuel told me my sister Louisa has a maze in her garden? And you promised me I could have one too?" Marie rose from her chair and went to the large silver urn on the sideboard where she drew steaming cups for both men.

"I must've been very much imbibed with the wine when I said it." Henri rubbed his temples. "Where's my coffee?"

Samuel laughed. "I heard ye say it. And you also said ye could never deny Marie anything she wanted."

Henri winced. "You didn't take advantage of me while I was defenseless, did ye? Just say it ain't so. Two of you against only me? I've to give up right now. And I haven't even had my coffee yet." He turned to Marie. "Where is my coffee?" She pointed to the cup beside him.

Henri took it and went to the doorway to the garden. He took a deep breath before he emptied the cup in a single gulp. He took it to the sideboard for a refill.

"Cook'll be right in with your breakfast. Smells good, doesn't it?"

"I feel better now except it seems last night I promised my wife a maze in the garden and I don't even know what Armstrong wants now or how much that'll cost." When he extended his lower lip in a pout Marie rang the bell to hurry the cook. As if she was waiting for Marie's signal in came their breakfast - sausage, bacon, eggs, hot biscuits, fruit preserves. The men helped themselves and ate while Marie watched. When Henri finished eating he wiped his mouth and sat for a moment. "Another meal to savor." He nodded to his wife and picked up his cup.

"You told me the maze has to be a small one with low bushes so no one could hide in it and leap out to attack us. And I said that's fine with me. I'd have the gardener come in to help plan it. I don't have to do it if you're against it now you're sober again."

Henri gave her a smoldering look and she burst out laughing. He shrugged his shoulders. "You win. Always do. Can't refuse ye anything." He turned to Samuel who was trying to avoid being drawn into their argument. "What do ye think Armstrong wants?"

Samuel sipped his coffee as he responded, glad the conversation returned to a subject more comfortable for him. "Usual thing I'll bet. English don't want us trading unless they can get their cut of taxes. That's why we all need to decide how it's to be handled. Don't want another brawl with him. It ain't seemly."

"Careful of that one," Marie said. "Got himself a reputation for being bad-tempered. Pleasant to me though, when he sees me about the town."

She gave her husband a mischievous look. "So I can go ahead with the maze? We'll have the only garden in Annapolis Royal with a maze in it."

Henri nodded. "I said ye could, so yes ye can." He looked at Samuel. "Bad day if the governor ever gets as good as Marie at getting what he wants."

"Not a chance of it with his temper."

"Man can't do his job makes anyone bad tempered," Samuel said. "Farmers at Minas and Chignecto goaded by certain Yankee traders to refuse to sign the same oath of allegiance as Armstrong got the Acadians here at Annapolis Royal to sign."

"Wouldn't be you doing such a dastardly thing," Marie said. A smile twitched at her lips.

"Damned if we do, damned if we don't. Always. What fools those British are to insist on trying to make people swear to do what they can't. Acadians would rather be damned by them than by their own people. But so far as they can swear to an oath they'll keep their word. No trickery there, just people who want their lives peaceful. Farmers every one." Henri drained the last drop from his cup. "So now we're to go and sit in the *Black Sheep* and tip a beer with the others? Right out in public? Won't it be like we're snubbing our noses at him? Whose bright idea was this? Yours?"

Samuel grinned. "Here we'll all be. Show of force only if he chooses to take it that way. Or he can talk to us as gentlemen. But I wouldn't expect so much of that from him."

"How else's he supposed to see it? Anyone invite him, tell him we're all to be there? Of course he'll find out about it and barge in all heated up to confront us all together. May even accuse us of plotting against him." Henri shook his head.

"That'd be his style."

"Some among us think they've things to say to him. Question is will he hear them?"

"Might do him good to listen for a change. We should've told him but he'll find out soon enough. He's got at least one spy among us who'll run out to tell him."

They left the house and headed for the tavern. At that hour of the day the place was theirs and most of the others were already gathered for the meeting. They greeted the Faneuil brothers, Adams, Alden, Blin and some of the smaller traders and joined a table. Samuel looked around at the room. It was full of mismatched chairs and tables collected over the years, the beams were darkened with decades of smoke from cooking fires and there were rows of tankards shelved above the kegs of beer. Even when the tavern was empty the air would still be ripe with the smell of stale beer and tobacco smoke. Now it was noisy with speculation about what would happen next. "This place could be in Boston," Samuel observed as he watched the men crowding in. The tavern keeper came over to them.

Samuel raised his voice to be heard above the room, "How many times do ye have men filing in like this to meet and drink away the morning?"

"It's what keeps the old place going. My father's before me and my sons' when I'm gone to dust. This here" – he waved his arm –"good business."

He went off to get their beer.

A man at the edge of one group so engaged in loud emphatic discussion they were oblivious to their surroundings caught the Governor's name and a few profane words besides. He rose unnoticed from his seat and made his way out. He ambled down the street and entered a small door at the back of a building.

Once inside the spy went to Armstrong's office and asked the young man who stood guard at the door to tell the governor he had some information. As he waited with his cap in his hands, he noticed a chair with broken legs standing in the corner and was reminded of the meeting held there a week earlier when Armstrong called the Annapolis Royal traders to his office to give them a dressing down about illicit trade. He had screamed at Henri, "Bancouer! Ye can stop the illegal business coming and going from your truck house. I know what you and your friends are up to." He had waved his arms at the men gathered in the room and shouted, "I've my eye on every one of you."

Then the Governor had turned and in one swift angry motion he had picked up his chair and smashed it against the floor, breaking the back legs and gouging the wooden floorboards. Then he hesitated a moment as if he was surprised the chair legs had broken so easily. His eyes had turned hard as stones as he looked at each of the traders and growled, "I'll break any one of you as thinks he can avoid paying his taxes due to the Crown!" His aide Robyn Jenkins had silently picked up the chair and removed it to the anteroom.

A shiver ran down his spine as the spy remembered how cold and hard the Governor's face had been at that moment. The chair still leaned in the corner where Jenkins had put it. It was just one more decrepit item in an already cheerless room. A large cobweb fluttered like a veil from the ceiling; motes of dust danced in the light that came through the large windows and the floor sagged in the middle where the planks hung suspended between the beams. The wooden framing around the fireplace was smudged with soot and the fire smoldered untended because the logs needed stoking.

Lt. Jenkins in his fine uniform didn't want to get his white gloves dirty. The guard wasn't supposed to lay down his weapon and leave his post for any reason. If he did and was caught, the Governor would use the excuse to lay on the lashes. It was a standoff.

The spy went over to the fireplace and jiggled the logs until a flame shot up. Then he reached for some wood and tossed it onto the bed of coals. Jenkins acted as if he didn't notice. The guard winced as smoke trailed into the room and irritated his eyes.

The man thought of his own predicament. He never intended to be anyone's spy. It had all happened at that same meeting. He had been the last to leave and Armstrong called him back. "And you, sir, ye think I don't care about the small folk like you, but you're the very people who know the most. You've the most to gain and the least to lose by cooperating. By a week from today you'll be back here to report something I haven't already heard or I'll throw you in jail."

Armstrong had his moods; many times they blew over and he would forget what he had said. But if he did remember, woe to the man who was lacking and the spy felt he couldn't chance that. Up until that morning he had nothing to report. But seeing all the biggest traders huddled over beers at the *Black Sheep* would certainly be news that would interest him.

The guard stood aside for the spy to enter the office and he saw the same stacks of papers on the Governor's desk as before. Armstrong sat before a gap in between the piles, writing with his goose quill. He dipped the pen in the inkwell and wrote a few more words before he put it down. "I was expecting you sooner. What've ye got to tell me?" The spy nervously whispered his news.

"At the *Black Sheep* then?" The Governor's laugh was angry. "I'll be doing some shearing over there." He buckled on his sword belt and put the weapon in its scabbard. "Come along, Jenkins. We've some men to meet on the King's business."

They made a noisy entrance into the tavern and the owner hurried over to them offering a table as he asked their pleasure. The Governor's glance swept the room; in a loud voice he observed to his aide that all the big fish were gathered in the same end of the pond.

"My pleasure ye say? That'd be having all you scofflaws" – he waved at the traders – "pay their just taxes to the Crown."

He smoldered as he looked at the studied innocence of the men's expressions. His anger at the thought of being duped by New Englanders – Englishmen they called themselves when it suited them – was near the point of exploding.

"Join us Governor, if ye wish to." Samuel rose and offered him his chair and Henri broke off telling some men about the meeting of the previous week. Warily they looked at Armstrong. He came over to their table and Jenkins followed a step behind him.

"So you'd be trading and never a coin for the King's taxes. I came to talk about scofflaws and tax evaders like all of you sitting in this room." He looked across the room. "Wipe that sneer off your face," he shouted.

"That's no sneer," someone called out from behind the governor's back. As he whirled to locate the offender another voice shouted from a large group sitting at a round table, "Just his usual phiz." Some raucous laughter followed.

The Governor's face reddened. "Jenkins! Take the names of those men."

Blin half rose from his seat, but seemed to think better of it and sat back down and muttered to his companions, "Last meeting it was my turn. Watkins can take the lashes now."

"Who're you accusing?" Samuel asked, trying to keep the tone of his voice reasonable.

"You for one," the Governor fired the words at him. "You run your ship up the bay, unload in Chignecto, and sell to the Acadians. Then ye take French stuff aboard and head direct for Boston and never stop to pay your taxes here. You think I don't know anything about it." He pointed to the others seated at the table. "You're all outlaws in that regard."

"What makes you think you're entitled to collect such taxes? We pay them where we land our goods, not where we're just passing through." Samuel stood ramrod straight. He was face to face with Armstrong.

"Anyone else think like Watkins here?"

No one spoke.

"Well, gentlemen. Then you'll either put in here from now on and pay your taxes or you'll be embargoed from carrying trade to any place in Nova Scotia outside of Annapolis Royal."

He pulled out the scroll he had been writing on when the spy came into his office and handed it to Lt. Jenkins. Armstrong told him to read aloud the terms of the embargo and looked around with a satisfied expression as the merchants heard the document and he savored its effect on them.

Samuel was furious and condemned the embargo to Armstrong's face. "What're you trying to prove? Don't you see what you're doing? You'll get no trade and no taxes and everyone goes hungry besides."

"I'll lay that on your tender consciences, gentlemen. Sooner or later, you'll do as I say." His face took on a smug look. He rubbed his hands together.

"You'll regret this," someone spoke up.

"Innocent people are who will suffer from it." Another voice joined in.

"It'll be the likes of you to suffer when you can't land your tax-evading goods to trade and sell and make your profits."

"When people go hungry they'll look to you for answers. What'll you tell them? On a matter of principle you stopped the ships from bringing the food in here?" Samuel held out his hands palms up and shrugged. "Folks are going to starve if you persist with this."

The Governor was enraged. "You'll all do as I say!" He pounded his fist on the table upsetting the beer the host had set down for him. He drew himself up to his full height and gave them an angry look before he slammed out the door. Jenkins followed as fast as he could.

"He'll regret this," Samuel shook his head.

"It'll take a few weeks before supplies run low enough to where people get really angry about it."

"You'll see some prime smuggling now."

"What about informers?"

"Let them starve if there are any so silly as to side with Armstrong."

To everyone's relief it took only a couple of weeks before the food ran out and the Governor had to back down. After that ships plied the Bay of Fundy exchanging goods as if there had never been an embargo.

One of Samuel's captains brought a cartoon of the Governor from a Boston newspaper and Henri made him put it in the fire as a thing that might be humorous in Boston, but in Annapolis Royal it would be seen as seditious.

He laughed at Henri's insistence to burn the thing. "No matter. That oath of allegiance will keep coming back to haunt us all."

Henri agreed. "Acadians must stay Neuter to survive. British fear what'd happen if the French beckon to them and the Acadians answer their call. The day will come when it'll all have to be worked out."

BEAUSEJOUR 1726

Jerusha's eldest daughter Aimeé was just finished with her morning chores and finally had a few precious minutes to herself. Soon she would fill the lunch pails to bring to the fields for the men's noonday meal. But for now she could sit on the bench under the huge oak that grew near the door and sew some stitches on the shirt she was making for her father.

She went outside and looked toward the meadows where her father and brothers worked to clean up after the harvest that left their barns filled to bursting. Jerusha was in the yard behind the house spreading out the wash with Virginie and Clarice. Aimeé sighed. Nothing ever happened to break the monotony of the everlasting round of things that must be done on a farm. She walked toward the barns. Even the animals were occupied – the horses were off in the fields at work with the men, the cows were far down in their meadow as if to shun human company; the sheep were in a nearby grass patch relentlessly snipping tender shoots with their sharp teeth. A large ewe and two year-ling lambs looked at her as she came to the fence and turned away when they saw she had nothing to offer them.

The surplus animals were gone, driven to Louisbourg. Uncle Jacques and his sons met them as they crossed the isthmus to Baie Verte and took the Bancouer animals the rest of the way to the fortress. Soon the farmers would start to slaughter their meat animals. The women would spend days cooking and preserving, make the blood puddings and collect the rest of the cabbages and ground vegetables to store in the root cellar. They would have plenty for the winter. Wood to feed the hearth was already cut and stacked nearby.

All was as it should be; and the deep blue sky that stretched above the land promised a warm and peaceful late summer day. Out to sea the morning mist was nearly all burned off. Aimeé sighed. If this was Eden – and many of the Acadians said so – it was certainly boring. She went back inside and packed the food and then went to the window and called to her mother that she was ready to go down to the fields.

"Can we go too?" her sisters chimed, eager to break their daily rou-tine. "We can carry the water jugs for father and the boys. It's a day to make anyone thirsty." Jerusha laughed at their eagerness. "Go on," she told them.

A few young swamp maples stood at the edge of the field in bril-liant red and gave a bit of shade. That's where the men would set down to wait for them. The girls started down the lane that led into the mead-ows and as they rounded a bend midway there was a prospect over the water where Aimeé usually stopped to scan the horizon.

Clarice's voice caught in surprise. "Look there. Do ye see it?" There was a ship far out and headed right for the Missaguash River that flowed past the bottom of their fields and separated Beausejour from the vil-lage of Beaubassin. Its snow-white sails were spread to catch every breath of the wind as it drove toward the shore. The girls stood watch-ing its dark hull cleave the water like a knife thrusting through a quak-ing and shimmering jelly, straight and true and coming closer and closer to them.

"Oh I do wish it's bringing our boys back from Louisbourg," Vir-ginie's voice quavered with excitement.

Aimeé pouted as she thought of her brothers' and cousins' freedom to go where they pleased. Having to behave like a young lady sometimes made her feel like a prisoner in her own home. She prayed that if she couldn't go seeking adventure it would somehow come to find her.

A flag broke out from the yardarm and unfurled in the wind.

"Ugh! British!" Clarice was dejected. "So much for anything good coming our way."

"The men'll probably have to go see what's about this ship comin' in here," Aimeé said, disappointed. Then a colorful banner unfurled from the topmast and the girls stopped to watch it break out in the breeze.

"Never saw that before," Virginie said. "Wonder what it means?"

They quickened their pace and in a few more minutes they reached the men waiting for them beneath the trees at the edge of the field.

"Did you see a British ship coming with a pennant flying? Ever see the like of that?" Aimeé asked as she handed over the pail of food. They spread out the ground cloth and the men delved right in and chewed hungrily on the bread and cheese and small joints of meat left from last night's supper. The girls speculated about the meaning of the pennant. They ate a few mouthfuls of food and sipped some water. They stood up to see how close the ship was to the shore. It had made good progress and was so near the mouth of the river it would have to drop anchor right where it was or risk being grounded when the tide ran out.

"It's not the way they usually announce themselves. Curious. For sure we'll know what they're after soon enough. Now go on back to the house. Take these empty water jugs with you." Guillaume hastened his daughters' retreat.

The girls packed up and began their trek up the path. They walked briskly at first, their talk all about the ship and what might have brought it to Beaubassin but by the time they got to the bend where they could get a good view of it, they were ready to rest and take a good long gander. The sails were furled but the flag and pennant still flew. Men lined the rails and longboats were lowering to take ashore some soldiers in red-coated uniforms, with drums and pipes and flags. A couple of officers with scrolls and ceremonial swords were already in another boat. A man climbed the rigging to the lookout platform and trained his glass on the shore. At first he looked at the village; a few men were gathered on the beach to welcome the boats. Then a flash of reflected sunlight alerted the girls that his glass was pointed at them. Quickly they rose from their places and picked up their burdens. They went the rest of the way around the bend and out of the man's sight.

"Mr. Jenkins, sir? What do ye see over there? Any pretty girls?" A soldier on the deck below called up to the man in the rigging who was holding his spyglass as if intent on something worthy of his concentration. He had moved to the edge of the platform to get a better look but now the girls were hidden in the trees. There was a farmhouse and barns farther up the hill; Robyn thought it must be their home. He saw men in the fields below. One of them stood up from his work and looked at the vessel. Then the farmer looked up at the hillside.

"Must've seen the flash from the glass," he thought, "Caught me looking at his daughters." Robyn turned his attention back to the man on deck.

"Saw some pretty misses but they run away." He put on a long face as he descended from his perch. "Maybe we'll see them at the Ensign's party." Just thinking about Ensign Robert Wroth's plan to invite the farmers to a feast with music and dancing put him in an excellent mood.

Just after they sailed out from Annapolis Royal Ensign Wroth explained the mission to everyone aboard the sloop. The Governor expected that in the spirit of camaraderie the Acadians would easily agree to sign the oath of allegiance to the new British King, George II. "Feast them, don't force them," – he told everyone that was what Governor Armstrong instructed them to do.

After he succeeded here, Wroth would be able to produce a list of signatures to show the Acadians in the other places they had yet to visit. That would convince all the others to sign for sure and make the job of getting each and every Acadian to swear to the oath a lot easier.

Wroth had already given the officers detailed instructions – march to a place and read the proclamation and then spend a bit of time to mix with the Acadians and encourage them to come over to Beaubassin to feast and dance. The officers were to go in their best dress uniforms and impress these people. Their errand was peaceful and they'd carry no arms other than a ceremonial pistol or knife.

He called out the landing parties and gave them each their assignment. Lieutenant Robyn Jenkins' detail was to cross the Missaguash River and go to the hamlet just up the hill from the landing place. He was to march up the same path where he saw those girls and stop at their farm. Wroth's nasal voice jolted him from his thoughts. "In a fog there, Jenkins? Come out of it and get moving."

"Yes sir!" he turned to his men and ordered them into the waiting boat. "Got another after you to transport," the coxswain told him.

"We'll be off directly you put us ashore."

All the way across the river Robyn studied the farm field and the lane. They would climb up to the top of the dike that edged the lower field and walk the path along it to get to the lane. He gave the men instructions to go straight up on the embankment when they landed and wait for him. Then he looked again at the lane. It wound secretly through the trees and came out into the open farther up; there it bent back in the direction of the house and barn. That was where the girls were sitting when he spotted them.

The boat bumped in the mud signaling they were finished crossing. Robyn waited for the soldiers to debark ahead of him and let the bow rise a bit higher. Then he ordered the oarsmen to push up onto the cobble where he could step ashore without getting his boots muddied. He jumped from the boat and followed the path his men had taken. Where the lane began he ordered them to follow him in file.

"Break out the pennant," he ordered. "Speak the cadence." When they reached the oak tree near the house Robyn gave the order to halt and stand at ease. The pennant trembled in the light breeze as he stepped up to the door and pounded on it with his gloved fist.

Inside the house Jerusha was putting away the last of the clean linens the girls had taken in and Aimeé stood by the hearth stirring a pot that bubbled a merry invitation to taste its contents. The smell wafted through the windows reminding Robyn how long it had been since he last ate a good meal.

Guillaume saw the boat when it set out to cross toward their farm and took a short cut through the woods to get back to the house. He appeared from behind the barn and asked the soldiers, "What brings you here?" Robyn turned away from the house and crossed the yard to speak to him.

Jerusha went to the window; the girls gathered behind her. "Isn't he the same man as had the spyglass?" Clarice turned to Aimeé with sparkling eyes.

"May be." The sisters strained to get a better look. "He's beautiful," Virginie squealed. Robyn heard her and turned beet red. "Look, he's blushing." She giggled and clapped her hands.

"Ye remind me of when me and my sisters was young and foolish over the men," Jerusha whispered. "And these be English, not even our own good Acadian men. Shame on ye."

"Perhaps my wife would join us and hear what ye have to say," Guillaume spoke up so the women would be sure to hear him as he went to the window and called inside. "Jerusha, the officer's got something to tell us. Come out and hear it."

Red-faced and stammering Robyn explained his mission. He told them about the great feast with dancing the English were to hold next evening in Beaubassin and invited the whole family to come over and join them. "Our leader Ensign Wroth wants to talk about the oath of allegiance to the new king. He thought the best way to do it was to invite everyone to come to a party. Wants all to have a good time and be friends. Will you come?"

They exchanged surprised glances; Jerusha gave a slight nod and Guillaume said, "Aye. We'll do." Robyn reached out and gave him a strong handshake.

Now he had his first success at dealing with Acadians. They seemed such good people. How hard could it be for Wroth to convince them to sign the oath? Then there'd be peace and an Englishman could be welcomed to court an Acadian maid. That officer he met in Annapolis Royal married an Acadian woman and her family had already made him rich beyond anything he would ever have been able to do for himself. "He has a good life," Robyn thought. "Why not for me as well as another?" He felt so buoyed up his feet barely touched the ground as he walked on to the next farm.

"Did ye never see the like of that?" Jerusha turned to her husband as the soldiers left. He frowned, wondering what the catch to it was and how much it would cost the Acadians when the time came for the accounting.

"Why'd they think to come here and ask anyone to sign their oath?" Jerusha muttered.

Guillaume gave her a perplexed look. "What do ye mean?"

"As I thought ye told me, we're living in French territory. They've a nerve to come over here and ask anyone to make an oath to them."

"True. But if we're to have a peace we all need to swear an oath of some kind. It's just that we can't let them insist it must be one that says we've to take up arms to fight against French and Indians."

"Why'd anyone swear to it if that's what they want?"

"Won't swear it; you'll see."

"Why'd any Acadian even listen to them asking us to swear to any oath of theirs?"

"Because we want peace. We're Neutrals, not French who come here to fight the British. If we're to survive them fighting each other, then we Acadians – all of us – must stay Neutral."

"Ye plan to swear such an oath?"

"I want peace here. I want to live a life without wars and fighting. I want to pass on what I have to my sons and they to their sons forever."

"Acadians are like a bundle of twigs. Bind them together and ye can't break the bundle apart. But break a few of them and soon the whole bundle breaks and ye can throw them all into the fire." Jerusha folded her arms and gave him a determined look. "Don't ye believe that's what'll happen when the French come asking for help next time? First one breaks off and then another and then there's a crowd of them. After those men go breaking their oaths, it's all the easier for the rest to join in. Men do what suits them. We'll never have a peace that gives us what ye want it to."

"I see your point," Guillaume said. "But what good is my word if I swear the oath to be Neutral and then break it the first time the French come asking? I believe we must all stay Neutral. It's all that'll save us in the long run. Because it lets us get along with everyone – Indians, French, English – as friend to all and enemy to none."

"I'd rather see you be right. Terrible day if something happens not included in your rosy scheme of how things are supposed to turn out. Troubled times have a way to find us and nothing's ever going to change that."

Inside the house the girls' excited chatter grew louder and louder. "We're going? Really going? To a party? With the English?"

"Calm down, or you'll all stay to home," their mother warned them with a smile twitching at her lips.

"Mother, ye wouldn't. Nothing ever happens here. Now here's this party. We have to go. English asked all of us to come. Ye heard him say that. Ye can't just leave us to home." Aimeé pleaded.

Guillaume turned to look at his daughter's flushed face and said, "Saw the flash off a glass when ye girls walked back up the lane today. Might've been that same one. Think so?"

Aimeé blushed. "Don't know, father. But my sisters liked his looks well enough. He seemed pleasant."

"Aye, girl. But that's when we most need to be watchful of the English."

"And of them inviting us to a party and then demanding we take their oath of allegiance," Jerusha thought. "He's a good man but he doesn't often enough see the traps that can hide inside of innocent-seeming things."

All the next morning the faint smells of roasting wafted across the river and tickled their noses until there was not even the slightest thought of anyone staying away from the party. As he bent to his work Guillaume wondered why the British kept harping on this oath as if it was a matter of life and death.

His thoughts touched on the enmity he had felt toward the English for Song Sparrow's death. That was long ago now and as he had looked at the young officer, a man of about his age then, Guillaume felt no resentment but rather amusement at the man's transparent interest in his daughters. Once he had been interested in another man's daughter. Had he been as obvious as Lt. Jenkins? The young man had a youthful breeziness as if not yet marked by war. Guillaume wondered whenever that happened what kind of man it would make of him. Was he the kind to don war paint and run with the *couriers du bois* like the Englishman who had come with his Indians and overtaken the camp that terrible day? He shook his head to rid himself of such thoughts.

By mid-afternoon Jerusha and the girls were ready; she came outside looking for him.

Jerusha laughed, "What a noise they make. I'd forgotten how important such a gathering is for young girls."

"Your head was never turned by such things as I recall."

She caught him winking at her as he spoke. "Ye were so determined to have your own way. Now here's three daughters just like ye bent on going to enjoy themselves. And why not? English may be there but so are all our neighbors. May even be some eligible Acadian men."

They walked down the lane toward the shore and crossed to the village where there was dancing to the music of English pipes and Acadian fiddles and everyone ate and drank their fill. After a while the men drew off to the side, joining in a discussion that began to turn serious. Ensign Wroth saw them gathered in a tight knot and chose that moment to interrupt the party and tell everyone about his official purpose.

He read the Governor's proclamation for the oath in smooth and pleasant tones, lingering over words about swearing loyalty to the new king and ending with a plea for all of them, British and Acadians to live together in peace. The Acadians marked Wroth's earnest features and thought he honestly believed he had just done all he need do to convince them to line up and sign the oath right then and there. They were courteous to him but insisted on having time to discuss the terms of the oath. The Acadian leaders withdrew from the festivities.

The English pipes struck up the music again and the fiddles followed suit; the young resumed their dancing. Lt. Robyn Jenkins was rigged out in all his finery and cut a splendid figure. His blue eyes and golden hair drew sighs from all the girls as he made his rounds dancing with one or another in the reels and jigs. Soon there were only three girls he hadn't squired through a dance and he approached them. Virginie was smitten. Clarice was infatuated. At last he approached Aimeé. He knew with a certainty that she was the one he was looking for, the girl in his spyglass who'd sat on the hill looking back at him. His bow to her went deeper than his bows to the other girls; his face pinked and softened to her and from that moment on he danced with no other.

One of Jerusha's friends nudged her in the middle of a sentence and pointed to the young couple. "Englishman's made all our girls wishful today, but it seems he's taken an extra liking to your Aimeé," and the women turned their heads to observe the dancers.

Jerusha turned to watch them. "Here's trouble at the doorstep," she thought. Aloud she said, "English're leaving soon. Then things'll quiet down." She turned back to her gossip, but kept an eye on her daughter and the officer who showed such interest in her.

The habitants returned with an unrolled copy of the oath. They gathered around Ensign Wroth and pointed to something they had changed; Wroth shook his head as if to refuse what they were saying. At last Wroth took the parchment from them, rolled it up and walked away.

As if this was the signal for the English pipers, they abruptly stopped playing. Then the fiddlers stopped and the music went quiet in the middle of a song. Like a curtain had dropped between them the end of the music separated the Acadians from the British.

Aimeé and her sisters reluctantly joined their mother. Taking many a backward look they started for the path that led to their boat. Guillaume stopped for a few minutes to speak with some of the men before joining his family and when he finished with them he turned and saw Robyn staring openly at Aimeé. His eyes pleaded with her to stay, and his daughter's face responded to the Englishman's beseeching look.

Guillaume went over and gently put an arm around her shoulder and whispered, "There's naught but trouble to fish in those waters."

Aimeé sighed. "But father, isn't this meeting about having a peace with the English?"

"Aye, if it can be done with our amendments to the oath they want us to sign."

"And if it is done and he asks to, can Robyn visit us?"

"Cross the first bridge and then we'll see what's on the other side of it. Seems a pleasant young man but British are not the best to look to for a husband." As Guillaume said those words to his daughter he thought of how Rising Hawk must have felt when he and Jacques asked to marry his daughters and how strange it must have been for him to give his daughters in marriage to men who came from a different world. The revelation moistened his eyes as he looked at Aimeé's hopeful young face and he tenderly squeezed her shoulder.

"We'll take this evening to consider what the British want," he told her. "Tomorrow we'll meet Ensign Wroth again and see what's to be done about the oath. He's thinking on some changes we made and it may be he'll give us something tolerable to sign. You'll see them leave directly they get what they want. Just the way they are."

That night everyone slept except Aimeé; she rose from her bed, dressed as quietly as she could and crept down the path toward the river's edge. The full moon in the cloudless sky looked like a pearl set against velvet. Grasses swished in the field as nocturnal hunters sought their prey and the hoot of a great horned owl sounded first from one place and then from another. A doe slunk deeper into the cover of the underbrush as Aimeé went down the path to the riverbank. A fish jumped and splashed the surface and she heard the faint sound of a boat moving over the water with muffled oars.

Aimeé melted into the cover of the trees and watched as Robyn Jenkins, dressed in a plain shirt and pants rowed toward the beach where he slipped an anchor into the mud and climbed out of the boat shoeless to wade ashore. He stood for a moment looking back toward Beaubassin, then turned toward the path and began to make his way through the grasses toward the fields. Aimeé gasped in surprise.

He turned at the sound and whispered, "Who's there?"

Aimeé had come down there but she hadn't thought about what to do once she'd got to the river except to stand and look out on it and wonder about the Englishman. Did he sleep or was he wakeful with thoughts of her? Now there he stood and why did he come rowing across if not to look for her? Did he see her coming down the moon-lit path in his spyglass?

"What're ye doin' here, lovely Aimeé?" he asked gently. "Do ye always come here to look at a full moon? 'tis a beautiful prospect itself and the fields and the river and you make it more beautiful still."

He stepped close and slid his arm around her waist but she backed away.

"Please don't be afraid. I wouldn't ever hurt you."

"Why'd ye come rowing across to here? What were ye thinking?" She wanted to hear him say he couldn't bear to never see her again, that he was desperately in love with her, that he wanted always to be here and never leave, never put that uniform back on and go off on that ship that stood anchored at the mouth of the river.

"We might be off on the tide tomorrow if Wroth gets his business done with your folk. You're so beautiful, even more now than this afternoon when we danced together. Foolish it may sound since we only just met but I can't bear to leave you. Just wanted to sit where I first saw you sitting and think about you. Maybe I've to leave forever when the ship goes." His eyes moistened. "Couldn't stand to never see you again. But I'm no real suitor for you, an Englishman and a soldier to boot."

Aimeé slid an arm around his waist and he embraced her. Softly he kissed her hair and her forehead and her lips. She felt her insides melt.

Nearby in the grass someone sneezed.

They startled apart and Robyn looked around. Had someone followed him from the ship? That couldn't be. He'd have known if another boat came across the river. It was someone on this side. Was it one of her brothers? He thrashed at the grasses to flush out the intruder and a small voice pleaded, "It's only me – Clarice. I saw ye leave the house so I followed you."

Aimeé sighed her disappointment they'd been discovered.

"It's very romantic to meet in the moonlight and whisper to each other," Clarice said as she stood up.

Irritation sharpened Aimeé's voice. "Some day I'll follow after you and we'll see how that suits you."

"It's all right," Robyn said. "It'll be light soon and I've got to get back to the boat before the watch changes. If we come ashore today I'll try to come and see you. But if not," he put his arm around Aimeé's shoulders, "if not you'll know there's an Englishman somewhere abroad in the world who loves ye." He kissed the side of her face, twisting a curl of her hair around his finger.

She whispered, "And you'll know that here's an Acadian maid that loves you."

She took Clarice by the hand and Robyn made his way back to the beach, shoved the boat away and rowed softly down the river to where his ship stood dark against the first coral flush of the dawn.

The family was already stirring when the girls came into the yard. Aimeé sent Clarice to the chicken coop to fetch any eggs already laid that morning and then went into the barn to sort herself. Inside the house Jerusha stirred the ashes in the hearth to start the fire." You're about early today," she greeted her daughters, noting the high color of Aimeé's cheeks. She took three eggs from Clarice's apron.

"I am, mother. Couldn't sleep too well so I got up and started to go about."

"Your father saw someone row across the river this morning." Jerusha gave her a questioning look.

"Did he see who it was?"

"Thought it might've been that soldier you liked so much."

Clarice couldn't keep quiet any longer and she danced about squealing, "It was him, mother. The soldier. His name's Robyn. I hid in the grass and I saw him."

"Oh mother, I wish he didn't have to go." Aimeé turned her face away as her eyes teared.

"So ye were down there and met him on the bank," Jerusha said, wiping her hands on her apron. "Ye know better than to do that. Before ye know it there'll be trouble. He's not the kind of man that makes a good husband nor any husband at all, no matter what ye think. Those men are soldiers, fighting and wandering. Let that one go. Once that ship sails you'll not see him back here ever again."

"But mother, I love him." Aimeé lifted her apron to her face to blot her tears. "He said he'd come back and ask to marry me. And I want to marry him."

"He'll never be back here once that ship's gone. You're too young to know it but they always talk about marrying. Then they don't and they leave you to wait for them while they're off saying the same thing to some other girl."

"But he's different. He means it. I know he does."

"Girl, you're foolish if ye believe that. Even if he did want to come back the British wouldn't allow it." Jerusha looked at her daughter, crying as if her heart would shatter and hugged her. "It's all right. There'll be another to come who'll love ye and you'll forget all about this one."

Aboard the ship, Robyn listened in dismay to the sailing orders. How could he see Aimeé if he couldn't go back on shore? She was perfect for him. He was sure that once he pleaded with her parents to let them marry they would accept him. Nowadays Acadian girls married English men all the time, he told himself. Love and marriage made better bonds between people than oaths of allegiance that no one wanted to swear.

He climbed into the rigging to look for her but there was no sign of anyone by the farmhouse until he saw Guillaume come down the path to his boat. Ensign Wroth and his men were already at the village. Robyn stayed in the rigging and watched the Acadians gesture as they talked with Wroth. Finally the Ensign rolled up the scroll he'd held out to them and the men parted. There weren't so many there this morning. May be they had no intention of signing. Wroth returned to the boat and allowed some of the other men to go ashore. Disappointed, Robyn went about the tasks assigned to him for the watch. Every so often he scanned the shore to see if she'd appear by the rock where he'd first seen her.

Aimeé sat at the turn of the path where she could watch the activity aboard the ship and saw someone at the rail that seemed to be searching the path where she sat. He waved. She stood up to wave back and he raised both arms and then turned away as if he'd been summoned.

Virginie came to find her. "Mother's looking for you to help make the dinner. Best come quick." She looked at the vessel but saw no one that resembled Robyn. "Did ye see him at all? Is he there?" Aimeé stood up and left her to examine the ship by herself.

Would he come back to her? Was it too much to hope for?

That night the ship still stood in the river. Men came and went from the shore. A messenger came to tell Guillaume and his sons over the age of ten to come to the town at ten o'clock in the morning. The promise to take up arms against the enemies of Britain was expunged from the oath and the Acadians were ready to sign it.

Wroth was in so good a mood he let anyone who wanted to go ashore. Robyn left the ship with some other men. After they wandered away from the beach and into the village he went back and took the long boat and quietly rowed across the river.

The full moon rising in the east was still pale and the light from the departing sun in the west colored the clouds with pink and apricot and rose as they promenaded along the horizon like a bevy of stately ladies sweeping yards of swirling silken skirts; the evening star brightened as the sky turned to twilight. Aimeé sat for a bit on her father's favorite bench just outside the front door of the house and looked out over the fields. She loved the view as much as he did, especially at this time of day.

She became restless and rose from the bench. She began to walk down the path and got as far as the rock when she saw Robyn coming toward her. She stopped and her hands rose to her mouth as if to stifle a cry; then she ran toward him. He opened his arms and caught her in his embrace and gave her a long searching kiss. He led her back down the path and into the trees where the long branches of a giant fir swept above a soft bed of needles and formed a protected bower. They lay side by side and exchanged whispers interspersed with soft kisses. Robyn leaned above her for a kiss and she moaned as his lips parted hers and her body arched against him. He kissed her throat, the place between her breasts, her nipples and knelt before her with his knees between her thighs. Slowly and gently he stroked her and then reached down to lift her skirt and lay on top of her. Her heat mounted and she grabbed hold of him and he thrust himself inside her bringing her to a fever and then releasing her. She groaned with ecstasy. "Oh my Love," he whispered. "My Love, my Love," and kissed her lips. "I'll come back to ye, lovely Aimeé and we'll marry." Gently he ran his fingers along her throat.

"Yes Robyn, oh yes. I'll wait for you."

The night brightened as the moon shone down on the meadow and was reflected in silver flashes as the tide rippled in the river and the light filtered through the gently swaying branches above them. An owl screamed as it swept on a field mouse. Startled by the nearness of it Aimeé reached for Robyn and his arms closed around her and they made love again.

Too soon the lovers had to take leave of each other, he to row back to the ship and she to make her way up the lane. Robyn parted with Aimeé at the rock where he first saw her through the spyglass. After one last lingering kiss, he started back down the path to the shore. He turned once and stood for a moment to look at her; she had not moved from the spot. She raised her hand and he blew a kiss to her. She caught it and blew it back to him. He forced himself to turn around and walk down the path when all he wanted to do was run back to her and sweep her in his arms and tell her of his passion and make her his wife.

Next morning the Acadians gathered to hear Ensign Wroth read them the oath of allegiance with all the changes the elders had agreed to. Then they lined up and made their mark or wrote their names on the paper that Wroth held out to them. When the signing was finished they drank a glass of beer and engaged in some friendly talk. After what he thought was a decent interval of socializing Wroth announced they had best get aboard their ship to catch the tide.

Aimeé went down to the turn in the path and watched boats rowing out to the sloop. A lump formed in her throat. Would she ever see Robyn again? She believed he would come back to her as he had promised. Now his ship was ready to sail and she saw the men swarm the decks and heard snatches of the shanty they sang as they raised the anchor, taking its rhythm to pace their work. She thought she saw Robyn aloft in the rigging but it wasn't him and still she looked with tears gleaming in her eyes. Then she saw him come to the rail. He waved to her and she jumped up and waved back. He disappeared behind a sail being hauled up the mast and when the sail was up high enough so she could see the deck again he was gone.

"As if our family didn't have enough to worry about," Jerusha was red-faced and furious and she shouted at Guillaume. "That damned Englishman got Aimeé pregnant."

Jerusha had never been so angry in her life; she stamped her foot on the floor so hard the crockery on the shelves rattled as if to add their disapproval to hers. "What came over her? She knew he'd go off and never come back. He took advantage of her. Now look at her." She scowled at her daughter, rolled up in a ball in the corner by the hearth and willing herself invisible.

Guillaume looked tenderly at his Aimeé and she hid her face in her apron; her shoulders shook as she cried. He walked over, bent down and rested a hand on her shoulder. Then he stood and faced his wife. "Oh, Jerusha how many ways does this girl have to be punished? Isn't it enough everyone'll know soon as they see her stomach bumped out?" Guillaume softened his tone. "She's young and frightened. She needs us to help her."

Jerusha wailed, "How could I have been so blind? Why didn't I do more to keep her away from that Englishman?"

"Because ye thought he'd go away and it would all come to nothing. As it should have." Guillaume kissed his wife's forehead and hoped to avoid a tiresome repetition of the arguments they began to have the day before when Jerusha noticed Aimeé's monthly bleeding had stopped.

Whenever she heard her mother begin to argue with her father about her Aimeé sought her escape by hiding in the bower where she'd lain with Robyn and tried to conjure his presence to bring him back to her. But each time she went there he seemed even farther away.

When the snows came Aimeé's misery became almost unbearable. She grew uncomfortable and snappish and found it hard to keep up with her chores, but they helped to steer her thoughts away from her troubles.

One night a storm came in off the bay and lightning crackled across the sky and a bolt hit the top of the tree that sheltered the couple as they had conceived their child. It ran down the trunk, splitting it in two; one side fell toward the river and shook the ground with a great thud. The other piece stood above the smaller trees like a charred and shattered mast. Pine needles ignited; cones fallen from the stricken tree burned and released their seeds. A rainstorm followed the lightning and soon doused the fire.

Aimeé's labor began when the first bolt struck; pain pulsed through her abdomen as the storm raged outside the window. As the rain blessed the fields once the crackling tendrils of lightning passed on Aimeé gave birth to a boy. Her heart blazed with love at her first sight of him. After her mother finished cutting and binding the umbilical cord she wrapped him in a blanket and gave Aimeé her son. She traced the small heart-shaped birthmark on his neck with her fingertips and the baby mewled. She stroked his cheek with her finger and he turned his head, his mouth seeking to suckle. She held him to her breast and he fell asleep, his jaws moving in rhythm with his newborn dreams.

Aimeé waited in vain for Robyn to come back to her; each day when she took the men their noon meals she brought the baby with her and sat for a time by the river. As he grew, Robert played about near the edge of the water while his mother's gaze sought her absent lover. Three years passed before she gave up her vigil. By then she didn't know if Robyn was dead or alive and had lost all hope he'd ever come back to her.

1732

Robert was very inquisitive; it seemed as if mischief lay in wait for him in every direction, setting its traps and lures around every corner. The first time Aimeé lost track of him she was frantic until she found him in the barn trying to climb the ladder to the hayloft. She grabbed him and smothered him in kisses. "What're ye doing, little man? Where do ye think you're going?"

Robert grinned and laughed at her. "Play with me, Mommy." He squirmed in her arms until she put him down.

"Stay near to me. Mind you." She tried to sound stern but it had no effect on him. Whenever she looked at her son she saw how much he resembled Robyn. "Best I marry and give him a real father and brothers and sisters to grow up with," she'd muse as she watched Robert playing. Her cousin Theo had recently brought someone to their farm, a widower called Modeste Etretat and at the end of the visit he asked Aimeé could he come back to call on her.

Thus, Modeste began to court Aimeé. Virginie, who was jealous of her sister, sang out in clear liquid tones as he rode into the yard, "Here comes Modeste courting Aimeé; When will a suitor court me?" He turned his head to see where the rhyme came from and smiled when he caught sight of Virginie moving away from the window and heard her giggling.

Modeste's thoughts took up the song, "And let such a man come soon and let him take her off to the moon!" Then he burst out laughing at making a verse that rhymed. Maybe it was true that love could make a poet of any man.

"Sssst!" Jerusha hissed at Virginie when she came away from the window. "You'll be having him think you're daft. And ye can stop pestering your sister." But Virginie ran out into the yard to confront him. "Ye liked my verse? Mother scolds me when I sing but I only do it to tease my sister."

"Hits the mark. May be that some day she'll do the same to you."

"Think so, Modeste? Think there'll be a man to come here to court me?"

Modeste was a few years older than Aimeé and had a little son of his own. But still she was nervous to have him courting her while Robert clung to her skirts. So it happened that one fine summer day when Modeste rode into the yard pumping up his nerve to ask Aimeé to wed him, Robert was taken from his mother to be cared for by his aunts.

Virginie soon became more interested in spying on Aimeé and Modeste than in taking care of her nephew and left Clarice to watch the boy. It was a warm afternoon and she took him out to the meadow where they lay down to look at the clouds, pointing out the shapes of animals or faces as they floated overhead. Clarice's eyes became heavy and soon she nodded off. Robert lay beside her for a few minutes before he got up and marched in a circle around her. She murmured something to him but didn't waken.

A bird flew past, its body a blur as its wings beat the air and fanned his face. He sneezed so hard he fell backward onto his behind and from his new vantage point he caught sight of a butterfly sitting on a flower and stood to get a closer look. It flew away and he followed it from blossom to blossom all the way down to the riverbank. When it fluttered across the water he looked after it until it disappeared in the grasses on the other side.

He sat down on the rock his mother usually chose for her vigils and mimicked her concentrated look. Then he lay flat on top of it with his face close to the water's surface. Minnows swarmed below him. He trailed a hand in the water as he had seen his mother do so often. The tiny lips of minnows tested Robert's small fingers with their tender questions as long as he held them still. The fish retreated beneath the overhang of the rock when he moved them and he played with them for a bit. The sky clouded over and was getting ready to loose some drops as the boy leaned farther over the edge of the rock to better see the fish.

A few minutes later Clarice awoke to rain pattering against her face. She got up and called for Robert and ran about in the meadow to see if he was lying asleep somewhere. She went down to the riverbank and saw a footprint where he'd stepped onto the rock but there was no sign of him. She ran to the house to give the alarm and the men ran down to the river as fast as they could.

Aimeé collapsed into a dead faint. Jerusha tried to revive her and when at last she opened her eyes she spoke in a voice that was thin and high and quavering, "Robert, my baby. Where's my baby?" She looked around and wailed, "Oh dear God, please bring my baby home. Please bring him back." Then her voice went deep under the weight of her grief and she moaned, "Where is he? Where's my boy?"

Jerusha wrung her hands. "Looking for him, the men. They'll find him." She tried to sound reassuring.

"He's gone. Just like his father. I'll never see him again."

"Don't go thinking like that," Jerusha said. "He can't be far. He's just a little tyke."

When Modeste and Armand came back, they said they found what seemed to be the print of a small foot in the mud but the rain had washed it down so it was hard to tell if that's what it really was. Armand had dived into the rushing water to search for Robert and the tide carried him upstream but there was no sign of the boy.

Aimeé refused to eat; when she tried she couldn't keep anything down. She couldn't look at her sisters without feeling angry with them for Robert's disappearance. As much as she felt it wasn't in her heart to forgive them she blamed herself even more for trusting them to care for her son.

Jerusha screamed at Virginie and Clarice and accused them of not caring about the little boy. "Whatever harm comes to him we've both of you to thank for it. What's wrong with you girls? You're never fit to be mothers. Who wants to marry someone so careless and foolish? Who'd ever have ye?"

When she and Guillaume were alone, Jerusha wept for the boy and for her daughter. "Who'd have imagined such a thing? We don't know if the poor boy is dead or alive or even maybe living with the Indians in the forest. Oh what'll we do?"

Modeste went home after the fruitless hunt for Robert was reluctantly called off. As soon as he got to Baie Verte, he went direct to Jacques and Patient Moon to tell them what had happened. Paul Dancing Crow was there and remembered how he had escaped death as a little boy because of his aunt's love for him. "Can I help find him?" he asked. They shook their heads.

"He's likely drowned and the body washed away by the tide in the river," Modeste told him. "Dead and gone that little one. All in mourning at Guillaume's place. Seems hopeless."

Clarice was miserable. Over and over again she blamed herself for losing Robert while he was in her charge. Jerusha berated her, screaming at the top of her lungs. Even her father who was usually easy with forgiveness had no kind word for either her or Virginie. Most of all Aimeé's sunken eyes and vacant stare, and the dry heaving sobs that broke from her chest when she thought no one was looking, haunted them all.

"What was Virginie doing to spy on Aimeé and Modeste? It was none of her business to do that but she's always prying into other people's affairs and then she gossips about whatever she overhears," Jerusha said to Guillaume one afternoon.

"Aye," his voice sounded flat. "Virginie was sorry for Robert's disappearance but she didn't take it hard like Clarice did. There's enough blame to go round this whole family."

Clarice felt isolated from everyone, scorned by her parents and her sisters and ignored by her brothers. She barely slept at night; when she did Robert came to her and begged her to please come and get him and bring him back to his mother. Clarice would awaken in a sweat, guilty and ashamed for what had happened. Day by day the black circles under her eyes deepened and fatigue and hopelessness wore her down.

One overcast morning when the air was heavy with the threat of rain, Clarice dragged herself to the barn. She saw her father's silhouette in the dim light of a stall near the opposite doorway and drew back against the wall and studied him.

When she sat on the bench outside the house that morning she heard a whispered conversation between her parents. She knew they had sent for the priest to ask his help for Aimeé. Father Girard was across the river in Beaubassin performing the last rites for old Pére Raymond and couldn't come right away. Clarice was afraid of the priest; whenever his dark eyes looked into her face they penetrated her with a power that made her soul feel dry and shriveled. Surely a priest with such godly power would never forgive what she had done. She was damned. Why would she want to live any more? That thought frightened her.

Guillaume stood by the doorway. A horse leaned from its stall and nudged him. He turned to the animal and absently stroked its face muttering, "What on earth are we to do now?" The horse snuffled. "Poor Aimeé withers away. Clarice is like a ghost. Even Jerusha sees their suffering and manages to keep her tongue in check. I feel so low and I don't know what to do. Poor Robert – is he drowned or please God, does he live? One child is lost and two others are near lost because of it. If the priest can't help us, I don't know who can." He stared into the horse's liquid brown eyes.

Clarice watched her father leave the barn and walk away. He didn't see her but what if he had? She didn't think he would come to her and hold her and try to comfort her. All this time that Robert was missing, he never tried to console her. "My life is over," Clarice thought. "No one loves me any more. No one cares how much I suffer for losing poor Robert. They just hate me and they always will because it's all my fault."

Inside the barn she saw a length of rope carelessly tossed onto a peg with its butt lying on the floor. She picked it up and studied it. It smelled of animals like it was used as a lead. She knotted it, imitating what she had seen her father do countless times and went up into the loft to pass it over a beam. She secured one end and put the loop around her neck, She knelt and blessed herself, said an Act of Contrition and pleaded for forgiveness for not being strong enough to bear her overwhelming sorrow and guilt. She jumped and fell unconscious to the floor, the wind knocked out of her. The knot held only long enough for the rope to leave an angry welt on her neck.

Father Girard heard something fall when he rounded the corner of the barn and he looked inside. Clarice lay in the dust on the floor with the rope swinging in the air above her. He rushed in and knelt by her. He put a hand on her forehead and with the other took her wrist and felt a pulse. The priest sighed with relief when her eyes fluttered. "Did I die?" she murmured.

"Nay, child. You're still here with us by the grace of God." Gently he lifted her up and carried her to the house. He called for help and Jerusha came to the door.

"Abbé," she said, "what's happened? What's happened to my daughter?"

"She's collapsed." He followed Jerusha to a bed in the corner of the room and gently put Clarice down. "Get some water, some cold cloths. She needs attention. I'm afraid she's very ill." The girl stirred and her eyes fluttered open; she saw Girard looking down at her and began to cry.

"Never mind," he said in a kindly voice, his dark eyes warm with concern. "It's all right now. Your mother's here." Jerusha rushed to the bedside and elbowed the priest aside.

"I'll take care of her now, Father." Jerusha laid a cold cloth on her daughter's forehead and then saw the rope mark on her neck. She hissed, "What's this? Clarice? What've ye done? What'll your father think when he sees this?"

"He'll think... He'll think...," she let out a sobbing breath and turned her face away. "I don't care any more what anyone thinks. You all hate me for losing Robert. It would've been better had I died."

"Hush, child," the priest said. "Don't think such. No one hates you. No one wants you to die." He looked at Jerusha as he spoke. "They love you too much to wish such."

Jerusha's face turned stony and she bit her tongue and said nothing. She kept dipping the cloth in cold water and wringing it out and replacing it on Clarice's forehead.

Abbé Girard watched her for a few moments and then went to find Guillaume.

After the priest finished praying with them for Clarice's recovery and Robert's safe return, Jerusha put Clarice and Aimeé to bed. Only she and Guillaume still sat with the priest. But for the crackling of the logs in the hearth there was silence. Girard cleared his throat and asked,

"Are ye surprised by what Clarice did?"

"Of course we are," Guillaume said. Jerusha only looked at Girard and frowned.

"Can ye offer your daughter forgiveness out of your love for her?" The priest spread his hands to include them both in his question.

"Hard to do that when I feel sometimes no one loves me," Jerusha blurted. "Hard to do that when I have to cry hidden away in a corner about something that hurts so bad as this. No one puts his arms around me and offers a shoulder to solace me."

Guillaume was thunderstruck. "How can ye say that? I do love you. I put my arms around you time and again."

"You're in the barn. I'm in the house. Each left to our own selves." She turned to the priest. "How could I know if he loves me when he has plenty to tell to the horses but he doesn't even talk to me?" She sniffled and pulled her skirts closer around her.

"Is there no love at all between you?" Girard's face was a mask of astonishment.

The fire was burning low and Guillaume got up to put on another log. "Of course I love you, Jerusha. Always have. But I'm overwhelmed. We all are. I've been selfish but now I see it. I've not put my arms around you or Clarice to comfort her and she feels all the blame for Robert and has all the sorrow. I've been so inward since we lost the boy I've never spared a thought for you."

Guillaume went over to Jerusha and knelt. He took her hands in his and held them gently, looking up at her with tearful eyes. "We can't see each other's thoughts. But I love my wife and children. There's no doubt." Neither of them moved. The priest watched, fingering his beads with his lips moving in prayer and a fragile peace settled on the house.

The embers glowed red hot and a log fell with a shower of ashes. A glob of pitch flamed up and burned like a faery torch and Girard cleared his throat and the sound brought Guillaume and Jerusha back to the moment.

"Sorry, Father," Guillaume said, "I should've offered ye a bed before now."

"In a minute. Would ye deem it'd help to send Clarice to the nursing sisters in Louisbourg, at least for a time? Could be she'd find her peace with this by devoting herself to prayer and to helping the sick.

Best she think about something else than the boy all the time."

Guillaume looked at Jerusha. "Wherever she is Robert's all she does think about."

"The nuns will care for her, and she might take to their work at the hospital. Maybe in time she'll want to stay with them. Try it for a year. Can't hurt her and it might be a help."

Jerusha pondered his advice. "No harm I can see for it except I'd miss her to help with the work here. But Virginie can add some of her portion. What do ye say to that, husband?" Guillaume nodded his assent. "But how 'bout Aimeé?" she said to Girard. "I'd think it'd rather be she you'd say should go to the nuns."

"Aimeé's had some time to mourn her boy. She's cried herself dry over it. For now she still hopes her son will come back. It's when she gives up hope for him there could be trouble."

"See some things better by the light of day," Jerusha said as she got up to leave the men to talk more if they wished. Guillaume yawned. "She's right."

The next morning the Abbé sat at the table with Jerusha and Guillaume. "I know how hard it's been for you but ye need to think of your daughters, and not always about yourselves. If you can love each other and your girls, you can find the strength to heal. Clarice, the poor soul has been like a scapegoat trying to carry the whole weight of the family's sorrows. She doesn't deserve that. She's shriven and her soul is pure again and full of our Lord's love and forgiveness. Her grief's too fresh for her to endure it on her own. For her to heal she needs love not blame."

Guillaume listened to him with his head bowed. "Aye," his voice cracked. Girard's dark eyes softened and he put an arm around his friend's shoulder. He looked over Guillaume's bowed head straight at Jerusha. "Forgiveness was the whole reason for Christ's sacrifice. Why else would He have given Himself up to suffer on the cross? What He freely gave we've no right to withhold." His eyes softened when her eyes moistened.

The last few days before leaving for Louisbourg were bittersweet. Clarice felt that by her decision she had regained her family's acceptance. Aimeé decided she wanted to go with Clarice and take vows so she could pray for Robert's soul in peace and quiet for the rest of her life. For a while she seemed brighter, but by the time Girard came back to collect the sisters Aimeé was once again the soul of dejection. "When my boy comes back I won't be here for him. I can't leave," she wailed. "He won't know where I am."

"If Robert comes home we'll send for ye right away," Jerusha insisted.

Girard put his arm around her. "Aimeé, I know it's hard to think of this. But just try to give Robert over to the Lord's care. Ask His help. Trust in Him." She buried her face in his cassock and wept. Jerusha's face went taut and Guillaume moved with all the lack of grace and strength of an old man when he lifted their trunk into the wagon.

LOUISBOURG 1732

The stifling July air was heavy with the promise of rain just as it had been for the past couple of days. Two-day-old laundry drooped from the clothesline and small biting flies hung about the garden defying anyone to try to weed the vegetable plot. The buzzing from the beehives rose to an aggressive level as if the insects would swarm at anyone who came too close. The nuns had no fresh sheets, no crisp vegetables and no honey.

Clarice put on her work dress and went to morning prayer. Then she breakfasted on bread and tea with the other novices. Since Clarice came to the hospital she had taken on the most menial chores as her penance – scrubbing floors, emptying night jars and other such lowly tasks. She felt those were the only kind of duties she was worthy to perform. She would be happy enough to live in seclusion; she never thought of it as giving up her freedom. She couldn't wait to exchange her novice's robe for the habit of the order.

Instead of laundering more things to add to the sodden linens already crowding the clotheslines, the Abbess sent her out to do the marketing and get a few things for the nuns' dinner. The novices took turns doing errands outside the convent; as much as the others enjoyed having the chance to see people and talk to the vendors as they squeezed fruits and considered vegetables, going to the market was a burden to Clarice.

She left the convent through a side door that opened into a small square that led to the larger one where the stalls and market carts were assembled and pushed her way through the crowd. The sound of her footsteps that seemed to echo so loud inside the cloister was no match for the noise of the peddlers hawking their produce and haggling over prices with anyone who stopped for a closer look at their offerings. Soon she sweated inside her scratchy woolen robe. Whenever she reached to test a fruit or vegetable for ripeness the vendor would toss out a price to try to get her to bargain.

She extended a hand toward a plump melon, fragrant and ready for the table.

"Ye know which's best. I can see that, Sister. A livre for it," a man leaned over his cart toward her. "See how juicy it is. Give it a sniff and ye know the flesh'll melt in your mouth." He winked and when he grinned at her she saw he had no front teeth.

"No thank ye," Clarice said. "That's too high to pay for such fruit."

A slight gray-haired woman whose cart stood next to the one whose produce Clarice first looked at turned to her with a ripe melon in each hand. "Sister, here's two for the price he asked ye for the one," she said as she thrust the melons toward Clarice's basket.

"That's more like it," Clarice answered the woman. "Make it three and I'll take them."

Now that she had her first purchase in her basket, she felt this would turn out to be a good morning's work and quickly done. As she tried to pass by some vendors to get some fresh haricourts a man jostled her and the melons fell from her basket and smashed on the stones, splattering them both.

"Why don't ye watch yourself," the man growled as he turned to face her. Then he saw her habit. "Sister, I'm sorry. Let me pay ye for them." As he dug into his purse and handed her three livres she thought Louisbourg surely did draw everyone to its doors for commerce, especially New Englanders. Clarice reached out to take the coins he offered her and then tried to hand him back the extra two he'd given her. "Only cost me one," she explained. "No point to you giving me extra." As she looked at him more closely she thought he seemed familiar but couldn't think why.

She went back to the melon vendor and then stopped at the cart that had the beans. She saw some peaches and plums that she knew the sisters would appreciate as an evening treat and bought some of those. If she found some courgettes there'd be more than enough to serve with the fish one of the local men brought to the convent each Friday. Her basket overflowed; it was time to go home.

A short distance away a group of New Englanders, including the man who jostled her gawked at something they saw in the market. He glanced in her direction and then stared. Clarice turned away and blushed. The other Englishmen reacted by pushing their way closer to her. The man who jostled her said, "I think I recognize her."

They were so close that Clarice overheard one of the men make a joke about his having a girl in every port he had ever visited. "You're the envy of the poor homely ones of us as hardly gets a second look."

She knew no Englishmen, but – there was the soldier who fell in love with Aimeé and gave her a child. She looked at him again and recognized Robyn Jenkins – Robert's father. She remembered how she and her sisters had spied on him and thought him so handsome. Now she only wanted to avoid him, but with her basket so heavy with produce it slowed her down. She turned away so he wouldn't see her face and moved so quickly that her robe swished around her feet and threatened to trip her.

But Robyn had already spotted her and raised his hand to get her attention as he pushed through the crowd and came toward her. Heads turned to watch. Robyn doffed his hat and bowed. "Do ye remember me at all?" he asked in a low voice, thinking how she'd been pretty as a girl but now her face looked ravaged as if she'd suffered. Now he wondered if he was mistaken about who she was.

"Are you Robyn Jenkins?" She was surprised by how much older he looked.

"Aye. You're Aimeé's sister, Clarice. I never forget a beautiful face especially when there's so many of them in a single family. How is she? And you here in a novice's dress? Do ye plan to take the vows?"

Clarice hardly knew what to say. "She's well. And yes, I am." She blushed as she shifted the weight of the basket hoping he'd take the hint and go back to his friends and leave her be.

"Did she marry?"

"Not yet."

"I told her I'd come back to her and never did." He became flustered and wrung his cap. "But ye already knew that."

Clarice said, "You shouldn't be talking to me about such. Aimeé's here in Louisbourg. You wish to talk about that, she's who ye want."

Now the basket felt like it was filled with rocks and she shifted it again to balance the weight.

Robyn hesitated. "What does she think of me? I mean could I see her? Would she speak to me?"

"You've had a son by Aimeé. Of course she'd see you," Clarice blurted. "Oh why did I say that?" she thought. The basket kept her anchored to the spot.

Robyn was astonished. "What'd ye say? I've a son by her?" He blocked her passage so she could not have moved if she had wings.

Clarice sighed. "Don't know why I told you that."

"I'm to go back to Boston in two days. I have to see her no matter what. Where's she living?" Robyn grabbed her arm, shaking the basket and shifting its weight again. He brought his face close to hers. "How can I be so near to where she is and not see the mother of my son? Is he with her? I want to see him too." Clarice's eyes clouded with tears.

"Please Robyn, let go of my arm. The basket's very heavy and I have to get back to the convent. The child's not here, just Aimeé. I'd have to ask her is she willing to see you and then the Abbess must approve it. Come to the hospital tomorrow when the clock's ready to strike the noon. I'll look for you at the top of the steps by the front door and give you her answer then. Be prompt."

She could scarcely hold herself together. "Not another word for him," she gritted her teeth.

He tipped his hat to her and walked over to where his friends waited. "No luck with that one, eh?" one of them said casting an irreverent glance at Clarice. Some of the French heard it and looked at her. She cast down her eyes and her face went red; she gripped her basket with both hands.

"Filthy English," a man spat as Robyn and his companions walked by his cart. "Why can't they respect the sisters?"

Clarice spent the next morning on her hands and knees scrubbing floors and thinking about what she left unsaid the day before. If she could just blurt it out to Robyn about having a son then she should have also been able to tell him the boy's fate. If it was unspeakable for Clarice to see him, what would it be like for Aimeé? She should never have said a word about it to her, just gone back and told Robyn she didn't want to see him. She was surprised when her sister agreed to see her faithless lover.

Aimeé reminded her, "I waited for him for three years praying he'd return. Now he has. Since he knows I bore him a child and he's asked to visit me, he wouldn't take 'No' for an answer."

As the hands of the clock moved toward the noon Clarice stopped to give herself a few minutes to clean up. She stepped outside the hospital just as the bell began to ring. As it pealed the hour she told Robyn the Abbess would allow him to visit Aimeé the following day. He was to come to the convent at one o'clock in the afternoon and visit her after mass was over. Exactly at the last clang of the bell she went back inside the building.

Robyn was disappointed he had no time to ask any questions. But no matter. He still could not believe his luck. Since Clarice told him Aimeé had his child and as much as admitted she had been courted but never married, his hopes soared. If that was true then whatever was she doing in the convent at Louisbourg?

In other circumstances Robyn knew the honorable thing for him to do would be to propose to her now. But he was married – to the only child of a very rich man – and his wife was barren. As much as they had prayed for a son and tried to have one, she couldn't conceive.

If Aimeé did have a child of his – and a boy at that – then Robyn had to convince her to let him take his son. If she was here and the boy was home with her family then how much did it matter to her that she even had his child? She could have others if she married. "But I never will," Robyn thought. "What a massive stroke of luck!"

He was so elated that he nearly danced in the street. The idea that his wife might not welcome his child by another woman never once occurred to him. He imagined she would wish to take his son into their home, and that Aimeé would give the boy to him once she understood what her son would one day inherit from his stepmother's family. What mother wouldn't want the best for her son and make any sacrifice to get it for him?

When Robyn came to the convent he was escorted into a small parlor with two chairs set across a round table. In the middle a large Sevres bowl filled with dried rose petals graced the room with a light fragrance. A fine Persian carpet covered the floorboards; paneling darkened by years of smoke from the fireplace walled the room except for a single open window that looked out to a small garden. Loose bunches of thyme and yarrow lay on the sill as if placed by someone outside collecting herbs and he could smell newly-turned earth and just make out the sound of a shovel beneath the music of nearby birds calling and splashing in a dish of water hidden among the flowers. Aimeé entered the room wearing her novice's robe.

"Robyn, it is truly you just as Clarice told me. Why have ye come to see me now and in this place? I waited years for ye but you never came back."

Robyn turned from the window and went to put his arms around her but the look on her face stopped him. She sank heavily into the nearest chair and scanned his face with dull eyes. "First Clarice and now her," he thought. "It's as if someone died."

"Dearest Aimeé, I missed you and wanted to go back to ye. But you knew I was a soldier and had to go off when I was ordered. This is the first time I've been anywhere near Acadia since that day the ship took me away from you. Then to be here and see Clarice in the market just by a happy circumstance – what a surprise!" He jumped to his feet; the chair was too small to contain his excitement and he paced about the room. "Imagine how I'm astounded when she says I have a son with ye and you're here and I can see ye if you wish it. And you're gracious to do it. I understand if you're angry with me. Couldn't blame you for that. But I'm so unbelieving the news – so wonderful that I can't believe it – I've a son. Tell me about him, Aimeé – please tell me all about him."

"Robyn, I loved you so much. How could I ever be angry with you? I carried your child, a little boy with a birthmark on his neck shaped as a heart." Her voice seemed dreamy and toneless. "I waited for you such a long time. Couldn't have any other man but you. What brings you here asking to see me after all this time? Is it only because you've heard about the child?"

He hesitated and thought of course she must be amazed to see him after all these years, so it might be better if he just told her the truth straight out. "After I left you it was some time and then I married. I never knew about our boy. How could I? Aimeé, I loved you truly and you were the one I always wanted to marry."

A sad look crossed her face and she turned her eyes to the window. "Got her with child then?"

"No. But her father found us together. After that I'd no choice. He wants a grandson but we've had no children and never will because my wife's barren."

"I'm sorry for you. But why did you stop to see me and tell me this? Couldn't you just leave well enough alone with me?"

He wished for it so much that he couldn't keep it inside him any longer, and the words rushed from his mouth. Please Aimeé. Do let me have the boy. Here you are in the convent, and someone else's taking care of him. If he can't be with his mother he should go with his father. That's me! Think of it Aimeé. No need to have another to take care of him. If ye stay here and take the vows, you'll not see him again. And if you went home and married you could still have other children. But I'm married and can't have even one. My wife and I'll raise him as our own. It'll please her father and the boy will inherit riches! Oh, Aimeé! Consider what a blessed day this is!"

Tears rolled down Aimeé's cheeks. "Robyn, I loved my son. I'd never give him up to anyone and especially not to you. You've never even seen him, never held him in your arms, never played with him or nursed him through an illness. All ye ever did for me or for him was to disappear and leave me longing for ye to come back for us."

"But, Aimeé, I told you I had to go. I never knew ye had my child. Whatever kind of man do you think I am?"

"One that could come here and confront me like this. Here I am made to suffer again by a man I loved and who left me and whose son I birthed." She pushed herself up from the chair. "Leave now if you ever had even a tiny bit of feeling for me."

Tears came to his eyes. "I came here thinking one thing and now I hear another. You won't forgive me and you won't give me the boy." He got down on his knees. "If you want to see me humbled for what I've done here it is." Aimeé went to the doorway and stood with her back to him; then she turned and came back into the room.

"Get up, Robyn, and listen. We've caused each other a misery that I can only begin to tell you."

Robyn pleaded, "But what could possibly be so sad and awful when you say I've a son? And whatever you say, the hope that could I ever have him to live with me all my prayers would be answered whether or not you agree to it now – that's all I live for since yesterday when Clarice told me about the boy."

She crossed herself and said, "Please, Robyn. Listen to me. The boy's not living."

Robyn dropped like a stone into the chair; his face fell and he whispered, "What? Not alive? How can that be? What happened to my son?"

"He's in a canoe in the river, tipped over, fell in the water and drowned before anyone could save him." She thought, "Why can't I tell him no one saw him fall and we never found poor Robert? But if I said that to him he'd have hope same as me; and if he believes the boy's still alive he'll seek me out again."

Robyn cast his eyes down and they filled with tears. "Wish I was there to save the lad."

"So did I wish and so you should've been if you truly did love me. Afterward I thought God gave him to me just to take him away and cause me to suffer more. Robyn, ye must leave me be. You've no place here. Your very name brings me only heartbreak."

Robyn bent forward in the chair, his elbows on his knees and his hands covering his face.

Aimeé said, "I'll pray for you. God may show you and your wife mercy. Perhaps he'll give her a child. Best she never knows about your son. I wish Clarice had minded her mouth and never said the words to torment you."

Instead of returning to her cell she went to the chapel. In the darkness she went down on her knees and then leaned forward to lie on the stone floor where she spread her arms out and wept. "Oh God," she prayed. "I was terrible in my lying. How could I be so high and mighty to him when I'm cast so low? Can You forgive me for what I said to him? Please let my son still live. Don't make him suffer for my lies." The cold of the stones seeped into her and her teeth chattered. A few minutes later Clarice came through the door and stared into the gloom. As her eyes adjusted she saw someone lying on the floor and went over and saw it was Aimeé. She pulled her head and shoulders up and embraced her to warm her back to life.

CHIGNECTO 1732

To the Indians who paddled their canoe up the river the boy seemed but a pile of rags carelessly tossed onto the rock; they looked about to see if there was anyone in the water but all they saw was the swelling motion of the tide pushing upstream.

Robert heard the sound of paddles dipping into the water and looked up to see the canoe. A man sat in the stern and steered the craft; a woman paddled in the bow. Aimeé had often told him when they sat by the river's edge that his father would return in a large boat. Robert thought this was not a big boat but he wondered if this could be his father and he sat up and focused his gaze upon the man.

The Indians were surprised to see the boy alone and scanned the bank to see who was with him. But they saw no one. "By yourself, boy?" the man called softly across the water. Robert stood up and looked at him and said, "Father?"

The woman stopped paddling to let the canoe drift toward the boy and beach on the mud; then she got out and came over to Robert. "What you're called?" she asked as she bent down to him.

"Robert." He stuck out his lower lip in a pout and looked over at the man who still sat in the boat. "Ye m' father?"

"Ye make childs with other wimmens?" the woman asked the man with a wide grin.

"Where ye be come here?" she persisted. Robert shrugged his shoulders. He didn't understand anything she said with her queer talk and turned away to walk back up the path but she caught hold of his arm and turned him back around. "Where ye be going?" she asked. Robert pointed toward the meadow and the woman looked around but she saw no one. "All alone, boy?" she said. He nodded. Clarice was asleep in the grass so he thought that meant he was alone.

"Come wi' me," she said in a pleasant voice; she picked him up and took him to the canoe and set him atop the pile of supplies and the couple eased the canoe back into the river.

Robert began to cry, "No want to go! No want to go!"

"Hush, boy. Ye be here all alone and the wolf'll come eat ye up."

The Indians paddled off just before the rain began to fall. Clarice woke and looked around for the boy. She came to the riverbank searching for Robert and when she saw his footprint by the rock she ran screaming to the house for help.

Guillaume and Jacques-Pierre ran for the canoe. Armand tracked along the bank and saw something in the water that looked like a patch of Robert's shirt and dove in hoping to find the lad. Guillaume and

Jacques-Pierre paddled right by a boat hidden in the grasses with a man and a woman and a little boy who crouched down because they told him they were playing a game of hide and seek with those men.

"Grandfather and Uncle Jacques," Robert pointed and popped up to wave and call to them but the woman threw a sack over his head and held him down. She looked at the man and said, "How much they pay for this one to come home?"

They drew the canoe out of the water after the searchers went past and hid it in the grasses. They picked up the sobbing boy and their sack of stuff and made their way into the forest to a path so narrow that only hunters knew of it. They went a short distance before the woman set Robert down. "You walk now Lost Boy," she told him.

The child looked at her and his lips trembled. "Want my mother," he sobbed.

"Ye be my boy now," the woman said. Her voice hardened. "Do what I tell you." She gave Robert a menacing look. Then she turned to her husband. "Maybe family pays ransom. Go find out who be they. They not want him back, he be my slave boy."

Paul Dancing Crow stood at the edge of the most decrepit camp he had ever seen. A trader told him about a family of outcasts who had a little light-skinned slave boy who was nothing but a rack of bones and said they had tried to sell the boy to him. Dancing Crow had come to rescue the boy he hoped was his nephew.

The man and his wife were inside a wigwam covered with old moldy hides and cracked, brittle pieces of bark. Fumes of sweet grasses, mixed with something else that gave off an unpleasant bitter smell wisped from the vent hole. Skinny children with barely a rag between them to cover their nakedness ran around outside like wild animals and the little boy was hoisted up and bound onto some sticks to wave his emaciated arms to frighten birds away from the sickly plants in the garden. There was no sign of anyone else.

He went to the opening of the wigwam and called out in a loud voice. "You been telling the people you've a slave boy to sell."

The man turned vacant eyes toward the sound of the strange voice and the woman cackled. "Little boy. I train him to do many things. Works hard, don't need to feed him. Eats dirt."

She staggered to her feet and came outside. She looked around and called in a raspy voice, "Lost Boy, you come here." Then she remembered she'd trussed him up to be a scarecrow and went over and untied him, letting him fall to the ground. The scrawny child lay where he had landed, his legs so thin Paul couldn't believe he could even stand on them. He was amazed the boy was still alive but steeled himself to show no emotion. "Scrawny one, not worth much," he said. "Close to used up, this one. Got others?"

"Not now. Soon. Others come. Parents not want them. Give them to us."

Paul picked the boy up. "No meat on him."

"Not sell him to eat, sell him to work." The woman cackled. "Run your wife errands. Feed animals, chase birds." She belched.

"Maybe." He was sickened just looking at the child. "How much for used up slave boy?"

"Not used up. Good boy. Gold coin."

"Crazy woman! He not worth that much. Here." He tossed a pouch at her filled with sweet grasses and tender tabagie leaves. "Best ye get for this'n."

The woman picked up the pouch. She opened it and sniffed the leaves. She went to her husband who lay dozing inside the wigwam. She shook him; he flicked his hand at her.

"He say yes. But money too."

Contemptuously and one at a time, Dancing Crow threw a few tarnished coins into the dirt in front of her. He bent down, opened his arms and took the boy leaving the woman on her knees scrambling and clawing for the coins and fighting over them with her children.

BEAUSEJOUR 1733

Some months had passed since Aimeé and Clarice went off to Louisbourg. Jerusha was spreading the wash across the bushes with Virginie. In the distance some people on horseback approached the far end of the meadows and she strained her eyes to see who they might be. "Coming here for certain," she remarked to her daughter. Virginie squinted. "Looks like a couple of Indians with some others."

Jerusha went to the barn to call her husband. He looked up from feeding the penned animals, and shaded his eyes with his hand. "I make it out to be Theo, Jacques, Dancing Crow, Patient Moon and Aimeé. She's holding a small one in front of her."

"Ye think they may have Robert?" Jerusha's face brightened.

"Looks like that's so. Especially as Aimeé's with them. Why else would she leave the convent?" He looked to Jerusha. "What's there to put out for dinner?"

By the time the horses stopped in front of the house the whole family was gathered. The men dismounted and Dancing Crow held his arms up to Aimeé and took the boy from her. "Now, Robert. Who do ye see?"

The little boy looked at the family standing around him and turned his face back into Paul's shoulder. Paul rubbed his back and whispered in his ear; then he gently turned the boy around. "Do ye see Gran'pa, Gran'ma, 'ginie?"

Robert squirmed in his uncle's hands and shrieked, "Mama, Mama!"

Jerusha stretched out her arms to receive her grandson. "Believed he's lost to us forever but now ye brought him back. And here's our Aimeé come home to us again."

"He a brave boy. Strong. Be proud of him. Loves his mama." Patient Moon said. "So good, I trade him for one of my boys." Theo groaned. "Mean I'd have to come live here?" He looked around. "Maybe, not bad. I'll do it."

"No ye won't, cousin. Now the boy's back, he stays," Virginie smiled at him. "But you could stay as well."

"Aye," said Guillaume. "Your mother wants to give you away, we'll take ye." His eyes misted over as he looked at his daughter and grandson, remembering how he'd taken Dancing Crow at Robert's age to live with Patient Moon, and how intensely he'd wished Paul could've stayed with him. His heart flowed over with gratitude to have Robert back.

When Father Girard returned from Louisbourg the following month, he went to Beausejour to tell the family that Clarice was already much respected at the convent for her devotion to the sickest patients in the hospital, and would soon take her vows.

"Paul found him," Guillaume told the priest in a husky voice when Girard asked how Robert was rescued. "Nearly dead, poor lad. Since he's home he's had no end of feeding and cosseting, but I see a darkness come over him when anyone asks what happened when he was with those outcasts. Then he seems like an old man; his eyes go dark and sometimes he just goes quiet and other times he cries but can't seem to tell us why." He sighed in resignation. "But as Clarice has found happiness I'm content for her sake."

"God's ways are mysterious to us. The child doesn't look like the same boy; but the Lord has rescued him and sent him home to you. You'll help him to heal."

"The poor lad's not the same boy, Abbé. Not at all. His uncle Dancing Crow found him in the nick of time."

No one saw Modeste Etretat make his way across the field. He felt a blessed relief that Virginie wasn't around to announce him by singing out his name in that high wavering voice he so disliked. The mere thought of that made him even more nervous than his reason for coming to Beausejour. Since Robert was rescued and Aimeé was finished with the convent, she was marriageable again. Modeste's desire to make her his wife had never abated even as the months of her absence had piled up one on top of the next. Mile after mile as he travelled to see her the question whether she'd now want him as her husband deviled his mind.

He dismounted and led his horse into the barn to remove the saddle and water and feed the animal and rub it down. He'd brought only the one horse but if she said "Yes" he knew Guillaume would send her and Robert home with him on a horse of her own. So much for practical matters. Once untethered from those he was free to float in the deeper waters of his hopes she'd agree to marry him and his journey would end with Aimeé becoming Madam Etretat. It had a nice sound, Aimeé Etretat. He wouldn't care then if Virginie chose to sing her heart out when they came to visit. She could start when they entered the farthest field. Then she'd have a sore throat by the time they got to the house. He smirked at the thought of 'ginie unable to speak and couldn't imagine it ever happening.

"Look who's come," a man's voice fell from the rafters. Guillaume stood in the loft above him. "Wondered how long it'd be afore ye looked up to see ye wasn't alone in here."

Modeste chuckled. "I was so worried about what you'd say when I asked could I propose to Aimeé that all the din going on inside my head was distracting me."

"Glad you're back to see her. What may come of your proposal you'll hear from her. But I'm all for it. Aimeé needs a husband and Robert needs a father to guide him up. If you're finished pampering that horse let's go see what Jerusha's got on for dinner."

BOSTON 1735

Guillaume knew his middle son Jacques-Pierre was an adventurer and not one to follow in his father's footsteps and become a farmer like his older brother Honoré. But the news that he and some of his friends thought they could get away with defying the governor's edict against trading directly with New Englanders took him completely by surprise. The boys took some goods from Henri's truck house without his knowledge or permission and sailed to Boston to trade them. They had rounded up some pieces of Saint Onge pottery, a dozen cones of sugar, and a couple dozen barrels of green fish and dried fruits. But what was worse was that Jacques-Pierre helped himself to a crate of French porcelain. They had no sooner sailed into Boston Harbor than the customs men swept down on them and impounded the goods and the sloop. The boys were thrown into a cell under the courthouse. As soon as he heard of it Samuel went to see them in the jail and speak to the magistrate. He sent word to Guillaume by way of Henri who sent a messenger on to Beausejour.

To the Bostonians the porcelain was considered quite valuable; in the possession of a bunch of young Acadians it was clearly contraband and Guillaume feared their arrest for being in possession of it. As Acadians their rights would be no different than those of an insect caught in a spider's web and he knew he had to find them before their youthful lark ended in a nightmare.

Guillaume immediately sent to the fathers of the other boys involved and asked them to meet him at Henri's truck house at Annapolis Royal. Henri hired Big Albert Denis, a fisherman familiar with New England waters to take them all to Boston aboard the *Emmeline*.

The weather began fair but the men set out in a bleak mood. The boat ran smoothly out the Annapolis River to the Bay of Fundy where it was taken by the outgoing tide and pushed along by a current running faster than the wind. On the horizon the Bay met the dark Atlantic beneath an endless bank of leaden clouds that seemed to hang so heavy they rested on the surface of the water.

The wind picked up as their boat swept beneath the edge of the cloudbank and the water surged and fell, twisted by random currents. Gusts of wind blew the tops off the waves and flecked foam down their backs; Big Albert struggled to keep them on course.

Outside the Bay the Atlantic swept them along a treacherous rockledged coast that seemed to come alive to menace them with sharp and dagger-like boulders that made the surf boil as if the rocks themselves frothed with anger that the boat kept far enough off the shore to escape them. Further west and south when the waves calmed some, Big Albert changed course and stood out to sea to give wide berth to the rocky peninsulas surrounded by shoals and reefs that ran far out from the shore.

When they passed the English fort at Pemaquid they saw its eighteen and twenty-two pounders protruding through the stone walls like huge nostrils. "Look there," Big Albert pointed. "That fort sees us and fires those guns on us, God himself can't help us in this sea."

As they sailed past Pemaquid, a line of squalls swept in from seaward and moved up the bay that opened to the west of them. Big Albert swore as he tried to make the boat point more to seaward. He nodded at waves breaking at intervals over sunken rocks, "That 'un's the Devil's Back. Get past it there's Devil's Knee waiting and then Devil's Elbow. Once a ship's in there and snags up on one of those Devils then the others grab at it and it's lost."

Bursts of wind and rain pelted them and then moved on, the sky clearing for a few minutes between squalls. A whale spouted to the east not far off their stern. The sounds of men's talk drifted up through the hatchway and a few minutes later the mate, a man named Bernie Richard, started playing a dirgey tune with his recorder that sounded like some graveside chant. The red eye of the setting sun peered at them through a rift that opened between the thinning clouds as if to mark who was abroad in such a wild sea. Richard seemed entranced by its bloody glow and his recorder music began a plaintive beat. The last notes no sooner trailed off than a moaning echoed from within the boat's hull. The sailors crossed themselves. "What've ye conjured with your music?" Henri's face was drawn with fear.

Again and again the strange moan built, each time ending in sobs as if something were in pain. Big Albert looked out over the water and saw a whale swimming toward the boat. It sank below the waves and then came up beside them and kept pace as they sailed. The fishy breath from its blowhole misted them and left them choking. The whale swam beneath them and again they heard the cries of grieving as if the animal suffered. They watched to see if it would broach to bat them down to a shuddering end with its giant tail or come up under them and try to tip their boat and themselves into the sea. After a time the whale's sobbing softened like those of a child that had cried itself out. Off their stern a flipper rose from the water and then the huge body arced across the surface and a dark eye studied them before the animal sank from sight.

Big Albert heaved a sigh of relief and said, "Heard once whales mourn for lost kin. Never could imagine it afore. Strange thing."

An icy current of air found its way under Guillaume's collar and a chill ran down his spine. He looked at the shore that was covered with an endless forest of firs lining the distant high-cliffed mainland. Nearby islands that were no more than enormous piles of adamantine rock rose out of a bottomless sea and on them the roots of stunted windswept spruce trees grasped for purchase like the claws of eagles. He thought of the many stories about battles fought between the French and the Indians against the English and how they had raided villages down this very coast, killing and scalping innocent settlers. Henri said he once overheard English soldiers at Fort Anne talk about how fiercely they hated the French for those raids. Guillaume shuddered to think of their harebrained sons carelessly snared in a net whose every strand was made of such vengeful loathing.

As night drew its mantle over them the last of the storms passed on and left the wind and water calmed. The sails that the wind had bellied taut to the bursting point now went empty and flat, and smacked against the mast. Now the men drew the lines in to hold the canvas steady so they could catch any faint breath of air. The evening star brightened above the masthead as the ebbing tide gently slapped the hull. Strange round iridescent fish glinted as the water moved them in gentle ripples and pooled them around the boat. Big Albert pointed to them, "See them some times after a storm goes by. Fishermen call them souls of men lost overboard." They leaned over the sides of the boat to look at them shining in the soft moonlight. Henri dipped his hand and raised a round little fish no larger than a coin that glinted silver in his hand and then lowered it gently back into the water.

A following sea pushed them past a group of shoaling reefs and low-lying islands. The barren treeless Isles of Shoals were used by both English and French fishermen. On one of the islands they could see the lights inside the houses of a small village. How Guillaume longed to be one of them for just a minute and sit beside a warm hearth with the smell of stew in the air and hear the chatter of children at his knee. But he was a stranger in New England, a castaway on a sea of trouble searching with his friends for their lost sons. Like a small mercy the scent of the island meadows followed them on the breeze and pierced them with sudden memories of home. Guillaume thought of Jerusha sitting outside for a bit after the evening meal was cleared away. He wondered if she gazed out at the bay and was she thinking of him and praying he'd find Jacques-Pierre and bring him home?

Big Albert steered for the darkened shore and as the boat passed from the lee of the islands the green fragrance of the meadows was lost in the salty tang of the sea. As they neared land the stringent odor of spruce and the familiar smell of hearth fires beckoned them toward a small break in the rocks that opened into a harbor where they decided to drop anchor and spend the night. Exhausted, they needed rest to re-gain their strength before approaching Boston.

The next morning Guillaume came on deck to see Big Albert look-ing warily at the sun as it rose like a bloodshot eye into a bruised sky, its reds and purples reflected in the oily water. The ship's mast stood black and tall against the clouds and towered above them like a mighty spear raised in defiance.

"Red in the mornin', sailor take warnin'." Big Albert looked grim. The crew pulled anchor and sailed with a light breeze that freshened as they rounded Cape Ann.

Outside Salem's harbor a whaler lay anchored, its bloody offal-cov-ered decks being cleaned by its crew. At one end its planks were being drenched in seawater by pumps and hoses as the crew scrubbed them down; at the stern, barrels of oil and reddish blubber were being of-floaded onto barges to be taken ashore. Hundreds of terns and gulls loomed, hovered, darted and dove into the water dragging pieces of flesh like kite tails into the grimy sky. The cacophony of their screams resounded in a hellish chorus. Downwind of them the stench was nearly unbearable. Big Albert changed course to sail wide of it and went a way to sea so their approach to Boston began from beyond the outer islands of the harbor.

As they neared the entrance they could see Boston's lighthouse and sailed toward it. Its weak light could not be sighted very far out to sea. Unlike the great lighthouse the French built at Louisbourg to welcome ships and help them steer clear of the rocks, this one seemed like a raised fist, a warning to strangers of more perils than hidden reefs and wily currents.

The lighthouse keeper sailed out in a small boat with a large red vane and hailed them. Big Albert turned his vessel into the wind and waited for him.

"Ye Frenchies?"

"Yes. Going into Boston."

"Ye need a pilot in the road."

"How's that?"

"The law hereabouts."

Guillaume shook his head to indicate he didn't understand what the man said.

"No ship enters here without a pilot. And I," he jerked his thumb at his chest, "be the aforesaid pilot. You're to follow after me." Aboard their vessel the Acadians spoke among themselves. Henri volunteered to go aboard the pilot's boat because he knew the place and spoke better English than the rest of them.

The pilot eased his boat to the side of the *Emmeline* and held out a line. One of the crew cleated it off so Henri could climb across. As he jumped to the pilot boat's deck the man said, "Twenty shillin's." He held out his hand for the coins and introduced himself, "Cap'n John Hayes." Henri put ten livres in his palm. Hayes looked at them doubtfully and then sighed, "Guess French stuff's all ye got. But it's only ten ye give me."

"We're but a small ship. Ten should do it."

Hayes spat over the side. "All right, I'll make it do."

He pushed away from the Acadian boat, trimmed sail and began to move up the channel ahead of them. Guillaume could just barely hear Henri answer Hayes as to why they had come to Boston. "Four silly lads we have, our sons. They thought to sail in here like they was home in Acadia and act like they're traders. Trying to find them. Heard anything about such boys?" Guillaume tried to catch the answer but the pilot boat slid further ahead and the words were lost to him in the wind.

Hayes scratched his chin and looked thoughtful. "Now ye say so," he turned his head to look at Henri, "I did hear something could be a week or two ago. French lads come in and thought to sail up the roads without a pilot. Foolish. Got themselves stranded." Hayes pointed out and named the larger islands and shoals where vessels had gone aground and broken up in storms. "There – that 'un claimed a fully loaded trader just home from the Far East and trying to come in here ahead of a big storm. Tried running straight into the harbor and drove up on the rocks instead. Sank. All hands. Cargo lost. That's where them boys was. Fisherman found them. Dead so I heard."

"French boys from Acadia?" Henri emphasized each word.

"That's what I heard. Same place as the other trader drove ashore."

Henri's back stiffened and he stared straight ahead with never a backward look to reveal any expression that held even the merest hint of what Hayes had told him.

The Acadians were glad to have the pilot to follow because it gave them time to look at the city they had heard so much about. Henri had come here and married so it was familiar to him. But except for Big Albert, who sailed in here once in a while with barrels of green cod the rest had never seen the place before. A bit further on the pilot boat turned a point west and dropped back a bit so the two boats were almost bow to stern as they passed a small island that seemed to be melting away. A weathered cross-like structure stood on its highest point. Pieces of chain hung from it gently swinging in the breeze. Hayes shouted, "Pirates' bodies strung up there in chains after they're hanged. Haven't had one in some years; last 'un went quite a time afore his bones finally give out and dropped down. Bodies buried there. Supposed to be a cursed place. Story goes that a mate accused of killing his captain, name of Nix, was hanged. Afore he's strung up the man says he's innocent and the whole island will wash away to prove it. Most gone now. Maybe he's right. Nix's Mate we call this place."

"Dead right," Henri said mordantly. Hayes slapped him on the back with a great horselaugh. He let out the sail a bit and moved a boat length ahead.

On another island there was a manned fort with walls of huge granite blocks called Castle William. A large British ensign flew above the ramparts. A few small boats were drawn up on the beach and tied off to posts set above the highest tide line. Cannon of all sizes bristled from openings in the stone near the top of the walls. Men in the sentry boxes looked at them through their spyglasses. "Have these men ever fought the French?" Guillaume wondered, but he didn't ask Henri to translate the question for Hayes.

They passed fishermen anchored out in the roads whose catch filled the air with the familiar tang of gurry. They sailed by a large British warship at anchor and saw some of its long boats being lowered to take some of the crew and marines ashore where waterfront taverns awaited their custom. As they passed one of the boats about to cast off its lines Hayes shouted something at them about having a care where they were headed. A chorus of laughter answered him.

"More men aboard her than all the French regulars in New France," Big Albert muttered.

Guillaume's eyes narrowed. "Aye. And looks like more people crowded into Boston than there are in all of Acadia. Look around ye. Never could've imagined a place so big and with so many people."

Sailing up the harbor they could see seven hills that rose up over Boston, most with large buildings. Looking through the glass Guillaume made out a large mast with a barrel attached on top of the highest hill. The pilot boat floated nearby. Hayes pointed to it. "That where you're looking to? Sentry Hill that, now most call it Beacon Hill. Barrel's full of tar. Light it and it makes a beacon to warn people something's going on."

There were many steeples in Boston and Hayes pointed out Cotton Mather's church atop Meeting House Hill. "Fire and brimstone he was."

"Aye to that," Guillaume thought when Henri shouted it to the Acadians.

The visitors gaped at the size and bustle of the waterfront and tried to count the many wharves that ran out into the harbor. Shipyards were busy with new-laid keels or vessels that looked near to being launched. They skirted a wharf that ran from a road that passed between what appeared to be storage buildings near the shore and extended out, Guillaume guessed for nearly a half mile. "Long Wharf," Hayes called back to them. "Up there's King Street. Next is Court Street. Court house and jail there too. End of the wharf and all along it there's counting houses, trade businesses. Weather's fine and people walk all around there in the evening, showing off their fancy clothes."

Vessels large and small surrounded Long Wharf. It joined with King

Street which led up to a brick building that Hayes called the "New Town House", built to replace an older wooden structure that'd burned down several years earlier. Guillaume's concentration was broken by Hayes' voice carrying across the water. "Where ye headed?"

"Samuel Watkins."

Hayes gestured toward two large ships; one with its hull the color of mahogany, the *Arbutus* was familiar to Guillaume because he'd seen it in Acadian waters several times. "Aye," he said pointing it out to the Acadians.

"Watkins all right." Hayes luffed his sails and hailed the vessel. Big Albert followed suit. A seaman came topside on the *Arbutus* when the pilot boat drifted near and asked their business. He gave Henri a hand up. Hayes called out "Luck to ye Frenchies" and they waved him off. Then the fishing boat closed with the larger ship and tied off to it and the rest of the Acadians were welcomed aboard.

They waited on deck while the sailor went off to find Samuel and tell him of their arrival. They stared at the city, wondering how they'd find their way in all that tangled maze of streets and confusion of people to find where their sons had been taken. The sheer size of the place and the busyness of it weighed on them and brought their spirits low, now that there was nothing else to distract them from their fears. There was no work to put a hand to and no water rushing beneath their keel. They were no longer driving to the rescue. They'd arrived and for the moment they didn't know what to do next.

Samuel was in the ship's cabin going over the bill of lading with his captain. He came right out to them, embraced Henri and clapped the rest of them by the arms and drew them together into a circle. "Ye must be frantic," were his first words. "Can't tell ye the whole story now. I'll send to the cook to get some coffee and food brought up for you. Wait inside here."

Henri gave him a puzzled look. "Sam? Are they alive?"

The men stood as if the world around them had fallen away and Henri's question was all there was left of substance or meaning. Samuel's face muddied.

"What say ye?" Michel, one of the fathers turned to Henri. "Why'd ye ask that?"

"Harbor pilot told me some young French men died on one of the islands when their boat was driven onto the rocks. Fisherman found bodies washed up."

A loud cry erupted from Guillaume's throat. "They can't be dead." Samuel grabbed his elbow. "Get hold of yourself, man. The boys're alive; they're at my house right now. Magistrate let me take them home from the jail yesterday."

"Sam," Henri asked, "What was the pilot talking about then? I thought it was our boys. Four lads, he said. French."

"Happened the week before your boys came in here. Then I heard about four lads taken and didn't think much but when I got the word they asked for me, I hopped right over. Wasn't them gone aground and their bodies buried over on the island - no, that was nothing to do with your lads."

The Acadians were nearly fainting by the time Samuel finished telling them that much. He led them to a different cabin than the one he had come from, where there were some wooden seats with cushions that felt good to sit on after the bare planks aboard Big Albert's fishing boat and the men sank into them to recover from the news. It wasn't long before the cook sent up coffee and biscuits. A few minutes later and wearing an apron stained with juices, he entered the cabin carrying a great tray filled with fried eggs, sausage, and ham. Relief fueled their appetites and stomachs that had known little food in the last few days growled like wolves. As one they dug in and ate until their cheeks fairly ran with grease and they felt restored. They left the cabin to stand on the deck and look at the city spread before them and speculate about their sons while they waited impatiently for Samuel to finish his business.

Boston was larger than Guillaume imagined and more of a town than he remembered even of La Rochelle. Nothing in Acadia was of any size or consequence compared to this and wouldn't be for a long time, Henri insisted. The place swarmed with activity. Boats emptied loads of men on leave from their ships and the waterfront grew noisier. He began to feel the hold this place had taken on his brother and felt at least a glimmer of understanding as to why Henri believed Acadia's future would lie with the English.

After an hour or so Samuel emerged from the captain's cabin and asked how they did and if they had lodging in the city. When the Acadians said they expected to remain aboard their vessel, he invited them all to come to his house. It would be a tight squeeze but they'd all fit.

He gave orders for the *Emmeline* to be tied up to his dock and had a man call for an extra carriage to take them with all their sea bags. They came ashore testing their legs and entered a large building that served as a storehouse. It had an office and a gathering room which he invited them to enter. "If I were you I wouldn't want to wait another minute to hear more about my sons," he began. "Ye already know the most important things." The Acadians nodded and told him how much they were in his debt.

"They came to Boston to trade some goods, without realizing there are rules to follow. Once they broke the first one and being French-speaking, they're arrested. When ye came into the harbor, a man come up to ye in a boat with a red vane on it?"

They nodded that was so.

"And ye gave him his wage to pilot ye in," Samuel said.

They agreed they had.

"Well, the boys didn't do that and the law requires it. There's a patrol boat that waits for such scofflaws. They overtook your sons and found them to be French. The boys either didn't understand they'd broken the law or refused to pay the fine for refusing the pilot. Whatever 'twas, that was enough for them to be arrested and their vessel searched. The cargo was nothing of too great interest except for the porcelains. When they tried to explain that stuff was theirs, the officers looked at them – their clothing, their small boat – and decided the goods were stolen and threw them in jail. Lucky they knew enough to ask for me and got someone to heed them. After they'd been held for most of a week I got word from the magistrate there were some French lads in the Boston jail that spoke my name. Couldn't imagine it. Went right over there to see what was what."

"There they were, themselves and their clothes filthy and sitting on the floor of a small cell with an open slit of a window and bars in it that let in a little light from the street. Couple of rats in the corner hiding behind the slops pail. Jacques-Pierre's overjoyed to see me and the rest of the boys, once they knew I'd help them promised me anything to get them out. I took the liberty to hire a lawyer for them, one that does regular business in that court. Reviewed all the information. Lawyer went before the magistrate and I sat in the hearing room right up front and watched everything. Boys looked terrible pale when they were brought in. Always a number of riffraff hanging around there, in winter mostly to stay warm but sometimes just to cause trouble. Heard murmurs of "French thieves" and "Hang the bastards" going around. Boys understood. Faces turned white as sheets. Told the lawyer to ask the magistrate to shut the talk down and he called to the bailiff to arrest the next man who spoke out."

"Lawyer explained the situation to the magistrate who looked each of the boys over as if he was trying to decide if he was hearing true. Called for witnesses so I stood up and faced the bench and swore to tell the truth. Looked around the room to see who was doing the talking among the lookers-on and recognized a man or two who'd worked in my yard. They saw I knew them and the heckling ended right then. Told the boys' story and attested that I'd seen such stuff in their uncle's trading establishment and expected he gave the porcelain to the boys and they decided on their own to come to Boston and try to trade or sell it."

"Magistrate called the lawyer before him and they spoke in low voices. Gavel went down. Decision was given. All goods and the sloop to be impounded and sold to pay for the boys' keep while they were in jail and pay for the lawyer's fees. Released the lads to my custody while they're in Boston and now you're free to take them home."

One of the other fathers erupted. "Those things're worth a lot more than what it costs to jail a couple of men and pay a lawyer. 'T was a cheat."

Samuel had a rueful look on his face. "Well might ye think so. But there's no other way you'd have your sons returned to ye. Else they might've been set to labor in the fleet and you might've never seen them again."

LOUISBOURG 1744

It was spring and well past the time when the Basque fishermen sailed into Louisbourg's harbor to unload the supplies that crammed their vessels before going out to fish the Banks. The Basques stayed out there all summer long, only came ashore onto nearby beaches to spread their gutted catch to dry in the sun. They never stopped fishing until they were loaded with barrel upon barrel of green cod. By the end of summer they'd sail back into Louisbourg and take on fresh supplies for their journey home to Galicia. For many years the system worked to the advantage of both. But this year the French looked in vain for the familiar sails to break the horizon and come to their relief.

Day by day Simon scanned the empty expanse of ocean. "Where are they?" he demanded of neighbors taking their turns to watch while they grumbled their fear of starvation. "Has to mean war," was the constant reply. "If that's so they won't come this year."

For the past few years every French ship that landed at Louisbourg brought word that war with England was imminent. After the first couple of times they heard it, people didn't stop believing it could happen but they stopped being so nervous about it.

But now the absence of the Basques was convincing evidence to the fortress that war was afoot, weeks ahead of the official declaration that arrived by fast packet from France. The only ship on the horizon, it was spotted far offshore and by the time it landed half of Louisbourg waited on the quay. "Is it war?" a babble of voices began to screech as soon as the vessel was within hailing distance.

"War! War at last!" a crewman in the rigging shouted to them and the cry was taken up by the crowd and went through the town like a wild fire spreading faster than the runner from the ship could carry the official declaration to the Governor. When he heard the shouts in the streets and read the document slapped into his hand, Duquesnel knew he'd have to act quickly to surprise the English.

He sent Francoise DuVivier with a small army to make a surprise attack on Canso. When the English were easily routed, DuVivier's victory opened the overland route all the way through from Acadia to Louisbourg and relief supplies flowed out of Chignecto like an undammed river and crossed the isthmus.

Simon no sooner heard the news than he packed up his gear and set off for Baie Verte to tell Jacques to load up a boat for Louisbourg. He went overland toward Canso and on his first night in the forest he was surrounded by a scouting party sent out by DuVivier's army.

His traveling companions slept by the remains of their campfire where only a few embers still glowed red and Simon had the watch. With the French takeover he wasn't expecting the rush of men who made a sudden break through the brush and overpowered him and the others. "Quiet," a voice warned them. "Make a sound and we shoot ye."

"Who be ye?" a low voice spoke in his ear as strong arms tightened a rope around his chest to pin his arms straight down by his side.

Simon whispered his name.

"What're ye doing here by Canso?" the voice demanded.

"Traveling by is all. Headed to my truck house at Baie Verte."

"Ye'll be telling that to the General."

"General who?"

"Ye don't know that ye don't come from Louisbourg," the man snickered and gave the rope a hard tug and Simon fell to his knees. "Get up, ye fookin' English spy." He yanked on the rope. Simon struggled to obey and was pulled by his captor through the brush. They entered a clearing where the rest of his friends stood bound as he was.

"English spies, be ye?" DuVivier looked each of them in the face. When he reached Simon, he gave a start. "Desjardins?"

"The same."

"What're ye doing here spying for English?"

"What makes ye think I'd do that? Risk my business for the likes of them? I'm not stupid but looks like some of your men are. Grab up good French and accuse them of that." He spat, careful to avoid Du-Vivier's feet.

"Release these men," the commander ordered. "Be more observant next time ye see it's Frenchmen trying to get some nod." He gave Simon a wicked grin.

"English still about?"

"Only the ones we captured. Getting ready to take them to Louisbourg. Where you headed?"

"Baie Verte. They should be happy to see you at the fortress. With all these prisoners ye take, ye'll need traders like us to send provisions over to help ye feed them. You'd best to not make us angry if ye want to eat."

BOSTON 1744

Henri was in Boston with Marie for a lengthy visit with Samuel and her sisters and planned to come home to Annapolis Royal aboard the Arbutus with a shipload of new goods for the truck house.

Boston had not yet heard that France had declared war and didn't know that French privateers were already out in force in the Bay of Fundy making the most of their foreknowledge and seeking English traders loaded with supplies to capture and send to Louisbourg.

As it neared Annapolis Royal the *Arbutus* was challenged by a French schooner that tried to take the wind from their sails and board them. The Frenchman closed on them and brought his ship near enough to use shouting trumpets. Foam sprayed across the bow as the vessels charged ahead.

"What d'ye think you're doing there?" Henri screamed, "Ye'll not be taking from the Bancouers. Want my goods, ye come to Annapolis Royal and pay good money for them."

"Should've known it'd be you, Henri. Trying to skin starving people with your prices. Be more'n us out here to chase your fine New England ships."

"Any want to try us let 'em come. We're bigger and have cannon. Blow 'em out of the water, even you French if any think to try something," Henri roared, one hand holding his trumpet, the other raised in a clenched fist.

The English captain listened to them shouting at each other and laughed to hear Frenchmen quarreling over his cargo; he was determined the privateer would get nowhere near it. The *Arbutus* could sail closer to the wind than the French ship and his crew kept her pointed high enough to sail just ahead of him. If they didn't hold her there and the Frenchman could close on her enough to take her wind and run up alongside, they would be in position to board. Then there'd be hell to pay, the more so because he carried an owner and his wife. Not to mention what Sam Watkins would do to him.

The vessels ran that way for a time with no gain for the French; both sail masters did everything they could to get the most from the trim of their canvas, feeding the ability of their helmsmen to point into the wind without luffing the heads of their sails and losing ground. After a time the *Arbutus* began to inch away from her pursuer.

The Frenchman was still reluctant to change course but after a time he tired of a game that held no promise of an easy prize. The threats and curses that peppered the air made the Englishman thank God he had armed the ship before it left Boston. He had sailed long enough to know that the rumor of war was as good as the fact if one's vessel was as ripe a prize as his. The captain was relieved when the challenger finally veered away.

"Good we're armed. Got a French ensign?" Henri shouted. The

captain bellowed the order to run it up the mast.

"Refreshing this breeze," Henri laughed. "Bring 'em on, the French bastards!" The English captain laughed, and remarked to the mate, "Ain't he a regular fighting cock when he's let loose from his ledgers? Got quick into the spirit of it, he did."

Standing at the hatch with one foot poised by the top of the ladder as he started to go below, Henri overheard the left-handed compliment and his chest swelled with pride. Marie was resting in the main cabin when he went down to look in on her and ask how she did.

"I heard all the shouting, Henri. What's that all about?"

"Oh 'twas only some silly French who thought they'd take us."

Marie sat up with a look of alarm on her face. "Oh my dearest, ye must leave such challenges to the captain. He's supposed to be in charge of that. Knows what to do to save us if it comes to a fight."

Henri looked down at his feet. "I guess I am getting too long in the tooth for such adventures," he admitted. "But wasn't it the best when I stood there in the wind and felt that racing hull under my feet and challenged that arrogant Frenchman to catch us, knowing full well he couldn't." He looked so full of himself that Marie couldn't help but call him on it.

"Ye're right. So what?" he gruffed back at her.

ANNAPOLIS ROYAL

The day after the Arbutus left Marie and Henri with all their merchandise on the dock and rode the outgoing tide to sail as fast as possible for Boston, DuVivier showed up outside of Annapolis Royal with a force of three hundred Indians including Dancing Crow's clan, along with some French regulars from Louisbourg and some Acadians. For a few days they stayed outside the town and menaced the British who they far outnumbered. Governor Mascarene had his hands full to prevent his troops from panic.

Marie heard scratching on the wood post outside their door that night. Henri opened it a crack and Paul Dancing Crow emerged from the darkness to slide inside and warn him and Marie to leave their house quickly. Paul was barely inside the parlor before he let loose a flow of words. "Indians fill woods all around here. DuVivier quarters his forces on Acadians. He wants Neutrals to join him. If they do the town must fall to the French."

"They'll depend on Acadians rising to help them and try to take the place without reinforcement?" Henri was dubious.

"DuVivier says two French ships promised. Supposed to come to fight. We tell Acadians if they wish to escape they must leave by night. Uncle, you and Aunt must take your people and go." Earnestly he insisted. "Please, Uncle. French are to give Acadians time to go. But when their houses go dark it signals the attack to begin."

"Paul," Marie choked back her surprise at seeing him. "You've risked your life to come here. Mascarene's like to have already sent to Boston for help. If ships appear in the harbor tonight they're more likely to be English." Marie embraced her nephew, and told him, "Watch out for that. You're a brave man, don't be a foolish one." Henri begged Paul not to try to come to them again. "It'd be a useless risk of your life. We don't want you to do that."

Paul slipped out the door and became just another shadow in the gloom. Marie stood with Henri at the sitting room window, looking at the lighted windows in the lower town. "Not tonight then," she murmured. "Gives us another day to prepare."

Next morning Henri ordered his helpers at the truck house to shutter the windows of every building as fast as they could, while Marie packed a few clothes and some food. Leaving the rest of the men behind to guard the house from looters, Henri and Marie took the maid and the cook with them to find shelter at the fort.

The next night the lower town was dark. The French attack came; fighting raged up and down the streets and buildings were torched. The British got the worst of it and civilians clustered inside the fort for protection worried what would happen if the enemy broke through British defenses. With burning buildings everywhere he looked, Henri constantly fretted about their house and the warehouses.

Abruptly the fighting stopped. Henri thought it meant DuVivier was waiting for the ships he expected from Louisbourg to sail up the Annapolis River with reinforcements.

Mascarene called on him to attend when a French officer came to present a truce offer. It turned out Henri knew the emissary – DuVivier's brother Joseph, who told Mascarene of the fleet and army that DuVivier expected to arrive from Louisbourg at any time. Joseph extended an offer to suspend hostilities until the French fleet arrived. Mascarene could decide then whether to surrender. Or if a British fleet arrived sooner the contest would resolve in Mascarene's favor.

"Of course, DuVivier's confident he'll win. Why else would he send this message and by his own brother?" Henri said to Mascarene after the meeting ended. "But if the French are really so strong, I can't understand why they don't just go ahead and take the town."

Mascarene agreed. He declined the offer and the fighting resumed.

A few days later DuVivier learned the ships that were supposed to come to his aid to take Annapolis Royal were recalled to fight English ships that now threatened Louisbourg. DuVivier and his officers argued and now the French were in turmoil. The Acadians who had joined them melted away. Ships began entering the river but DuVivier hesitated to leave until he knew for certain they were the enemy. One of his officers screamed at him, "Who else could they be? You haven't listened to us – those're English. Retreat now before they land." But DuVivier accused the man of being a coward and he ordered his men to stay and fight.

A large band of Abenaki Rangers led by John Gorham of Cape Cod rowed ashore to break the siege. They mounted a fierce attack on the Indian camps, killing women and children and mutilating their bodies. DuVivier finally retreated after the Indians fled.

Henri prayed that Paul and his family escaped but there was no way he could know and frustration fueled his temper. "Why do the French always try to compromise us? Why do they come here and attack the British without the means or the will to see it through? I understand DuVivier's ordered to drive the English out of Acadia but the French just don't countenance the Acadians wouldn't – most of them – break an oath, even one forced on them by the English," Henri raged as he paced his parlor.

Marie listened, knowing her husband's fear for Paul Dancing Crow and his family was the root of his anger. Paul was like a son to both of them and she would give anything to know he was safe.

"Why do the French always come here and expect the Neutrals to rise up with them against the British? They may think there are so few British here that with the Neutrals' help, they could drive them out. But Annapolis Royal is only an outpost to all of New England and they'd never tolerate such. The English will always send ships and men from Boston. French need to understand that. But they never seem to take it into account."

She was only repeating what Samuel had said to Henri time and again. Her husband had said it back to her brother during so many of their conversations, but it still darkened his face with anger because he could never convince Jacques or Guillaume of it. Surrounded by French, they had little contact with the English – other than those New Englanders who were happy to keep things just as churned up and confused as ever they were in Chignecto, so they could keep on making money from trading goods. His brothers couldn't see beyond that to understand the game that was being played. If Jacques didn't subscribe to Neutrality, Guillaume was adamant for it and believed that it was all the protection the Acadians needed to get along with the British. Henri thought they were both behaving like fools.

After several weeks things settled back to almost what passed for normal and the first merchant ship came in from Boston. With it were some old friends, Caleb Jameson and Zachariah Warren who looked in to see how Marie and Henri had fared.

As they toasted their luck with some fine claret and conversed late into the evening, their talk inevitably turned to how the British planned to push the French from the shores of the New World. "Back in '20, Mascarene even sent a letter to the Board of Trade in London saying Acadians should be removed from Nova Scotia," Caleb said.

"But ain't that old news by more than two decades?" Zach answered. "How serious could that be? Unless you think he'd write the Board of Trade about this latest episode to ask it again?"

"Whichever it is, it's still disturbing to hear. Mostly for us who try to live here in peace with all of them," Henri said. "Wouldn't have ever thought a Huguenot governor would promote such a business. But after the French standing under arms and threatening to take the town it's easy to imagine the idea coming back to lodge in Mascarene's brain now as a way to settle things."

Next morning Henri and Marie sipped their coffee and brooded. She asked if he thought the governor could seriously entertain the notion to send the Acadians away. "We could just go to Boston," Marie shrugged. "Mascarene has a house there. We might buy one near by him and be neighbors." She smiled at the thunderclouds gathering in his face. "I'm teasing you, Henri."

"Last night Caleb and Zach said the only reason it wasn't done then was a new Minister in London who didn't want the colonies always at war and draining the treasury."

"If money's involved I believe that'd keep anything from happening. I'm not a trusting woman when it comes to how men act who hold the purse strings. Present company excepted of course." She arched an eyebrow at him.

Henri became thoughtful. "That policy and the fact they greatly outnumber the British here, has protected the Acadians for almost thirty years. British can't even collect taxes from them and of course no one's out there volunteering to pay. Must be a real aggravation to them when no Acadian money's going into the governor's coffers."

"Without the French nearby to frustrate them wouldn't the Acadians make better accommodation with the English? After all this is their mother country and not France," Zach said.

"True," Henri replied. "French on Ile Royale are little more than distant cousins to us. They come over here to hold the possessions of the French king but Acadians live here as Neutrals and must keep in accord with everyone. It's not an easy thing to pick a way through those thickets but so far we've done well by our trade business."

Caleb said, "Speaking for myself I believe both the Acadians and the English don't want to see it all just go up in smoke."

Of course that was the answer if things were really as they thought – namely, that it made sense for the English to want to protect the economic success the merchants were all enjoying and not see all that prosperity dashed to bits. It soothed them to think it so.

1746

Marie was surprised when Henri came home in the middle of the day. "Dear man," she purred, "ye haven't done this in a while. Are we to rest together this afternoon as we used to?"

"Something terrible has happened, and I want to talk it out with you."

She raised her eyebrow. "Ye look all flustered. Could ye use a glass of whiskey to calm your nerves?" She went to the sideboard and came back with a healthy pour for each of them. She rested her glass on a wine stand, smoothed her skirt and when she was settled, she looked at her husband and said, "Tell me what the matter is."

"Remember those rumors of a great Armada sailed from France to attack Nova Scotia and revive Acadia? Well here's a letter come from Samuel," he handed it to her. "He says everybody in Boston goes around in fear of any ship that even comes near the harbor."

Marie skimmed the pages. "A lot of yelling against the French. More preaching from the pulpits and cries against Papists raised by the church folk. Still it's only rumors, but fear of French invasion seems to be having a powerful influence in Boston." She was perplexed. "What's to come of this, do ye think?

Henri shook his head. "Like a gambler that makes one mighty swoop of the dice, all or nothing. All these years we wait for the French to come with such a force and try to take back Acadia. Now see what a predicament they've stirred up."

"Will it be war again?"

"Got word this morning at the truck house," Henri continued. "Single ship drifted into Chebucto harbor. Acadians went to the shore to see it. Ship's filled with diseased men. Acadians fear a contagion and won't go near to give any help. Sailors shouted about great storms at sea that destroyed the whole fleet in the middle of their crossing."

"French came right enough, just not as they planned to." Marie read more of her brother's letter. "Sam says that Shirley's going to send more Massachusetts men to Nova Scotia. Five hundred English to sail from Boston for Annapolis Royal."

"Yes. Mascarene told me about that. He can't support so many of them here. Sent to ask what we could provide them from the truck house. Even with what we could send over there, they still won't have enough supplies to keep them all at the fort. So Mascarene plans to quarter them on the Acadians. He'll send them on to Grand Pré. Let them spend the winter there and eat up Acadian stores."

"What's it mean that the English go there?"

"British build fortifications at Grand Pré and they'll have another stronghold to lock Nova Scotia in their grip. French'll never allow it. Just ye wait and see, m' love."

Henri paced the room. "Heard Mascarene say he wrote again to the Board of Trade advising removal of the Acadians from Nova Scotia so they could be replaced by English Protestants. It sickened me to hear it. That could've only been the wash-back of DuVivier's threats. When the day comes for one power to succeed over the other, I can't see France being the one to prevail."

Henri took a good hard swallow and the whiskey burned all the way down. "My brothers off there in Beausejour and Baie Verte don't heed my views or my fears. Jacques with his Indian ways, believes the English are their enemies, bent on wiping them out."

"You think that's where Paul must've gone when the militia shipped in from Boston?"

"More likely took his people there than to Beausejour. Guillaume's in some kind of rosy cloud where he believes the oath's enough to save the Acadians from having any conflict with the English so long as they all stay Neuter and don't support the French when they come to attack." He put down his glass and looked over at Marie. "I've asked Samuel to buy a small house for us in Boston near his own, where we can go to if it comes to such trouble."

Marie sat still and a stricken expression spread across her face. "I always enjoyed to go back to visit in Boston and stay with Samuel or one of my sisters and visit my nieces and nephews. After all these years I must've become a true Acadian because now Boston sounds such a grim place and so full of hateful people." She studied the design in the carpet on the floor in front of her. "Could this really come true?" Her troubled eyes lifted to meet his face.

"I see that if the Bancouers are to survive this battle between England and France over who owns this country, we must be sided with the English." Henri swallowed the last drop in his glass, and walked outside into the garden to light his pipe.

GRAND PRÉ 1747

Snow drove into Jacques-Pierre's face and threatened to blind him as he hurried to keep up with the man ahead. It clung to his hat and his hair, tiny icicles crusted his beard in a circle around the warm exhalation of his breath and the head strap that harnessed him to the sledge these last few hours left a red welt that stung as wet snow drove against his skin. He would soon trade his place off to one of the other men from Chignecto who had joined to fight with the French.

On the last day of their journey large flakes began to fall from a sky filled with clouds that bulged like overstuffed bales of dingy cotton. The army of men on snowshoes alternated with each other to pull sleds loaded with guns, knives, ammunition and food as they ran urgently forward. The flakes thickened and by the forenoon the going became rougher and runners began to stick, threatening to overturn their burdens; snowshoes turned to hoops of ice.

"It's madness," Jacques-Pierre thought. "French army comes looking to get volunteers to throw the English out of Grand Pré. Say without the English are driven off now, when spring comes they'll charge right across Chignecto to kill and burn and loot. Here's our farm right in their path. I believe that and I have to go with the French when they say it's best to stop them this way. My cousins Albert and Theo say it too."

The storm thickened and the world turned solid white. There was no time to think about anything but pushing onward and hope the officers up ahead knew where they were going. At dusk the snow let up a bit and when they stopped to rest someone saw a glimmer of light directly ahead and shouted the news. The men headed for it, cheered by the thought of food and warmth and a dry place to rest. The faint smell of roasting meats that came to them down the wind drew them on and they followed it intent as the Magi who followed Bethlehem's star.

A large barn and then an outbuilding and a farmhouse gave shapes to blankets of snow. Animals nested in their stalls by mangers filled with hay and from the house the light of a host of candles flickered through the windows and inside music and dancing sounded. Smoke swelled up from the chimney and melted the snow that fell into it and released tantalizing smells that wafted like incense into the yard. Under urgently whispered orders they spread out around the house and waited for deVilliers' signal to act.

With ice forming on the windows as fast as snow melted on the glass, all anyone could see of what was inside were swirling colors. DeVilliers pushed through the falling snow to make his way toward a window and when his gloved hand wiped a bit of the glass clear, he saw a wedding celebration going on inside.

He went around to the front and pounded with all his strength on the large oaken door to be heard above the noise. The music stopped and voices rose in alarm and then hushed as the door swung open. Tables stood laden with the remains of the wedding feast. Bride and groom clung together in the midst of the crowd, astonished by the sight of the snow-covered army with their fur hats and beards rimed with ice. The man who'd opened the door looked out; he was too amazed by the sight to either speak or move.

"Melanson! It's DeVilliers! Help us, man! We've come a long way to remove your uninvited guests. Need food and shelter." Men rushed outside to help and before long every soldier was quartered among the houses that were still home to Acadians.

DeVilliers and his officers put their heads together with Melanson. "All the houses taken by the British are on the opposite side of the river," he told them. They stepped outside, and Melanson waved to where some lights twinkled through the falling snow. "They stand close together along that ridgeline. Two dozen wood houses. And over there," he paused as he pointed again, "a great stone mill house their officers took for themselves."

"What about ships?"

"Standing down at the wharf. Loaded with wood to build blockhouses, and weapons and powder to arm them. Guards aboard. Be careful not to alarm them."

As they sat by the fireside thawing their bones and eating the remains of the feast, supplemented with bread, cheese, and hard cider, they formed their plan and attack parties were designated.

Back out into the storm they all went and trudged heads down to their posts. The snowfall was starting to tail off but it still swirled heavily enough to cover their advance. Each man relied on the one ahead to know the path and Jacques' party finally arrived at the house they were to attack. Once in position they'd be ready to go at half-three. Faces, lips, fingers and toes tingled and stiffened as the deep cold found them again. Officers ordered them to be still once they were in place and to neither move nor speak lest they be spotted by a watchman.

But no one stood outside watching in the blizzard. The English were all inside asleep at their hearthsides. They were warm and full with eating and drinking.

Jacques-Pierre chafed his hands and thought, "Came a long way running on snowshoes for this. Young officers are full of themselves to make this long slog to go attack the fookin' English in the middle of winter. French are a mad race of men to come this godforsaken night and take them on. Who else would think to do this but the fookin' French? Acadians are home in their warm comfortable beds, but for those like me and Theo and Albert that come along to toil with the French." He stamped his feet and rubbed his gloved hands to encourage circulation.

"So thick out here we could walk right up to the house and bang on the door just as bold as ye please and they wouldn't know we was there 'til they opened. Even if they was looking out for us they'd nivver see us till we was on them. Can't hear a shot nor see a man right in front of ye in this storm."

As the men looked enviously at the glowing hearth inside their target, a large mound of snow slid from a tree and hit the roof with a loud thump. Shouts erupted inside, the door flew open and an armed man came out. Voices called to him; he answered that he saw nothing. He walked back and forth across the front of the house as if to go through the motions of looking for any enemy trying to creep up on them. Then he stepped a little away from the house to relieve himself before going back inside. The men weren't hidden that far from where he stood. Albert was even so close he could see the heat rising off his steaming piss, and had to put his face down into the snow else he might be spotted. The skin on his face was frozen to the bone before he heard the door slam shut and dared to look up again.

Theo rubbed his face to revive any feeling. "Half three o'clock in the morning, deVilliers said. Dear God, let it come soon!"

Muffled shots thudded through the falling snow. The attack was on and they ran to the house. Albert raised his axe and battered down the door. It swung open and a shot rang out. He fell, his forehead grazed by a bullet. The Englishmen tried to load and fire again but the French came in fast, screaming and shooting. From the corner of his eye Jacques-Pierre saw the blade of a sword slice through the air toward his shoulder and jumped back; a gun fired from somewhere and he heard a shriek. The sword clattered to the floor as the man fell with his shoulder smashed by the impact of a bullet fired at close range. Men in nightshirts screamed as they grappled with their attackers, yelling obscenities and slashing with knives at close quarters. An arm was ripped open from wrist to elbow; the joint of a finger arced through the air and hit a man's back as if to summon him to turn about. He did and he fired. A bullet pierced his throat in return and blood gushed from the wound as he slumped to the floor. At last the English surrendered. The French collected their weapons and the survivors worked as best they could to bind up the wounded that lay where they fell on the blood-soaked floor.

Albert's wound was quickly bandaged. Boishébert appeared in the doorway and shouted for them to follow him. Theo stayed behind with his brother to guard the prisoners. Bloody footprints tracked out the door into the snow as they picked up their arms and ran after the young officer. He led them down to the mill house where the English were packed inside; many of them were wounded. It was only a matter of time before they would run out of food and water.

The French had them surrounded, and let off a volley; some of the leaden bullets flew through the narrow windows; others smashed against the stones and the French stopped firing to wait the British out.

DeVilliers was shot in the first assault, his left arm shattered; the French packed him and a young officer who had also fallen aboard a sled and took them to a nearby home for help. La Corne ordered Boishébert to take the ships. He handpicked a group of men to follow him to the wharf, where they overwhelmed the soldiers protecting the vessels, and cut off any British hopes of making a retreat by sea.

In the forenoon, the British looked out on the French surrounding their stone fortress and decided to make a break for it. They threw open the doors and charged out into the waist-deep snow where they became bogged down. After firing off a round of shots and being fired on in return, they retreated back inside and the French waited with their patience growing thin.

Treated for his wounds by a surgeon, Edward How recovered enough to dictate a message to La Corne about arranging a truce. Their meeting was brief – the British bullyragged, claiming more than they knew they had any chance to get and fired broadsides of demands at the French who countered by knocking them aside like so many shuttlecocks.

"We take our ships, sail back to Annapolis Royal," How insisted.

La Corne stood fast. "We keep the ships and everything aboard."

"We take one ship to transport the wounded. We keep the food supplies on that ship."

"Prisoners stay. Supplies stay. We keep the ships."

"Wounded go back with us. March out with colors. Supplies enough to reach Annapolis Royal," How ventured.

"No colors. No supplies."

"We march to Annapolis Royal with supplies enough to get us there. Every man promises to not bear arms against the French for three months."

"Twelve months' parole."

"Six months. We march with our colors."

The men stared at each other, their faces hardened. Finally they struck an agreement.

Before they parted the English invited the French to dine with them. La Corne entered first as the guest of honor. After him How was carried in on his stretcher. Wine was brought out and La Corne uncorked a bottle; he handed it to another officer to pour and French handed glasses to English, passing them around until each man held one. After the first toast to salute their truce aides ran about offering refills as the recent enemies matched each other glass for glass. The leaders spoke together and the officers started by calling out loud good-humored toasts and as they became involved in conversation, their voices dropped and they changed topics. La Corne asked How, "When do you think the British will intrude again into French territory?"

How responded, "You can't be serious. This isn't French territory – it's British by the last treaty and well ye know it."

La Corne laughed cheerfully. An officer seated nearby stopped talking and looked at the two men. Others saw him and the room fell quiet until La Corne noted the silence and raised his glass. "It won't be long before we're out fighting each other again. Let's enjoy ourselves now." A chorus of "Ayes" answered and the room once again buzzed with conversation. To his aide La Corne muttered, "It's but a thin veneer, such camaraderie between natural enemies."

On the next morning French regulars lined the snow-packed road as the redcoats marched away from Grand Pré with their flags flying and drums beating.

Nine days later when the French pulled out they left the Acadians feeling let-down and angry.

"After all that," Jacques-Pierre said as he trudged back to Beause-jour with his cousins and some of the other farmers, "Who'd ever want to volunteer to go help the French? You'd think they'd leave a garrison of some kind."

"Officers say their forces're spread too thin all across New France. Now this is settled, they're called back to Quebec to go fight someplace else," Theo grunted. "Likely it's that western frontier Boishébert's always mentioning."

"Never get rid of the English if the French can't hold on to what they take," Jacques-Pierre kicked away a clump of snow that'd fallen into the trail. "When I was in Boston in '35, I never saw so many regulars in one place as the English had there. French never kept up to their numbers."

"Can't hang on to what they take, why don't they just go away and leave us to make our peace with the English?" Albert muttered.

Theo replied. "Acadians swear to the oath and try to stay neutral. Been workable so far."

Albert said in a voice edged with sarcasm, "Then along come the French regulars like they're out to save us. They drag us into their fights and win or lose, it's always the worse for us when they leave."

"Don't know," Jacques-Pierre said. "Been this way so long as I been alive. My father recalls back to the time the French owned all of Acadia. Then the British came and after they took Port Royal there was that treaty that gave Acadia to them and left our place sitting on the boundary with the French. Since then nothing's ever been the same. Most like it never will be again."

GUILLAUME, his Book, 1747

At today's dawning there's a song sparrow. Once it would've been something of great significance to me to see that bird but I've seen so many over the years that I've forgotten when it was that I no longer felt it was my dear Song Sparrow's spirit bird. This one sat near me on a bare branch and trilled so sweetly, such a long and beautiful song that for the first time I felt a lightness of my body as if I could ascend and fly off with it.

I turned my eyes to survey the broad meadows where patches of snow sparkled in the sunlight and looked across the red mud toward the sea, gone so far away when the tide's low and felt how my life has been as one great turning of the full moon tide and now it pushes back toward whence it arose.

I think about the years of hard work that carried me forward to the crest of my achievement. Now I fear that everything I fought so hard to build stands on quicksand and may soon disappear. I feel a twinge of pain. I've felt them before. They always pass. I sit quietly on the bench near the doorway where the sun always warms me and wait with less patience than I had yesterday.

Jerusha comes outside. "Are you well, husband?"

"It's nothing." I wish to reassure her but now I'm glad that some time ago I finished telling my story to my family. She casts a doubtful glance at me and returns to her chores.

Jacques-Pierre went off to fight the English at Grand Pre with Theo and Albert. Each day I wait to see them return safe.

- Translation by Liam Butler, A.B., M.Ed., Ph. D.

PART II

INTERLUDE

I met Liam Butler in the bar at the Marriott. He was already sitting at a table when I came in; he stood and waved to get my attention. "Glad you called me. I wanted a chance to talk with you." As he pulled out a chair and helped me settle in we exchanged the usual pleasantries.

"Guillaume's diary has sparked a lot of interest and I'm grateful to your uncle for letting me publish it." He smiled and raised his palms. "So – your thoughts about what I read last night? I assume you've looked over the copy I gave you."

"Of course I did. Did you think I'd just toss it into my briefcase?"

"I hoped you wouldn't do that. But if you had I'd have felt awful." He looked concerned, and said, "Don't be afraid to tell me what you really think. Please."

That encouraged me to keep talking and open up to him. "I liked it. But it was more than that. The way you read it gave me a whole new way of looking at something I thought I already knew everything about." I said more to describe how I felt as I watched him read and how wonderfully he used his body in telling the story. I said it was like watching a dance choreographed to emphasize Guillaume's words. He warmed to that.

"There's something about the diary that brings it alive when I work on it. But last night's reading was my first when there was a family member present. I felt like Guillaume himself was there. That sound crazy?"

I laughed nervously and admitted there were times when I was digging into my research that I experienced the same sort of thing. "It always makes me feel like I'm on the right track." I said and watched his face relax into a smile.

He used his considerable charm to draw out more and more of what I felt as I watched and listened to him and we got so absorbed we didn't even notice when the waiter came over and slipped menus in front of us.

If I thought Liam was attractive the evening before, now I found him irresistible. He must have felt the vibes because he looked around and saw the dining room had filled while we were talking and asked if I'd rather keep the rest of our conversation private and order lunch from room service. He'd seen something on last night's menu that looked good to him and that wasn't on this one. I arched an eyebrow; he threw a fistful of loonies on the table and we went upstairs.

Later that afternoon we decided that instead of rushing back to Henri's home in North Carolina I'd stay another week and travel with him up to Caraquet to look around the Francophone area bordering the Baie de Chaleurs and meet a historian from New Brunswick who was speaking there about her own work. I was a little put off about the idea of meeting a woman professor. Since I had no real claim on him yet the best I could do was go along for the ride. I would at least have a chance to find out how we might wear as a couple – assuming we became one.

It was just a couple of days later that I realized I couldn't leave him because even though he told me he loved me while we were having sex and I believed he meant it, I worried that I'd lose him if I didn't stay with him. He was already a whole lot more to me than a casual fling and I needed to know what I was to him before I got in over my head.

The professor he planned to see was Liz Daiell. She was the athletic one with the red-gold hair who bent his ear at the Halifax reading. It turned out to be a meeting quickly ended – for her. Liz spoke just long enough to introduce Liam and for him to climb out of the audience, take over the microphone and become the center of attention. What he did to her couldn't have been more obvious if he'd just gone up and given her the elbow.

Liz came over and sat down with me to watch him. She shrugged her shoulders and said she wanted him there to help increase her turnout but not to take over. "I'll have to be more careful about who I invite to my talks if I can't take being upstaged like this," she admitted. "I spent a lot of time planning this. Just not for him to show up and grandstand."

The green-eyed monster in me grinned and when I asked if she was new at this, she admitted that she was. She looked so down in the mouth I had to feel a tiny bit sorry for her. Then I wondered how many others like her might wander into his life and realized I couldn't let myself become complacent about my budding relationship with him.

We moved in together after that, settling down for the school year in a suburb of Boston where he taught a wide-ranging course about 18th century relationships between the North American colonies and their mother countries. There was a heavy emphasis on the influence of European politics on New France and New England and how that morphed into the present day relationships between the US and Europe. It sounded so formal and scholarly when he read the course syllabus to me that when he finished and gave me a self-satisfied look, I joked that the write-up made him sound absolutely infallible – like he was some Pope of North American history. He ate that right up.

On the other hand my stuff was more limited in scope – to the story of the Bancouer family. So Liam took the larger stage and I the smaller taking insights from his research and applying them to my work-in-progress.

Toward the spring I felt my breasts becoming tender. Liam mentioned that I was beginning to look like a cherub out of a Rubens painting right about the time I realized I hadn't had a period for a while. We had gone to a party a couple of months earlier. We came home late that night and dropped into bed. That was the only time we'd ever had unprotected sex. What are the odds?

We had already scheduled a trip to Beausejour in late May to see if we could identify the place where Guillaume's house stood on the hillside below the reconstructed fort and agreed that was the perfect place and time to have a wedding.

We saw the storm clouds gather out over the bay and by the time our small wedding group was assembled, there were a few drops. But as I opened my mouth to say 'I do' it came down in buckets, so we ran up to the fort and took cover in the visitors' center. The sky finally cleared enough for us to make it back to the hotel.

Something went wrong in the final trimester and the baby was stillborn. I've never really recovered from it and still don't want to talk about it. I can't bear the memory of his tiny body wrapped in the white gown that should have been used for his christening, lying on the padded satin inside the small white coffin.

For a long time afterward grief divided us and Liam and I lived as strangers. Once he came home late from giving a talk to some graduate students and when he came in the door and hugged me I smelled alcohol on his breath. When I pulled away from him there was a long blond hair from the lapel of his jacket stuck to my cheek. All the anger at the loss of my child gathered in a knot inside me and fed the rage brought on by that hair I plucked from my face. At that moment I hated him and demanded a divorce. He must have been waiting for me to say it; without another word he packed a bag and walked out the door.

Papers went between my lawyer and his and for a long time that was our only contact. My anger turned to sorrow and the flashbacks became less frequent. As the months went by I was able to settle into a routine and focus more on my work than on my loss. The dreams I had about my child nestled in my arms while I comforted him with lullabies slipped further into the past and by the next year I felt I was coming out of it. One day at the bottom of a huge pile of mail, underneath the catalogues I found a legal-sized manila envelope with the papers that said the divorce was final.

On the morning I felt that I was ready to take up my work again in earnest and finish writing the Bancouer family story, I felt something that's hard to describe. I felt like a bulb that's sat frozen in the earth through the cold winter months and when the sun comes to warm the soil, it reaches up and pushes away the clodded darkness that's been both its sanctuary and the barrier to its rebirth into the world. Like the surge of life in new green tips touched by light for the first time, I felt a connection with Guillaume. Like folding a paper so the top meets the bottom I felt as if what happened in his life touched mine in that instant – when his grief at losing the only woman he ever loved to the very depths of his being had to be put behind him so he could marry Jerusha and give her all the love and attention a wife was due – and in that moment the sacrifice he had to make to fully live out the rest of his life became as real to me as my own.

That night I was awakened by a beam of light travelling across the wall of my bedroom. Sometimes the tugs on the river use searchlights to check how close they are to a mattress and that's when this kind of thing happens. But this time I saw – and this wasn't some ghostly image on the wall because it was clear enough for me to read it from across the room – the initials "A.B." and the date "1755" next to them. I was wide awake now. I got up and went to the wall to get a closer look but the light went out and when I turned on my table lamp the wall was just the usual wall. I didn't know what to think about what I had just witnessed. Since I was fully awake now, I went to the kitchen and made a pot of coffee. Then I turned on the computer and checked my email and found one from Liam sent just a few hours earlier.

He and Liz found something they knew I'd want to see – "A.B. 1755" carved into the wall of a cell in the old prison on Georges Island in Halifax Harbor. That made my skin crawl. I jumped up from my chair and knocked my coffee cup to the floor; that brought me to my senses. My mind churned as I mopped up the mess. If those really were Armand Bancouer's initials, they would be the evidence that Guillaume's youngest son had indeed been one of the Acadian delegates imprisoned there. For years and years now I've believed that was true because Armand and his wife Cecilie were exiled to North Carolina aboard the *Providence* when it sailed from Halifax in December of 1755. I just never had any evidence to prove it. Of course I wanted to see it for myself and put my fingers into the ridges of those initials etched into the rock. Liam said that Liz had tickets for the three of us on one of the historical society vessels for their annual visit to Georges Island and that it was she who invited me. Not him? I wondered.

A few days later I saw a news clip of them – Liam was being interviewed about his latest publication. He looked young and vibrant but Liz's face looked drawn and pale like she had a cold. He wore a pair of rimless glasses that I knew he didn't need because he has perfect vision, but they complemented his appearance. All I had to do was look at him to know his book would be a best-seller.

I could have asked them to send me photos of the carving but instead I flew to Halifax. I did it as much to satisfy my curiosity about how Liam and Liz were together as to see the letters and date etched into the stone. In my heart I already knew those were authentic.

Just the sight of her as I entered the arrival lounge told me he had used her up and already had other women in his life. After the divorce I began to understand him as someone who thrives in a relationship where he's always on top of things, never responsible for anything and, God forbid, never the one who's vulnerable. I wondered if that was something society teaches boys to expect and girls to cope with – or just something in his genes.

Liz seemed excited to see me because she thought she was the one who made it possible for me know for sure Armand had been one of the delegates, and said she couldn't wait for us to go out to the island together and have our picture taken with the carving. I said nothing to contradict her or dampen her spirits. I would have sounded insane if I told her about the searchlight and the writing on my wall.

By the time they took me to the airport to fly home to New Orleans I thought Liz looked like she was just about at the end of her rope. On the other hand, Liam seemed infected with some kind of new energy. I recalled that while we were on the boat crossing over to Georges Island I felt like I was watching two people whose neuroses had complemented each other for a while and now they didn't. It gave me the creeps just to think about but he was her problem now. And it was high time I got back to living my own life

A few weeks later I got another email from Liam. He and Liz were back to going full steam again. Their time frame began in 1749 with the first mention of their ancestors in the army records and since it included the years leading up to the Deportations they wanted to know if I'd consider merging our projects into a single publication.

I tossed off a tongue-in-cheek reminder that I was working on a family history based on the experience of the Bancouers, whereas he and Liz were working on a more serious kind of publication. But if they would consider an honorable mention in my book as one of the many sources to whom I owed my humble thanks, or having their names appear on the cover beneath mine – in smaller typeface of course – either of those would work for me.

He was such a publicity hound that I figured him not getting a top billing would be enough of a non-starter to make him just drop the whole idea.

The more I thought about it the less it made any sense to me that they would ever even ask such a thing, but when he emailed back after a few days and said they talked it over and were serious, I agreed to use whatever they provided me to expand my story to include theirs with the same understanding as I had with him earlier. My bottom line was that this book was my project and I would stick to my genre.

I never expected them to agree. And when they did, it didn't seem right that they gave in so easily to my demand for their diminished billing. Liz told me some strange story about how my work and my ideas would help them find some new path through what she called their 'academic miasma'. I knew they didn't need my creative efforts for what an evening sharing a good bottle of wine could give them – unless for some reason they were at a dead end and Liam felt trapped and was making them both so miserable that she was desperate for help to find a way out. I was genuinely sorry for her if things had reached that level. I suffered plenty during my marriage to him but at least I was spared that. I remembered the high-pitched sing-songy child voice he used when he felt cornered or when he was angry and about to do something reprehensible that he'd later refuse to acknowledge his responsibility for. Maybe he had talked to her that way and it scared her as much as it had me when I carried our child and I first heard that voice.

Here's what they doled out to me to work with: His ancestor was Sean Butler, a captain in the British army. Hers was Hugh Daiell, a major. There was a round lead ball slightly flattened on one side and some strands of black hair Liz found under a false bottom in an old trunk in her attic. She had been so excited about that find that she dropped everything else to come to Halifax to show them to Liam that night at Schooner Books when we both met him for the first time. I recalled she had a folded piece of paper in her hands that I thought had her name and contact information written on it. I thought she was just making a pass at him and missed the rest of it. Now that Liz brought it up, I don't recall him mentioning any of it to me. Ever. I emailed back and said I'd take a shot at it. Pun intended.

PART TWO: 1749 -1754

LONDON 1749

Etienne Massé tried to ignore the pounding on his shop door but it just got louder and more insistent and men began to bellow for him to open. He feared a return of what happened in his village in France when two old men argued the sins of their Protestant and Catholic grandfathers several times removed and a Papist mob surged through the town and killed Huguenot families and fired their houses. He just barely managed to hide himself and escape to England. Even now he believed Death yet stalked him, determined to find him no matter where he fled.

When he banged on his friend the apothecary's door that terrible day it swung open, its lock broken. The place was thoroughly ransacked and the shopkeeper and his family lay garroted with the pockets of their aprons slashed and the fabric hanging loose where it had been torn by grasping hands looking for coins. The smell of feces and bodies just beginning to rot hung in the room.

Instinct pushed him face down to the floor between the woman and her children; he closed his eyes and willed himself not to vomit. Papist vigilantes came in the door and looked around and then moved on to the next house. The pressure of a footstep on the floor and the light rustle of movement told him at least one man still lurked. Perhaps he had even heard Etienne hammer at the door and seen him enter. Etienne willed himself to lie still for what felt like hours after the intruder's weight no longer bent the boards.

The apothecary had taken a liking to Etienne and treated him as an apprentice. He showed him how to make potions and poultices and sew wounds. Now he had no more lessons to give but his fate showed Etienne he must escape from France before the fever of persecution spread.

He took the apothecary's implements and whatever herbs were left in their jars and put them into a pack. He knew his friend had concealed some coins – that must have been what the intruders sought. Beneath a floorboard that stuck out from under the edge of the counter he found the apothecary's hoard.

He took the dark woolen jacket from the clothes peg at the back of the shop and put several of the smaller coins in his trouser pockets, a few more inside the herbs in his pack and the rest in a pouch sewn inside the jacket's lining. Cautiously he peered out the door and saw burned buildings that still smoldered; a crosstree that could have held a sign or a noose leaned from the side of one.

The smell of charred wood mingled with that of roasted human flesh hung over the town like a miasma floated up from Hell. Grimy shapes black as devils poked through the ashes with sticks and pitchforks to search out any odd valuable that might have survived. All that day, hour after bloody hour the dark underbellies of sooty clouds smothered the town and spattered occasional raindrops polluted by columns of ash-filled smoke.

Like a gourmand inspecting a tray of morsels before making his choice a single large crow strutted among the bodies that lay as they had fallen on the road. When Etienne stepped outside the bird flapped away in loud protest of the intrusion and he pushed back into the shadow of the building, worried he might have been spotted. But the street was empty and as the day retreated from the town Etienne followed after it.

Filled with grief, he paid little attention to where he was headed. At La Rochelle he found an English trader and stood near the dock to watch it load. Satisfied there were few crew members and none were French, he climbed to the rail as the last box was carried on and offered the captain some coins for his passage. He boarded just as the vessel cast off to sail for London.

From the moment the ship was away from the dock Etienne stared at the widening gap of water knowing that his feet would never again tread the soil of his native land. For the next few days the strong speech of working sailors punctuated with curses was the first clash of men's voices he had heard since the day the Papists murdered his family.

Even before the sailors finished tying the dock lines Etienne's fugitive feet touched the soil of England. A man hailed him as he dropped to the wharf and called after him to stop. Heavy footsteps sounded on the wooden planks but Etienne ran faster, driven by fear and not caring where his legs carried him as long as it was away from the waterfront and whoever was in pursuit. He rounded a corner and came upon a market with stalls of produce and vendors hawking beer and hot pies. The spicy smells made his stomach growl and he slowed to make his way around bystanders and weave through the crowded square. Women with baskets made their way among the carts arguing prices with this farmer and that. He pushed his way through the noisy crowd whose language was hard and strange and stopped once to look behind to see if he was being followed. Just as he did a man a little way behind him stopped at one of the carts and began to finger the produce. He raised his head and looked straight at Etienne.

He shrank back and turned into an alley where he could watch the man. After a few minutes he saw him make a purchase and go off in the opposite direction without a backward glance. Etienne waited until the man left the square and then he slunk forth to buy food and drink with French coins, pointing to a meat pie and a mug of beer. The hawker looked at him strangely but took his money without complaint.

He ducked back into the alley where he thought he had a safe vantage to watch the market-goers. As he bit into his pie he noticed a movement in a window above him; a woman held a curtain aside and looked down at him and then turned her face as if to speak to someone.

Etienne slipped around the corner and a beggar who sat hunched against the wall reached up to grab the pie from him. Etienne snatched it away and ran off. The beggar cried after him, "Shear off a bit to share it with a sharp-set old man, for Christ's sweet sake."

In his panic he turned back toward the waterfront and it was then he found himself in a quiet lane. He stopped and looked around. A man walked past and offered a friendly greeting before entering a printing shop. Etienne heard the sound of the press and voices mingled in conversation. He noticed a narrow empty storefront wedged into the recess between the printing shop and a bakery whose clientele were mostly women. It felt like the perfect place for an apothecary shop.

Two windows looked out from a pair of narrow doghouse eaves that jutted out above the entrance. Etienne thought he saw the dim flicker of a candle inside and banged on the door. A wizened face looked down at him; in a quivery voice an old man asked, "What do ye want?" His lips pursed as he gave Etienne an intent look.

"Ye the landlord here?"

"And what if I be?"

"Look at this place ye wish to rent?"

The shutters closed with a bang and Etienne heard slow footsteps and the sound of a cane descending. The door groaned opened and the old man stood before him. Etienne was surprised to see a yarmulke covering the crown of his head. A wiry tangle of white hair escaped from beneath it and haloed his wrinkled face and a thin beard sparse as the worn pelt of an old squirrel draped down his chest. His blue eyes had the filmy look that Etienne had seen often enough in elder folk whose sight was disappearing; clothes that might have been new castoffs a decade earlier still served their purpose. Veined hands that seemed too large for such a frail body rested on the handle of a cane that looked like it might also serve as a cudgel.

The man lowered his voice. "Ye nivver see a Jewish man afore?"

Etienne was startled by the question. "Once when I was boy. In the market in my town there was a Jew that sold rugs. Some boys tried to take his head cover and my father called for them to stop. Later he spoke to me about it: 'As fathers speak so the sons act,' he said."

The old man nodded. "Ye be Papist?" He peered into his face as if he read the answer before it was even spoken.

"Huguenot." Etienne swallowed.

The old man pulled a large key from his pocket and offered it to him. He backed up to the bottom step and with both hands on the top of his cane he slowly let himself down. "Take your time. Wait right here," he said when he was settled. "Up and down too many times together has got too hard for my old carcass."

Etienne bargained with the landlord who showed surprising strength in negotiating for all that he seemed so fragile. Back and forth they went and at last they agreed on two shillings a week. Etienne would clean the place out to suit himself. That was hard work, but for the first time in many months he forgot his fear of being followed. He settled in and with his knowledge of herbs and his soft-spoken manner he soon became a neighborhood fixture.

Two years had passed since that day. He suffered fewer nightmares now and had even begun to believe that in Protestant England he had finally escaped persecution.

Now it was happening again – men pounded on his door in the middle of the night and shouted for him to open.

The landlord unlatched his window on the floor above and yelled at the men outside to be silent and be gone. One of them shouted they needed the apothecary to tend a wounded man. The old man slammed the window shut and pounded his cane on the floor to rouse his tenant.

Etienne warily opened his door a crack and looked out. On the threshold two men supported a red-haired giant who stank of beer and grinned from ear to ear as he cradled a gashed and bleeding arm. "Anyone follow ye here?" Etienne was anxious.

"Can hardly walk them others," a Scottish voice slurred.

"Bring him in." Etienne nervously stepped outside to look up and down the lane to see if anyone watched. "Bring him through and lay him down." He tried to swallow his fear and willed himself to act like this was any other man brought for him to tend and not the fearsome intrusion it seemed. He led the way into a small room with a cot that was curtained off from the front and lined with shelves filled with bottles and tins. A small table with a chair sat to one side.

Drunk as he might be, Hugh kenned Etienne was a Frenchman from his accent and his mannerisms. Etienne read his thoughts and looked the carrot-haired man straight in the eye. "Huguenot. From France, two years since. Name of Etienne."

"Ye'd be the bleedin' Devil for all I care." He slurred and mangled his words. "Patch m' wound so I c'd go back there 'n fight 'em. Show 'em who's fookin' better'n who."

Hal and John, the two men who brought him in, lifted him just far enough to pull his shirt off and then eased him back. Hugh struggled to raise himself but Hal planted his fist in the middle of his hairy chest and held him down. "Going nowhere. All o' them other coves arrested by now. How much help for that arm do ye think ye'd get when you're thrown in jail?"

Etienne looked around for a couple of candles. He took a straw to get a flame from his lantern and asked the men to hold the lighted candles and move them as he instructed so he could inspect the wounds.

As Etienne worked Hugh rambled on, his tongue thickening as he spoke. "Go t' taverns 'n drink th' glory of old times. Brawl wi' Britishers as think they're better'n Scots 'n have t' say so. Had t' settle it." Etienne shook his head; the corners of his lips twitched.

"I'm going to make sure this is the only place you're hurt." He began to poke and squeeze to look for any broken bones but the gash was all the damage he could find. He turned to Hal and John to ask whether they had the strength to hold Hugh down while he sewed up the wound in his arm.

Hugh choked back a curse. "I c'd beat 'em both silly, wi' m' bleedin' arm tied behind m' back," he taunted.

"Listen to that would ye? The Carrot'd ding us culls?" Hal chuckled. "And he says that after all we done to save him from fibbin' wi' them bit coves."

Etienne looked puzzled and John laughed. "Hal meant we deserve better, it being as we pulled him away from his fight with them rogue soldiers afore he got worse beat."

Hugh belched. "He's bloated." Hal grimaced and waved his hand in front of his nose.

John laughed, " 'Tis indeed the breath of stinking fish."

Etienne bent over Hugh and said, "Listen to me. Nothing's broken. I'm going to clean the wound with some vinegar and it'll sting. Then I'll sew it closed and your friends will hold ye down 'til I finish. In a few days the wound should be healed enough for you to pull out the threads. If the arm seeps or turns bad, you come back to me at once." Hugh nodded and looked solemn.

Etienne took up a pair of thin hooks and drew lengths of thread through the small openings at the ends. When Hugh saw them whatever shreds of bravado he had left deserted him. "They implements used to torture?"

Etienne tried to reassure him. "Don't worry. It'll hurt some but you'll heal. Then you'll forget this ever happened."

Etienne nodded to Hal and John. "Quickly." Strong hands grasped Hugh's shoulders while Etienne worked to close the wound. Then he dabbed it with vinegar and wrapped the arm in a clean bandage. Hal and John sat him up and pulled on his shirt and jacket. Then, even though his head still swam Hugh tried to stand and lost his balance. His backside hit the cot as he went down.

"Don't be so quick," Etienne said. "First let your friends help you to sit on a chair. Wait 'til your head clears before ye try to stand."

John brought the chair over to where Hugh sat on the floor. On a count of three he and Hal raised him up and placed him on the seat. "Lookin' dimber again like his reg'lar self," Hal said. Etienne turned away and began to wipe the hooks clean; the pungent smell of vinegar filled the room and made their eyes water.

Finally Hugh said he felt strong enough to leave and asked the apothecary's fee. "Come back when you're healed," Etienne told him. "Then we'll settle it." He led the men to the door and let them out into the night. When Hugh turned to look back the shop had disappeared. The light they saw when they came that way earlier was gone and the buildings on both sides of the street stood dark.

After a week Hugh could feel the stitches growing tighter. The wound itched and was uncomfortable so he set out to find the Huguenot. Hugh wondered about him as he did his best to retrace his steps, tramping down a couple of blind alleys before he found his way to the apothecary shop. There seemed to be no one inside but Hugh pounded on the door anyway and thought he heard some movement. Above him a shutter opened; the old man looked down and shook his head and then disappeared.

Hugh heard a door inside the shop open and close. Through the window he saw the apothecary approach. He was covered from shoulders to shoes by a leather apron.

Etienne recognized the shock of red hair and opened the door.

"Everything healed?"

The smell of what seemed to be burning herbs perfumed the air inside the shop. "I'm making a medicine. Could ye wait a few minutes 'til it's finished?"

He left Hugh to browse the shop while he went back to his workroom. The same bottles and flasks that gleamed so mysteriously in the dark of night like vessels of magical potions, looked harmless by day. They were all labeled: rosemary and other familiar garden herbs like St. John's wort, sassafras and digitalis. There were jars of leeches and even some with spiders spinning webs. Hugh knew what the leeches were used for and he had heard of spider webs used as a gauze on wounds that festered but this was the first he ever saw of anything like this. A tray of instruments lay on the counter; there lay the hooks used to sew his wound that had healed as quick and clean as Etienne had promised. Nearby was a large jug of vinegar. A bowl of it was set to cleanse the air. He heard the door again and Etienne appeared without the leather apron.

"Quite a business," Hugh said.

"Aye. Now sir, how's your wound healed?" Hugh removed his jacket and slid his arm from the shirtsleeve. "Wound looks good and healthy. Might sting when the stitches come out as the skin's grown over them a bit."

Hugh sat on the chair and gritted his teeth. A few drops of blood oozed when the deepest stitches were pulled. "You'll have a scar," Etienne said as he worked with sympathetic hands. He asked, "What's a Scot to do in London?"

"Serve with General Cornwallis," Hugh told him. "He's going to Nova Scotia to begin a new settlement. Halifax it's to be called."

"What kind of place is that, Nova Scotia?" Etienne prompted him to explain to distract him from the sting of the stitches being pulled.

Hugh laughed. "Once belonged to French, but British took it over. Now Cornwallis's leading two thousand settlers there to build a new town. Lot of them are soldiers and sailors mustered out of the services."

"And you're one of those?" Etienne said.

"I stayed in the army. Good man, Cornwallis. Fine leader."

"Sounds like all the settlers are to be men."

"What do ye mean by that?"

"Strikes me that if there's to be a settlement supposed to take root, there'd be women going along, families. Just men, no women? How's a settlement to last that way? Who's to do the cooking? Who's to keep the men happy? Men without women or families can leave any time they want."

"Some of them are married, some have children. But Cornwallis's mostly looking for single men to go. Lot of them signed, men who served with him and mustered out after the wars. Not afraid to work."

"Sounds to me more like he's trying to raise an army than build a settlement."

Hugh rubbed his chin. "Huh. Didn't see it that way."

Hugh toyed with the thought of asking was Etienne interested in such a venture. Surely an apothecary would be a desirable trade to have in a new settlement. The man seemed as good as any surgeon when it came to sewing wounds. Could likely set bones as well. Had a gentle manner unlike some of the butchers that served as doctors in the army.

Etienne asked, "What do ye expect of Nova Scotia? Deem it'll serve ye better there than here in London?"

"There's some fighting with French and Indians. Governor's taking a number of troops along to protect the colony. British promised land and a year's supply of food to settlers. By next year's harvest each has his own crops to keep him through the winter."

"But does that make it a better life? What about fighting?"

"Look," Hugh proposed, "Ye decide to join on, you'd go with the whole might of the British empire behind ye. Place's ours by treaty. We're going to take it all over from the French. They're to go out. That make it safe enough for ye? Catholics all gone? No more churchy wars?" A look at Etienne's face softened his tone. "Once the British secure the place nobody has a thing to worry about. If ye choose to go over with me then I'll look out for you." Hugh caught himself before he reached out to chuck him under the chin as he would to reassure a troubled child.

"Nova Scotia's meant to be under Protestant rule is it?"

"Already a colony of Britain, so yes to that. But French Papists live there now. They're who we're meant to replace. Governor Mascarene's in charge until Cornwallis comes. French Huguenot like you. Army talk has it he's fair to all. Been understanding of the French but not so as to let them rule him. When we get there with Cornwallis and all the new settlers he's bringing, it won't be long afore you'll see it all change."

"I'd have to know more about it." Etienne wondered what he must be thinking to say such a thing.

Hugh perked up. "Can't see a reason British would refuse to take ye. Unmarried man and ye have a trade."

After he left the shop Hugh realized Etienne hadn't even asked him for payment. He threw back his head and laughed. The apothecary couldn't be much of a businessman if he didn't have his hand out to get paid for doing honest work.

NOVA SCOTIA

They sailed from London in May, Hugh with his few assorted belongings and Etienne with all his stocks of herbs, instruments and potions. Cornwallis sailed aboard the Sphinx, a fast sloop of war that outpaced the rest of the fleet and was across the horizon before the rest of them even weighed anchor.

After the first day at sea the fleet of thirteen ships was so scattered that no one could see the whole of it. The *Everly*, the transport that bore Hugh and Etienne was among the half-dozen ships of a small flotilla that bent to the wind in company.

It wasn't long before someone learned Etienne was an apothecary. After that a growing line of men waited each morning to consult him about various remedies and complaints. Hugh thought that because it seemed he could cure most ills Etienne would easily establish his trade in the new town. But on a ship with hundreds of men Etienne felt nervous and exposed and was bothered by nightmares. While he could restore others' health he could not seem to heal himself of his troubled dreams.

The officers slung their hammocks in a compartment between decks separate from the settlers. After the first night aboard, the men who slept below decks near Etienne complained of his screaming when a nightmare took him. Hugh moved his hammock and slung it next to Etienne's; that seemed to comfort his friend. But on the first night he lay there, Hugh awoke sensing a presence that lurked in the shadow of a beam near him. He lay still as if asleep and gradually the face of another officer, Sean Butler emerged from the darkness. His sharp-featured face with its deep-set black eyes and the hair that gave the 'Black

Irish' their name were unmistakable. As Hugh watched Butler his lean whip-like body reminded him of a coiled snake ready to strike and made it obvious why Butler's men called him that. They only spoke it behind his back but Butler knew of it and bragged about it to his fellow officers. He liked the nickname but the word was out among the soldiers that he would kill any man he heard speak it.

Butler stood looking at the rows of hammocks; sleeping men as far as he could see filled the darkened space. There was no mistaking Etienne's small body twisting in his hammock or Daiell's red hair. Butler heard the men refer to him as "The Carrot" and knew that Hugh had laughed when he found it out. Butler could not forgive that he would accept such a common nickname.

Butler stared at Etienne with an expression on his dark face that looked like a sneer, as if there were something he found personally objectionable about him. Hugh lay there and watched him lean forward like a predator casting its shadow over a sleeping quarry. Soon Etienne began to twitch as a nightmare took hold of him and the Snake pulled back into the shadows. In the instant that Hugh rose to reach over and touch his friend's arm to quiet him Butler vanished.

"You're down there asleep and I'm up here bleeding to death! What keeps you?" Butler paced at the top of the ladder that went down the hatch to where the seamen's hammocks were slung and howled as if each drop of blood that oozed from the gash on his arm would be his last.

"See," he croaked with his throat dry, "I could bleed to death waiting on ye." Etienne climbed out of the hatchway dragging his instrument box behind him. The sky was washed clean by the rain that pelted down during the night and the wind still shook spatters of water from the rigging like the drops of blood that flew from Butler's wound when he waved his arm.

Men looked up from their tasks to see what the ruckus was all about and a voice asked, "Why's he want the apothecary? Should go straight to the doctor when he's got something sounds that serious." Another answered, "This one's sober and awake." The men stifled their laughter and bent their heads back to their work.

The line of men waiting for their various miseries to be tended to compacted into a half-circle to watch Butler's performance. Etienne pulled himself together as the icy fingers of his old fears began to pry at him and he cleared his throat and said as evenly as he could manage, "Pray let me see the wound, sir."

Butler extended his arm and looked around him with the expression of a spoiled child who had just got his way. "See," he said, "Managed to cut myself as I'm about to take my razor to shave. Would ye be so kind as to sew it up and bandage it?"

Etienne took hold of Butler's wrist and turned his hand to get a better look. It was a clean cut and not even a very deep one but blood still pulsed from it. He wondered if Butler had squeezed his forearm to keep it flowing and then was shocked by the thought. Still it reminded him of something else he had seen that was like that. It didn't look quite right for something accidental.

"What kind of fate put this man on the same ship as me," Etienne's mind flashed to the day when his friends had pulled a frog from the village pond and proceeded to torture it. He winced as he recalled one of the boys saying, "Pa told me the Bible says such critters as these are here for us to use as we want." Butler had the same expression of dark intent that he remembered seeing on the boys' faces when they looked at the doomed frog.

"Well?" Butler bent his face close and looked Etienne in the eye. "Is it serious?"

"I can mend it," Etienne looked away from Butler and took a deep breath as he carefully opened his instrument tray and his box of herbal concoctions.

Butler looked at the men standing in the line now circled tightly around him and waved the wounded arm to make them back away. "I've better things to do than stand around dripping blood."

"Odd kind of thing. How'd it happen?" Etienne ignored the bluster and drew Butler's attention back to the gash.

"Ship lurched. Lost my balance as I'm swinging the razor to begin to shave and reached out to steady myself. Next thing I know I'm bleeding."

"Would ye care to sit, Captain?" Etienne rose from his stool. "I've all I need to do the job right here."

Butler took the stool and the men pushed back to give the apothecary more room to work. Butler looked at his audience and said, "Let's see what kind of job the Frenchie can do for this." He gave Etienne an unpleasant look. "Better be a good one."

Etienne swabbed vinegar on the wound and Butler flinched. He used his fingers to press the edges of the cut together and the bleeding slowed and began to dry. Their faces were so close they could take each other's breath. Butler watched him intently and Etienne's face twitched with a nervous tic. Butler leered, "Make ye edgy to tend an officer's wounds?"

"A little," Etienne admitted. "I'm always concerned to do my best to help anyone who's hurt." He tried to keep his voice from rising out of control as he chose a straight needle and a piece of black thread to sew the skin together.

In a low voice Butler asked whether he had a tot of whiskey to dull the pain. Etienne said barely loud enough for the men nearest them to hear that he had none but would send a man for some if Butler wished it.

"Don't need it," the officer asserted in a loud voice and turning toward the men waiting for attention. Etienne bent to his task, pulling the thread delicately through the flaps of skin and Butler inhaled sharply at each prick of the needle. When Etienne finally finished Butler stood up and examined the closed wound. "It'll heal all right?" he blustered.

"Aye. Usually do. Come back when ye begin to feel the stitches itch so I can take out the threads and let it finish healing." Butler stepped away and looked at his arm as if to judge Etienne's work.

Then men waiting for the apothecary straightened up and the first in line stepped forward. "Watch yourself with that one. Got a bad reputation. Bully-rock, he is. No one else here says any different about him," the man whispered his warning.

Etienne was startled to hear him speak so candidly about Butler. "Careful mate," Etienne muttered. "Don't want to be overheard saying such things about an officer." He looked up at the man's open face. "Don't want you to find trouble ye don't need."

The man looked at Etienne with a grin, "Who'd there be to patch cuts and bruises if anything was to happen to you, matey?"

Later when Etienne stood on deck with Hugh and talked about the day he mentioned Butler's cut he sewed up and the comment the seaman whispered to him. "I still can't help thinking he did it to himself but that doesn't make any sense."

For a moment Hugh thought about telling Etienne how he saw Butler watch him during the night but thought better of it. Why add that to his fears?

"Man's a hector and got himself a reputation for striking from behind," Hugh warned. "Careful of that one."

"Men call him "The Snake" behind his back. I see it's less about his looks than about how he is with other men," Etienne said. "They're cowed by him. Just being near him made me nervous and afraid of him."

"Aye. Takes no prisoners so to speak."

"Why do his superiors put up with him?"

"See him as a man gets the job done. Don't care how. Officers like me see him as he is. Still have to work together with him." Hugh shrugged. "Just the way it is with the Army."

As the Everly approached the Nova Scotia coast the men saw a shoreline of endless unbroken spruce and hemlock extending right down to the water. The navigator brought his charts out on deck to confer with the captain and the mate. They thought they were near the harbor but they couldn't spot the break in the trees that signaled an entrance. The ship continued along the shore and the officers used their glasses to look out for it. The watch high up in the rigging sighted a fishing vessel out on the horizon ahead of the ship and shouted word to the deck. The captain ordered the helmsman to bear down on it.

The fisherman was ready to cast its nets when its captain saw the oncoming ship flying the British ensign and turned into the wind to wait for it to come along side. Amid a great clatter of idled sails the *Everly* shouted to the fisherman and asked their help to find the mouth of the harbor at Chebucto.

"Aye," came the answering shout. "You're on a course that took ye by the entrance a few leagues back." More shouts were exchanged and the sailing master on board *Everly* ordered a change of course to seaward. They ran away from the land for a time and then came onto a new course going landward.

"There," the navigator shouted. "See where there's a large island with a channel in beside it?" The sailing master nodded. "Go beyond that island to where another opening shows." The helmsman made a slight change of course and as they ran up the first channel the navigator pointed, "There. Ye see it? That's where we go in and turn up into Chebucto." The vessel steered into a passage between two headlands covered with spruce that blended to appear unbroken from offshore and the passengers lined the rails to get their first look at their new homeland.

An osprey sailed in the strong currents of air high above them, crying as it sighted a fish and dove alongside the ship. As the hawk rose with its struggling catch in its talons, a chorus of screeches and squawks heralded the abrupt departure of a flock of birds from a tree next to the water. Another osprey screamed and plummeted from on high and it too made a catch.

The preacher shouted, "Glory to God! We're here and what a wild place this is!" A great cheer went up; some of the settlers uncovered and bent their heads in prayer. A warm breeze came from the land as if to welcome the sea-weary travelers with scents of spruce, cook fires, and fresh-cut timber.

The sailing master's voice boomed and the canvas fell to the decks and was instantly grabbed up and made fast. The ship coasted forward losing speed and the passengers let up a mighty cheer; the men ashore paused in their work to watch the ship and answered with shouts of their own.

"Where ye been?"

"Ye bloats get lost?"

"Lot of fookin' work waiting for ye!"

"Ye bunch of lazy sods!"

"Get off that boat and get to work!"

The passengers laughed and jeered right back at them and waved their fists.

"Anchors away!" the mate shouted as the ship slowed. The crew let the anchor chain run and it plummeted through the water to catch the bottom and bring the vessel to a stop. A cannon boomed an echoing welcome from the deck of the *Beaufort*, and a signal flag ran up its yardarm to invite *Everly's* captain to report aboard.

LOUISBOURG

Abbé Jean-Louis Le Loutre found himself rescued from captivity again, this time by the treaty signed at Aix La Chapelle to end the latest war with Britain. "Bother!" he exclaimed thinking of how he'd crossed the Atlantic on his way home to France only to be taken on the high seas by the British and thrown into prison. Now, whether by a stroke of luck or an act of God – he preferred it to be the latter but either would do – he was free again and returning to Acadia on board La Chabanne with the new Governor of Louisbourg.

When Governor Des Herbiers first saw the priest he thought the prisoner's pallor of his boney face was the most remarkable thing about him. At first sight Le Loutre seemed a man worn down and care-ridden who would have all he could do to minister to his flock, if he even survived the passage.

"And where are they located?" Des Herbiers asked when they were first introduced and the Abbé mentioned his numerous Indian converts.

Le Loutre's sallow features warmed. "My Indians are in Shubenacadie now. On my return we'll move to Beaubassin to face the British across the Missaguash River, which we recognize as the disputed boundary between French and British territory."

"Ye sound more a military man than a religious," the Governor laughed. 'Your face takes on lively color as ye speak. Your enthusiasm for conflict belies the uniform ye wear." Then he was taken aside by his aide and glanced once or twice in the direction of the priest as the aide whispered in his ear. "Helped the Governor of Quebec did ye? So you're one of the warlike Jesuits. One time I'd like to hear your experience of that."

The Abbé gave the blessing each evening when the governor sat with his chief officers at dinner in the captain's cabin. Once Des Herbiers remarked how the French would overcome the English threat now that the treaty returned the great fortress at Louisbourg to them. "New Englanders must be furious at the British for giving Louisbourg back to France," he laughed. "I'd be were I them looking at such a towering threat so nearby to my country."

Le Loutre rubbed his hands in anticipation. "I deem ye plan to give them trouble." The Abbé was delighted by the thought of it and was all set to expand when one of the officers cut him off and turned the talk to the politics of the French court and the latest gossip.

On a day when the sky was clear and the ship sailed an even course the governor had a bit of respite from the demands of his administrators and the priest found him pacing the deck and happy to take up their talk where they'd left it off.

When Des Herbiers asked him point blank Le Loutre admitted that he had orders from the Bishop of Quebec to restrict himself to tending his flock. But he had also met with the Governor of Quebec and the military leaders. When Le Loutre outlined to them the ways he could help their cause by deploying his Indian converts to attack the English they wasted no time to enlist his help. He had left Quebec excited about his new role in leading the Indians against the English settlers. But before he had a chance to act on it he was taken at sea by the British and thrown into prison. He saw every reason now he was released to offer his help to the new Governor of Louisbourg.

"How do you propose to do that?" Des Herbiers seemed amused.

"My Indians will attack them at their work; they'll burn their buildings. They'll take away their stout English hearts to plant themselves on French lands," the priest exclaimed. His face glowed with anticipation.

"What would the bishop say if he heard ye speak such?"

Unabashed the Abbé replied, "He'd say I was to mind only the spiritual needs of my flock. Bring more savage souls into God's Kingdom. Forget political things and encourage the material things our people hold dear such as their land and their livestock, and especially their children's inheritance of all they own."

He touched the Governor's arm. "Isn't that what the French also seek – to hold firm to what the Acadians have already achieved?"

Des Herbiers mused, "Back in France and especially in my meetings with the King and his Ministers, all I heard was how important it is to build up the French empire so as to possess and hold all of New France and beat back the British. It takes real fighting men to do that. But I find there are only so many of those and I hear there are only enough of them at Ile Royale to hold Louisbourg safe."

"Aye that's so. And that's where my Indians can help. The Acadians worry about the British coming to push them off their land and put down their Protestant settlers. British want the land for themselves and their own kind and they'll take it any way they can get it. So we have to act now or how will anyone be able to stop them?"

"I take it you'll help us then? You'll put your Indians to harass them? You'll help the government? Needn't report any of those doings to the Bishop at Quebec."

The priest's dark eyes flashed as the Governor's request sparked a renewed purpose of his mission. He felt a surge of gratification at Des Herbier's belief in him. "We'll drive the British out. You'll see how we will."

At Louisbourg Abbé Le Loutre stepped from the ship into the long boat that would take him ashore and admired the sight of the fine stone fortress. He thanked God for its return to the French. Now that they had the fortress back, he would have protection closer by than Quebec for his mission in Acadia.

The harbor of Louisbourg was filled with English transports loading to take the British governor and all his people to Halifax. In all the buzz and excitement of the French Governor arriving to take back Louisbourg, no one noticed a priest stepping ashore to slip off into the countryside determined that soon enough the French would see what the Indians could do under his leadership.

HALIFAX

"Look there," Hugh pointed to the ships emerging from the fog as they came up Halifax harbor. Men and women lined the sides of the vessels and the crews knocked down the sails and furled them as the hulls slid through the water like a pod of great silent whales. As they dropped their anchors there was a babble of excited voices.

"Where'd they come from? They the folk from Louisbourg, ye think?"

"Must be. Who else?" Hugh counted the vessels. "Settlers with all their gear."

"Good thing," Etienne said. "Of all that come with Cornwallis the most that stayed are married men. As I thought when ye told me about this scheme."

Hugh looked at Etienne's smug face. "What're ye, some sage as predicts the future?"

"Merchant ships come from Boston to trade and take off men who can pay for passage to New England." Etienne shrugged, "Simple enough."

"One way or other it's rescued now with these folk. They know how to plant a new town. Done it all before."

From the deck of the *Beaufort* Cornwallis watched the ships come in, grateful for the people they brought. "At last we'll have Englishmen who understand what's to be done here," he said to his aide, "and enough of them to do the job. Raise the signal flag for Governor Hopson as soon as their anchor's down. Louisbourg's loss is to the gain of Halifax." Cornwallis's face relaxed into a confident smile. Hopson and his settlers would know how to get Halifax off to a proper start.

The Beaufort had a spacious cabin that Cornwallis used for his meetings and councils. Outside the sun reflected from the water and made a rippling of light across the ceiling.

The handful of Acadians who came to welcome him were held outside the cabin while the departing governor, Paul Mascarene read the copy of the oath of allegiance as it was signed by the farmers in 1727. He emphasized the words that were supposed to be omitted – the infamous exclusion about not having to bear arms against the enemies of the British Crown, notably the French and the Indians, supposedly written outside the margins of the document that Ensign Wroth had agreed to in order to get the Acadians to sign the document. Mascarene could clearly be heard through the bulkhead; as he read he was interrupted several times by heated exchanges between Cornwallis and his advisers.

The Acadians' faces showed no emotion as the talk went on inside until they heard Cornwallis insist the Neutrals must swear to the full oath. "They're subjects of the British sovereign, they hold land in the British province of Nova Scotia and of course they must swear to be as loyal as any other of the King's subjects. I can see no excuse for anything else." There was a murmur of agreement as the doors to the cabin opened and the Acadians were invited inside.

Brief pleasantries were exchanged before Mascarene read them the new Governor's declaration that contained all the things they expected to hear: they were chided for aiding the French contrary to their stated neutrality; they could continue to hold their lands and enjoy the free practice of their religion if they would help the new settlers the British were bringing to Nova Scotia; and, they must now take the full oath of allegiance to the British king.

One of the delegates drew a scroll from his wallet and presented it to Mascarene to hand over to Cornwallis.

"This is a letter signed by one thousand Acadians who agree to abide by the oath as it's already been sworn in Governor Philips' time. We've lived in peace with the British and the habitants wish that to go on as it has been. We're farmers who work the land; our crops feed us all, English and Acadian alike."

"Ye feed the French as well," Mascarene said, beetling his brows in annoyance.

"Aye, we've some trade with them. None's left to want."

While Cornwallis looked over the document the only sound in the cabin was the gentle creaking of the boat's timbers as it floated on its anchors. Someone coughed. Cornwallis exchanged an angry look with the man he came to replace as if he thought to reprimand Mascarene for being remiss in his duties to let things get to this pass. Then he turned his attention back to the Acadians.

"Remember," Cornwallis raised his voice. "You've had some three decades and more to go about as ye chose. Now there're new Englishmen come to build a settlement and there'll soon be more to come after them. We must keep the peace between us. To keep the order all in this province must swear the same oath – the full oath. Every subject of the King must be on the same footing and obedient to the same laws."

"We've been faithful to our oath. It's been a time of peace for English and Acadians. Why can't it stay like that?" The Acadian spokesman stood firm on his principle.

"I've just told you. The law can't be one thing to one man and a different thing to another. Surely you could understand the import of that. Now you must go back and explain that to the rest of your people. We mean to have peace in Nova Scotia and every man of this province sworn to the same oath of allegiance. It's only for pity of your situation and lack of experience in government that we try to reason with you. Otherwise it'd be a matter of our command and your obedience."

Once the Acadians were in the long boat and heading ashore the Governor growled his disbelief of what had just transpired. Paul Mascarene's laugh had a bitter edge. "Gives you a taste of what I've experienced in my forty years here."

Edward How nodded his agreement to the question when John Gorham asked Cornwallis why he would ever allow the Acadians to remain in Nova Scotia.

"Even if I'd the means to send them away as some wish, where'd they go but straight to the French and swell the ranks of their army?

Why give them that advantage?" Cornwallis shrugged. "The situation's just plain exasperating."

In October the screams of men working at a mill in the settlement of Dartmouth carried across the harbor and Hugh went across with a detachment. By the time they got ashore four men lay dead, one was dragged away by the Indians and one managed to escape by hiding in the woods. That one shuddered as he spoke. His wounds still bled and his voice quaked as he told of an Acadian called Beausoleil who led a gang of Indians that was urged on by the priest Le Loutre.

Etienne was tending to a sick officer in the cabin next to the Governor's office. He overheard the messenger deliver the news and Cornwallis order him to ride to Annapolis Royal for two detachments of troops to come and patrol the roads between Halifax and Grand Pré. Next the Governor dictated a written order for Captain Butler to take a large detachment and join the men coming out from Annapolis Royal. He emphasized to Butler that although they held the same rank, as the more experienced officer Captain John Handfield was to be in charge of all the troops. Etienne breathed a sigh of relief. Life was always easier for him when the Snake wasn't around.

It was quiet for a few minutes and then he heard a scraping sound as the governor pushed back his chair. The door to the cabin where Etienne tended the sick man opened and Cornwallis started at seeing him still there. "Overheard the news, did ye?" he cocked an eyebrow at Etienne.

"Couldn't help it, sir. But ye know I wouldn't spread it around."

Cornwallis' face twitched. "Well. Seems that now you're here there's something I've wanted to ask you."

Etienne stood up and faced the Governor. "What is it, sir?"

"We need a man to spy on the Acadians. Are they true to their word? Do most of them wish to keep the peace or are they becoming warlike? That's what John Gorham's telling me. Of course I know he'd use any excuse to take his Rangers out to look for trouble. I don't want to start anything with innocent folk but that one they call Beausoleil is already a prime troublemaker. Then there's that Papist priest Le Loutre. When he came here he was smooth and agreeable but now he's deceived me. I see he's just another one out to make trouble for us. We need to know what's what among the Acadians. Will ye help?"

"But I know some of them and they'd recognize me. Even if they didn't, the way I speak isn't as the Acadians do. Their language is different than mine so right off they'd be suspicious of me."

"But what if you pose as a priest new in Acadia? Survived a shipwreck down by Sable Island? Ye row to shore in a beat up longboat and land somewhere down on the eastern coast. Ye know Acadians'll help a priest. Even the Indians would offer to help you."

"Ye make it sound too easy. But what if I'm caught by British forces?"

"You can't tell them who you are or who sent you out. I'll put out a notice to the garrisons they're to send me any priest they take. That way I'll know if they do get you and I'll have you back here."

"What am I to tell Hugh Daiell?" Etienne looked mournful. "He's the one who talked me into crossing over the ocean and coming here in the first place."

"He'll be your contact. He'll know where ye are and what you're doing. If ye get into any trouble, Daiell will be the one responsible to get ye out." Cornwallis answered. "So there. What do ye say?"

"I'm only an apothecary and not made for such work." Etienne said with a tremor in his voice.

"I've no one else to send on such a mission. Need to have someone reliable. And we have a great need for such information. Can't order you to do it, but would ye think about it?"

"Could I talk it over with Hugh to see how it'd work if I did agree to it?"

"Of course." Cornwallis turned so Etienne wouldn't see the smile that creased his face.

In the officers' barracks, Butler crowed to Hugh, "Governor gave me a mission. Bet you'd like it yourself." He hesitated as he saw Hugh was unmoved by his news. Then he took a different tack. "Maybe you just want to stick close by here to be with your Huguenot boy. Afraid to leave him if someone else comes along and takes him away from you?"

"What do you mean by that?" Hugh's face darkened with anger.

"Plain enough. We all see how ye spend so much time with him. More than with your fellow officers."

"My time's none of your business."

Butler shrugged and turned away as if to dismiss him.

"Don't ever imply something unless you're ready to discuss it,"

Hugh's voice was a low, menacing growl. "Act like a man not some cark-ing snot."

Butler looked around at him. "You threaten me?"

"Are you making ignorant talk about me?"

"Governor doesn't want his officers fighting." Butler picked up his pack.

"Nor does he want an officer to provoke one."

"I'll see you when I come back."

"Yes, you will." Hugh spat on the floor at Butler's feet and stalked away.

Butler's guide led his detachment across country, following Indian paths to the Shubenacadie River and then turned toward Piziquid where they were to meet the troops from Annapolis Royal. When his scouts re-turned to report after a day of tracking through the woods ahead of the column Butler called a halt.

"About a league ahead of us there's a river called Stewiacke joins this one. Le Loutre had a large camp near here with many Indians. Appears they're all gone now."

"All of them?" Butler asked. "Any stragglers hanging behind? Good if we can get a prisoner." He recognized the name of the priest as the one the Governor wanted in chains more than anyone else. Wouldn't that be an important catch? He speculated if he could bring Le Loutre back to Halifax whether Cornwallis would promote him for it.

"No sign of anyone." The scout watched Butler's face guessing his thoughts and wondered if he thought it to be such a simple thing to catch the Jesuit who had already outsmarted better men than him.

"We'll have men to take the point and guard the rear as we go on." Butler went down the line telling his soldiers there could be Indians about and to keep a sharp lookout. Then he went back to the head of the column and waved them forward.

Word came to Halifax a fortnight later with an Acadian bringing in a wagon loaded with produce that a detachment of soldiers was am-bushed near the Shubenacadie River and the officer in charge was taken captive. Word went around; it was sure to be Butler. Hugh laughed as he told Etienne the news and slapped him on the back, "Takes care of that one sure enough. Lot of folk here be relieved when they hear this news. Not only you."

"Something I need to tell ye," Etienne said quietly.

Hugh turned his full attention to his friend. "Something wrong?" he asked.

"Could be. Cornwallis paced around like he had something on his mind and I could overhear him that time when I sat with that sick officer in the next cabin. When the patient fell asleep I was about to leave but first Cornwallis opened the door and asked me to come into his cabin. He asked me a lot about France and why I came to be here with the British." Etienne took a deep breath.

"Well, what'd he want? Don't keep me hanging."

"He asked would I put on a priest's robe and spy among the Acadians to see what's going on. I said I'd think about it. Wanted to talk it over with you. You're to be my contact here should I decide to go."

Hugh's face paled. "You don't know the danger of what he's asked ye to do. The French should they discover you, and British if you're captured and someone recognizes you, they'd both hang you as a spy. You'd be at double jeopardy. I'd say to tell him ye can't go."

BEAUBASSIN 1750

"Germain look what's in this pouch the Indians got hold of. Two warships ordered to sail with troops and materials for building a fort at Beaubassin." Le Loutre rolled out the plans stolen from a British courier and spread them across the table that served as his desk. "They come here," he put a finger on the spot that marked the village, "land their ships and get on shore to build a fort. Sure to demand the Acadians to help them."

"Ye think they'd do it? Help the British?" Germain rubbed his chin.

"British will remind the Acadians of that oath they all swore and that where they live is British ground. Then what do ye think they'll do?"

Germain stared at the plans. "They'll work for either side so long as they get paid for it. Cornwallis began the Halifax settlement and some went there to help build houses. Some helped the French over to Beausejour to build their fort." He put his finger on Beaubassin. "Draws the British here to do the same thing this side of the river. Acadians are caught between the French and the British if they stay here."

"We're thinking in agreement. Now the question is how to prevent that."

Germain scratched his head. "Seems too harsh a measure but the only thing I can see to do is we send the habitants away from Beaubassin. The British come and find nobody here, they can't demand anything of them."

"Acadians would never be willing to leave if we tried to reason with them," Le Loutre looked into Germain's eyes. "Time would be wasted with their talk and protests and then the British land here and it's too late to move them away."

"We'll have the Indians to help us. And when the Acadians argue we'll threaten to excommunicate any who keep to that cursed oath. That'll right enough put the fear of God into them."

As the month of April began and the farmers should have been working their fields the weather turned dark. Squalls blustered overhead and brought rain in wind-driven torrents. The priests went about the village and found the habitants of Beaubassin snug in their houses. After some stern arguments with their elders the priests ordered each family to pack the belongings they wished to save and take themselves and their animals across the river to Beausejour.

On the day after the priests finished making their rounds, they said the final mass in the small church of Notre-Dame-de-l'Assomption and Abbé Le Loutre preached a fiery sermon against the British and any Acadian who still kept to the oath of allegiance. After the final blessing they lowered the bell from the steeple and sent it across the river to Beausejour to show the people the Abbé meant business.

"Now go," Le Loutre screamed at the farmers who had just helped take down the bell and still stood outside the church in a hesitant knot. "Go before we burn this entire place to the ground!"

Germain went about the village yelling at the people, "The British are sailing to Beaubassin! There's worse to fear from them than to lose your houses if ye don't get away now!"

At first the villagers still resisted. "They'd nivver," one of the habitants insisted. "British can't just drive us off our land after we kept to the oath and been complaisant with them."

"Traitor," Le Loutre screeched, his voice going hoarse. "Ye don't deserve the sacraments, any one of you as clings to that oath. False to your own people ye be." The man quailed as the priest growled at him. "Go now or stay and watch the place burn."

Black smoke issued from a house at the edge of the town. "See that?" the priest stared down the group of habitants that gathered around to support their neighbor. "This is what's going to happen all over here. When the British come they'll find there's nothing left for them to take at Beaubassin."

The men looked where the priest pointed. "I see no sails of warships! There are no British here! It's you are destroying our homes! Why do you do this to us?" one of the habitants demanded.

"There's a whole fleet of cursed British sailing to Beaubassin right now! Be in this bay any time now!" He grabbed the farmer by the shoulders. "Get out before they come! Take your family! Cross over to French territory!"

Germain gave the signal and the Indians fired the thatch on more of the houses so that a pall of thick black smoke smeared the sky overhead. Then they torched a storehouse and the farmer ran for water to douse the flames devouring what was left of his grain. "Ye'll starve us all to death!" the man screamed.

"Better it burns than the British get it," Le Loutre snarled and ran after him and grabbed him by the shoulders. "Do ye think we'd leave anything behind to help the enemy? Any food ye leave stored here will go to their tables to feed them. Animals ye don't take are left for them to use. Don't want to lose any then ye must drive them along with ye!"

The farmer opened his mouth to protest and Le Loutre snapped at him, "Stand here and argue about it and ye'll lose everything. Ye've no time for that. I've been telling you." Le Loutre turned to the men who had run to help their neighbor throw water on his burning storehouse. He raised his fist and shouted at them. "Get away from here! Everyone!"

"Abbé," Germain called, "The habitants are going too slow. Fire's going to catch them up if they don't move quicker."

"I know what'll send them along. And now's the time to do it." Le Loutre ran off to the church and took some brush from a pile the Indians gathered and lighted a torch from the flames of a burning house.

"God help us all and forgive me for this," he muttered as he raised his arm and took his aim. He tossed the lighted kindling through an open window, and it landed against the dry wood of the altar where it caught with a rush of flames that licked at the timbers as they climbed up the wall. He called one of the Indians to bring another torch. He took it and held it to the doorway and watched the flames run up the outside of the building.

"Habitants see the church set to fire, they'll go safe across before the English come," he said to himself as he stepped away from the building. He fingered his beads and watched for a time while the church burned, ignoring the people who pushed by him in a panic and drove their animals toward the river.

BEAUSEJOUR

When the first puff of smoke rose above the treetops Jerusha was in the yard to collect the wash she had strung across the bushes earlier in the day. "Guillaume, quick! Look over to Beaubassin! The place is all afire!"

He pushed himself up with his walking stick and lumbered down the path to Aimée's rock with the smell of smoke growing stronger as he went. He could scarcely believe his eyes when he looked at the burning village. Flames licked the sides of houses and thatched roofs flamed like torches only to collapse into ash within minutes. He was shocked to see the black forms of the priests directing the Indians who ran around tossing firebrands onto the roofs of houses. Flames gushed from the windows of the church and some Indians took axes to smash parts of walls left standing where everything else around was already burned to smoldering ashes. The destruction sickened him.

Below his perch the river stood at low tide, the banks hemmed by wide margins of red muck. A silent stream of people burdened by their possessions churned through the mud along the path on the opposite bank, followed by sheep, horses and cattle. Smoke billowed outward from the ruins as the sky filled with rain-gathered clouds and soon the promised deluge pounded down as if Nature herself wished she could save the place and wash it clean with her tears.

The sight of priests chasing the habitants away from their homes horrified Guillaume. He couldn't ever imagine such a thing. Weren't the British and the French trying to settle the matter of the border between their provinces? Hadn't the English encouraged the Acadians to wait until the decision was agreed to?

Guillaume remembered how he heard the priests insist the British lied to the Acadians. The habitants pleaded with the priests what did it matter as long as they honored their old Neutrality? The Abbé answered with threats of excommunication for anyone who still kept to the oath and the priests who were charged with tending their flock of believers to bring them to salvation through the love of God now seemed bent on destroying the very lives of their people. Guillaume saw his world set to flames and turned upside down.

Like dogs herding sheep the priests drove the people along the shore to where they could ford the river onto French territory and a stream of refugees began to appear at Beausejour, most on their way to find refuge with relatives or friends who lived farther up in the marshes. Finally there were only those left who had no other place to go and the priests took them around to the habitants and asked each household to take in the very folk they'd driven from their homes.

To Guillaume's door Germain brought a couple with six small children. The adults were exhausted and confused by the tragedy that had wiped them out. The children's faces were tear-streaked and smudged with dirt; all of them wore neatly patched clothes grayed with ash and grime. Their eyes fixed on Guillaume, the parents silent and with a defeated look as if they felt themselves the culprits rather than the victims of the tragedy and must now face a judge about to pronounce sentence on them.

The littlest boy wore a cap that looked to have been handed down through his brothers; the woolen fabric was worn thin, the dye that once colored it was long faded by years of shielding its wearers from the elements. It sat on his head like a badge of boyish honor and his hair stuck out from the sides in a wild profusion of tangles.

In his heart Guillaume saw Jacques-Pierre at this one's age, scraped and torn by brambles as he played at being a hunter or explorer. How many times had he taken one of his boys in his arms and kissed his wounds to make them heal? Of them all, this boy's expression was the only one that was clear and untroubled. Would he, with the look of a child who would reach to experience everything that came his way as an adventure grow up to be another Jacques-Pierre? "Pray he doesn't change," Guillaume thought.

"Fire jumped to our roof. Precious little we could do to save the house," the man broke the silence and reclaimed Guillaume's attention.

He and Jerusha stared at the refugees and were horrified by their plight. "Can ye help these people, my friend? The British are coming in their ships," Germain continued his plea. "What else's there to do? They're coming to build a fort over there" – he pointed toward Beaubassin – "and that puts everyone in peril. Folk have to come over to French territory to save themselves. We burned the buildings to keep them from being used by the enemy."

Guillaume started to speak but Jerusha interrupted him. "Perhaps we can make room in the barn for them. It's a sorry offering but not much else we could do with a family of our own to worry about."

"Yours are all grown up now," the priest persisted. "Couldn't your boys share some space out in the barn and let the little ones sleep in the house?"

"We'll manage something," Guillaume said gently. He looked at the lines of fatigue etched in the priest's face. "We'll make it do." The couple burst into a tirade of thanks.

"All well enough," Guillaume told the man, "but I can see the day and not too far coming, when we've all to leave this place and take ourselves away from here." He mumbled to himself as he led the way to the barn, "and I hope to nivver live to see it."

In September when the British sailed up the bay and anchored near the remains of Beaubassin, they faced an army of French regulars and Indians led by the priests Le Loutre and Germain, who came up from behind the dikes that lined the shore and leveled their weapons at them.

Under fire, the British landed a detachment on the back of the peninsula, got around behind the backs of their attackers and routed them. They nearly captured both priests.

"Too bad," Lawrence remarked when he heard the report. "That would've been a good day's work." He looked up from the plans for the new fort. "We've got to build this soon as we can and settle in for the winter."

"The French have taken the best outlook over there at Beausejour," an officer remarked.

"Would've been the perfect place for us to put our fort," Lawrence agreed.

"But ain't that French territory?"

"Believe the French boundary claim that's so. Believe our claim the British own everything over to and including the St. Croix and maybe even to Pentagouet." He smiled. "I know which I believe and if it ain't true now I plan to make it so and the sooner the better."

BEAUSEJOUR

GUILLAUME, his Book, 1754

The heads of the giant oaks at the far end of the pasture stand against the deepening twilight like tufts of purpled wool. When I finish my supper and go outside the house, where once there were only open fields I see the French fort at the Beausejour ridge facing the British Fort Lawrence across the Missaguash River poised like two castles on a chessboard waiting for players to settle down and begin their game. Where only the calls of birds settling at twilight and the voices of animals in the barn once broke the silence men's voices carry down the wind.

Watching the trees fade I wonder do the souls entering the hereafter leave this world in such a way, melting from one place to take form in another? Once Jerusha and I leave our land to go live with Honoré's family will there be so little trace of the Bancouers left behind at Beausejour and of all we built here by the sweat of our labor?

In the morning Jerusha and I must leave this house forever. Armand will come to take us to Honoré and Marthé's home in Tatamagouche. Honoré's my second-born but he's Jerusha's first-born son. She cosseted him so much as a boy that when he went off on his own during his eighteenth year, she was as heart-broken as a girl jilted by a faithless lover. I tried to comfort her. I explained that boys must leave their mothers to become men, as I did when I was even younger than him. But she wouldn't hear it.

So quick is the time to pass. Now he's a married man with grown children, and Jerusha must learn to take her place in Marthé's household. Outspoken women, those two and I pray for a peace there such as I have enjoyed here, sitting on a bench by the kitchen window and hearing the soft tones of women's contented humming only interrupted by the clatter of crockery, just the familiar sounds of a harmonious household and none other. And I pray the dear God to hold back what I most fear about the future.

- Translation by Liam Butler, A.B., M. Ed., Ph. D.

The treetops were no more than dark patches against the last glimmer of light and then only if Guillaume squinted his eyes to search them out. Night settled around him and wrapped him body and mind in a darkness that turned his thoughts inward and sped them to the vexed question of what it would be like for the Acadians if the rumored expulsion ever came true. If the Acadians now agreed to swear the full oath of allegiance without the exception of 1727 as the British demanded, wouldn't that save them from exile? He drew on his pipe and pondered as he'd done time and again. But no matter how he turned the question around, he couldn't imagine the British would be willing to let them off so easily.

Just a fortnight ago the Abbé Germain came to hear confessions and say mass for the few Acadians still living near the forts. Guillaume found him sitting on the bench in front of the mass house that was to be burned the next morning when the torch was taken to his own home and spoke to him about the oath.

"Don't ye believe you've to be bound by it any longer," the priest said looking up at Guilluame. Struck by the intensity of his gaze Guillaume stammered, "Why do ye say so?"

The priest's eyes flashed as anger ruled his face. "English are our enemy. Always have been though many were slow to see it. Why'd anyone believe they had to swear to be loyal to them?"

Guillaume said, "For some who swore they did so because living in British territory means they're subjects of the British king. By law wasn't that what they had to do? Do ye say to those like me they're to believe some oaths are sacred and others are not?"

The priest sucked in his breath making a sound like a sob. Then he answered in the voice of a parent grieved by the sin of a child as if speaking of it took all his effort to keep patient. "Those things ye hold in your breast as truths are revealed by what ye do with others, by your deeds and words of trust – those things tell ye be an honorable man. Not any oath demanded by the British." He folded his hands in his lap as if to indicate he was finished with the matter.

But Guillaume was filled with a built-up store of anguish and ignored the priest's dismissal. "Abbé ," he said, "I did take the oath. If I forswear it and run about threatening the British then I break my given word. If I break my word then I'm not the man I believe I am." His voice rose and his words came faster. "If I'm not who I believe I am then who am I? How will my family know me? Would they trust any of my promises if I broke my word about something I've said over and again was as important to protect our lives as this oath?" The words poured out of him before he even realized what he was saying.

The priest recoiled. "It's what ye believe in your heart that makes you the man you are, not keeping a faith with what ye thought was once your duty but can't be any longer. Neutrality has outlasted the need for it. British don't care any more if ye keep to their oath – that's not to say they wouldn't chastise ye for breaking it – but they've no more respect for it. They'll use it to run roughshod over you as ever it pleases them to do and they'll make ye suffer for it. But with or without the oath, in your own heart you're as steadfast as ever. It's just that what the British want from you changes from time to time. What they want now may go far beyond what you pledged when ye first took the oath and ye may not be ready to give it."

Guillaume felt what the priest said was completely foreign to him and he didn't want to credit any of it; it turned upside down what a man was taught all his life to believe in. Beaubassin was burned. The priests' mission was no longer to preach love and forgiveness but to burn Acadian homes and drive the habitants over to French territory, incite them to fight the British and excommunicate any of them who disagreed with the priests about Neutrality.

A man could lose his way if he followed with that kind of thinking. It came to him in a flash and it felt like this was the nub of it all: Le Loutre was besotted to have the French rule over Acadia again. Because he believed his influence could make it so the Abbé was leading the Acadians down what Guillaume believed was the path of their destruction and Germain followed his orders.

As he had done every night after his talk with the priest he turned Germain's words over in his mind. The only answer for the Acadians had always been Neutrality, and they'd clung to it all these years. So far they had survived the threat of exile by walking a narrow and perilous path between two mighty empires ruled by kings who sat on faraway thrones. Now Le Loutre's actions threatened to tip the balance against them and Guillaume couldn't just take back his oath and do what the priests wanted without giving up his belief in himself as a truthful and honorable man. He was vexed.

It was years since he gave up the illusion that either the French or the British would ever leave them to toil in peace. The oath the Acadians had already sworn contained no words that could be used to force them to fight against the Indians or the French. Guillaume signed it when the British came to Beaubassin in 1727 because in his heart he believed that only by pledging their Neutrality – regardless of whose territory they lived in – and keeping faithful to it would the Acadians manage to survive.

From the start the British used the oath to try to bend the Acadians to serve their purpose. Were the British any worse for doing that than the priests were for forcing the people to forswear the oath by threats of excommunication? The British used their government and the priests used their religion to lever the habitants to do their will. He wrestled with it time and again. Was he being faithful to what he truly believed, or was he being just plain stubborn by clinging to what was truly past?

He thought how his sons must see things. Men of his own generation believed that the oath was their best protection but it was too subtle and fragile an argument in these mixed-up times for their sons to accept. The younger men seemed to see how the oath amounted to no more than a pile of ashes and Neutrality was no shield of protection to their way of thinking. He wondered if he could ever learn to accept that.

The bitterness of abandoning their family home the next morning made his heart feel as shriveled and sere as the ashes of Beaubassin lying compacted in the soil under the heel of the British fort. He cupped the bowl of his cold pipe in his hand and stared at it as he remembered his first sight of Acadia. So much had changed from those days. He knocked the ashes from his pipe and watched them scatter onto the ground. He hoped if the Acadians were exiled from their land, he wouldn't live to see it happen.

A blanket of stars filled the cloudless sky; he looked up at them and wished he could rise to fly off into their depths and lodge suspended among them, remote from the looming struggle. The kitchen had been quiet for some time; the hearth was banked for the night and again Jerusha called him to come to bed. He pushed himself up from his bench, stretched to relieve his stiffened joints and trudged inside to spend his last night in his own home.

Dawn painted the tattered clouds like so many flags with the glorious

colors of a new day and then the sun went high enough to leave them
bleached of their rich hues. Armand walked alongside the horse as it
pulled the wagon up the bluff toward his parents' home thinking about
how the Bancouers had gone from lives of contentment to lives measured by their suffering. From a distance he could see Guillaume standing in the dooryard gazing out over his empty fields.

The last pieces of baggage were soon loaded onto the cart and the
house stood empty. It looked sad and forlorn, like an ancient relative
holding out his arms begging to be taken away with them and not be
left behind. The kindling crackled and they smelled the wash of smoke
from the fire started at the back of the house to light the torches that
would be set to the thatch once they were on their way. Guillaume
looked away from the house with his jaw clenched and Jerusha held a
handkerchief to deny her eyes the sight of something beyond the suffering of mere pain. Armand handed his parents up into the wagon. He
pulled on the harness to start the horse to walk and the cart creaked
slowly out of the yard. Jerusha turned for a last look and seemed about
to run back to plead with her nephews to stop but Guillaume tightened
his grip on her hand and said something to distract her.

Armand guided the wagon slowly over the rutted roads. His concern for his parents made him conscious of the way the cart lurched
and bounced when he urged the horse to move a little faster. The pots
and pans and crockery Jerusha had lovingly used over the years to prepare her family's meals chattered and banged as they went along. She
carried her Sevres teacup in a handkerchief tied to her bosom and when
Armand noticed it he recalled the cup his father used with the chip in
the bottom that'd smoothed and dulled over the years. Guillaume examined the chip when it was new, wondering how he'd been careless
enough to have caused it. Armand didn't dare tell him it flew from its
perch when Jacques-Pierre wrestled with him and sent him flying
against the shelf where the crockery stood.

When they reached Tatamagouche that evening, Honoré and his
family brought them into the house to sit on real chairs with soft cushions. After a bowl of soup to warm their insides Guillaume and Jerusha
were put to bed and soon fell asleep.

"Ordeal for the old folk, eh?" Honoré squinted at his youngest
brother.

Armand shrugged his shoulders. "Mother began to cry as soon as she was in the wagon. Hard on both of them to leave it all behind. The boys torched the roof just after we left. Then they went and helped the priest light the mass house roof. Smelled the smoke for a while before the wind changed and took it away." He noisily cleared his throat.

The brothers went outside with their pipes and murmured late into the evening about their memories of growing up at Beausejour and how they helped to cut and place new thatch when the roof needed fixing and whitewashed the walls because their mother wanted everything clean and bright and the times they went adventuring in the woods and fields. They wondered what had become of Paul Dancing Crow; there was no news of him or his family since the attack on Annapolis Royal a decade ago. They knew only that he and his family had not come to Baie Verte. Armand's eyes teared as he thought back to the days when they were all younger and life had not yet begun its real business with them.

Next morning Guillaume awakened to the bustle of a working farm. He lay there with Jerusha still sleeping beside him but after a few minutes he got up and dressed. Marthé directed him to the hand pump that stood near the door for water to wash his face. He felt barely awake when a visitor came bearing some freshly baked loaves. Marthé saw her and went outside calling, "Cecilie, come inside. What've you got there?"

"Mother sent you some bread she baked this morning. Said you've guests and could use it." Cecilie handed Marthé the basket.

Armand heard their voices and came to see who was there to visit so early. He didn't know all of Honoré's neighbors; this was someone new to him, but when he looked at the girl he felt as if he had known her all his life. Marthé noticed the way they stared at each other and asked, "Have you met each other already?"

"Where do ye come from?" Cecilie asked him after they said their names. "I know I've seen ye hereabouts before but ye don't live near."

"I've a farm over by Maringouin, where the surf pounds against the rocks and the tide runs in from miles offshore and when there's a storm the waves can touch the tops of the highest hills around." The nervous words spilled from his lips with the speed of the tidal bore running up into the river.

"Pa says that here we're well away from all that, especially places where storms can flatten the crops and the British might sail up and cause mischief. Does your wife fear such things?"

"I'm widowed," Armand said sadly. "But it's a fine place to farm and to fish."

Cecilie gave him an appraising look. "I'm glad to meet you but I've to go back to mother. She's waiting for me to help her with the cooking."

Armand took a hesitant step toward her and searched her face. Something powerful flowed between them and set every nerve in their bodies atingle; he took another step closer and she still didn't retreat from him.

Cecilie looked at him directly and Armand said, "I've come here to bring my parents. They're to stay with Honoré and Marthé but I've to go back home to my own place."

Mathieu heard the voices and smiled in anticipation as he came outside the house. Mathieu was in love with Cecilie since they were children and planned to marry her. He went to her father once to speak to him about it but the old man told him, "My daughter needs a husband who's established himself and can properly care for her." Then as if he thought to take away the sting, he added, "You've some time, son."

But the naked longing he saw in his uncle's face as he looked at her stopped him in his tracks. Then he saw that she looked back at him the same way and their faces told Mathieu his time had run out and Cecilie was lost to him. Tears filled his eyes; he crept away unnoticed.

She looked at Armand as if no other person existed in the world. "Mother told me I'm to come right back home and not inconvenience you."

He stared at her wondering how such a lovely creature could ever be a bother to anyone.

"She still thinks of me as a child," Cecilie laughed nervously when he spoke his thought. "Although that's far from being the case."

Armand pulled himself together. "I hope to see you again before I leave."

"That's of course up to you, however ye wish."

"Perhaps I'll come to thank your mother and father for their kindness to my family." The longer he looked at her the more he was determined to take her home to Maringouin as his wife. He thought, "And while I'm there I'll lead around to ask them for your hand in marriage."

Her face softened as if she heard his thoughts and she said, "I'd be glad of that."

PART THREE: 1755

MARINGUOIN   (June)

Armand was awake. He had been so ever since the moon set and the last shreds of night returned to darken the sky. Cecilie lay peacefully asleep; a smile passed over her face as her hand moved to her breast. How lucky he had been to marry her. He felt as if he had come to life all over again, with his youth returned to him and he ran his hand down her body, his touch light and sure. She stirred, opened an eye and he bent and kissed her and the flames he had thought were banked now burned anew. If ever there was a paradise on earth, he was sure it was here and now.

After a time he rose and went outside to feed the animals pastured in the dooryard. It was then he saw figures in the mist hanging off the shore. He rubbed his eyes but this was no trick of the fog. A fleet of British ships filed into the bay to drop their anchors behind Cap Maringouin. He counted thirty-eight vessels in addition to three naval ships showing British colors. Troop ships and their escorts could only mean they came to attack Fort Beausejour and wrest the land from France. Had the Boundary Commission finished their work? Had it made England the master of all Acadia? But there'd been no courier bringing such news.

"Cecilie, wake up," he spoke from the doorway. "The British have come with a whole fleet of ships. Means nothing good I'd say. We must warn the fort. They can't know these ships are here all hidden by the fog. So many it's sure they're bent on making an attack. You've to come with me. When they send troops onto shore it'll be too dangerous here for a woman alone."

PONT a BUOT

The men lay in wait above the gutted bridge wondering when the enemy would show their faces. The air was still so burdened by the stink of charred timbers that Robert thought he might never again breathe clean air. He remembered how he and Mathieu went to Beausejour five years earlier with their uncles Armand and Jacques-Pierre to stand up against the British.

Then, and not even a year since, as Armand drove Robert's grand-parents away they helped Jacques-Pierre set fire to Guillaume's house. He had seen his uncle hesitate with the torch crackling in his hand, and the tears in his eyes when he threw it onto the thatched roof. As the house burned to the ground its ashes seemed to spit out lifetimes of memories as they popped and smoldered. He would never forget the sight or the smell of that. The stench of the burned bridge just down-wind of him thickened in his throat and made him cough.

Up the ridge beyond the French positions lay the homes built by the Acadians forced out and chased across the river when the priests burned Beaubassin. Some of the uprooted families came back and planted themselves there so they could cross the bridge and still work their land on the British side of the Missaguash. Even the dire threats of the priests could not force the habitants to completely abandon the farms that had fed them so generously for three generations. What Le Loutre wanted them to do, to go higher up in the marshes to dike less productive soil on the French side of the river made no sense at all to the farmers, especially now with the large number of refugees that had to be fed.

Whenever the Acadians asked the British about their intentions they sang the siren song about waiting for the Boundary Commission to agree where the line between British and French territory lay. Then the Acadians who lived on the British side of the line would just swear the full British oath of allegiance and life would go on much as it did now. The farmers who listened to that wanted to believe that swearing the full oath was the biggest change they had to look forward to.

When they told Le Loutre what the British said he shrieked at them, "It's lies, all lies! Why do ye believe it? Don't ye see what they're up to? They're to divide ye from your own people! Put you under their law! They'll tax you and make ye live dirt poor."

But it didn't change their minds and since it was the priests and not the British that burned Beaubassin to the ground, the farmers stayed convinced they'd soon make their return and rebuild their village. Now push had come to shove and what the British intended was out in the open for all who had eyes to see.

Mathieu and Robert were among the men charged with wielding the torches to light the roofs of the Acadian houses if the French or-dered a retreat from their position. The Indians lay down the hill near the French, ready to rise up and fight alongside them. Above them on the ridge in front of their houses the farmers made barriers of tree roots and branches that the soldiers said were worthless protection against cannon shot. The farmers hovered behind them, and stayed well out of the range of musket fire.

Jacques-Pierre gave them the once-over when the decision was made to burn the houses if there was an order to fall back. "Those fools will run the minute the first shots are fired."

The evening was peaceful and the men murmured to each other there might not be another like it before the English came to attack the redoubt. The river swelled with the inflowing tide; swallows whirled in the air above its muddy edge and the men waited for signs of the British approach. Sentries lighted their pipes to drive off insects, careless if there might be an enemy spy lurking nearby. The men watched for any sign of boats riding the current and scanned the open stretch of marsh on the bank opposite the redoubt.

Ensign Baralon was charged with defending their position. "They nivver come as Indians and French do in thin lines and each man moves tree to tree. They be noisy and out in the open to boast their numbers." He spoke to someone dug in next to their position.

"This was French mounting an attack, there'd be Indians come with canoes on the current and getting to shore somewhere down the bank; then they slink through the woods to attack and cut the enemy's throats in the middle of the night," Robert whispered to his uncle, his eyes lit with excitement.

"Still could be, if they've got Rangers with them," Jacques-Pierre mumbled. "Not like Grand Pré back in '47," he thought. A shiver ran up his back as he recalled how he'd lain in the snow that freezing stormy night waiting to attack at half three in the morning. "Fookin' nightmare that was," he muttered.

Robert whispered, "None but animals moving in the grass." He tensed and rubbed the birthmark on his neck. An owl hooted from the dead branch of a tree that hung out over the river and the men became edgy. As the bird swept down on a meadow vole there was a nervous chuckle when someone whispered, "Business as usual."

At midnight they were relieved from duty; Robert felt like he'd barely slept when the dawn chorus awakened the marsh and the men stirred and broke their fast and resumed their vigil.

In the forenoon a messenger came from the commandant at Fort Beausejour to warn Baralon of a large force of English marching away from Fort Lawrence. The messenger repeated De Vergor's orders — hold ground and at all costs prevent the enemy from crossing the river.

An hour later a sentry sent back the word, "English're comin'! Hear 'em a league off, they're so noisy."

Robert's eyes flashed. "Wait'll they see they can't get across," he chortled.

"They'll expect that," Jacques-Pierre replied. "They'll have planks with them to try to rebuild the bridge. It's how they work." The marsh birds fell silent; after a while the faint grump of booted feet accompanied by the rhythm of pacing drums could be heard. The noise of the advancing army grew louder and then the first of the redcoats broke from the cover of the forest. A stream of soldiers with weapons shouldered marched into the open where the road tracked the edge of the marsh.

Baralon ordered the French swivel guns to take their aim at the British line and screamed the command to fire. The Indians rose; their blood-curdling war cries temporarily confused the enemy. Robert's lips tightened into a menacing grin and his eyes darkened and he gripped his gun. Muskets and swivel guns opened up from behind the redoubt but the shots flew over the heads of the enemy; only a few were downed before they could kneel to load and return the fire.

Monckton roared for the British cannon to be brought up and the French soon found themselves on the receiving end of heavy fire. Cannon balls struck the redoubt and disabled the swivels. Baralon shouted orders to fire the Acadian huts and retreat. The French fled through the woods throwing the useless swivel guns into a bog and firing intermittent rounds from the cover of the trees at the British who brought forward the wooden planks they carried from their fort to span the river.

FORT BEAUSEJOUR

Thomas Pichon was privy to every piece of mail that came and went from the fort. As the secretary of both the commandant and the priest he understood the whole fabric of plans and activities at Beausejour. And he knew how the British valued that kind of information. Without it they would have no warning of Indian raids planned against them or of French troop strengths or even how useless were the commandant De Vergor's and the engineer De Fiedmont's time-consuming and fruitless arguments over the defense of the fort. That was not to mention the intelligence he had provided them about Le Loutre. The priest had drained off all the men he could get and sent them farther up in the marsh to build dikes, leaving few pairs of hands behind to work on buttressing Beausejour's defenses. Pichon hoped that when all of this ended – with the British masters of Beausejour of course – he'd be richly rewarded for his efforts.

A commotion at the gate drew the commandant's attention. De Vergor looked up from the dispatches, disappointment and anger coloring his face faster than the fog rose over the river when he saw what was happening.

"Damn it! What the hell is this? What's fookin' Baralon's men doing back here?" He slammed his chair back and went out the door.

Pichon looked through the window near his desk and watched De Vergor advance on a stream of men pushing by the sentries to get into the fort. The commandant was only midway across the parade ground and already screaming his rage.

Pichon was pleasantly surprised by how easily the British had forced these men to turn their tails and run. His last letter to Captain George Scott, his contact at Fort Lawrence, sent before the British assault began included a compendium of the French plans to protect Beausejour. Colonel Monckton must have found it all useful in planning his attack. Pichon got up from his desk and went outside to see what was happening.

The men at the gate who clamored to get into the fort were ordered to defend the redoubt. Pichon knew a retreat was not expected to happen so soon even in the enemy's wildest expectations. The British must be really kicking some ass out there for these men to be back at the fort so soon after they were ordered to hold the crossing. Pichon hoped it meant an early surrender so he could go over to the English and not have to spy on the French any more. That had become all too tiresome. He dreamed of a post in Philadelphia, a city where an enlightened man would find himself welcomed.

Enraged shrieks brought him back to the present as De Vergor's voice carried clear across the parade ground from where he screamed curses at Ensign Baralon and jabbed an energetic finger at his chest.

The Ensign was only a junior officer, young and untried and Pichon had thought De Vergor mad to entrust him with the most important element of the French defense – that of keeping the British on the other side of the river. Now the French could never hold the fort against them. The man yammered his explanation. "Nothing we could do. They started with their cannon, got us good with a couple of shots and put out the swivels so we're down to muskets. Fookin' useless Acadians run over the hill to get out of range. Then they're gone. Fookin' Indians yelled war cries and loosed some arrows and then they're all gone too. How'd we suppose to hold off the whole English army without help and we all get killed?"

"That's the point, don't ye see it? It's your duty to fight to the death if ye must and keep the enemy back on the other side of the river. Miserable fookin' fool! Get out of my sight," De Vergor fumed.

Pichon knew what would be next to come. De Vergor was furious his simple strategy to protect the fort had collapsed so easily and his face burned like an ember in a bonfire. He stomped toward Pichon and shouted, "Get De Fiedmont and the priest. Bring them to my office. Right away!"

Pichon drew back a step.

"Do it now!" De Vergor shoved Pichon and he stumbled; then he regained his balance and ran for the supply building where he'd last seen the engineer.

"What's this?" De Vergor demanded of De Fiedmont. "Our positions so defenseless? How'd that get to be this way?"

"What d' ye mean, 'how'd it get this way'? You've heard me complain over and again there's no fookin' men to do the job to buttress the fort and the redoubt to make them defensible. What'd ye expect? Acadians don't work when we have any here to help. Then the Abbé takes most of them off up river to build fookin' dikes and no one's left here to work at the fort." De Fiedmont gestured to the priest, who sat watching the interchange. Le Loutre heaved his shoulders with a theatrical sigh.

"When the Abbé gave orders to burn Beaubassin and forced people to move across the river to the fortress, I fookin' begged both of ye, give me men and materials to strengthen the walls." De Fiedmont was going hoarse with irritation. His voice cracked. "But no, the priest insisted all the men had to work the fields to grow crops. What good's that to us now? Unfinished dikes. Not even a crop to harvest. At least when they drive us out the fookin' British won't get no use of any of that!"

"You've both been too busy making yourselves rich by selling off the stores in the warehouse – which were purchased to feed your men – to care about anything else," Le Loutre countered. "Is it any wonder no one wants to work when they see you scooping the gold into your own pockets?"

Pichon thought he looked like a pot that was about to boil over and worked to contain himself from laughing at the image of steam bursting from the priest's ears. And, as with all these tirades the longer the shouting lasted the more hopeless and diminished De Vergor became, and the more that drove De Fiedmont to scream and curse in frustration. Once they reached the climax of their dispute it'd slump to the usual conclusion. The changed tone of their voices reclaimed Pichon's attention.

"I went to France to plead with the King himself for funds to build dikes so our people could settle on new land and farm it," the priest's voice sounded reasonable but his face was filled with rage. "And he saw fit to support what the people need to live. But not you if ye can't make money out of it."

De Fiedmont's voice became a growl. "Beausejour falls to the fookin' English, what good are any damned dikes? King's gold or no, French and Acadians will all be gone." His shoulders slumped as if he felt the end was coming and his voice trembled. "Why put the people to labor at a foolish task that'll fall to the advantage of the damned English if the fort's lost? What's wrong about setting the men to build defenses to protect the fort before ye start in to build useless dikes?"

Le Loutre's face twisted, "People need to live. Can't live if they can't farm. Why can't ye see that?"

De Fiedmont spoke as if the argument no longer even mattered. "What I see," the engineer fought to control the anger in his voice, "is if the habitants ain't here to live on the land because the fookin' English took it over, none of your damned schemes matter even so much as a tittle."

"But the habitants will yet be here even if the fort's taken," Le Loutre insisted.

"Ye don't see it, do ye?" De Fiedmont said. "Beausejour falls and the English take all of Chignecto. They'll burn and pillage and the habitants will be killed trying to escape. Then the English will stand at the walls of Louisbourg. And if we can't hold this fort it'll be we who'll be blamed to let that happen."

Pichon's eyes widened as he thought, "He's really given up hope the fort can hold out. Now he and De Vergor will be more concerned to keep hold of their ill-gotten gains than mount defenses against the British." A shiver went up his spine as he thrilled to the thought of the coming British victory. "The sooner Beausejour falls the sooner I'm away from these bloody fools and collecting the pension the British promised me."

Pichon smirked as he listened to the argument and wondered, if these men were the leaders of men willing to die for France, would he have been so quick to turn his coat and spy for the enemy? But what had really driven him to spy was that none of the French had ever been willing to give him his due. He knew he was a better man than they were ever willing to acknowledge. Pichon could never understand why they valued men like the commandant who were nothing but empty uniforms and trusted them to lead. But the British were different. Pichon knew they recognized his worth.

De Vergor's face flushed. "Now it seems I'm to lose my command because we're to be swept away by the British. De Fiedmont's right – but what's any of it matter now? We're lost."

"Aye. So it remains to stiffen the men in their will to fight when the English come outside our walls." Le Loutre said. "Speak to the men. You're still their commandant. Tell them we're Frenchmen" – he thumped his fists against his chest – "patriotic and proud. We'll fight and die here before we give up our fort."

"And you're the priest who's out there every day giving the same men your own separate orders and threatening to excommunicate them if they don't do as ye say. You go and tell them they're better off to die in this miserable Hell-hole than give it up. Maybe they'll listen to you, but I don't believe any will. We'll only see more of them go over the walls to escape."

De Fiedmont wrung his hands. "We'll put up as good a fight as we can. But the British have more men and weapons. And soon as they get close enough, they'll fookin' have us. Only question is how fookin' many are to die afore it happens?" He went to the door and turned to De Vergor. "I'll send some men out to see where the fookin' English are and what they're up to. Beausoleil wants to take some men to try and take a hostage. Maybe we could learn something."

"At least that one knows how to fight," De Vergor sniped. "Send him out." The commandant stood with his chest thrust forward in a dandified pose. When De Fiedmont was out the door he turned to Pichon. "What time's my dinner to be ready?"

Early the next morning De Vergor sent for Pichon to meet him in one of the bomb-proof shelters. Concussions from English cannon fire shook the ground and loosened clods of soil from between the support beams in the roof. Pichon hated being underground; he didn't like the earth close around him and its rank smell of decay. Leave that for the dead so far as he was concerned. A shower of soil landed in his hair and he shivered. Quickly he raised his hands to brush away the dirt and it brought him back to a time that he and a couple of other boys played around an open grave in the churchyard. One boy who was older and larger pushed him in and threw some handfuls of dirt on top of him. He screamed for help but the boys ran off and left him alone to try to scramble up the side. He dislodged clods of earth as he tried to climb out only to slide back down and finally he sat in the bottom of the grave, exhausted. He decided to try climbing slowly up the side, scooping out places to hold his feet and moving gently from one hold to the next. He fell forward when he got to the top onto solid ground. For a month afterward he suffered from nightmares and from that time on he was terrified of being buried alive.

De Vergor was speaking to him. "I've sent riders to Quebec and Louisbourg for help. We'll only have to hold out long enough for the first relief to get here. Then we can pound them from the fort and from the rear. We'll have them in our grip." He sounded hopeful. Pichon gave him a skeptical look. "Think we can hold out long enough?"

De Vergor grimaced as the engineer came into the shelter. Pichon wanted to escape from the two men as fast as he could. He knew that what was going to pass between them would occupy them for some time and they'd never miss him. He eased away from the building confrontation and started back to his desk.

A messenger who'd ridden hard and fast from Louisbourg waited for him by the door. The man greeted Pichon and handed him a letter.

He turned it over, saw the seal and was certain he could guess the message.

"Know what it says?" Pichon asked.

"Nothing that'll be a help to ye, I wager," the man replied coughing. Pichon sent him off to the kitchen for something to eat and drink. With a resigned sigh he put the letter in his pocket and went slowly back to the shelter to hand it over to the commandant. By the time he got there the priest had arrived.

"The Unholy Trinity," Pichon thought. He stood outside and listened to the tone of their voices until there was a pause; then he stepped in and extended the letter. De Vergor looked at him hopefully as he took it. He broke the seal and read it silently and his face clouded with anger. "No help's to come from them. They're besieged by New England ships and can't get any troops out of the fort. No men to spare if they could. We're to wait for help from Quebec." His hands shook. The priest stared at the governor with glistening eyes.

"What're we to do then?" Pichon voiced their general concern.

The engineer shook his head. "We've not the stores nor water nor powder and ball to last long enough for help to come from Canada." He looked De Vergor in the eye and his voice rose to a shout. "Too much time and men have been diverted away who should've been put to work to protect us from being fookin' attacked," he slammed his fist down on the table and shifted his eyes to the priest. The familiar argument was in danger of erupting all over again. De Vergor deftly headed it off. "After all it isn't as though we're at war, our countries. We've been attacked in time of peace." He made it sound like the complaint of a reasonable man astonished by the unimaginable.

A cannonball struck the curtain on the opposite side of the fort, shattered a section of wooden pickets and drove into the packed earth.

"Don't seem to stop the fookin' English that sentiment." The engineer snorted with disgust. "Damned Acadians, they're all so nervous they can't tell a fookin' fart in the dark from a cannon shot. Either one's enough to send them running over the walls. Said if they stay to help us the English will hang any of them caught here with us. We should've been building up our fookin' defenses, but instead," he spat in disgust, "we're fookin' lulled to sleep by thinking we're at fookin' peace." He rolled his eyes and brought them to rest on the commandant's perplexed face.

Le Loutre held up his hand to stop the engineer from stalking out of the room. "If ye say I'm to blame for it then so be it." His voice was meeker than either of them had ever thought possible. "I say we more need to decide what's to be done now we've to defend the fort and all these men inside." He looked at De Vergor. "They need to rally to what they're supposed to fight for."

Pichon stared at the priest. "You really think if he" – he pointed to De Vergor – "was to go out there to tell them it's better to die defending this place for France than to give it up to the British, they'll rally to that? Ye think that won't send the whole lot of them over the walls and off to disappear into the forest?"

Le Loutre spread his hands like a suppliant. "Be that as God wills."

"Makes no fookin' sense to me." The engineer got up and left. Pichon's eyes followed him for a moment and then he slid outside and walked away.

Le Loutre and De Vergor faced each other inside the bomb-proof casement. Where the beams that held the structure in place were seamed with earth, the smell of the soil that leaked through was like that of an open grave. The priest's hand was raised as if in blessing when a bomb hit the opposite shelter dead on. Men inside it screamed and shouted in agony.

A soldier came to the entrance of their casement to report to De Vergor who slid back into his seat, his eyes staring at the priest's face. "What do ye say now about dying here, Abbé?" He jerked his thumb toward the destroyed casement. "Like those unfortunates?"

Le Loutre's face filled with fear. "Are they all dead?" He emerged from the casement and stood before the opening to look at the bloody scene spread out before him. Some of the bodies lay outside the destroyed bomb shelter, others were buried inside. Father Etienne was already there to pronounce the last blessing as rescuers dug out the dead and wounded.

Soldiers ran helter-skelter inside the fort with no other apparent purpose than to avoid being hit by the next mortar shell whenever the British chose to fire on them again. Pichon came to see if De Vergor was hurt.

"They're good marksmen." The commandant chose his words to sound dismissive but De Vergor seemed as if he was already defeated. "We've no hope of help from Louisbourg. And Quebec's too far away.

We may have had a chance if we'd kept them on the other side of the river. But now fookin' Baralon's let them come over and build another bridge so close to us they bring over all their cannon to pound us with, I think we have to surrender before we lose any more people." He seemed as if lost in a trance. "Yes, we've no more choice so that's what we must do."

Le Loutre was frightened by De Vergor's hopeless tone. If the commandant planned to surrender at the first opportunity then what would be his own fate? He was wanted by the British and he couldn't allow himself to just fall like a ripe fruit into their hands. He knew the British blamed him for the ambush that killed Edward How back when Fort Lawrence was new and he commanded the Indians at Beausejour. No question about it but they itched to get him in their clutches and had a price on his head. What would they do to him if they did capture him? They cared nothing for the Catholic religion and had no respect for priests so he didn't have the lever of their beliefs to manipulate them. His thoughts took a dark turn and he shuddered at the thought of torture and of another imprisonment. He wanted France to win this war but he shouldn't have to suffer martyrdom to make it happen. Maybe his bishop was right that he should have kept to providing for men's souls and not act like the soldier he was never ordained to be.

Now the British had them surrounded. It was too late for him to run for it with his robes flapping, without them seeing him a mile away and chasing him and taking him down. What would he do?

He saw a woman run from one building to the next. Her direct purposeful movement through the milling sea of confused men caught his eye. The answer was so simple it amazed him and he went after her. His lips moved in silent thanks to God for showing him his escape. He followed her to where a small group of women, Acadian wives who had come to the fort with their husbands – all dressed in the grays and browns of plain homespun clothes, some with a touch of lace about the collar or a white cap or shawl edged with a bit of lace to relieve the drab colors of their dress – huddled in a corner inside the storehouse.

"Daughters of Christ," he whispered as he lifted his hand to bless them. "There's naught for ye to fear from the enemy. They'll not harm you. They don't make war on women. They'll let ye leave in peace."

One young woman sniffled. "Is that true, Abbé? We're told they're devils and if they take the fort, oh, oh,..." and her voice caught and she burst into tears.

"And our husbands who came here to fight with the French? Will they be hanged as traitors as the English threaten? Oh what'll we do?" The whispers became sniffles and sobs.

"No, no, no. The Governor will see they're pardoned. He'll insist they're released."

The weeping stopped as the women heeded his answer. "You'll all be reunited with your men, no fear of that."

"But what're we to do? How're we to get out?"

"You'll go out in advance of the French after the fort's been surrendered. The Commandant will arrange it all in the terms of surrender and the British will accept it." The women looked relieved. Then he gave a great sigh. "It'll be a different story for me, a priest," he said in a quiet voice.

"Oh, Abbé. Surely the British wouldn't hurt you, a man of God?" One of them spoke and the rest gathered around him, concern written all over their faces. "They've put a price on my head but don't ye worry about me. I'll be all right."

Their faces filled with alarm. "Can't we do something to help you?" one woman asked.

"Perhaps… perhaps ye may," he spoke very slowly as if he'd just thought of something. "No, I can't do that," his voice was so soft he seemed to be speaking to himself.

"What is it, Abbé? Tell us. Is it something we can do for you?" A woman's face, furrowed with concern, was only inches away from his. He squeezed a tear. "I couldn't ask that."

"What couldn't ye ask, Abbé? If God plants a seed in your thoughts isn't it because He's about telling ye he wants ye to do something?"

He groaned. "I just thought – no, I can't say it."

"But ye must tell us so we can help ye."

He cleared his throat. "If I could dress in woman's clothes then I might have a chance the British devils wouldn't see me leave. I could leave the fort with all of you."

"You'd lead us?"

"No, good wife, I'd go among ye, as the least of you brave women."

"Yes, Abbé, yes. Of course. How simple it'd be. I've an extra dress."

"And I've a shawl."

"Ye could wear this." A woman blushed as she held her best lace cap out to him. He shied from it.

"Not your prettiest cap for an old crow like me. Ye must wear it yourself. All I need is a dark shawl; something old is best."

"See how easily you're dressed?" another said as she handed him the garment. Then she laughed. "Tuck in your crucifix, Abbé." He looked down, dismayed. They'd spot that for certain. Then they'd really make him a laughing stock.

"You'll go like Joseph taking Our Lady Mary off into Egypt to escape Herod's men. Walk with me, Abbé and carry my babe."

"Bless you all, my daughters. We'll watch for our chance to leave. Father Etienne will stay with your husbands and leave when they go."

The British officers sat easily on their horses and watched the French march from the fort with their flags flying and drums beating, going out along the north road toward Baie Verte where they were to board English transports to take them off to Louisbourg.

"A brave sight," Colonel Monckton was sarcastic. "March better'n they fight." He looked over his shoulder to ask the men behind him, "Anyone find the priest?"

"Not a sign of him." Captain Scott replied. "It may be he's among these so-called Neutrals. We'll go man by man to search him out."

"Your spy said be sure and get his chest. There's stored all kinds of secret things supposed to make our hair curl." Monckton snickered. "Wonder what all that could be? Find him and bring him to me."

"Men already searched his room and found no chest. Gone somehow, like him."

Monckton turned to Colonel Winslow. "Never did find if your farmers could put up a fight."

Winslow's steady gaze did nothing to discomfit the younger man. "We came here willing enough to help. It was them that couldn't oblige us."

Monckton snorted. "Take a detachment of your militia to Fort Gaspereau and accept their surrender. Maybe you'll find the priest there."

Major Robyn Jenkins looked at the prisoners standing around on the parade ground inside the fort, all supposed to be Neutrals and all of them under arms contrary to the oath. Anger and sadness for these hapless men warred inside him. How could the Acadians be so blind they

couldn't see the tide was running against the French? They were foolish to answer the French call to arms. That should have made them
traitors to the British crown, a hanging offense. But under the conditions of surrender they were to be forgiven, even the young priest Father Etienne who was taken right after the British entered the fort. At
first they thought he was the Abbé. They arrested him and passed him
on to Major Hugh Daiell for questioning, as Lawrence ordered. Monckton and his men were disappointed to find he wasn't Le Loutre after
all and furious that the man they wanted made his escape. The young
priest seemed dazed by the news that Le Loutre went off and left him
behind. "No honor among thieves," one of the officers muttered and
they all laughed.

Hugh had to control his delight to discover that Etienne was safe
and that he was accepted by the Abbé, although Le Loutre didn't seem
to trust him enough to take him along when he made his escape.

"I didn't see him leave. I don't know how he got out of the fort.
When the surrender came, the women left first and then the officers
and men came out." Etienne frowned as he described the scene to
Hugh. "Had to be he disguised himself. But how'd he manage it, and
where'd he get away to?"

"That's easy enough," Hugh said. "Was it me I'd head for Louisbourg by the quickest route. Take the road to Baie Verte, was I in disguise. Then go by boat to Ile Royale. Monckton's sent that New
England colonel, Winslow to take some troops and look for him along
the road north. Take the surrender at Fort Gaspereau. Any luck he'll
find him." Hugh grabbed his shoulders and laughed. "Ye did your mas-
querade so well that French spy Pichon nivver kenned who ye are.
You've told me a lot that says Pichon sometimes invented and decorated what he told us. Monckton's pleased to get the measure of his
worth. He says you're to keep on making the rounds of the Acadians
and learn whatever ye can. Soldiers and officers don't know you're our
man, so be careful with them. Butler's here if you've not noticed. Don't
let him get close enough to recognize you. Nivver can tell what murky
stuff rules in that black soul of his."

As Etienne walked back to where the Acadians were being held he saw
Major Robyn Jenkins standing deep in concentration. He wanted to
speak to the officer if only because he seemed a decent man. Three

Acadians who were the focus of Jenkins' attention stood nearby. One had his feet wrapped in cloths. Etienne was curious to see what was the reason so he went over and asked the man if he had no shoes.

"Not that, Father," Robert said. "Infection. Feet swelled up. Just have to wait it out."

"I've a salve made from pine balsam that could help you. Got the recipe from some Indians for frostbite cure but it does much else. I'll look in my satchel and bring ye some." As Etienne turned to go he noted that Major Jenkins still stared at the young man he just spoke to. He saw the officer's face soften and wondered what he might be thinking. Then he noticed Captain Butler looking at Major Jenkins as if to make note of his interest in the young man. Etienne shuddered as he remembered how he felt when Butler gave him that same appraising look, as if he was searching out a meaning for something he didn't quite comprehend. Etienne recalled the anxiety in Hugh's voice when he warned him about Butler and turned away.

Jenkins stood like a statue as he relived memories of the days he had traveled with Ensign Wroth in '27 to get the Acadians to swear to the oath. He wondered how many of these men had taken the oath of allegiance, but then it occurred to him that most of them were too young to have been more than babes in their mothers' arms back then. If his son had lived might he be here among them? As the thought entered his mind he felt there was something familiar about the lad with the bound feet that drew his eyes like a magnet. The Acadians walked off to join some of the other men milling around and waiting for whatever the British would do next. Jenkins shook off his thoughts and went over to where Monckton was gathering his officers to give them their orders.

An unexpected thought came to Jenkins when he looked at Monckton – with the strength of troops now at the governor's command, between his British regulars and the two thousand militia Colonel Winslow brought with him from Massachusetts, the British could wipe the province clear of the French. Jenkins was startled by the insight, but the more he turned it over in his mind, the more he saw how this situation developed into a strategy for taking action to sweep the Acadians out and do away with the French threat at the backs of the British. It was just the sort of thing Governor Lawrence, once he recognized his advantage would insist had to be done. And what better chance would ever present itself than now?

Jenkins felt someone next to him. His sergeant cleared his throat to be recognized and asked was he ready to review the captives?

Jenkins ordered him to stand the Acadians in ranks and then march them past single file to throw down their arms. As the prisoners moved by some of the other officers came over to watch. Jenkins saw men pass by who looked familiar to him, maybe even brothers or sons of Aimeé Bancouer, the woman he'd loved and whose face he thought he could still conjure. He forced himself to focus on the men's faces and the growing pile of weapons, noting they were fowling pieces and squirrel guns and not the weapons of fighting men. It was pathetic the way the French had compromised these farmers.

Captain Sean Butler came over to stand beside Major Jenkins just as Mathieu's turn came to surrender his gun. "Stop!" he bellowed. Jenkins asked why he'd yelled at the man. "Looks like he might know something," Butler answered.

"Well?" Jenkins gestured. "What're ye waiting for? Go ahead and ask him."

Mathieu looked at his feet and waited.

"Where's the priest?"

Mathieu dropped his squirrel gun onto the pile, "Over there tending to the wounded." He motioned toward Etienne's back.

"Not him. That other one – Le Loutre. You know who I mean."

Butler moved in front of Mathieu to block his way. "Look at me." His black eyes bored into the captive.

"Where'd he get to?" Butler insisted.

A chill ran down Mathieu's spine and his knees went weak. He felt as if he was being overcome by a darkness that sprang from deep inside the man and threatened to suck the life out him.

"Ain't seen that one." He could barely manage to get his voice above a whisper.

It seemed an eternity to Mathieu before Butler finally stepped aside and ordered him to move along.

Jenkins watched Robert as Butler questioned Mathieu and saw his eyes go dark with anger. He saw in Robert's expression the rage of a man untethered from the world around him – the blackness of eyes opened to the very bottom of the man's soul. He remembered the same look in the eyes of a soldier who had a narrow escape from death. He had judged that as an experience powerful enough to rule the man for the rest of his life. Jenkins shuddered and drew his eyes away from Robert's face to resume his search for Le Loutre.

The next two men gave the same answer. Butler turned to Jenkins. "They all say they saw no priest. Jenkins, do ye think it's possible Le Loutre disguised himself to throw us off the scent?"

"Captain Butler?"

"Yes?" the raptor-like stare unsettled Robyn for a moment. Then he said, "Please address me as 'Major Jenkins'. You know the proper etiquette."

"Yes sir, Major Jenkins." Butler was clearly annoyed by the reprimand.

Jenkins hesitated before he continued. He had just thought of a way to get rid of Butler and finish his search without that officer's unwelcome comments and interruptions.

"All those men we caught, we've rounded up to single file and drop their weapons. So far there's been no man that matches the description of the priest. Fewer left of the Acadians now. Could it be he changed clothes and went with the French officers when they surrendered?"

"That's it! He disguised himself and got away from us." Butler stalked off and Jenkins knew he was headed straight to tell it to Monckton. His lips twitched as he tried to control a smile. The General's aides weren't simple. They'd likely already solved the mystery of the Jesuit's disappearance for themselves.

Jacques-Pierre, Mathieu and Robert joined the group of prisoners milling about in the center of the fort. "Can't stay here," Jacques-Pierre insisted. "Rumor says English are bringing a ship to take us all away. Once they get us aboard there ain't no way to escape."

"Ye see the Abbé? The way that officer looked at me and questioned me I thought he was the Devil himself come looking for the priest." Mathieu shuddered.

"Not after the attack. If the British had him, he'd be somewhere locked up. They wouldn't still search for him." Jacques-Pierre stared at Butler's back as he strode across the parade ground toward the gate.

"I saw him," Robert said quietly. "In woman's dress. Went with them. Clean out the gate ahead of those useless French."

"Ye sure 'twas him?" Jacques-Pierre demanded. "Or was it just the ugliest female ye ever did see?"

"Seen him enough that I should know him," Robert insisted.

"We got to get out of here fast as we can."

As evening came they mixed with the crowd of habitants milling about and began to edge over toward the breach in the wall. Etienne was tending a wounded man nearby; Mathieu went past him, slipped through the breach and knelt down to wait for a diversion some of the Acadians were to make to distract the sentry. Then he was gone. Jacques-Pierre and Robert were about to follow.

"Hold there! Stop!" A sergeant whose white breeches were smeared with dirt and whose thick dark eyebrows drew together in a scowl, waved his rifle at them. Jacques-Pierre called, "Lookin' for a place to take a piss is all." The soldier used his rifle to nudge them toward the waiting officer. Major Jenkins looked them over. He told Robert to comer closer and asked, "What's your name, lad?"

"Robert." He looked down at his bandaged feet.

Jenkins thought if his son had lived he'd likely be his age and his voice coarsened with emotion. "Last name?"

Robert looked up and met his eyes. "Bancouer."

Now Robyn was deeply shaken. When he last saw her in Louisbourg Aimeé told him their son had died, but as he stared at Robert he wondered if he saw a heart-shaped birthmark in the grime smeared on his neck. "Where'd ye come from?" he demanded.

"Baie Verte."

"Always there?"

"Lived at Beausejour before."

Robyn felt as if a hammer hit his chest. Was it pure coincidence? During the British advance on the fort he had looked around to see if he could identify the place where he and Aimeé had lain together, but the houses and barns that had once stood there were no more than piles of ashes and there were no more stands of trees along the path that came up from the river. Nothing about the place was recognizable. It all felt foreign to him.

The Acadians waited. Jacques-Pierre danced a broken jig, hopping from one foot to the other.

"Go on, fellows. Answer nature's call, ye say ye must."

Robyn needed time to think. Again he wondered could this man be his son? Did Aimeé deceive him? He couldn't imagine her doing such a thing. His impetuous demand for her to give up his son to him had made her angry although she had tried to hold it in. But when she had told him the boy was dead she was so listless and her voice was so low and so sad that he had believed her. But what if this young man truly was his son? She mentioned a birthmark on his neck that looked like a small heart, one side larger than the other. He saw Jacques-Pierre and Robert relieving themselves by the wall of the fort and when he looked away from them he saw Butler's eyes fixed on him. He frowned and Butler turned and walked up the steps to the sentry box.

Robyn decided he had to settle the question for good. He would seek the boy out and get a good look at that smudge on his neck; then he would have his answer, one way or the other.

Now Robert was standing among a crowd of prisoners over by the breach in the wall. He had seen men do that before and recognized it as an unmistakable sign they were going to bolt. He should call out a warning to the guard but instead he turned his back and walked away.

A shot boomed from the sentry box. "Got one of 'em running for it." Some of the British soldiers cheered. The black plume in the officer's hat identified the shooter as Captain Sean Butler. "Make good target practice," he called. "Better than rabbits. Send me another."

Robyn was horrified. Who was shot? Was the boy dead? Wounded? He ran to where the sentry stood by Butler, who squinted into the gloom.

"There's the body. Remarkable shot, sir." The sentry pointed and handed his spyglass to Butler.

He took the glass and held it for a moment. "A Frenchman name of Voltaire said, 'God is on the side not of the heavy battalions, but of the best shots.'" He cackled. "Didn't think I was so learned or so capable did ye?" He turned to Robyn and winked. "We've got both the shots and the men. Here you are Major. Take a look for yourself. Want to try if ye can make the shot good as me?"

Robyn was aghast to hear Butler brag about shooting an unarmed man in the back, never mind his boast. Did Butler think to make him an accomplice to such a foul deed? His hand shook as he took the glass and put it to his face. He thought he saw a movement. Before he even recognized his thoughts he prayed, "Please God, don't let my son die." Why'd he pray like that? Wasn't his son already dead? But if he wasn't, could that be his boy out there lying dead or wounded? Robyn had to know if the downed man was the one they called Robert.

Butler was still talking. "They're traitors, after all. Should be going to hang. That one's saved the trouble of jigging about in the air."

"What're you talking about?" Robyn was upset and now he was getting angry. "Monckton's given them the pardon as was in the terms of surrender. You know it as well as any officer here. Whatever you think of them, you've no right to shoot them down."

"Look at them," Butler pointed to some men clumped together in the middle of the parade ground. "All look alike don't they? How'd ye tell one from the other? All look like Frenchies, not like us." He spat in disgust. "Can't even put up a good fight."

"Maybe it's as you say but once a man surrenders it's unlawful to shoot him. What's the glory in that, to shoot an unarmed man in the back? Murder's the crime of sneaks and bullies. Anyone who does things like that doesn't deserve to be an officer."

Robyn Jenkins climbed down from the sentry box and barked at his sergeant to come with him. The young priest Etienne came over carrying his pack of ointments and bandages and asked could he help. Jenkins gruffed, "Come along then. Be quick about it."

From the sentry box Butler watched them get ready to go. "One ye know where to find, Major. Best go with your pistols primed in case there are others out there who find you," he grinned but his eyes were cold and angry. He shifted his gaze away from Jenkins and stared at the priest, who reminded him of someone but he couldn't think who it could be.

"I don't need your advice, Captain," Jenkins shouted angrily at him. The twilight was deepening as they made their way across the field.

Mathieu hid in the brush while Robert wept with his uncle's head cradled in his lap. He noticed the sound of grasses being thrashed and saw indistinct shapes coming toward them. "They must be looking for us," Mathieu whispered, noting that one of them seemed to be wearing a robe. "Could be it's that priest, Etienne."

"Ssst!" he expelled a breath between his teeth to get Robert's attention. Before he could warn his cousin the three men were on him. The sergeant leveled his pistol. Jenkins knelt beside Robert and looked at Jacques-Pierre. He recognized the man who'd said he had to go take a piss. "Went a long way for that, friend," his voice was gentle. "Don't matter now."

As his eyes flicked to Robert's face he believed he saw a heart-shaped birthmark on his neck and his emotions nearly got the better of him. The boy held Jacques-Pierre's body tight in his arms, sobbing and moaning. Robyn wanted more than anything to put his arms around Robert and embrace him as tenderly as the boy held his friend but he controlled the urge to do anything more than look on.

Etienne knelt by the body, gently closed the eyes and spoke the final blessing. He put his hand on Robert's arm and asked, "Was he your friend?"

"My uncle." Robert's breath caught in a sob. Etienne squeezed his arm and said, "Now he rests in God's peace."

"Major Jenkins? Keep looking to see is there another?" The soldier kept his pistol leveled at Robert.

"No," Jenkins said. "We'll go back to the fort now." He had just opened his mouth to speak to Robert when Mathieu broke from his cover and threw his arms around the sergeant. The pistol waved with the movement of his arm and nearly flew from his hand but his finger caught on the trigger and it fired and hit Robyn in the forehead. Blood and brain matter sprayed and splattered Robert's face and the front of his shirt and a metallic taste met his tongue as Robyn collapsed against him and knocked him down.

Mathieu hissed, "Look what you've done. Killed your own officer." He dropped his arms and the sergeant jumped free of him and snarled, "You did it. Grabbed me by my arms and made me fire. His death is on all of you. You're outlaws escaped from the fort and I'm arresting you now. You'll come back with me. The priest saw what happened. Witnessed it, he did and he can't lie about it. There's not a judge as would-n't hang ye for this."

Robert reached for the pistol tucked into Robyn's belt and pointed it half-cocked at the soldier.

The man's face drained. "Ye wouldn't dare shoot me."

But Robert fired and the man dropped to his knees, and crumpled onto the ground.

Mathieu looked back toward the fort. "Best we be gone."

He and Robert stripped the soldiers' bodies of their weapons, coins and ammunition and even took their boots. Mathieu pulled at Etienne's sleeve. "Come with us. English come out here and find ye, they'll put the blame on you for what happened. Here, give us a hand. Carry some of this stuff." Robert thrust the small hoard of their gleanings at him and Etienne automatically pushed it into the pack he carried. Mathieu and Robert lifted Jacques-Pierre from the ground and they went off into the forest.

The next morning Major Robyn Jenkins and his sergeant were missing when the roll was called. Captain Butler volunteered to organize a search party and go out to look for the missing men. When they reached the place where the sentry had last seen shapes of men out in the field the night before they found both soldiers lying dead of bullet wounds next to a bloody bed of flattened grass but the Acadian's body was gone.

Butler said, "They didn't shoot each other. Acadians had to have used their own weapons to kill them." He voice rose in indignation. "That's an outrage! Look! They even took their boots!" He poked around some more. "That priest was in on it with them. Good riddance."

All of a sudden it came to him – that was no true priest. It was the apothecary, Daiell's friend, masquerading as one. Butler's eyes lit with pleasure. Soon as he had the chance he'd take Etienne; he'd squeeze the truth out of him and he wouldn't do it gently. Probably implicate that bastard Scot. Serve Daiell right for consorting with him. "French are French," Butler thought," Papist or Huguenot all of that race are enemies."

Butler walked about, excitedly whacking the grass with a stick. "Why are there only two bodies? Where's the Acadian I shot?" Like a hunter determined to find the carcass of his kill he looked for telltale signs the body was dragged off – a trail of blood on flattened grass, drag marks in the dirt. There was nothing. He knew he'd brought the man down. Saw him with his own eyes. There was all that blood on the smashed-down grass near the other bodies – had to be from the man he shot. Acadians must have carried him away. He'd ask Colonel Monckton could he take a party in pursuit. Now Major Jenkins was done for, maybe he'd get a field promotion out of this. He felt he was at the start of a very good day.

TATAMAGOUCHE

GUILLAUME, his Book, 1755

The warmth of the evening as the sun begins to set and the delicate light of the moon in its early phase make me sigh with contentment as I look up at the heavens and admire the beauty of it. I take a long draw on my pipe and fall silent, suddenly feeling myself enclosed in a great love. Sometimes over the years I've felt Song Sparrow's presence but never as strong as now. Radiant warmth eases my limbs and I feel as young as if the years had never flown by. Memories of faraway times flood back and consume me – how beautiful she was, how desirable, how loving and passionate our embraces were, how I wound my hands in her thick black hair and tasted her lips and how she bore me a son, a strong, handsome son. Now nothing's left to me in this living world of my love for her and hers for me. I squeeze back the tears.

A hand touches my shoulder. I think it's her come back again to comfort me, but then it's Armand's voice I hear.

I open my eyes. The pipe has fallen from my hand but it was already empty. I'd finished smoking the last of the tabagie. Dancing Crow always brought that for me when he brought his family to Beausejour to visit us. How long has it been since his last visit? When would he come again? My thoughts turn to him, my first born son and I try to push aside the memory rising to remind me he was lost in '44. I come untethered and my eyes flow over with tears and my old man's mind wanders to catch at straws in the wind.

- Translation by Liam Butler, A.B., M.Ed., Ph.D.

Jerusha screamed, terrified by the sight of Guillaume slumped over the table. He had refused to hear a word of whatever else Robert and Mathieu had to tell until he knew why Jacques-Pierre didn't come home with them. He was an old man and had suffered a bad shock when Paul went missing after the French tried to take back Annapolis Royal in '44. Mathieu knew it was the news of Jacques-Pierre's death that had done for him and he wrung his hands, guilty that the news he had given his grandfather had brought on his collapse.

Armand came on the run and eased his mother back into the house; then he and Mathieu lifted Guillaume from the chair and carried him to his bed. "He's alive," Armand called out. Jerusha got some damp cloths and knelt by the bedside to press them to Guillaume's forehead.

Mathieu backed himself into a corner and slid down onto the floor to watch. Robert came to the doorway, looked at his cousin slumped over and saw how his grandmother leaned over his grandfather with sobs catching in her throat. He went outside and sat by the doorway.

Each time Guillaume struggled to speak Jerusha whispered, "Save your strength." Tears ran down her face and she wiped them away with the backs of her hands. Armand pulled her to her feet and gently sat her down by the bed.

"Mother," he began and then lapsed into silence. What could he say? He knelt by his father wanting to believe his spirit was still housed somewhere inside him. He took hold of his hand to chafe the color of life back into it.

After Guillaume drew his final breath, a quiet broken only by Jerusha's sobs settled on the house. She knelt beside her husband, held his hand and smoothed his brow, pleading for him to awaken. Armand pulled her to her feet, folded her in his arms and drew her away from the body to a seat in front of the hearth. Jerusha stared into the flames that flickered as low against the charred wood as her own spirit breathed inside her.

Armand brought planks from the barn for the laying out and began to prepare his father for burial. As he washed the body his fingers traced the network of scars on Guillaume's arms and chest. He rubbed herbs against his father's skin and placed Paul's carved bird around his neck. A few years back a trader came to say he had met Dancing Crow in the western forest. Paul had entrusted him with the necklace to carry to his father at Beausejour. After such a long silence Guillaume was elated to think Paul still lived, although the trader would say only that he was far away in Canada. Armand reminisced as he fingered the necklace and its touch now shocked him into realizing Dancing Crow would never have parted with it while he was still alive. He wondered about the trader, who he was and how he knew where to find them. Could he have been Paul's own son? He stood with his hand resting lightly on Guillaume's chest and considered that possibility.

Guillaume never said anything to indicate he thought Paul was dead and for a time he wore the carving around his neck. Then he put it away. Armand thought for a moment about when it was he did that. Finally it came to him that it was just before he told them about his life before he married Jerusha. When Guillaume spoke about Song Sparrow putting the carving around Paul's neck on the morning of her death, he reached to his throat and a shadow crossed his face and that was when Armand saw it was missing.

His father believed it was a talisman and he'd stripped himself of its protection – like a soldier laying down his arms in surrender – before telling them of his life as Song Sparrow's husband. As he spoke of her death Armand saw grief and anger come back to rule his father's face as he lived it all over again. After the passage of so many years the horror of it still had a power over him that none of them ever realized. When Guillaume finished the telling he was shaking. Jerusha embraced and held him until the tremors passed.

Armand's mind cleared and he became aware of his mother standing beside him. "What's this?" she hissed; her eyes widened at the sight of the carving.

" 'Twas Dancing Crow's. Ye recall a trader brought it to father some time ago. Told him Paul's still living. Remember how happy father was to hear that?"

Jerusha stared at it. "Belonged to her first." Her voice quavered. "He told me how Paul came to have it on the day she died. Now he'll have it with him always." Armand's arms went around his mother's shoulders as she leaned into his chest and wept.

"Would you like to put something with him so he'll have that too?" She stopped crying and her face softened. She untied a ribbon with a carved locket of two tiny flowers and a rosebud and took it from her neck.

"He gave me this when I told him I carried our first child." She held it up and looked at it with a shuddering sigh. Then she leaned down and fastened it around her husband's neck as if to make it a nest for the bird.

Armand looked at the threesome image and wondered if, when his father made it, he saw Song Sparrow, Paul and himself as he carved the wood. Best his mother to believe that it was a token of his father's love the he had made especially for her.

"I was so jealous of her when we first married. My brothers couldn't understand why he ever married the Indian woman in the first place." Jerusha dabbed at her nose. "Better I learned it all at last. Oh God," she wailed, "He can't be gone."

"Remember how he and Paul would go off to the forest when he came to visit?" Armand squeezed her shoulders. "Once I saw them with their heads together and talking like he nivver seemed to talk to us. I was so green with envy."

Pieces of a log burned through the middle fell down and the wood piled atop it shifted, sending sparks flying from the hearth to land on the floor. Armand turned toward the disturbance, stamped out the burning chinks and rearranged the logs as best he could. He made sure the kettle was still safe on its crane and stared into the flames for a moment or two before he heard his mother call him back to her.

Armand continued his story. "Took me some years but one day I said how I'd seen him and Paul long-ago and how I'd felt. I told him that even after I'd only been a father myself for less than a couple of weeks before my wife and child died, I knew how it felt to have a son taken away from me. But I also realized that if I married again and had more children that grieving wouldn't make the love I felt for the rest of my family any the less."

"I was the reason Paul went away," Jerusha said. "I know your father nivver spoke of it, and all this time he nivver forgave me for it neither. Such a silly young fool I was to think I could make that part of his life go away when he took that child back for his aunt and uncle to raise. But Paul kept coming back over the years and every time Guillaume saw him, it reminded him of what he'd lost. 'T was like a wound that couldn't heal. He could be forthright about all else and especially loving of you children but when it came to showing me the love he should've had to give his wife, he couldn't do it because all those years it was always still hers. And I knew it."

Armand remembered how his own grief had so numbed him that he had believed he could never love another woman. It was years after his wife died that he met Cecilie and at first sight he loved her completely. She wasn't another Jeanne-Louise but someone altogether different and who he could love simply for who she was. He wasn't at war inside himself because of trying to love two women at the same time – and one of them dead. For the first time he understood how burdened his parents' lives had been. The love their children took for granted his mother never believed offered her the same shelter. He felt a deeper sympathy for her.

He chose his words carefully, hoping they would comfort her. "Father told us the suffering of his grief did mend. Mother, he didn't expect ye to be her. He knew he couldn't do that to you. But nothing could keep him from loving Paul and sometimes feeling a deep sadness for his mother. Father had to learn who you were as a woman and accept you and love you for it.

"When I became a widower I grieved but not the same as he did. Seems a long time ago but it's only now I've learned to love another. Jeanne-Louise died differently than Song Sparrow. Father must've felt guilty for leaving her that day as I felt for not being able to save my wife and our child. Sometimes I think it costs so much to heal from that kind of guilt it spoils all else good that comes after."

His arm circled her shoulders. Guillaume lay at peace on the cedar plank as if he heard and approved every word they spoke. Armand interrupted the silence, "He told ye it was all right. That he loved you from the very first and always would."

She searched his face. "Ye believe that?"

"None of who raised Paul mattered so much after a time. When Dancing Crow was little Father's love for him was a longing, grasping, needing kind of love. It all changed when Paul became a young man and their love grew into that between equals, how a good father wants to love his sons. But no matter how Father loved Paul it never took any of his love away from the rest of us. Especially you, Mother." He hugged her.

She stood by and watched him wrap the burial shroud around his father and settle his body back onto the plank. As he rubbed the cedar and the fragrance of the forest breathed back at him, Armand thought about the pages of Guillaume's journal – words the priest sometimes wrote for him when he came to Beausejour – that he found in the chest with Dancing Crow's carved bird. He could almost see a vision of his father as a young man on the hunt, when he stalked animals through forests of spruce and hemlock, and cast lines to fish in a sea covered with sun pennies. "Aye, father," he whispered and bent to kiss the familiar cheek. He rubbed the cedar again and inhaled its essence.

ANNAPOLIS ROYAL

The housekeeper opened the door to Captain Handfield. She was surprised by his visit so early in the morning, but welcomed him in as if there was nothing unusual about it. She wondered if he came to tell Henri what the British intended for the habitants.

The whole town seethed with wild gossip about the fall of Fort Beausejour and of expulsion for all the Acadians. None were to be excused, people whispered, not even those who had given daughters in marriage to English men and made them rich beyond what they could do for themselves. She scanned Handfield's face for clues.

Henri rose from his seat as the officer was ushered into the parlor. "Ye look grim, my friend. What's happened?"

Handfield replied, "It's the Governor's order. None of my or any other officer's doing, and I'm sorry to be the one who's to tell you. You'll understand how this affects me. I wanted to warn you of what could also happen to you."

Henri's face dropped. "Then it's true, the rumors about expulsions?"

"Yes. No matter how any individual Acadians have befriended the British cause here, all are to be transported out of the province. The proclamation is to be officially made within a fortnight. Even my wife's family and the families of all others like hers. It'll be a sad life for her to stay here without her folk, not to mention her worries about what may become of them. I didn't wish to tell you this, but I know you must be expecting such news."

Henri got up and called to Marie. "Come join us, sweetheart. You've to hear this as well."

Handfield stood when she entered the room. "Madame, I assure you this is none of my doing, but still I'm charged with the duty to carry it out." He hesitated and Henri nodded for him to continue. "You're not to tell anyone what I'm about to say. I'm placing my trust in you by telling this to you early."

Then he told them the news they were expecting but still afraid to hear.

Marie sank down onto the sofa. "So it's true and now it's to come about?" She looked at his careworn face and asked, "You're saying we can't stay here? But we're British."

"Madame, it's your husband you should worry about. Only he's affected by this but I'm certain you wouldn't want him to be taken away without you to go with him."

"What? Henri's as good as any Englishman. Everyone knows that, especially after all these years." Anger and fear warred in Marie's expression. Henri's face turned spectral and he sank deeper into his chair.

"I'll see if there's a way to get permission for him to stay here if you wish that. But don't expect too much. They may relent on your husband as they did for my wife but the proclamation will say all Acadians are banished and all goods are forfeit to the crown, so they may refuse to let you carry furniture and the like if you decide it's better to go away from the province."

"Ye can't just take away what belongs to a British citizen."

Handfield's face blanched. "I'm concerned for your own good above that of your possessions. I'd no luck to help my wife's parents nor anyone else of her family, neither them nor their goods."

"Would you let us leave here aboard our own ship when the *Arbutus* comes back?" Her lips trembled as she verged on tears.

"I wish I could say," the man answered. "Better if she sails in before the proclamation's read so it gives you the choice. I shouldn't have come here. But I wanted to warn you so if ye decide it's best for ye to leave Annapolis Royal then you needn't be here when the soldiers come to collect your husband."

HALIFAX (July)

Word came for the Acadians' appointed deputies to assemble at Halifax, so Armand packed his bag and prepared to leave Tintamarre. As Cecilie helped him she asked what he expected would come from the meeting.

"Dearest," he cleared his throat and began to broach something he felt was hardening into a certainty. "I don't know what the British think to do with us once we're in their hands, but should the worst happen I fear there's a chance I may not come back here."

Cecilie threw her arms around him." Then don't go."

He grimaced. "I've no choice. I've been called to act in concert with the other delegates. We'll try to forestall any harsh treatment the British have in mind for us."

"You're just like your father," she threw down the words like a challenge.

He looked down at the floor as if searching the nails to see if they were properly set into the floorboards. When he looked up at her his eyes softened and he said, "If you mean to ask do I feel I've a duty then I must answer that ye know I do."

Cecilie caressed the side of his face. "I'm afraid it'll be the end of us, the British decide to act. Now ye speak your fear, I confess I've felt the same way since the day we woke and saw those ships setting anchors off Maringouin. It's like we're rooted up and blown from our own pasture like a bale of wild weeds and driven here and there by the wind, never to settle back in our place. Is that what this'll mean to us? To nivver have a home to go back to?"

Armand kissed her. "It'll have to be decided sometime, what the British are to do about the Acadians. Governor's called us to come to Halifax. We must go and put forward our best case."

"And what if ye don't come back? And what if I'm already carrying your child?"

He gave a start. "Are ye?"

"It's too soon to tell, but it could be."

He crushed her to his chest and kissed her forehead. "Then this is the worst leave-taking I've ever had." He took a step back, his hands on her arms. "You're not sure?"

"All I'm saying is that it may be." She gave him a defiant look. "Some things won't wait on you carrying forth your so-called duties."

Armand was perturbed but his mind was already made up. "If I don't come back ye must stay with Mathieu. He'll help you." She looked at him in disbelief. "Then you still mean to go?"

"I must. I'm a chosen delegate. It's my duty to go and speak for the habitants hereabout." He gave her a speculative look. "You'll forgive me?"

"What's a wife to do else than that?" Cecilie kissed his cheek. "But if things are as bad as ye think, what if I'm not here when you come back?"

"All the more reason to stay with someone who'll protect you as best he can. I'll speak to Mathieu before I go. One more thing. You've seen the pages where the priest scribbled my father's thoughts?" She nodded. "If ye have to leave would you please try to save those as being dear to me." His voice softened. "They're all I have left of him."

Armand traveled through the forest to Baie Verte to look in on his uncle Jacques and tell him the news. But when he reached the truck house it was as empty as if no one had ever lived there and the fishing boats were gone. For the next couple of days Armand saw only a few Indians hunting in the woods as he travelled.

As he passed by the hamlets, he learned some of the delegates had already come that way and weren't far ahead of him. The next day he came upon some men traveling with one of the priests. The habitants were going only as far as the next village but Fr. Etienne was headed for Halifax and asked Armand did he mind if they traveled together.

The following day found them talking about the coming meeting and guessing at the Governor's intentions. "I'm hoping for the best," Armand told Etienne, "but I'm worried about how things might play out. We need to think differently now."

"What do ye mean? Acadians have always trusted in their oath of Neutrality to see them through any hard spots. Seems to have worked pretty well for them."

"Acadians have always stood by their Neutrality and you're right about the past. But now what's to happen? Aren't you supposed to insist to me that the oath's no good for the Acadians any more? I thought all the priests were agreed to what Le Loutre said."

"I didn't agree with him. In fact, he was so exasperated with me — I was with him at Beausejour — he made his escape when the British took the fort and left me behind. Haven't seen him since. That's how I come to be wandering. I heard the delegates are off to Halifax. Thought I could be a help in some way if I went there." Etienne gave Armand a half-smile. "Maybe the Abbé thinks the joke's on me, but I feel my feet stand solid on the ground when I treat with people simple and direct. Convoluted thinker, that one."

"We buried my father just before I left. He took the oath in '27 even though he lived in French territory. In '50 when the British built Fort Lawrence, the priests insisted he must give the oath up because the time when such things counted was past. For my father and the other old men who took the oath back then and stayed Neutral, it was a matter of keeping to their honor to keep their families safe. Many of the delegates still believe Neutrality is the best shield against whatever the British might try to do to the Acadians."

"Do ye think they'd refuse to take the full oath, if Governor Lawrence demands it?"

"Likely they'll hew to the same cant as always. If they do I think they misread the Governor's intentions. That's my big concern with this meeting – what's to come out of it, if the British don't get what they say they want." Armand frowned.

"So you think they'll use what the delegates say, if they insist on keeping to the old oath, as the excuse to act against them?" Etienne frowned.

"Look what Le Loutre's done to have his way with the habitants. You think the British be any different? Any of them, French or British – they'll use who and what they must to get what they want. I can understand that and maybe the other delegates can too. But will they do what they must to save our people from the British sending us all to exile?"

Etienne was dismayed. "Sounds like most of the delegates have made up their minds to stick to the old way."

"It may be moot if the British are on the march against the French regardless. They took Fort Beausejour. I'd call that unmistakable evidence they plan to have all of the old Acadia for themselves. The question is whether they'll leave any room here for the habitants."

The next day another group of men headed for Halifax caught up with them. As they trudged ahead the conversation shifted to how hard a line the delegates should take to preserve their Neutral status. Etienne looked at Armand's bitter expression, remembered their earlier conversation, and thought there were few Acadians who seemed to fully credit the peril they faced. And for those who did understand, did any of them imagine there was anything they could do about it?

Etienne parted with the Acadians, and hoped this was the last of his priestly masquerades. He looked forward to once more only being the apothecary to Halifax and to his reunion with Hugh. As they had grown to know each other better their friendship had deepened to devotion. It was the first time in Etienne's life other than with the apothecary who'd trained him back in France that he'd enjoyed such a friendship. Hugh was a generous man willing to live and let live and Etienne breathed more freely when he was nearby.

Etienne's thoughts turned to the Snake who controlled his men like a puppet-master and bullied anyone who tried to gainsay him. A chill ran up his spine as he remembered the dead Acadian at Beausejour, shot in the back. Just like Butler to do something like that. If Butler ever recognized him, he'd think he had license to act as he pleased. Etienne shivered and remembered the old superstition that someone had just walked on his grave. Hugh once compared Butler to a cannon that got loose once on the gun deck of a sailing ship as it tried to maneuver. Hit anything in its way as it rumbled about, then stove in part of the hull and plunged overboard before the gun crew could capture and tie it down.

Etienne trusted Hugh and looked up to Cornwallis but now that Lawrence was governor, his original mission of spying on the Acadians had gotten more dangerous than ever. Colonel Winslow's New England militia was abroad in force and were a danger to Etienne when he dressed in his priest's robe.

When he first put on the cassock he felt hidden and safe in it but now it marked him out for capture or worse. With Fort Beausejour taken and the imprisoned Acadians held at Fort Lawrence, and Winslow's militia everywhere in Chignecto, Hugh promised Etienne he wouldn't have to go to spy again now that Lawrence and the Massachusetts governor William Shirley had made up their minds the Acadians were to be exiled.

July 28, 1755 was a day of brilliant sunshine; the air was clean and clear right out to the horizon. The sun beat in through the opened windows of the antechamber where Armand stood with the other delegates, packed together to wait for the summons to enter the meeting room.

Governor Lawrence spoke to the council at some length of General Braddock's defeat at French hands and his death in the Ohio territory. Some of the councilors erupted into shouts of outrage that grew louder and louder until they were interrupted by the banging of the gavel. Lawrence's news had them in a proper stew about the possibility of the French and Indians rising up on the frontier between New England and New France and at least one voice shouted that the next thing would be the French would arm the Acadians and goad them to revolt against the British to take back Nova Scotia. An angry chorus of "Ayes" erupted.

Then Governor Lawrence said that he and Governor Shirley of Massachusetts whose militia was still in Nova Scotia formally requested the Council to end this dire threat to their provinces and vote to send the Acadians away unless they now agreed to swear the full oath of allegiance without reservation to the British crown. The time for half-measures was past. England and France were always at war on the western frontier; if war came east to Canada and Nova Scotia and the French armed the Acadians, they'd have a standing army ready to attack the British right at their backs.

If the Acadians would accept only the amended version of the oath as they always had in the past, he would have all the delegates thrown into prison on George's Island and plans for deporting all the Acadians from Nova Scotia would be carried out. Transports were available at Boston to sail to Nova Scotia and take them away.

"What if they agree to the full oath and swear it right here in this chamber before the council? You'll call off the deportations?" One of the members shouted to be heard above the babble.

"They won't agree; they never have in the past. They'll say they've no authority and have to go back to their villages and get everyone else's agreement first."

"They've stalled before so ye think they'll do it again?" another councilor shouted.

"Mark my words."

"So when they refuse to swear you'll arrest all of these and send them out to George's Island?" the first councilor persisted.

"That's what I propose to do."

"But what if they do agree? What'll you do then?" another voice shouted.

"Have them swear, then make them to understand everyone else must swear the full oath before a specified time or we deem they all be French citizens. As such they're all exiled from this province."

"Why play a waiting game? It's never worked before. The more time they have to think about it, the more time they have to organize and gather arms and get the French in here to help them fight."

"That's why we have to conclude this business right now," Lawrence insisted.

From time to time the sound of a voice rising in agreement or dispute and an occasional word filtered through the walls. The longer the delegates waited the more agitated they became.

Armand thought of his leave-taking from Cecilie. Both of them were too upset to do more than hold each other in a wordless embrace before he set off. With the fighting at Beausejour, its fall to the English and the Acadians being held under arrest inside the fort it was too dangerous to try to get back home to Maringouin. Now he thought he might never again return to his farm.

Whatever happened to him now, he knew Cecilie was safe. Mathieu had promised that he and the others would protect the family while he was away at Halifax. Mathieu did ask if Cecilie should go to stay with her own people but Armand had responded that now she was his wife, she belonged with the Bancouers.

"We did our best by them," the man standing next to him whispered as if he could read his thoughts. Armand sighed. He thought it unlikely the delegates would be arrested, but you never could tell what might happen. At least the women of his family would be protected even if he could not be there to help.

"What else's there for us to do but stay Neuter?" another shrugged. "Our farms are here, this is our country. Why'd they think we'd want war with anyone?"

"Le Loutre runs about the countryside with his Indians and has the British scared silly."

"Aye, he's what did it." Anger shook the man's voice.

"Heard nothing of the priest since Beausejour's taken." Armand looked around to see if anyone would speak up to contradict him.

"Rumor went around he dressed in women's clothes and got out afore the British could clap him in prison." Someone snickered at the thought of the priest in disguise and nervous laughter rilled through the room.

"Aye and they find all those farmers there in the fort as swore the oath and they're under arms with the French. Don't help our cause, them hotheads."

The door to the meeting room opened and revealed the council seated inside behind a long table. All conversation stopped. The delegates positioned to see into the council room noted the set expressions of the men that stared back at them.

"Please be quiet out here," the sergeant-at-arms said. "Your voices can be heard quite plain. Governor Lawrence will call you inside soon. Just be patient a bit longer."

Armand thought, "They've already made up their minds and it's written all over their faces. No good's to come of this."

He whispered to the man next to him, one of the Minas delegates summoned to appear earlier and kept imprisoned until this meeting, "What do ye suppose they'll do? Send the Acadians over to Louisbourg or Ile St. Jean?"

"What they did to us as come here ahead of the rest of ye, was throw us in the prison on George's Island to wait for ye to come along. I'd say they plan we're to be taken away and if they don't want us here because they're afraid of us rising, why'd they send us over to Louisbourg to give the French more men to support the fortress? Don't make sense, ye think some about it."

The latch clicked as if a hand was placed on it from the other side, but now hesitated. Voices ceased; everyone stared at the door.

The delegates' defeated expressions were more eloquent than words could ever be as to what they expected was about to happen. But a few still showed the fire to argue in favor of Neutrality, if they were given half the chance. Armand thought it well if they didn't all go in to face the council like a herd of sheep harried into the pen. If they could muster the ability to reason they might fend off the decision they all feared.

The door creaked open and the Acadians spread across the threshold into the meeting room. The sun stood higher in the sky and the room was brilliant with light pouring in through the tall casements. A large portrait of King George II looked down on the crowd. Known as a hard and businesslike sovereign, his painted face, with eyes that seemed to follow the viewer, held an expression meant to intimidate and accuse all within its purview. Other than the portrait, the long table, and the chairs occupied by the members of the Governor's Council, the room was unadorned. To the Acadians the place was as barren and uncompromising as the British themselves.

The council members sat grim and silent as the habitants scuffled their way in and packed together. Most of them seemed diffident toward the council, as if the Acadians had already guessed the purpose of the meeting and felt resigned to what they knew they could do nothing to help. Others seemed ready to burst with words barely held in check. Every face was etched with worry.

Lawrence looked around the room. When he saw Etienne he checked his gaze, remembering he had asked him to wear the cassock here as a special favor thinking his presence among them would keep the Acadians calmed. His eyes passed to a farmer standing a few ranks back. Here was someone he remembered from previous meetings, a man who could marshal his thoughts and knew how to construct a sensible point of view. Agreeable or not – that was another matter. Armand looked impassive as Lawrence's eyes lingered on him. The Governor wondered what he thought to stand thus and see the disaffected expressions frozen on the faces of the councillors. Likely he already guessed their intention. He read exhaustion in Armand's features and noticed the black mourning band tied around his left arm. Lawrence wondered how he would take the decision about to be given.

The Acadians crowding into the room were mostly leaders of their villages. Back home their families and neighbors waited to learn what the Governor wanted of them. The men shifted nervously trying to read the expressions on the implacable faces that stared back at them and a carking silence settled on the room. Lawrence rose and asked the clerk to read the decision of the Minas deputies for the record. When he finished Lawrence looked at the men standing before him and asked, "What say you?"

A few voices answered. "No unconditional oath."

"We've sworn Neutrality and kept to it."

"Already gave ye what ye wanted. Need no other oath."

"We agreed to keep faith with what we swore to in Governor Philips' day."

Those who spoke out looked around for support and some "Ayes", more or less hearty were heard. But many of the delegates remained silent as if they knew their fate was already sealed.

Governor Lawrence turned to his council. They nodded their unanimous agreement and he pronounced his decision. The Acadians were under arrest, to be removed to the prison on George's Island and await deportation. A door at the other end of the room opened and a detachment of guards entered to clear the chamber and escort the Acadians down to the docks.

As soon as the habitants were outside and the door closed, the council resumed its meeting and took up the matter of where the Acadians were ultimately to be taken. The Governor again stood up to address them. "Foolish to send them over to the fortress at Louisbourg to swell the ranks of the French." He looked at the faces of his councilors and saw them nod their agreement.

"They think that's where they're going," the Governor said. "There's a rumor among them to that effect. Best they've no idea what we've planned for them." One of the councilors started to speak and ask the obvious question but Lawrence cut him off. "It's best we distribute them among the other colonies. We can't allow them to reconstitute as a nation. Divide them and send them to live among English settlers so they'll have no opportunity to gather in large enough numbers to become a force that can ever act against us."

A voice rose, "Where be the ships to take them away?"

Someone else asked, "Who has the contract for their transportation?"

"Orders are sent to Boston even as we speak. Our agent's already confirmed the firm of Apthorpe and Hancock has ships ready to sail. First of the transports will go to Chignecto where the rebels that went to help the French at Beausejour are held under arrest."

One of the councilors muttered to the man next to him, "Ain't that the firm that employs William Shirley's son-in-law?"

TATAMAGOUCHE   (August)

Tattered clouds hung like rotted winding cloths in the smoky stagnant air above the burned village. One bore stains with the likeness of eye sockets stretched into hollows as deep as the sky itself.

One day earlier the sun warmed the habitants' faces as they welcomed Captain Abijah Willard and the hundred New England troops he led and exchanged pleasantries with them. English and Acadian faces were wreathed in smiles. Laughter exploded from clusters of men, English and Acadian together, as jokes were made. The farmers opened their arms in hospitality to the New Englanders and gave the soldiers bread fresh from their ovens, milk and butter, sheep to slaughter and roast for their dinner and places to sleep in their houses and barns.

Now there was nothing left. The English went off in contempt of the homely village, setting fire to the very buildings where they fed and sheltered and left them to be reduced to no more than piles of steaming ashes and charred timbers. They took the men away with them as prisoners but having no orders about what to do with the women and children the soldiers forced them to stay behind.

At the rear of the long column they used their rifles to push back the screaming women who tried to follow their men, calling out for them to come back. Marthé ran after Honoré and Aimeé after Modeste, crying to the deaf ears of the soldiers, "What shall we do without them? How will we live without our men?"

Jerusha prostrated herself on the ground and pounded the soil with her fists. "Come to me, Guillaume, take me to you. Don't leave me here. Help me to die now and be with you."

Cecilie wrapped her arms around her mother who lay near Jerusha and keened for her husband. The women shrieked and wailed until they were exhausted and by the time they had only dry sobs left to wrack their breasts the men were as absent as if the earth had opened up and swallowed them down.

As night came on Cecilie and some of the younger women assembled a lean-to, to shelter the old women who still moaned and wrung their hands.

The next morning Marthé and Jerusha spoke out in favor of building a more permanent shelter. That way they could all stay together right where they were because the men knew where to find them whenever they managed to escape. Few of them had ever been anywhere else in their whole lives and could not imagine how they could ever leave a place that was all they knew of the world and where their lives were so firmly rooted.

The younger women said if they stayed right there the soldiers knew where they were and could come back for them. The older women argued with the younger and couldn't agree what to do. Some of them went to poke through the ruins of their homes to look for anything that might have escaped the fires. Swarms of flies buzzed around them as they searched, rising up and resettling on singed and burned animal carcasses.

When none of the men returned on the second day, more of the women succumbed to hopelessness. Cecilie felt that if she stayed there for even one more day, she'd give in to despair and lose the will to go find help. On the third day, as she was ready to leave, Mathieu and Robert walked out of the woods into their camp. The women mobbed them and demanded their help.

"What happened here?" Mathieu was surprised to find the village in ruins and the women left on their own. "British come and burned the place down and marched all the men away?"

Jerusha began to cry again and Robert held up a hand to shush her and said, "We've no time for that Grandmother. We've been past Baie Verte and Remsheg. Burned to ashes same as here, except there are no folk about. We come fast as we could to warn you but we see we're too late. At least we found you. Now we got to make up our minds what to do next and crying won't help with that."

Cecilie stepped forward. "I thought to go to Cobequid to look for help. Ye been there? Know any news of that village?"

"None we heard of. But not been there, neither." Robert turned to Mathieu. "We go with her? She can't go alone. Not with so many English all about."

Mathieu asked, "Where did ye think to go?"

"You've told us how the British burned Baie Verte and the villages near there so it makes no sense to go that way. Go toward Beausejour and you'll see English everywhere. I think the safest direction is toward Cobequid; maybe there's help to find there. If not I keep on toward Halifax. Armand went to meet the delegates there. I mean to find him and bring him back here."

"But what'll we do if ye leave us here?" Jerusha wailed. "And what about your poor mother, Cecilie? You'll leave her alone too? Oh what'll we do?"

"Don't you see, if we all stay here and no one goes to find help it's certain we'll have no aid nor protection. Someone's got to go. Maybe there's folk at Cobequid who can help us. If it's so then we ask them to come here and rescue you. Then I go as fast as I can to Halifax and bring Armand back with me."

"What if they do send help?" Mathieu asked her.

She repeated what she'd tried to explain to the women. "Perhaps if we can get help from Cobequid to get over to Ile St. Jean or Ile Royale, the French can help us. Can't stay here to wait for the English to come back and sweep us up like they did the men."

"I think the men are being marched to Fort Lawrence." Robert pondered. "It's possible some could escape."

Jerusha's face brightened. "There, ye see? My grandson thinks it's just as I said – we don't have to leave. We just have to be patient and wait for them to get back here to us."

Mathieu said, "I doubt it, Grandmother. They may not get to come back here even if they do escape. Then what'll ye do? I know ye want to hope for the best but ye can't wait on the men to find a way to rescue you. That ain't about to happen now the British have them. And it's the first place the British would look for any of them who escaped."

He turned to the women and searched their worried faces. "Better if we can find help from another quarter. Robert and I'll go with Cecilie to Cobequid. Near enough by we can do it in a couple of days. If there's anyone still there we may get help. Then we'll take stock of how things are."

They found Cobequid still untouched by the English and the habitants going about as if everything was normal. Cecilie wondered if they would believe the news about the destruction of the other villages. But telling their story gave focus to the Cobequidians' simmering anxieties about what would happen to them and their village when the English came. Word went round and like a lake full of fish drowsing one minute and leaping into the air the next to escape advancing predators everyone scrambled to leave as fast as they could. They promised as they fled to search out the women and children hidden in the woods at Tatamagouche and take them across the bay to Ile St. Jean where they would all be safe with the French.

Now Cecilie's worry was all about how to find Armand. Mathieu and Robert insisted on staying with her. Two Cobequid youths offered to come along at least to guide them through the marshes. They stuffed bread and cheese into their packs and headed for the river where Olivide and Josef's fishing canoes lay hidden in the thick grasses.

They hadn't gone far from the emptied village when they heard the sounds of an army advancing by the road and pulled their canoes deep into the reeds to hunker down while the soldiers marched past.

"Thank God you came when you did," Josef whispered. "But for you everyone would be caught up and taken away." As soon as the enemy reached the village, there were shouts and gunshots, and then the first smell of burning thatch reached them. Flames burst into the air above the houses and soldiers shouted and ran about beating the bushes in the nearby woods; a search party came down to the river and the Acadians made themselves as small and inconspicuous as they could, hardly daring to breathe. After taking some whacks at a few stands of reeds, the soldiers decided no one was hiding there and went away.

Evening came and cook-fires blazed; the smell of roasting meat tantalized the hidden Acadians. The English prepared to spend the night in the few buildings left unburned and the fugitives heard the banter and laughter of men who knew the darkness concealed no threat to them. They poled their canoes out of the reeds into the river and paddled off in silence.

As the first streaks of dawn lightened the sky, they hid their canoes, to set out on foot. Soon they met a band of Indians. After a few minutes' talk, they learned the delegates were being held in the prison on George's Island in Halifax Harbor. English soldiers were spread out across the country between Halifax and the main Acadian villages at Minas, Annapolis Royal and the forts in Chignecto. Cecilie told the Indians she sought her husband and spoke his name, but they had heard no mention of him.

Cecilie's nerves were delicately balanced between hope and fear and now she despaired of ever seeing Armand again. She put on a brave face and said she was willing to go to the British and even beg them to put her in prison if it meant that she and her husband could be together. To hear that made Mathieu gnash his teeth. He nearly took her by the shoulders to shake some sense into her but Robert saw his intention and laid a hand on his arm to stop him.

With every step they took toward Halifax, Mathieu wanted to turn them all around and run from the British, if only he knew some place they could find refuge. Olivide opined that things were even more dangerous than they first seemed at Cobequid. Cecilie turned on him and demanded to know if he wanted to go back there.

"I was just saying. Anyway, you know the place has burned. What's the matter with you, anyway?"

Robert gruffed at Cecilie, "No matter what ye think, it's just plain foolhardy to walk up to any English. It may be you've noticed they're hunting fugitives – people like us? We'll go the rest of the way with you, but we scout things out before we show ourselves or talk to anyone about how can we find Armand or plan how to get to him."

When they were as close as they could get to Halifax and still be under cover of the forest, Mathieu insisted they settle down to watch the road for a time and see who passed by; the few people they saw coming and going were all English.

"I might as well just walk out of the forest and ask the next person who comes by us where to find the Acadian delegates." Cecilie threatened after they had waited one full day and part of another. "Unless you thought of a better idea."

"Let's all work this out together before you just go off and do the next silly thing that crosses your mind," Robert insisted. "Ye can't just rush out among the English without ye put the rest of us in danger of being taken. Give us a thought," he growled. "What happens if they catch us? Then who's left to help you?"

"It took us a long time to get here. Let's not defeat the purpose of it by going off half-cocked." Mathieu looked stern. The looks on Olivide and Josef's faces told her she could expect no support from them.

"All right," she agreed. "I'll wait, just not for much longer."

HALIFAX

Cecilie awoke confident she'd find her husband that very day and she convinced Mathieu to go with her along the edge of the woods to scout the waterfront. "Look," Mathieu pointed to a figure standing near a dock. "It's Father Etienne. What's he doing there?"

"Those women with him look to be Acadians. And they've baskets that look like they're loaded with food. Think it means he's taking them to the Acadians over at the prison?"

"I'll ask him," Mathieu said.

"No ye won't – who looks there sees a priest surrounded by women. One extra won't be noticed, but a man would stand out right away."

Etienne didn't acknowledge her until she came up to him and when Cecilie asked what they were doing, he turned to answer and noted her as a stranger to Halifax. "We're taking food over to the prisoners at George's Island." He looked her over. "You're new here. Where did you come from? And with all the soldiers abroad, how did you ever get here?"

"I walked like anyone else. My husband's come here with the delegates. Hasn't come home, had no word of him and I'm worried sick. So I come here to find him."

She asked the women circled around to look at her, "What're you doing here?"

"Husbands come to build some houses for the British. Put over on the island when they finished. Soldiers let us cross here and collect food to bring it over to them and the delegates. They know we won't leave our men."

"Possible he's over there." Etienne pointed to the island. "We're just ready to sail." He bowed to the other women, "Would ye mind if we try to reunite a husband and wife, name of...?" Cecilie spoke her name and the women tittered. "We're all curious to see is a husband waiting at the island for her."

Etienne led them to a small sloop tied up at the end of a dock and handed the women into the boat; they untied the lines and he hoisted the sail and shouted, "Cast off for George's Island." He grabbed the tiller and pulled in the mainsheet and the wind pushed the sloop off the dock.

"Father, what are you really doing here?" Cecilie asked as the boat settled into a fast steady passage.

"English let me stay on sufferance. Helps if I talk with the delegates. Bring some of their wives over with food and take letters back and forth. Keeps their spirits up. What's his name, your husband?"

"Armand Bancouer. From Maringouin, over by Beausejour."

Etienne became excited. "He gave me a letter for you." He reached into the pocket in his cassock but his hand came out empty. "Must've taken it out. Has to be in my chest. I'll bring it with me tomorrow. He's on the island. That's where he gave me the letter. Wish I had it with me to give you now. Tomorrow for sure."

Now Cecilie could hardly contain herself. When the boat was tied off she was the first to jump out and had to force herself to wait long enough to help unload the food baskets.

After the women went their separate ways Cecilie followed Etienne inside the prison to where they found Armand sitting on a bench. He looked up when he heard their approaching footsteps and rose slowly as if he saw a ghost. Her eyes glistened with tears.

"It's really me. I'm here, Armand. Put your arms around me, I won't melt away like some creature made of fog."

His voice barely rose above a whisper. "They say they're sending us away. I thought I'd nivver see ye again." Tears claimed them both for a few moments. "Did Father Etienne give my letter to you? How'd ye get here?"

Cecilie dried her eyes and pointed to the priest. "He brought me over. But I've a deal of news to tell you." She took some bread and cheese from one of the baskets.

Etienne said, "I'll come back to you when I've finished here."

"How'd ye ever get from Tatamagouche to Halifax?" Armand looked at her like he feared she'd disappear if he so much as blinked his eyes. She whispered the story of the village burned by the English with the men taken away and the women and children left behind in the forest to fend for themselves. He squeezed her hand and his eyes teared. "What can ye tell me of my mother?"

"She wanted to stay right there because the men would know where to find them if they managed to escape. She wasn't the only one who insisted about that. I couldn't agree it was right. What if the soldiers came back? So I promised I'd go and seek for help."

He nodded, and said, "But ye didn't come all the way to Halifax by yourself?"

She whispered how Mathieu and Robert avoided the English and found the women and children left behind at Tatamagouche. Then came away with her.

Armand was silent for a time, sifting all the things she told him. Then he said, "So it's happened, what that red-haired officer told us. None of us wanted to believe it. British let the Minas delegates go home; said it was because they wanted families to be together. We prayed they were being released and we'd soon be set free, too. But a few days ago Major Daiell said boats already came and loaded Acadians on board and took those away to exile. Now the talk is about the British ruining the land, burning all behind them, leaving it empty." He paused and she traced the curve of his lips with her finger. "If they're transporting the Acadians to exile now, they'll bring a ship here to Halifax to take us away too. I'll nivver see any of them again – my family, my home. You're all I have now and if you go away from me, I may nivver see you again. Then I've no one."

"But likely the women are gone off to Ile St. Jean or Ile Royale by now and the French protect them. I believe the Cobequid folk kept their promise." She looked at him as if to memorize the landscape of his face. "I must go back with Father Etienne and the other women. They believe I got here all on my own and want to help me however they can." She reached up and smoothed a lock of hair back from his forehead. "I just want to be with you but I can't leave Robert and Mathieu without them knowing I found you. It's not fair if they wait for me and chance capture, with all they risked to bring me here. Then I'll come back and stay with you."

GRAND PRÉ   (October)

When Colonel John Winslow led his men away from Beausejour after his formal request to the Governor to be reassigned from Monckton's command was granted, he had no idea of the duty Lawrence planned to assign him to carry out at Grand Pré.

The last of the deportation ships were leaving Minas Basin for the Bay of Fundy and now the transports stood far out from the shore with their sails spread across the horizon destined for different ports, to scatter their human cargo among the colonies of New England and farther south. According to Lawrence's plan, that would prevent the Acadians from ever again gathering as a people strong enough to threaten the English.

It was a terrible experience for Winslow, one that began long before the day the orders came for him to send his soldiers to call in the men and boys from the fields to attend a meeting at the church of St. Charles-les-Mines. Once the habitants were inside the soldiers locked the doors. Then Winslow stood before them and read Governor Lawrence's order announcing their deportation and the confiscation of their farms, crops and livestock by the British Crown. He could still see their shocked faces; their shouts of dismay and anger still echoed in his ears.

Winslow thought he and Captain Murray, who was charged with the deportation of the Piziquid habitants, kept their Acadians as peaceful as they could and therefore under control. Winslow had stretched the limits to treat his charges as well as he thought possible: he let the Acadian men out on parole, twenty each day to go home and be with their families. When those returned twenty more could go. He let the families come to the church to visit their men and bring them food. When news of the rebellious Acadians under Monckton's charge in Chignecto reached his ears, Winslow became nervous about the same attempts to rise up happening at Minas. His prisoners greatly outnumbered his forces but his instinct to treat the people humanely paid off.

The transports arrived a month behind schedule and each added day they had to hold the Acadians while they waited, food supplies got tighter. Winslow had to listen to the habitants wailing and pleading ever louder against the British plan to send them away. Deep down Winslow might have sympathized with their situation, but as the officer in charge of a large group of exiles he steeled himself to do his duty and remained adamant against their entreaties.

When the deportation ships finally came, they used each high tide to get in close to the beach and load the exiles on board. The women were subdued, the men's faces wreathed with frowns; only an occasional muttered word escaped pursed lips, as if all the words and pleas they had stored inside to argue their cause were drained out of them.

Now that the Acadians were gone, his mission was done and the anger he held at bay at how he and his New Englanders had been used since his first confrontation with Monckton at the capture of Fort Beausejour bloomed inside him. Winslow had raised his militia on the basis of his popularity as a commander, calling up men from Cape Cod, Marshfield, Andover and Boston to come and help the British capture the French fort. Once that was accomplished, Governor Lawrence should have released the New Englanders to go home, as he had promised Governor Shirley, so they could go back and tend their farms. Now they could only hope that others had helped their women and children take in and store their harvests. It was an injustice to the New Englanders, but the Acadians were even worse off. They would never enjoy their harvests, but Winslow would go home to have his, and it would feed his family through the coming year.

Along the shore Winslow saw loaded carts with oxen still hitched to them, animals used to the caring touch of their vanished owners, and now left behind to die standing in their traces. At least he could send some men to cut the beasts loose so they could forage. The farmer in him rebelled at the cruelty and wasteful brutality that added mockery of the careful husbandry of the helpless Acadians to their awful fate of losing their land and almost everything they owned.

A line from *Lamentations* came to him: "How doth the city sit solitary, that was full of people?"

He turned his horse away from the view of the ships going over the horizon and headed toward the road, his thoughts again on the experiences he and his militia had had with the British regulars since landing in Nova Scotia.

The professional soldiers, the regulars always thought they were better than the colonial militias. But it was only with the help of New Englanders that the British accomplished their purpose to remove the so-called Acadian threat from Nova Scotia.

Winslow wondered what had ever made him think that any of them, beginning with Lawrence and Monckton and working down the ranks, would thank him for bringing more than two thousand Massachusetts men to Nova Scotia, a force that greatly outnumbered the British regulars who had taken their help and divided his men, attaching them to regiments of regulars and all the while disparaging them.

Winslow thought the British truly must not understand the effect of how they treated the colonial militias and wondered what would happen if they ever brought a fight to New England soil.

COBEQUID   (November)

Butler had his orders just that morning – he could still smell the ink it was so fresh – to take his men to search for Acadians who'd escaped the deportation ships. He was to go toward Cobequid and round up any of the habitants he came upon, bring them back to Halifax and send them to the prison on George's Island. The transport was scheduled to arrive soon and take the rest of the delegates away. The more Acadians they could pack aboard it, the better.

"Send them colonial militias home and leave the mopping up to the professionals," he crowed as his men readied to leave the fort. He rode out with his troops, following the same route as when he went out to meet Handfield in '49, when he was taken prisoner by the French and later exchanged at Louisbourg. When the British were ready to take the fortress back, he believed his knowledge of it would be important; maybe it would even earn him the promotion he yearned for. He thought he had deserved one after Jenkins was killed, but that prize was given to the Carrot and Daiell was now a major. It galled Butler that he had lost out to him, but his time would come and when it did there would be no Hugh Daiell to stand in his way. All he needed was to goad the man to a duel to see to that. Dueling was forbidden but what was the worst they would do to him? Slap him on the wrist?

This time he'd be extra thorough about scouting his route. French regulars were still ranging about; he had heard that officer called Boishébert was the leader. They could pop up anywhere. Just when it seemed they were nowhere nearby, the French would jump out from behind the trees yelling and shooting.

They went along the Stewiacke; Butler urged them to move faster to get beyond the place of his earlier ambush and they came to where the Jesuit's church once stood. The place reeked of desolation.

He decided to set down there to make camp and ordered the men to light only small fires, and post sentries. One of his sergeants remarked that when Acadians still lived there, the soldiers were always welcomed, housed and fed, and how empty it was without that hospitality.

Butler sneered at the man. "Took comfort from the enemy, did you?" And the sergeant replied, "They weren't called the enemy then. They were always naught but farmers."

That night as clouds raced across the face of the moon they heard the movements of animals hunting in the forest. A wolf howled far away and the voice of a great horned owl echoed across the emptiness to sound like an advancing army of winged predators.

When the smudged red eye of the dawn broke the horizon, it quickly disappeared behind a dense ridge of clouds so dirty they looked like they could rain down ashes. The camp began to stir and Butler opened his eyes to another day of searching. They'd keep on toward Chipoudy, where the Acadian Beausoleil was rumored to be in hiding with a large group of refugees.

At the first village they came to that morning they poked about in the ruins and looked for evidence of recent visitors. All they found were animal tracks – fox, raccoon, skunk – so they continued on their way. They'd traveled a good part of the day and the sky had cleared to a deep empty blue when he saw an orchard in the distance. The fruit on the trees was lit to a bright red by the afternoon sun and would attract anyone looking for food. Butler decided on a cautious advance in case someone was there.

At the edge of a field that looked like it had been partly harvested before the Acadians were taken away, spoiled shocks of grain lay on the ground where the farmer and his sons must have left them to go to the local church to hear the governor's proclamation. A flock of black birds that picked at the seeds still left in the fallen heads of grain took off in a great flutter of wings as the soldiers approached. Butler noticed there was evidence that someone had returned there and taken more of the harvest. And now he thought he heard someone in the orchard; he motioned his men to silence.

Indistinct female voices carried down the wind to them and Butler waved one of the scouts to go and take a look. After a short time, the man returned and said there were a few women with some children, picking apples.

"Does it mean others are nearby? Men as well?" Butler hissed.

"Very like to be. But none that I saw by the orchard."

He motioned to his men to pull back from the edge of the field, and go into the nearby forest to where there was a clearing and then he gathered them around. "I want to know if there're others. We'll stay here tonight. No fires. Scouts are to follow those women and see where they go. We may sweep up a whole village of them."

Just before midnight the spies returned. "Small inlet not far from here. Settled in this side of it. Only a few houses. Looks to be a dozen or so – men, women and children. Couple of canoes on the beach. Didn't see any watchman."

Butler roused his men. "We'll leave now. Move quiet and set ourselves under cover. We'll bring them in." He thought that if he took enough prisoners he could go back to Halifax. Maybe Lawrence would send someone else out to hunt and find the next batch.

In the pre-dawn light the last soldier took his place in the ambuscade.

A man emerged from one of the huts, yawned and stretched and went into a bush to take a piss. He finished and went back inside. A child came out next, then one or two others. A woman came out of another hut. The casual innocence of their movements triggered the predatory blood-lust that rose in Butler whenever he waited the last few seconds before the charge sounded to launch him into battle.

The soldiers rose up all at once surrounding the Acadians who froze in their tracks and stared at them. Someone fired a round and then there was no stopping the soldiers and people were shot down as they ran from their huts. Some older children tried to jump into the water and swim away but they were shot and sank below the surface.

Butler drew his sword; he smelled the gunpowder and a red mist rose up and clouded his vision and a hatred for these strange folk took him over. He ran among the fallen, laughing and hacking at their bodies. When his eyes cleared he looked around at the carnage.

Butler ordered the soldiers to look and see if any Acadian was still left alive.

"Who fired that first shot?" he shouted.

" 'twas me." A man who looked barely old enough to wear a uniform came forward. "Thought I saw a flash from a gun barrel."

"I never gave the order to fire."

"I saw a weapon pointed direct at me and fired to defend my self."

"Search the place for weapons," Butler ordered. "A few squirrel guns would be evidence to report they fired on us first."

The soldiers scattered to rummage around the huts. "We'll find them, sir."

When they were finished searching they fired the huts. He ordered his men to form their ranks and when he walked down the line and searched their faces, he knew there was no way the story of what happened here could be kept under wraps.

HALIFAX

Cecilie got out of the boat and walked with the other women only as far as the nearest grove of trees, to a concealed clearing. One of the women told her about it, and said that she found it a fine place to be private with her thoughts. Mathieu and Robert waited for her there.

She explained how she had seen Armand and decided to stay with him and share whatever fate brought them. She told them her duty was with her husband and until the transport ship came to take them away, she would stay with the other Acadian wives and bring food across to the prisoners.

"But ye can't do that," Mathieu insisted. "He'd want you to stay with your family, with us. He asked me to take care of you. There has to be a way to get him out."

"He's my husband. I'm carrying his child. We need to be together, wherever that may be." Now Cecilie was crying.

"You're pregnant?" Robert asked, his voice sounding strange and foolish. "How can that be?"

"I'm a married woman. That's what's supposed to be. A woman's meant to bear children and make a family for her husband."

"I know that," Robert said. "But aren't ye better off to stay with us and we find how to spring him out of that prison?"

"How'd ye think to manage that? It's such a fortress with all the soldiers about. Not to mention the currents and the tides. Indians won't even try to help them. That's how risky it is. Why'd you chance such a dangerous thing? You'd just get yourselves captured."

"We'd do it for you," Mathieu insisted.

Robert tapped him on the shoulder. "She's right, ye know. We'd all end up in there waiting for the ship to come for us. And what about Olivide and Josef? They've come here because of us. Not right to get them into some madcap scheme that gets them captured."

"What does any of it mean any more?" Cecilie trembled. She put her hands to her face and tears came streaming down. Mathieu reached out to put his arms around her but she shook him off.

"If I go back with you to Tintamarre do ye think the women and children will still be there? Or will they've left to go hide somewhere safe? No, I've to stay with my husband and he's over on that island. At least I know where he is and I can be with him. When the ship comes here to take the Acadians away, I've got to go with him." She sniffled.

"So ye say we're to leave you here? I'm to leave you and chance you'll be all right because they'll let ye be with your husband?"

"Ye must. It'll be too dangerous to roam these woods alone. Such talk as I heard over there – soldiers are free to say how they hunt our people down to ship us away. Some are even shot. How can we resist what they're doing to our folk?"

"I don't want you to go away from me. It's selfish I know, but I love ye."

"Oh, Mathieu. The time for that is past. You have to find another to marry and make a family with." She turned to Robert. "Do ye hear what I say? Goes for you too."

Mathieu stood like a stone. "So ye believe I have to just go and leave you behind?"

"It's the best thing. I'll be with the women here and with Armand over on the island. One day we'll be gone but we'll be together. As it should be."

Robert hugged her. "Good bye, then. God take you in his care." He withdrew a few steps and looked at Mathieu as if to encourage him to make his own parting with her.

But Mathieu looked at Cecilie as if he saw his life dissolving in front of him.

"You'll get over it," she said, "and one day we may find each other again. We have to hope we Bancouers aren't all lost to each other forever."

Mathieu put his arms around her and gave her a lover's kiss. "It's that I love you so deep and long for you every day of my life. Did you forget how we pledged ourselves to each other when we were young? I felt like I was already married to you. Then Armand comes along and everything changes. I don't understand how I lost you to him." He squeezed his eyes to hold back the tears.

Cecilie opened her mouth to insist he stop that kind of talk, but she understood where his words came from because she too had felt that way about him before she met his uncle. She didn't know why it happened but when she looked into Armand's eyes that first time it was like falling off a cliff into a different world and finding herself in a place she had not known to exist before, one that felt right to her, that felt secure and lasting. And in just a matter of seconds she knew Armand owned her heart and she could never love anyone else as she loved him.

"I carry his child," she said in a soft voice. "How can I deprive him of seeing it born? It isn't as if he doesn't know about it. Remember how he's already lost a wife and a child, and for how long that haunted him. We'll suffer other things when the British send us away but so will many others like us. How could I add to his burdens by leaving him alone now?"

"But I love you and your child. I'll protect you both. And we'll be free."

"You know I could nivver leave him. And because I love him being faithful to him is all my freedom."

She looked at Mathieu, his face full of the naked longing that she would realize he was the one she needed and the one she should love, and let him take her away from where Armand lay lost and hopeless in that prison. He was already doomed to exile and Cecilie knew he would understand if she didn't go back there to choose that same fate for herself and her child. Mathieu stood silent and gazed into her face and waited for it to fill with love and open to him. As the moments passed with only the look of sorrow in her eyes, he understood it was not to be.

One minute Etienne was making his way through the empty forest and in the next he was surprised by soldiers chasing him in hot pursuit. He held the priest's habit bunched in his hands and ran as fast as he could. He was wearing the garment again, just until the transport ship arrived, to escort the Acadian women who brought food over to the island each day and then he could give up the cassock altogether.

He had been asked that morning to take one last assignment on the road, by a messenger who said he came from Hugh. But where he searched for the young family reported walking toward Minas he found no one. He thought about the women crossing to the island without him, and wondered how Cecilie had found her way to Halifax without being taken by a patrol. That had to be more than luck. She certainly didn't come on her own. He finally remembered to put her husband's letter in his pocket, imagining how her face would fill with pleasure when he held it out to her.

He felt the pounding of feet getting closer and Etienne ran for his life. The land which was filled with the radiant color of fall when the Acadians were put on board the transport ships and taken away to exile, now stood leafless and empty. He had seen oxen dead in their traces, still attached to carts that yet stood in the red mud at the high tide mark on the shore, where they had hauled family goods for loading onto the long-gone ships. He had passed farms where crops were burned inside the barns; where sheds, pens and farm houses had gone up in smoke; and where farm animals had been slaughtered. The smell of decaying flesh mingled with that of charred wood and incinerated crops reached out to some distance from farms and villages and drew scavenging animals in from the forest.

He was running out of breath and there was no place to hide. They began to close in on him and one of them sprinted across a clearing, caught the back of Etienne's cassock and yanked him to the ground. The others caught up and hauled him to his feet. They pulled off his robe and bound him and threw him naked onto a mound of twigs and leaves. After the noise of the pursuit silence descended on the forest. The men were winded from the chase and sat a little way off from their captive, talking about what they had been ordered to do to him.

A drifting bank of clouds intermittently covered the face of the afternoon sun, its rays bursting through openings to pick out a tree or a hill in clear golden light. A shaft of light illuminated the priest.

They stopped drinking the whiskey from their canteens long enough to consider the figure of their victim lit by the heavenly radiance, but even this beatific sign was not enough to compel them to either offer Etienne a drink or to stop what they were about to inflict upon him.

They pulled him upright, bound him to the tree and made the scalp cuts on his forehead and temples. They jeered at him, poked him, slapped his face, and punched him.

Etienne pleaded with them to stop. But when he looked at their mocking faces he knew it was no use. He recognized Butler's bullies and knew they followed his orders. They searched his robe for anything of value. Armand's letter and a few coins were all they found. The letter was written in French – they couldn't even read it but they decided to take it as evidence to prove the priest was spying on the English. They waved it in his face and screamed he was a traitor.

Then someone cut and peeled back the skin from his skull, taking it right to the bone. Blood gushed down Etienne's face, filling his eyes and blinding him to which of them pulled on his hair and his skin and who it was that finished cutting his scalp. They executed the deed in a blood-lust fury fanned by the sight and smell of their victim and his pitiful whimpers. Holding up the scalp, one of them gave an impromptu version of an Indian war whoop and danced about while the others laughed. Then another untied his body and Etienne toppled to the ground. They kicked him; at first each impact brought forth a grunt and then no matter how hard the blow, only wheezes. They spat on him and left him to finish his dying. The letter fell from someone's pocket and landed in the leaves.

Josef and Olivide heard a man's screams and the voices that laughed and taunted him. They crawled through the brush toward the commotion in time to witness Butler's hectors take Etienne's scalp. They heard the sound of his skin being torn from the bone and the metallic perfume of fresh blood carried down the wind to them. Olivide had all he could do to keep from vomiting and Josef pushed his face deep into the packed leaves to escape the horror.

The murderers finally tramped off into the forest shouting drunken curses at each other. There was a brief fistfight over the scalp and it changed hands with a burst of laughter and then the noise receded. A bird twittered from a nearby tree and the boys crept to where the priest lay. Olivide saw the letter lying near Etienne's body and picked it up. There was nothing to be done for the priest now other than to bury him; gray-faced and shaken they went to find Mathieu and Robert and guide them to where the naked body lay.

The assassins brought the scalp to Butler, first hesitating at the door of the officers' barracks to look for any sign of Daiell. When they didn't see him they came inside and handed it over. "Here's the rest of him and evidence of him being a spy, as ye ordered us," their leader said. He handed the scalp to one of his men while he dug into his pocket for the letter. "Had a letter but must've fallen out when we were about finishing him off."

Captain Sean Butler was dressed in his red coat with its brass buttons and insignias polished to a gleam and his white breeches cleaned to perfection. He was revolted by the bloody mass the men tried to press into his hands.

"What're ye bringing this in here for? I'm dressed to meet with the Governor. Can't go to him with blood and muck spattered on me. Careful with that thing. Couldn't ye think to toss it into a rag and save it aside, bring it later?" he snarled at them. "See that cloth over there? Drop the hair on top of it and then put it here." He pointed to the table. They scurried to do as he ordered and put the bloody prize in front of him. Butler dug into his purse for the coins to pay them the scalp bounty and tossed them carelessly onto the table. The coins bounced and fell on the floor and the assassins went down on their hands and knees to scoop them up.

After his bullies scuttled out the door, Butler looked at the grisly trophy and spoke as if he imagined Etienne or his ghost could hear him. "Should've come to me instead of the Carrot. I'd have been able to take care of ye and you'd have been together with me. But no, ye loved that doltish Scot." He squeezed his eyes and brushed off the tear that ran down his cheek. Then his voice hardened and shook with frustration. "Fool ye were to choose him when 'twas I ye should've turned to for protection." He stared at the scalp and his voice softened and took a higher pitch. "Once you were such a pretty boy. Now look at you. Hope ye still think the Carrot was worth it."

When Hugh returned to the fort, Etienne wasn't in his quarters so he went to look for him and heard a rumor that a priest had been taken and was found to be a French spy and been killed because he resisted arrest. He recognized the soldiers who were involved as Butler's hectors and questioned them about it. When they told him they had given the priest's scalp to Captain Butler, Hugh was too stunned to press the men for details. Instead, he went right to Butler's room in the officer's barracks and confronted him.

"What d'ye want with it?" Butler sounded uneasy when Hugh asked to see Etienne's scalp. Hugh called upon all his strength to keep a hold on his temper.

"I'm asking you to show it to me," he repeated.

Butler saw through his effort at self-control and taunted him. "No reason I should."

"Then we'll settle that with Governor Lawrence." Hugh turned away as if to leave and Butler gave him a strange look but produced the scalp and unwrapped the cloth that covered it.

"Here's the traitor's hair."

Hugh's eyes darkened with pain and anger. "What makes ye call him that?"

"That's what I deem he was."

"Well you're wrong," Hugh growled. "Your bullies killed our own man. Someone set him up – must've been you since it was your hectors that chased him down and killed him."

Butler shrugged. "Where's your proof? Besides, he was impersonating a priest, ye say? Maybe it was God who meted him out the punishment for his impudence."

"How'd you know to tell your men he was dressed as a priest?"

"I saw him before in priest's garb. He was in Fort Beausejour after we took it. Ran off with the two Acadians that killed Jenkins and his sergeant. Why wouldn't I recall it? Proved he was nothing but a turncoat spy for the French. My men found him and caught him. Gave him what he deserved."

"You're wrong and you know it." Hugh strove to control himself. "Etienne's identity as a priest wasn't supposed to be known. It was nobody's business to chase him down and kill him." Hugh forced himself to look at the bloody scalp. "The Governor needs to know that Etienne was killed by your men as he carried out his duty. I'm asking him to make an inquiry as to how it happened that you gave the orders to run him down and take his life."

Hugh knew Butler was guilty but he had no witness. His thoughts churned as he stalked away and headed for Lawrence's office.

What if he was wrong about Butler? He felt like he was locked in a closet with smooth bare walls that sealed him off from seeing the truth. What if it was done at the Governor's order? But then, Lawrence was direct; he would have called Hugh on the carpet as Etienne's contact, and had him arrested and thrown into a cell and dealt with right there. Hugh believed Etienne's death was a personal vendetta, one that pointed straight to Butler.

He had seen Butler look at Etienne more than once with eyes black with either anger or lust. He'd seen that look in men's eyes often enough to believe the two were rooted in the same ground. He recalled when they sailed aboard the *Everly* how Butler watched Etienne as he slept; then Butler contrived to get his attention by cutting his arm, claiming it was an accident and had to be sewn up. It was a strange way to act unless Butler lusted for Etienne and tried to make it known to him. Etienne was always sympathetic to a wounded man and the thought of him being manipulated that way left Hugh shaken to the core.

Suddenly he understood the meaning behind Butler's senseless remarks about their friendship – he doesn't get what he wants, then he's jealous and thinks all manner of things. That makes a bully like him doubly dangerous. Hugh drew in a troubled breath. It was a sordid game, one that was always played outside the rules.

The Governor's large office was furnished with only a writing table and a chair. A portrait of King George II hung on the wall behind the desk, between tall windows that looked out onto the parade ground. A spider worked busily on a web, connecting one corner of the portrait with the edge of the window frame. Sunlight streamed through and dust motes danced in the beams. The governor sat with his back to the light, so at first Lawrence's face was mostly shadowed. Outside, a cloud passed across the sun and the room was briefly darkened. Lawrence's face and that in the King's portrait were clearly visible side by side for a few moments. Lawrence invited him to speak, and George II peered over his shoulder at Hugh with eyes that seemed to question his right to exist. The sovereign's mouth was set, not in the customary expression of mild benevolence, but in a curl of displeasure. It seemed as if whatever the Governor might say would have this King's automatic approval.

Hugh pulled himself together and reported Etienne's loss and what he had already learned about it.

"Spies are always in danger of death or worse. I'm very sorry he died at our own hands, but those men couldn't know who he was or what services he rendered to us. They found him in the forest dressed as a priest; they called to him and he ran away. We can't punish them for acting as they did."

"We must let it go? Without investigating how his identity was compromised?"

"Do you have evidence that it was?"

"Not yet, but I believe it very likely was."

"Let it go then," Lawrence was firm. "Only we're to know that. I'm sorry your friend was killed, but there's nothing else to be done. Etienne Massé died in the line of duty. Let it go, Daiell." The governor's tone had turned harsh. Hugh saluted and left Lawrence's office dejected that he had no satisfaction from the interview. And if that was possible, he felt even worse about Etienne's death.

Lawrence sat for a moment as if to contemplate what he had just heard. Could it be possible that Butler learned about the spy, then betrayed him and set his bullies on him, as a man not willing to be identified had whispered to his aide? It was a vendetta, the informant had said, but he could give no reason for it. A man who would take such an opportunity to address a personal grudge would be capable of other things. The slaughter of that village of defenseless Acadians that he summoned Butler to answer to came to mind. Shouting from the anteroom interrupted his thoughts and he sent his aide to investigate.

Sean Butler stood in the middle of the bare room in his best dress uniform. A fire burned in the small grate, but it was not enough to take away the chill. Next to him stood his aide holding his newly brushed hat. Hugh felt shabby by comparison, and out of sorts by what had passed between him and Lawrence.

Butler seemed to ignore him so Hugh chose to return the compliment by passing them by and leave the room without recognizing them. Butler swung around to face him; his cold black eyes focused like a snake's examining a mouse before striking at it. Feeling at a disadvantage, Hugh stared back at him. Butler shifted himself to block his way, fixing his eyes on Hugh's face. "Ye look distressed, man. More bad news?"

"Nothing I'd want to discuss with you."

"So ye told Lawrence about your boy's death, did ye?" The words punched the air and landed like brass knuckles on Hugh's fragile self-control.

"Who asked you?" he growled, taking another step toward the door.

"Saw his body. Made a right mess of him, they did."

Hugh stopped in his tracks. "What'd you say?"

"Just that the men told me what happened, so I went out and saw it for myself. Got what traitors deserve, he did."

Hugh's face went black as a beet and he spoke through clenched teeth. "Etienne was no traitor and you know it."

"So you say. We can't ask him now so we'll never know, will we?"

"When did you know he'd gone out?"

"I heard the same rumor he did, about a poor family in the forest that needed help."

Hugh exploded. "So it's true as I heard. You meddled with Etienne, what you had no business to do. You gave the order to send him when you knew I wasn't there to gainsay it. Something needed doing, it could've waited. Acadians're gone now. What'd be the difference?"

"Acadians ain't all gone. As ye know had ye the eyes to see." Butler smirked.

"Who exactly was it that killed Etienne?"

Butler giggled. "So what if he's killed? Happens all the time. What's one less of them French traitors? They're not important. It's us who lead the men that count."

"Ye make me sick." Hugh stomped away but the poisonous seed of revenge was rooted in his heart just as surely as if Butler had physically opened his chest and planted it there.

Lawrence's aide stood in the doorway, a witness both to the encounter and to Butler's provocations and shouted, "You, sir! You're wasting the Governor's time with your nonsense. He's finished waiting for ye."

Butler licked his lips and his voice took a conciliatory tone. "You're right. I stand corrected. Why'd I want to keep the Governor waiting for such business as this?"

Hugh's retreating back went rigid as if he was shot and he fought to control himself.

The officers' quarters were empty. Etienne's scalp, caked with dried blood, lay just as Hugh had seen it, as if Butler intended to leave it out for display. Hugh wrapped the cloth around it and stuffed it inside his jacket. Back in his own room, he undid the cloth and held the scalp in his hands, staring at it until he heard the sounds of someone entering the barracks. Quickly he rewrapped it and placed it in his trunk.

Butler was pleased that his taunts hit their mark and preened with satisfaction. Now Daiell was browned, he could be goaded into challenging him for a duel. He gloated to think how he would have his way about that. Butler took his hat from his aide, set it on his head, and entered the Governor's office.

Lawrence looked up from his desk. Butler saluted, smartly doffed the hat and tucked it under his left arm. Its plume trailed down like a curl of black smoke.

"Well, sir," the Governor began, "Since you've been in my command, you've developed a reputation for the way you treat the men, not to mention how you behave to your fellow officers."

Butler stood and waited for Lawrence to continue. "Major Daiell was just now with me and I asked him some questions about the death of Etienne Massé. I want to know if you had anything to do with that."

"No, sir," Butler spoke easily. "But it was my men who found him in the forest in a priest's dress. Thought he was a traitor. They chased him and killed him. Brought back the scalp. Was meant to be taken as proof he was dead."

"They had no orders from you or anyone else to take his life?" Lawrence asked.

"None I know of, sir." Butler stared at the portrait on the wall behind Lawrence.

The Governor went to the window as if stepping away for an interval to judge the value of what the Captain said. Then he turned and looked at Butler again.

"I hear that when you're sent out to round up Acadian drifters to bring them back to hold for deportation, you've caught nary a one. Yet I hear stories of dead bodies lying in the woods where you were sent to search."

Butler was surprised by the shift of his questioning.

"What've you to say to that?" The Governor waited for his answer.

"Most Acadians we've found were armed. Last ones fired at us from ambuscade. Hit a couple of my men; nearly got me. But God was with us. He protected me. "

"That's ridiculous," Lawrence was annoyed. "We already confiscated the Acadians' weapons. If they still have anything, those're no more than squirrel guns. That brings me to ask about the people ye came on at that village the men are talking about. I hear it was a massacre of mostly women and children, and you're the officer who ordered it."

Butler looked at him with the mock innocence of a small boy caught with his hand in a biscuit jar. Lawrence waited for an answer. "Were ye going to tell me what happened? You weren't sent out to kill people, just find them and bring them in."

"One of my men thought he was threatened by a musket. Fired to save himself, he told me afterward. First shot fired, the rest of them volleyed. Before I knew it, Acadians were dead. Every one of them. We checked afterward to find if any still lived."

Lawrence drew himself up to his full height. "You're responsible for your men's actions. And for your own. Soldiers are trained to fight men armed against them, not murder civilians and then go hacking their bodies to pieces."

Butler was nonplussed. His face quivered like he remembered the preacher's did when he sent his voice low and soft to make the congregation listen for his words. "I've nivver experienced the like of it," he began in a whisper. "It was like a cloud come over us," his voice began to rise, "and our blood heated" – now he was shouting – "and a voice cried, "Kill them all" Like sometimes we hear when a battle begins." He looked at Lawrence. 'Sir, I believe it's God's voice urging us on to do His work."

Lawrence was so shocked by Butler's answer that for a moment he was too stunned to speak.

"Preposterous," he spoke the first word that came to mind. Then he thought about men in battle and how each side always believed they fought under a divine mandate when they met their opposites on the field. If they didn't believe they served the Deity and fought for a purpose greater than themselves, how could they face death as bravely as most soldiers did?

At the same time he recognized this was no battle, but an ambush set to trap innocent unarmed folk. He refused to let himself be drawn down a path intended to change the facts to something that more suited Butler's purpose. He already knew enough about Butler to see he was capable of such manipulation of facts.

"You'll be confined to the fort until I say otherwise." Now he'd made that decision Lawrence looked Butler over – the impeccable uniform that was the badge of British integrity belied by the black eyes that seemed a portal into darker depths and the sneering expression that habitually resided on his face.

"Well he's Irish after all, and had to come here because he fathered a bastard on a nobleman's daughter," Lawrence thought, "as if that's excuse enough for this kind of thing." His expression changed. "You're dismissed," he said in as neutral a tone as he could manage.

When Butler returned to his quarters, he saw the bloody scalp was missing. He expected the Carrot would come back for it. Now all he could think of was how to maneuver Hugh Daiell to challenge him to a duel. He would find a way to provoke him in front of witnesses. He could be arrested when Daiell was killed. But if he could prove Daiell instigated it, he'd get off Scot free. He laughed at his own pun until tears filled his eyes.

HALIFAX (December)

Mathieu and Robert found Olivide and Josef wandering about in a troubled haze, careless of their safety. They told of witnessing the priest's murder and Olivide held out to Mathieu the letter Etienne was carrying. He opened it, recognized Armand's signature and tucked it into his pocket.

Then they went to where Etienne's body lay. The cassock was on the ground nearby and they fetched it to wrap the remains and carry them away for burial. They worked in silence as they dug his grave, carefully lowered his body into the loamy earth and scooped handfuls of dirt over him. When they finished gathering and piling rocks on top of Etienne's grave they stood around it and prayed for his immortal soul.

Then Mathieu said, "We have to go back and tell Cecilie the priest is dead. I'll give her Armand's letter he was carrying."

Olivide and Josef insisted, "We can't stay here no more."

"Every day it's more likely the British'll catch us. Then what?"

"It was horrible what they did to him." Their words flowed like a wild torrent rushing from a broken dam. They had had more than enough of wandering where the enemy always surrounded them. They had witnessed the young priest's terrible death and had to bury him afterward, his body all bloody and broken. What happened to him could happen to them. Their eyes widened as if they recognized their own mortal danger for the first time.

Josef insisted, "Don't go back to Halifax. We need to be quit of this place."

But Mathieu was steeled to do what he believed was his duty and he convinced Robert they had to return to Halifax, even without Olivide and Josef, and give Cecilie the letter and tell her of Etienne's fate.

When they got to the grove where they last met her, they saw the whole place was deserted. Across the bay the sloop that took the women back and forth approached the dock at George's Island. The transport sat at anchor; boats plied back and forth from it, ferrying people and supplies.

"That must be the ship come for them. *Providence* I make its name to be." Mathieu's eyes filled with tears and his voice shook.

"She'll not be back here," Robert interrupted him. "We need to go. Sun's burning off this fog. Someone's sure to spot us, we don't leave." Robert put his hand on his cousin's arm. "High time we was gone away from this cursed place," Robert insisted.

"Father Etienne should've been to the island and gone aboard the transport." Mathieu shuddered at the memory of the broken body they'd laid to rest. "All he ever asked was what could he do to help you."

"I've nivver seen such a vicious killing," Robert said. "But he's gone now. Think that officer with that big plume on his hat had something to do with it?"

"Wouldn't have been anyone else," Mathieu insisted. "Remember what happened at Beausejour when we escaped? Jacques-Pierre's shot in the back? Father Etienne came out with that other officer that got shot by accident? The priest helped us carry Jacques-Pierre to the woods and bury him. He was a good man and there're some as can't stand such decency. Good man like the priest makes that kind look worse to themselves." His fingers touched the letter still in his pocket.

"Ye do think it was that officer questioned you about Le Loutre?" Then Robert's voice dropped. "Same one who shot Jacques-Pierre."

"Him or his men. Same thing." Mathieu paused. "We stay to watch the ship go. Then if she ain't come back here, we leave."

"No," Robert was firm. He took his cousin by the shoulders and looked into his eyes. "She's already gone, Mathieu. She ain't nivver coming back. We're to leave now."

Butler watched for his chance to bait Hugh and it wasn't long before he found it.

"Where's your little friend gone to now?" He came over to Hugh in the officer's mess and whispered it into his face.

Hugh stood up. He was the taller, and looked down at Butler. "Say that again?"

Butler waved his hand as if to strike Hugh in the face. Instinctively Hugh raised his arm to ward off the expected blow and Butler leaned forward and grabbed his wrist. He shouted, "He struck me!" Heads turned to look at them. "I didn't," Hugh shouted. "He's trying to provoke me."

Now that they had everyone's attention, Butler raised his voice and taunted him. "Here's a prime coward among us. And now his little boy's been killed. Did ye know that apothecary Etienne Massé masqueraded as a priest? Went among the Acadians? Supposed to be a spy for us? What was he really up to?"

It was more than Hugh could stand. He had had more than enough of Butler's taunts and shouted his challenge. One of the other officers, Captain James Danforth, stepped forward and offered to be Hugh's second. No one came forward for Butler. "I've my own man who'll stand by me," he scowled at the snub.

Hugh went back to his room. The challenge had dissipated his anger and now he knew he had to concentrate to prepare himself. As he brushed his coat and polished the brass buttons, he thought about how Butler, who had a reputation for dueling maneuvered him to make his challenge. Hugh had only ever been called out once and then it was fists. He came away the winner, with cuts and bruises but no broken bones. After that experience he wasn't one to go seeking such contests.

The scalp lay under the false bottom of his trunk; he took it out, unfolded the cloth and stared at it. If he was to die for his friend then he wanted Etienne with him when it happened.

Unaccustomed to the apothecary's needles, he pricked his fingers over and over as he worked around the clots of dried blood and clumps of hardened earth that glued the tangled hair together to sew the scalp to the inside of his shirt. He finished his work and held the shirt up to look at it. He put it on; bits and pieces of dried blood and dirt scratched his skin as he paced the floor and thought out every aspect of the duel. He tried to get some rest before he had to face what the morning would bring, but each time he closed his eyes, Etienne's bloodied face stared at him.

He finally fell into a troubled sleep, and in the early hours of the morning he entered a nightmare. In it, he was bound to a tree near the one the bullies tied Etienne to. Butler stood near them in his dress uniform wearing an enormous red hat with a huge pluming black feather; he taunted Hugh to watch them torture and kill his friend.

Etienne was terrified and strained against his ropes to lean toward him. He cried, "I'm caught. Help me, Hugh! They've bound me, like the jealous, hate-filled rabble that bound my Christ." He gave a long anguished wail. "I'm no traitor. I did what they asked me to. I helped the British. Now these fools treat me like some turncoat because I dressed as a priest to do their bidding. These devils deny the truth. They don't care what I say. They understand it's me, Etienne, they torture."

Hugh screamed, "No! It's all a mistake! Let him go!"

Butler turned and the face that looked at him from beneath the brim of the red hat became a death's head.

Etienne shrieked, "I'll suffer as my Lord did. When death comes they say the everlasting Love of God cradles the spirit. Will it draw my soul to the Light?"

The Death's Head growled, "What if you're wrong? What if it's the Dark that claims your soul? Ye refused to love me. Why should anyone save you? You've no hope no more."

Hugh screamed, "No, no! Let him be. He's innocent!"

"I die at the hands of this mocking rabble. Must I love them so I can be redeemed? They take my cloak, my coins, even my hair that they ripped from my scalp and divide the spoils among themselves. Their laughter makes me afraid. Who comes to rescue my soul? Hugh, I cry to you. You're the only one on earth who ever loved me. And I loved you."

The Death's Head turned its stare to Etienne and growled, "Ye loved him but ye had no love for me."

Etienne screamed, "Look at me, Hugh! If ye ever loved me then save me, dearest friend."

Hugh woke in the predawn darkness covered with sweat; his face was drenched with tears. When he was a child back in Scotland the adults told in hushed voices of spirits who roamed the moors crying for someone to give them vengeance. Now Etienne called to him from his dream. Once the selkie had found him it'd never let him go until he'd either done its bidding or been killed trying. He must win the duel with Butler to release Etienne to find his eternal rest.

Hugh was worn out and nervous when he met Danforth just before sunrise to walk out to the appointed place. From time to time, men who had a private grievance came and locked horns to take off pressure. But as the aggrieved man, Butler had chosen pistols over fists.

A light snow had fallen overnight from skies that remained overcast with great leaden lumps of clouds. A merciless chill permeated the air and the men shook as the damp cold deepened its hold on them, penetrating coats and uniforms to wrap its icy fingers around their bones. As early as Hugh and his second were, Butler already waited for them and he was wearing the red hat with the flowing black plume. His nasal snarl greeted them. "Want to get this over with. Don't you? Freeze to death before we settle this, we dilly-dally 'round here."

Danforth took Hugh by the shoulders and turned him so they faced each other. "Don't let him get to you. He'll try to throw you off your stride by talking nonsense or saying things he knows will hurt. Forget about everything but the duel."

Hugh nodded. "Hard for me to forget what he caused done to Etienne."

"Ye can't think of that now. Remember Butler's a bully and he's a crack shot. Ye need to be better than him. Compose yourself. Rest of us depend on ye."

Butler broke into raucous laughter. "What're ye waiting for? Ye need a conference? Danforth, maybe ye need to teach him how to hold his pistol."

"Pay him no mind," Danforth said. "Ye hear how nervous he is. Take your time. If he can't hurry you it throws him off his pace."

Robert and Mathieu had taken cover for the night in the grove near the dueling site. At the first sound of movement at the clearing, they took notice. They slithered through the underbrush and watched Butler stand with his second and talk about a duel with another officer they called the 'Carrot'. When Hugh arrived with Danforth, they recognized him. Mathieu whispered, "He's the one in Armand's letter. Was their guard over at the island."

Robert's teeth chattered. "Here's our chance to get Jacques-Pierre's killer. Looks like he's out to get himself another victim. Let's get him now. Get away afore we freeze to the spot." Mathieu saw the darkness fill his eyes and put a hand on his arm. "He shoots the red-head, then you get him – and I shoot the second." They hunkered down to watch.

The duelists were ready and stood back to back. The seconds called out the paces in unison. Just before they reached ten, Butler turned and in a single fluid motion, raised his pistol and fired. The lead smacked Hugh in the chest; he staggered and just barely managed to stay on his feet. His breaths rasped as he tried to raise his weapon.

"Hold steady, man," Danforth shouted. "Concentrate. Raise up the pistol."

Butler's second screamed, "Turn yerself, sir. Silhouette." Butler looked ashen.

"Foul," Danforth yelled. "Cheat!"

Robert spoke to his cousin in a hoarse whisper. "Shoot a man aforetime when he's not looking. Just like he got Jacques-Pierre in the back. He's to die this day."

Mathieu cautioned him. "Wait and see what the Carrot does. It's his fight this time. Let him finish it if he can."

"Coward," Danforth spat. "You're not a man, Butler. You're naught but a rank miserable fake and everyone knows it."

Hugh slowly raised his arm and tried to pull the trigger but the pistol grew too heavy for him; his arm lowered, and he collapsed. Two crisp shots from behind the trees echoed in the cold still air. Butler cried out as he fell to the ground mortally wounded, and writhed in pain. His second lay motionless.

Danforth turned toward the direction of the shots and shouted, "Shoot me too?" A crow cawed in the distance and others took up its cry, as if their endless repetition fading away into the forest would force a response. But no other voice answered.

"There's no weapons here but dueling pistols. Only one left not discharged." He held up Hugh's pistol and waved it in the air. Danforth hoped the assailants, whoever they were, would take that as an invitation to leave and he heard a rustling that could have come from a light breeze rattling the dry leaves on the branch of a nearby oak.

Danforth knelt beside Hugh and opened the bag of bandages he had brought along. Hugh's teeth chattered as Danforth put his hand against his chest. A wad of something that felt like horse hair padded the inside of his shirt. Danforth pulled it open and saw the bullet had passed almost through the wadding, struck his chest just above a rib, and left a slight wound – the bullet had broken the skin but had not gone inside; he exhaled in relief and then drew back in surprise as he recognized the wadding he held in his hand was a human scalp.

Hugh remained unconscious. Danforth plucked the bullet from the wound and put it in the pocket of Hugh's jacket. Then he pulled out a length of bandage, tore open Hugh's shirt and wrapped it around his chest to bind the wound and hold the rib in place. Hugh stirred as Danforth laid the scalp on top of the bandage and wrapped his coat around him.

Danforth's teeth chattered as he began to speak. "Won't get us much to pursue whoever it was that fired. We've no weapons to fight them if we do catch them. They're gone now, the more's our luck. Butler and that bully of his are dying; it may be they're already dead. Good if they are. Those two devils deserve it."

He turned his head toward the bodies. "I'll look to be sure, then go and get help to get ye back." Danforth walked over to where Butler and his man lay. "Gone," he shouted. He took their coats and brought them to cover Hugh. "Be back fast as I can. Hold on, Hugh. You're to recover from this."

Hugh lay there, his face slack and pasty as Danforth ran toward the fort. He whispered, "Now it's done and ye can rest, Etienne," just before he fainted.

Danforth found a wagon and a man to help bring Hugh back. The doctor pushed his way through the crowd that was gathering around the cart because someone was circulating a rumor about a duel. They moved Hugh onto a stretcher and carried him inside the barracks.

Danforth told the crowd about the duel and showed them Hugh's pistol with the round still chambered in it. Once they'd heard the story a couple of soldiers took the wagon back to the dueling place to see if Butler and his crony were dead. They returned with the two bodies bouncing in the wagon bed as it came along the rutted road. A burial party was hastily assembled to give them to the ground without ceremony or farewell. The red hat was laid on the stones atop Butler's grave; a light breeze puffed out the black plume and it danced against the freshly turned earth.

A few days later Hugh was on his way to recovery, and Governor Lawrence and his aide came to the barracks. Hugh tried to rise from his bed and stand, but Lawrence told him he didn't demand military courtesy from sick and wounded.

"But there is a reason I've come to see ye now." Lawrence looked at him and frowned. "There are penalties for dueling. I know you're well aware." Hugh nodded and cast down his eyes.

"This is a most unusual case. The men all know what happened, at least Danforth's story's going about, and he's the only witness. Was your friend's scalp really fastened inside your shirt? They're saying it saved you from being killed."

Hugh leveled his eyes at Lawrence. "Etienne deserved to know he was revenged, or I was killed for his cause. As for the other, I do believe it was him who saved me."

"They're saying Butler deserved what he got, however strange the way it happened." Lawrence shook his head. "Seems there are Acadians about whose teeth haven't been drawn. Thought at first it smelled like something Beausoleil would do, maybe to revenge that village where Butler killed all those people, but rumor has it he's far from here over at Chipoudy."

"Why would the Acadians just up and shoot him?" Hugh wondered.

"Regardless of that, I have to make a decision about you. I can't have the men going back to dueling with weapons to settle grievances. If you stay at Halifax I'll have to demote you back to the rank of Lieutenant and you may never advance from it again. I can't let what you did stand as example to justify the men can duel and get away with it."

"But I'd never tell a man it was right to duel."

"It's not what they hear ye say, it's what they see you do they take as their example."

Hugh opened his mouth to protest but Lawrence raised a finger in reproach. "Let me finish. If you agree to go to another post, you keep your rank. Danforth's already made up his mind he'll stay a Captain and go to Boston. Maybe you'd like to do the same. Think about it. The *Arbutus* is bringing supplies to Halifax; she's due in a few days. Ye can tell me then which you choose."

EPILOGUE

After telling about Guillaume's death I felt the past begin to wane, like a door was slowly swinging closed to return them all to the privacy of the hereafter. I wondered if it was Liam's translation of his journals that brought Guillaume back at those moments when I know I had communion with him. But now my book is finished. I have to get back to living in the here and now and tend to some unfinished business.

I try not to think about this much less talk about it. I've never told this to anyone before and I wasn't planning to start now. Just before our son should have been born, Liam's voice when he talked to me began to change. And when he spoke about the baby it turned into a sing-songy child's voice and whenever he said anything about the baby coming I thought of a jealous sibling waiting for the birth of a child he already thought of as a rival. That made me worry he might have wanted to hurt the baby even while it was still inside me. He didn't force himself on me physically, maybe because he knew I'd fight like a tiger to resist him. But after the doctor told us he'd lost the foetal heartbeat, Liam stopped the weird behavior and became very sensitive to my needs. I wanted to ask the doctor if he thought a baby could be scared to death when it was inside the womb, but something told me not to. Maybe if the answer to that question was "Yes" I would have had to shoulder another burden – whether or not I had the strength to forgive him. I'm glad I never did ask because I think I already have enough to cope with without having to face that. I still mourn for my baby but the times are fewer and farther apart. Mostly I just can't let myself think too much about it any more because when I do it hurts too much.

As soon as I had the first draft of my story finished, I sent it to them. Next thing I knew they were doing the history thing again. When the e-book version of my family history was published, Liz produced a note supposedly written in the 19th century that gave credence to the story that I thought I had invented. I still want to know if she made it up to give them another reason to hold a press conference and try to drag me into it, or could it be real? She sent me a copy. Judge for yourself:

"October 1875. Jericho Corner, Maine
The story about my great- great-grandfather is like to be true, just as it was passed down to me. Six score years ago Major Hugh Daiell was challenged to a duel

by Capt. Sean Butler. Both were army officers at Halifax, Nova Scotia. Butler fired early and wounded Daiell. There was a scalp sewn inside his shirt that belonged to a friend killed by Butler's men. A Huguenot's scalp saved Hugh's life, was the story told over and over at the fort for years afterward. My grandfather told me he remembers when he was a boy he heard his father tell that Hugh was buried with his friend's scalp tucked inside his uniform coat.

We think the Huguenot's death was the reason he challenged Butler to the duel in the first place. Butler was cut down at the dueling site by fire from unknown persons hidden nearby. Hugh came to Boston after that. Later he married the widow of John Danforth. They had two sons, my grandfather Hugh and Ethan. My father told me his uncle was named for his grandfather's friend, Etienne Massé. Both boys served in the Revolutionary War. Ethan was killed in 1778 at a battlefield near Saratoga, New York."

Hugh Daiell, 4th

It gives me goosebumps every time I read it. I would have liked to include it in my book, but it's about her ancestor and someday Liz may want to write her own family history.

And since Liam hasn't made a public peep about it I suspect he at least believes it's the real deal. If it was *his* letter about *his* ancestor, he'd have published it all over the place – in a heartbeat. Some day I'll corner Liz and ask her about it. For now they're having another good run of publicity so neither of them has the time for an idle chat with me.

Now that I'm finished with my book and my family history is done there's not much reason for them to stay in touch, but I'm sure I'll still hear from them once in a while. And I expect I'll get the answer to that letter of hers one of these days, probably when I least expect it.

TIMELINE

1696 British capture the French privateer Pierre Maisonnat called Baptiste and throw him into prison in Boston

1697/8 End of King William's War. Peace between England and France

1702 Massachusetts Governor Dummer threatens to hang Baptiste as a common criminal

1704 Deerfield massacre. French take Rev. John Williams and his family to exchange them for Baptiste

1710 British take Acadia and rename it Nova Scotia. Port Royal is now Annapolis Royal

1711 Abraham Gaudet leads farmers to attack British troops in Chignecto (area of the present border of Nova Scotia and New Brunswick) near Beaubassin.

1712 French settlers come from Plaisance (Newfoundland) ceded to Britain along with Acadia, to found Louisbourg.

1725 Prudent Robichaud suspended in chains for welcoming Indians in his home.

1727 George II succeeds to the British throne. Acting Governor Armstrong sends Ensign Wroth with a delegation to persuade the Acadians to sign a new oath of allegiance.

1744 War declared between Britain and France. French take Canso but fail to take Annapolis Royal.

1745 French go to attack Annapolis Royal and the English take Louisbourg.

1746 D'Anville Armada of 70 ships and 8000 men sail to retake Louisbourg and free Acadia from British. Storms at sea and disease ravage the fleet and the remnants return to France. Massachusetts Governor Shirley sends 500 militia to Annapolis Royal. Nova Scotia Governor Mascarene sends them to quarter on the Acadians at Grand Pré.

1747 French and Acadians drive English from Grand Pré and they retreat to Annapolis Royal.

1748 War ends in Europe. By the treaty of Aix-la-Chapelle fortress Louisbourg is returned to France.

1749 Cornwallis leaves London with 2500 settlers to build the new town of Halifax in Nova Scotia. (Ca. 1748-9) French build a fort at Beausejour.

1750 The priests Le Loutre and Germain drive the Acadians from Beaubassin and burn the village. The British build Fort Lawrence where Beaubassin stood.

1754 Charles Lawrence becomes Governor of Nova Scotia. Death of Edward How at the hands of Indians incited by Le Loutre.

1755 Fort Beausejour is taken by British regulars under Robert Monckton and the New England militia under John Winslow.

1755 Acadian deportations begin.

GLOSSARY OF TERMS AND DEFINITIONS

aboiteau - dike, built of wood of hollowed-out trees, with a leather flap at the end. The flap opens to drain water from the marshland and closes when the tidal flow pushes against it to keep seawater out.

Baie Francaise - Bay of Fundy

ban-lieu - the distance of a cannon shot. Houses were not allowed to be built within the radius of a cannon shot of a fort.

bit cove - tough guy

bloated - smells like a stinking fish

bully-rock - bad bully

carking - worried, fretful

carrot - red headed person

cull - fop, silly person

dimber - pretty

ding the culls - beat them silly

fibbing - fighting

habitant - dweller, or inhabitant; in this case, Acadian

Hector - cowardly bully, one of a pack of 'Hectors'

Isle (or, Ile) St. Jean - Prince Edward Island

Isle (or, Ile) Royale - Cape Breton Island

Pentagouet - French fort; the site is near present-day Castine, ME, settled by the French early in the 17th century. Southern-most point of

Acadia.

phiz - face, short for physiognomy

Riviere St. Jean - St. John River

Selkie or Silkie - a spirit that usually appears as a seal in the sea, and comes on land as a man

sharp-set - hungry

St. Criox river - forms the present US/Canada boundary between Maine and New Brunswick

sutler - middle man who buys merchandise from the producer and sells to the army or truck houses at a profit, sometimes inflated

swivel gun - small-bore cannon carried by one or two men, field mounted and turned to fire in any direction

truck house - trading post

LIST OF CHARACTERS

FICTIONAL

ACADIAN (HABITANTS OF ACADIA/NOVA SCOTIA) AND INDIAN

BANCOUER:

Guillaume (1680-1754) – emigrated from France with his brothers Jacques and Henri in 1698.

Song Sparrow (1687-1704) – Guillaume's first wife, daughter of chief Rising Hawk and White Heron, sister of Patient Moon.

Paul Dancing Crow (1703-1744) – son of Guillaume and Song Sparrow.

Jerusha Ruisseau (1686-1755) – Guillaume's second wife (m. 1707)

Guillaume-Honoré (b.1708) – first son of Guillaume and Jerusha.

Marthé – wife of Honoré

Mathieu (b. 1732) – son of Honoré and Marthé.

Aimeé (b. 1710) – first daughter of Guillaume and Jerusha.

Robert (b. 1728) – Aimeé's son with Robyn Jenkins.

Modeste Etretat - Aimeé's husband (m. 1732)

Jacques-Pierre (1711-1755) – second son of Guillaume and Jerusha.

Clarice (b.1714) – second daughter of Guillaume and Jerusha.

Virginie (b. 1716) – youngest daughter of Guillaume and Jerusha.

Armand (b. 1720) – youngest son of Guillaume and Jerusha.

Jeanne Louise Montard (1719-1743) – daughter of Pierre Montard, first wife of Armand Bancouer, died with her newborn son of childbed fever.

Cecilie Duchesne (b. 1734) – second wife of Armand Bancouer (m. 1754)

Jacques Albert (1678-1755) – Guillaume's older brother.

Patient Moon (1688-1755) – wife of Jacques, sister of Song Sparrow.

Albert (b. 1710) – oldest son of Jacques and Song Sparrow.

Theo (b. 1713) – second son of Jacques and Song Sparrow.

Henri Edouard (1684-1758) – Guillaume's younger brother.

Marie Watkins (b. 1695) – wife of Henri Bancouer, sister of Samuel

Watkins.

Evangeline (1975-) – Geraldine's daughter; Henri's niece.

Geraldine (1950 -) – Evangeline's mother, Henri's sister.

Henri (1955 -) – Present day descendant of Guillaume via child of Armand and Cecilie, born in North Carolina in 1756. Family custodian of Guillaume's journal.

BREAU, Ismael – habitant of Grand Pré.

CORMIER, Jean – habitant of Annapolis Royal.

DENIS, BIG ALBERT (ca. 1735) – captain of the fishing boat *Emmeline* that took Guillaume to Boston

RICHARD, Bernie – mate aboard the *Emmeline*

DESJARDINS, Simon – manager for the *Compagnie du L' Acadie* in New France, later became the Bancouers' partner in trade.

DUCHESNE, Cecilie (b. 1734) – second wife of Armand Bancouer.

ETRETAT, Modeste – husband of Aimeé Bancouer (m. 1732) and stepfather of Robert.

FLYING SQUIRREL (d. 1704) – disgruntled suitor of Song Sparrow.

HÉBERT, Ambrose – captain of the *Fleur de Lis*.

Aboard the *Fleur de Lis:*

Adam, the purser

James, the mate

Michel, the navigator

LE BRUN, Pitre – recruiter for the *Compagnie du L' Acadie*

MONTARD :

Pierre-Jaspar – captain in the French army, sailed aboard the *Fleur de Lis*

Jeanne-Louise (1719-1743) – daughter of Pierre-Jaspar, and first wife of Armand Bancouer

RICHARD, Bernie – mate aboard the *Emmeline*

RISING HAWK (1665-1720) – Mi'kmaq chief and father of Song Sparrow and Patient Moon, Guillaume's first father-in-law, Jacques' father-in-law, died in a raid on New England fishermen at Canso in 1720

WHITE HERON (b. 1660) – Rising Hawk's wife, mother of Song Sparrow and Patient Moon

RUISSEAU :

Benoit (1660-1730) – Jerusha's father
Marie-Josephte (1665-1732) – Jerusha's mother
Jerusha Ruisseau - Guillaume's wife from 1704-1755
SMILING OTTER – clan shaman, friend of Rising Hawk
THERIOT, René – habitant of Grand Pré

BRITISH AND ENGLISH (OF NEW ENGLAND)

BUTLER:
Sean (1723-1755) – Captain in the British army, came to Halifax in 1749 with Cornwallis; ancestor of Liam Butler.
Liam (1978-) – Professor of History, Acadian history specialist. Descendant of Sean Butler's son born out of wedlock.
DAIELL:
Hugh (1732-?) – British officer, came to Halifax with Cornwallis in 1749, Liz Daiell's ancestor.
Liz (1985-?) – Professor of Canadian studies, Acadian history specialist.
DANFORTH, James (1733-?) – came to Halifax with Cornwallis in 1749, friend of Hugh Daiell, his second in Hugh's duel with Sean Butler.
JAMESON, Caleb – Boston merchant, friend of Samuel Watkins
JENKINS, Robyn (1705-1755) – British officer who came to Beaubassin with Ensign Wroth in 1727. Aimeé's lover, father of Robert.
MASSÉ, Etienne (d. 1755) – Huguenot apothecary, friend of Hugh Daiell who comes to Nova Scotia with him and impersonates a priest to spy on the Acadians for the British.
WATKINS:
Marie (b. 1695) – sister of Samuel and wife of Henri Bancouer
Samuel (b. 1693) – Boston merchant, business partner of Henri Bancouer. Marie's brother.
WARREN, Zachariah – Boston merchant, friend of Sam Watkins

HISTORICAL

FRENCH AND ACADIAN

D'AULNAY, Charles de Menon (1604-1650) – contested with La

Tour for control of Acadia.

BAPTISTE, see Pierre Maisonnat

BEAUSOLEIL, see Broussard

BOISHEBERT, Charles Deschamps de (1727-1797) – French officer at Grand Pré in 1747; fought in Nova Scotia after the expulsions to protect Acadians who escaped deportation; also fought on the 'western frontier', contested territory between New England and New France.

BONAVENTURE – lover of Loiuse Guyon, Madam Damours de Freneuse.

BROUSSARD, Joseph dit. Beausoleil – escaped deportation and led attacks against the British in New Brunswick and Nova Scotia.

DES HERBIERS, Charles de La Raliere (1700-1752) - Governor of Louisbourg from 1749 to 1751.

DURAND, Justinien (n.d.) – Pastor of Port Royal/Annapolis Royal from 1704 to 1720.

DUVIVIER, Joseph Du Pont (1707-1760) – led attacks on Canso and Annapolis Royal in 1744, fought in the Seven Years' (French and Indian) Wars.

FIEDMONT, Louis-Thomas (Jacau) sieur de (1720-?) – engineer at Fort Beausejour.

FRENEUSE, Madam Damours de (Louise Guyon) (1668-?) – lover of Bonaventure, mother of his illegitimate son.

GAUDET, Abraham – Habitant of Missaguesche who led an attack on the English in 1711 near Beaubassin. Fled to Canada, returned in 1713.

GERMAIN, Charles (n.d.) – Pastor of Beaubassin 1745-1748, helped burn the village in 1750.

GIRARD (n.d.) – Paster of Cobequid, 1743-1750.

GUYON, Louise – see Freneuse

HERTEL, Jean-Baptiste, sieur de Rouville (1668-1722) – led the raid on Deerfield, Massachusetts in 1704 to capture Reverend John Williams.

LA CORNE, Louis (1703-1761) – second in command of French troops at Grand Pré in 1747.

LA TOUR, Charles (1559-1665) – see d' Aulnay

LE LOUTRE, Jean Louis (1709-1772) – Jesuit priest who supported the French cause against the British in Nova Scotia; captured and imprisoned three times by the British for agitating against them;

burned Beaubassin in 1750 to chase the habitants across the Missaguash River onto French territory; threatened any Acadian who kept to the British oath of allegiance with excommunication, and torture and death at the hands of his Indian converts; believed to have been the architect of Edward How's death.

MAISONNAT, Pierre, aka "Baptiste" (1663-1714) – French privateer captured by the British in 1702 and released in 1706 in exchange for the Rev. John Williams.

MAUDOUX, Abel (n.d.) – Pastor of Port Royal from 1694 to1702

PAIN, Felix (n.d.) – Pastor at Port Royal from 1701 to 1710 and at Beaubassin from 1710 to 1713, and from 1715 to 1724.

PICHON, Thomas (1700-1781) – secretary of de Vergor and Le Loutre at Beausejour; called the "spy of Beausejour".

VAUDREIL:

Philippe de Rigaud, Marquis de (1643-1725) served as Governor of New France (Canada and French Louisiana) from 1703 to 1725

Pierre Francois de Rigaud, Marquis de (1698-1778) served as Governor of French Louisiana 1743 to 1753, and of New France from 1755 to 1760, when Canada was ceded to Britain.

VERGOR, Louis du Port Chambon, sieur de (1713-1775) - commander of Fort Beausejour in 1755 when it fell to the British; later involved in the fall of Quebec.

VILLIERS, Nicholas Antoine Coulon de (1708-1750) – in charge of the attack on Grand Pré to reclaim it from the British, where he was seriously wounded.

GOVERNORS OF ACADIA

BROUILLAN, Joseph de (1651-1705) served from 1700 to 1705

SUBERCASE, Daniel d'Auger de (1662-1732) served from 1706 to 1710 when Acadia fell to the British.

VILLEBON, Joseph Robineau, Chevalier de (1655-1700) served from 1690 to 1700.

BRITISH/ENGLISH (NEW ENGLAND)

ADAMS, John – New England trader in Acadia

ALDEN, John – New England trader in Acadia

BLIN, James – New England merchant with business in Acadia

BRADDOCK, Edward, Major General (1695-1755) – came to North America in 1755 as commander of British forces with orders to take Fort Duquesne, Fort Niagara and Fort Necessity from the French. On his way to Virginia he met with Governors Shirley of Massachusetts and Lawrence of Nova Scotia who told him about the Acadians and how they could be armed by the French to attack the British from the rear unless they were deported. Braddock agreed and approved it, adding it to his agenda against the French. It was the only one of his initiatives that succeeded. Braddock was wounded in the Battle of Fort Necessity (where George Washington served as one of his aides) and he died a few days later, on July 13, 1755. Word of his death flew to Boston and Halifax, arriving when Lawrence was to meet with the Acadian Delegates. Braddock's death hardened the resolve of both Governors, Shirley and Lawrence to carry out the expulsions.

CHURCH, Benjamin (1639-1718) – militia leader from New England who attacked Acadian settlements as retribution for French and Indian raids carried out in New England. Vescaque (Westcock) was one of the villages he destroyed in 1704 as retribution for the Deerfield massacre. Promoted scalp bounties.

FANEUIL, Peter (1700-1743) – wealthy Boston trader active in Nova Scotia; gave Faneuil Hall to Boston in 1742.

FANEUIL, Benjamin – Peter's brother.

GORHAM, John (1709-1751) – his father organized, and he carried on, Gorham's Rangers to fight the French and their Indian allies. The Gorhams hailed from West Barnstable, Massachusetts and recruited men from Cape Cod to fight in Acadia.

HANDFIELD, John (1700-1763) – married an Acadian woman, Elizabeth Winniet (b. 1713). He was officer in charge of the deportations from Annapolis Royal in 1755.

HAYES, Captain John (n.d.) – Boston Harbor lighthouse keeper and pilot, 1735.

HOW, Edward (1702-1754) – New England trader and soldier, trusted by all sides; wounded at Grand Pré in 1747; died outside Fort Lawrence in October 1754 in an ambush reputedly set by the Jesuit Le Loutre.

MATHER, Reverend Cotton (1663-1728) – one of several Boston Protestant ministers who preached destruction against the Catholic

Acadians of Nova Scotia.

MONCKTON, Robert (1726-1782) – Lt. Colonel of British regulars. In charge of the capture of Fort Beausejour in 1755. He was Lt. Colonel John Winslow's superior officer, as Winslow was a colonel of the colonial miltia. Monckton was in charge of the Acadians at Chignecto and of their deportation in 1755.

NOBLE, Arthur, Col. (d. 1747) – led the British against the French attack at Grand Pré in 1747, and was killed there.

WILLIAMS, Reverend John (1637-1718) – the Deerfield massacre was carried out to capture the Rev. Williams and his family to provide prisoners to exchange for Baptiste, who was held in Boston and under threat of being hanged as a common criminal.

WINSLOW, John (1703-1774) – Lt. Colonel of Massachusetts colonial militia. Raised 2000 men in 1755 to go to Nova Scotia to help the British take Fort Beausejour. Governor Lawrence kept the militia on after the fort was taken and used them to carry out his plan to send the Acadians to exile. Winslow was in charge of the deportations from Grand Pré.

WROTH, Ensign (n.d.) – led the 1727 expedition to have the Acadians sign the new oath of allegiance to Britain when George II became king.

GOVERNORS OF MASSACHUSETTS (selected names)

DUDLEY, Joseph (1647 – 1720) served from 1702 to 1715
DUMMER, William (1677-1761) served from 1723 to 1728 and 1729 to 1730
SHIRLEY, William (1694-1771) served from 1741 to 1749 and 1753 to 1756

GOVERNORS OF NOVA SCOTIA (selected names)

PHILIPS, Colonel Richard (1661-1750) served from 1715 to 1739
MASCARENE*, Paul (1684-1760) served from 1740 to 1749
CORNWALLIS, Edward (1713-1776) served from 1749 to 1752
HOPSON, Peregrine Thomas (d. 1759) served from 1752 to 1754
Also served as Governor of Louisbourg from 1746 to 1749
LAWRENCE*, Charles (1709-1760) served from 1755 to 1760

also served as Lieutenant Governor before being made Governor

LT. GOVERNORS OF NOVA SCOTIA (selected names)

DOUCETT, John (n.d.) served from 1717 to 1725
ARMSTRONG, Lawrence (1664-1739) served from 1725 to 1739
COSBY, Alexander (1685-1742) served from 1739 to 1740

Book Discussion Group Suggested Questions:

1. What effect would the deportations have on the deportees? Their children? Their descendents?

2. Can you understand the British point of view for the deportations? How?

3. What do you think would be the effect the deportees would have on the locations they were deported to?

4. If you were among the deportees, what would your concerns be?

5. How different would the US be today if the French had colonized it and kept control?

6. Why were the Acadians deported?

7. What was Guillaume's personal conflict with the oath?

www.ingramcontent.com/pod-product-compliance
Lightning Source LLC
Chambersburg PA
CBHW020946260626
47169CB00006B/1850